# Praise for *Scotch River*

"A captivating story with fresh and original characters ... Linda Little has written a splendid novel."

—*The Globe and Mail*

"Written in sweeping lyrical prose, the novel is particularly evocative in its descriptions of the land. For the majority of the novel, Little's cast of supporting characters sustains the reader's interest—so much so that following their misadventures almost feels like watching a train wreck. Particularly intriguing are members of the Holmes family, infamous for their poor judgment and destructive tendencies."

—*Winnipeg Free Press*

"*Scotch River* is a fresh, startlingly original novel that should please any fan of good fiction ... A wonderfully written, satisfying novel, its captivating story [is] threaded with vivid imagery and a powerful sense of place. Its main merit, though, lies in its true reading of human folly, of the secrets we harbour, of the resentments we nourish and of the lies we tell ourselves in order to survive."

—*The London Free Press*

"Nova Scotia writer Linda Little has crafted a superb novel about memories, the pull of home and the need to connect."

—*The Hamilton Spectator*

"Little manages a feat too rarely accomplished in literary fiction, which is to lace the pages with lovely phrases while at the same time compelling you to turn them to find out what happens next … Little has such empathy for her characters that in the swirl of perspectives we glimpse the hopefulness in each lonely heart and come away moved."

—*Literary Review of Canada*

"Little returns now with *Scotch River*, another not-to-be-missed tale of coming home to Nova Scotia."

—*The Sun Times* (Owen Sound, Ontario)

"Linda Little is a natural storyteller with a gift for acute and quirky characterization. These two rare talents combine to make *Scotch River* a highly unusual and absorbing novel about lost souls in pursuit of the meaning of family."

—Guy Vanderhaeghe

"Reading *Scotch River* is sort of like a stylized blend of Cormack McCarthy and Annie Proulx, with a little Gordon Lightfoot thrown in for soundtrack purposes."

—*The Daily News* (Halifax)

"Little captures the small, bitter indignities family members heap on each other; the secrets, the lies and the new lies to cover old lies; the lies we tell ourselves and the lies we tell others."

—*Quill & Quire*

PENGUIN CANADA

SCOTCH RIVER

LINDA LITTLE's first novel, *Strong Hollow*, was shortlisted for the Books in Canada/Amazon First Novel Award, the Thomas Raddall Atlantic Fiction Award and the Dartmouth Book Award. She has lived in the Ottawa Valley and Newfoundland, and now makes her home in River John, Nova Scotia.

# SCOTCH RIVER

# RIVER

*A Novel*

# LINDA LITTLE

PENGUIN
CANADA

## PENGUIN CANADA

Published by the Penguin Group

Penguin Group (Canada), 90 Eglinton Avenue East, Suite 700, Toronto, Ontario, Canada  M4P 2Y3
(a division of Pearson Canada Inc.)

Penguin Group (USA) Inc., 375 Hudson Street, New York, New York 10014, U.S.A.
Penguin Books Ltd, 80 Strand, London WC2R 0RL, England
Penguin Ireland, 25 St Stephen's Green, Dublin 2, Ireland (a division of Penguin Books Ltd)
Penguin Group (Australia), 250 Camberwell Road, Camberwell, Victoria 3124, Australia
(a division of Pearson Australia Group Pty Ltd)
Penguin Books India Pvt Ltd, 11 Community Centre, Panchsheel Park, New Delhi – 110 017, India
Penguin Group (NZ), cnr Airborne and Rosedale Roads, Albany, Auckland 1310, New Zealand
(a division of Pearson New Zealand Ltd)
Penguin Books (South Africa) (Pty) Ltd, 24 Sturdee Avenue, Rosebank, Johannesburg 2196, South Africa

Penguin Books Ltd, Registered Offices: 80 Strand, London WC2R 0RL, England

First published in a Viking Canada hardcover by Penguin Group (Canada),
a division of Pearson Canada Inc., 2006
Published in this edition, 2007

1 2 3 4 5 6 7 8 9 10   (WEB)

Copyright © Linda Little, 2006

Canada Council   Conseil des Arts
for the Arts   du Canada

*We acknowledge the support of the Canada Council for the Arts which last
year invested $21.7 million in writing and publishing throughout Canada.*

*Nous remercions de son soutien le Conseil des Arts du Canada, qui a investi
21,7 millions de dollars l'an dernier dans les lettres et l'édition à travers le Canada.*

LIBRARY AND ARCHIVES CANADA CATALOGUING IN PUBLICATION

Little, Linda, 1959–
Scotch River / Linda Little.

ISBN-13: 978-0-14-305267-8
ISBN-10: 0-14-305267-5

I. Title.

PS8573.I852S36  2007    C813'.6    C2006-906274-9

Visit the Penguin Group (Canada) website at **www.penguin.ca**

Special and corporate bulk purchase rates available; please see
**www.penguin.ca/corporatesales** or call 1-800-810-3104, ext. 477 or 474

*To my parents,*
*James and Barbara Little*

# CHAPTER ONE

CASS HUTT COULD NOT FEEL the land beneath his feet. Stone-cold sober and reeling around on nothing as though his flesh speckled out into air, as though ghost legs propped him up. He pulled off his boots at night and ran his hands down his calves, feeling skin on skin, seeking to reassure himself. He rubbed his feet hard, one at a time, ran his palms back and forth over his soles. He massaged his toes until grubby black dirt and pungent boot sweat permeated his hands. He rubbed his hands together, absorbing the smell. On his bunk, he lay back perfectly still, resting on the edge of something dark and dangerous, and fell asleep with his arm draped over his eyes.

In the morning he saddled up and headed out with the others. Sometimes he tried to speak with them like he remembered speaking in years past. When chance allowed and he knew he could not be observed, he would slip off his horse and pat the ground, rub the earth between his fingers, knock on his boots. He hadn't drunk a drop since he left Tacoma and still his feet would not touch the ground. And he feared the deadening of his flesh was spreading higher up his calves, its fingers reaching towards his knees. His will had grown heavy and unwieldy and wanted only to sleep. It wasn't just that Lionel was gone, it was that Lionel had taken with him some untouchable, unnameable thing. At night when Cass dreamed, it was always of falling, of water and salt and emptiness.

Most of the day they spent cutting heifers, but Cass was as useless as a city kid. One of the others rode past shaking his head. "I know you got your troubles but, Christ, you're embarrassing a good horse."

The boss missed Cass at the corral, sent another ranch hand around with the message. The guy found him stretched out on his bunk, barefoot, forearm covering his face.

"Casper, is it? *Casper* Hutt?"

Fury jerked from the pit of Cass's stomach to his Adam's apple then fizzled, floated off into empty space. He let his arm fall, turned blank eyes to the man, who waved a postcard in the air between them.

"You got registered mail."

"That?"

"Course not. You take this to the post office. You have to sign for it." He handed the notice to Cass. "Hey, you sick or something?"

Cass twitched his shoulder in a move that might have passed as a shrug if he hadn't been lying on his back. He tucked the card into his shirt pocket and buried his eyes behind his arm again, willing the fellow to disappear.

Nearly a week passed before Cass managed to prod himself into town. He got a haircut, wandered into a store and bought razor blades and socks, found the post office card in his wallet and remembered. Curiosity eluded him but at least he understood he ought to be curious, and that was something. At the Cotton Creek post office he exchanged his card for a bulky little envelope that he retreated to his truck to open. From the covering letter he read that old name, Casper Hutt, and his address at the One Bar None. He struggled to pull a few words out of the scramble that followed. Our, to, April. Address. If you, it, thank you. He would ask Lionel … no. No, he would not.

Accompanying the letter were two little bundles. One had several sheets of typing stapled inside a cover of heavy green paper. *Dead,* it said on the front. Was the word "dead"? Perhaps it was something left to him by Lionel. Then another bundle, four sheets of lined school paper folded together. Handwriting covered both sides of each sheet, an endless trail of ink looping across line after line in an impossible clutter of corners and curves. The paper crumpled and bruised between Cass's rough fingers. He shifted his eyes to the typing again. The more he stared, the more the letters bent and twisted. Sold to, it said. A headache bloomed at his temple.

He drove home and stuffed the envelope into the kit bag under his bunk. Several times a day the package crossed his mind. He tried to care and couldn't. He hauled hay to the herd. He pulled calves. And he lay on his bunk and did not care.

He was lying on his bunk when the boss, a proud old rodeo man, found him and started in on him with an awkward mixture of kindness and anger. "Do I pay you to lie in bed? It's Coleman, for godsake! Everybody expects to see Cass Hutt, the great bull rider, in Coleman. It's practically next door! And it's not as though you're doing any good around here."

Cass clawed at the edge of his emptiness. With a great shrug of willpower he tossed his few things into his kit. It didn't take long— Cass lived packed. With the morning light behind him and the air still brittle with the night's chill he drove west into the hills towards the Coleman rodeo. His truck had developed a rattle under the hood that he could not be bothered to investigate. He hadn't driven ten miles when he pulled off the road simply because he could not bear to go on. The hopelessness of the venture overwhelmed him. He no longer belonged to his life. The idea of riding a bull was as preposterous as the idea of taking flight. Or of sitting in a truck on a roadside, or of standing on a prairie trying to believe in some dead thing beyond the sky. His eyes slumped to the kit bag on the seat beside him and rested there for minutes, perhaps hours. When his eyes focused again he pulled the pack to him and rummaged for the buried documents, laid them out before him. Never mind the handwritten pages. The typed bundle he examined again. Dated October 15, 1963. A name and address. "Sold to"—he was fairly certain of these words. Perhaps the word on the cover was not "dead" but "deed." The word "river" he recognized as well. Another name and the same town listed again. Sss. Kuh. Oh. River. Noh. He looked away before the letters could knit tangles in his head. He repeated the sounds aloud. An odd watery feeling sloshed through him, as though his joints were not attached to each other. This had nothing to do with Lionel. He pulled out his wallet and flipped through the empty cellophane windows where family photos were supposed to be kept. He tugged his birth certificate out of its sleeve. Yellow crumbs of dried plastic flaked off and fell into his lap. Carefully he placed the remnants of the card next to the address on the document. Scotch River, Nova Scotia.

Long ago Cass had worked his way out west. People always said this as though it were a social advancement, like "I worked my way up through the company." He had left almost nothing back east. In Nova Scotia there had been … he had been … Words disintegrated. Once he had watched a man cut a bull rope in half. He no longer remembered why the man had done this, but the image haunted him, then and now—a grip, a length of plaited rope, then nothing. All that hold and nothing to hold on to. Two parts of nothing. Somewhere he must have left some frayed hank of rope a person could lash himself to.

He turned the truck around and drove back the way he had come, slowed at the turnoff to Cotton Creek. But why return when the ranch was nothing but someone else's cattle and horses and earth that he could no longer stand on? He continued east past Lionel's gravesite, a hole filled with bones like the grave of every other dead man. He passed the home of Lionel's real family in Lethbridge, a huge boxful of people from someone else's life. Cass drove until the sun blazed red in his rearview mirror and the rattle under the hood had become a roar. At Gull Lake, Saskatchewan, he pulled into a garage. He sat in his truck rubbing his shins then his feet, pressing his fingers into the boot leather. He would spin off the planet, he was certain, if he couldn't get his feet on the ground.

He sorted through his things, chose carefully, shrugging into his heavy coat with the sheepskin lining, taking the new socks and razor blades he had ignored since the day he bought them, leaving his bull rope, gloves, rosin. He took his bedroll, his slicker, left his spurs and his watch. He sold the truck at a ludicrously low price to the Blackfoot Indian who ran the garage, pocketed the cash, tugged his knapsack off the seat and slung it over his good shoulder. He bought supplies at the general store across the road, packed matches, jerky and hard bread, tea and whisky, bought a canteen, a can opener, a groundsheet. He set out east along the train track across the Saskatchewan prairie, listening to the soles of his boots on the railroad gravel, trying to will sensation up his legs. The soles of his boots landed on every second tie.

Bro, Lionel used to call him. Short for brother. Of course it was a joke—my little brother. With Cass six foot two, broad and flat, and Lionel barely up to his shoulder, compact and quick like a bull rider ought to be; Cass with his dark eyes and silence and Lionel with his tussle of red curls and his quick friendly jabbering. "I think they're brothers." The ride came at him again in the wind blowing always against his face and this time he walked into the memory without hesitation or fear. Horseflesh, manure, blood and furious muscle, the taste of dust, the smell of rodeo that was his air, water and solid ground for months of every year enveloped him as though he had never smelled it before. He felt the hovering of the body, mere flesh, soft tissue, suspended over the horns of that spinning bull. He felt the space evaporate, the horn pierce the skin, a dagger thrusting upwards under the rib cage, the splash of arteries. He felt the physical surprise behind his eyes, heard the loudspeaker and the ambulance, felt the jostling of paramedics. The packed dirt of the rodeo arena pushed itself into his knees, drove itself between his fingers, billowed up his nostrils.

A leaden plunger forced downwards through his rib cage then puke spewed everywhere, up his nose, dripped through his fingers. Insistent hands on his back, faces swirling in and out of his vision. Off in the background his name, and "I think they're brothers." When he woke in the training room Lionel was gone. Taken. And he was not.

All around him now space rolled out forever. There was no shelter from the vastness of the prairie, nor did Cass seek any. At night he simply stopped and ate and slept. In the morning he hoisted his pack and faced the sun. Somewhere beneath his feet steel rails pointed, whispering, *This way*. Thirty, forty, fifty miles a day. When trains, needles of direction, lumbered upon him from behind or bore down on him from miles away, he stepped aside and walked with their company for the minutes it lasted. There were gophers and, from time to time, trotting coyotes. In the spring sloughs ducks and geese landed, fed and flew off. Intermittently, falling-down wooden grain elevators grew from specks in the distance to small towns. Sometimes large new steel elevators had been constructed to take over from their wooden ancestors, sometimes not. Cass walked behind the backs of towns, filling his canteen from back-door taps, saying nothing, moving on. Saskatchewan melted into Manitoba. Wapella, Moosomin, Elkhorn, Virden. The crisp promise of April blew over and around him in the constant wind. When the sun shone, his Stetson shaded his eyes and neck. When it rained, his slicker shed the water, and when the April winds whipped up one last snow squall, the sheepskin lining in his heavy coat kept him warm.

Tracks joined tracks joined tracks as he approached the spiderweb of Winnipeg. As tracks sidled up to one another, parallel, close but never touching, he felt the man he had been walking beside him just beyond reach. A slice of this physical dislocation, the feeling that he was not attached and could fall off the planet, this was not entirely new to him. Several times a year throughout his western life a restless loneliness welled up in him, spherical and empty. Urgency, a kind of survival imperative, overcame him. When this happened he headed out for Calgary or Edmonton, or any American city if he was on the road, even Winnipeg a few times. It didn't matter. Everywhere he found his city men.

Cass never refused money if it was offered, though it wasn't their money he was after. It was their need, desperate and demanding, that raised him up, that fed him. They wanted him lean and raw in jeans and dusty boots. They spotted him leaning up against a bar, a bus shelter, a tree, with his Stetson in his hand. They met his eyes, hovered, looked away. When they glanced back, they were his. These men always had a place in mind. They were men who planned. They had money, expensive haircuts, clean soft hands, strong teeth, bodies rounded with success, bones well padded with luxury. They all wanted Cass in charge, to feel his muscle mount their will. They all wanted to lose themselves in him. And in those seconds of ultimate passion they loved him like a god and like a son—like salvation. They loved him to the center of his soul and down through the core of the earth, fleetingly and utterly, though of course not at all.

Many men he met only once or twice. A few were regulars. He collected all their pictures in his mind, gave them names. The one he called Puppy always loosened his tie slowly, pulling it out from his neck, letting the knot fall askew several inches from his Adam's apple. His wrist always twisted right around when he opened his collar button, creating the little vee at his throat. The tie was navy with red cartwheels. Or green with yellow arrowheads or red flecked with chocolate. He never took it off, always left it hanging like a leash around his neck. Another one hung his jacket on the back of a chair, smoothed it down and patted it. Harris tweed, the man had said the first time, and Cass, thinking the man had introduced himself, answered with a name of his own. He remembered the rich confidence of the laugh, of the explanation, of the introduction almost, to the jacket. Harris Tweed wanted spurs and he kept a pair hanging on one of the bookshelves that filled the room from floor to ceiling, winking at Harris Tweed over the heads of serious men and guileless acquaintances. After a visit with Harris Tweed the smell of ink and paper and furniture polish sat in Cass's nostrils for hours. The one he called Butch drove them out of the city in a four-by-four to his father's section of wheat and crouched there naked and whimpering and begging for the lash of the belt. Butch always called him Sir and paid him so much money Cass couldn't spend it without feeling the burden of the guilt it carried. Cass always returned to the ranch whistling.

Winnipeg swelled around him now. Cass left the tracks and headed downtown, sought out a familiar spot on Main Street, dropped his pack and leaned against a building. Perhaps this was all he needed. Perhaps this time was the same as all the others, only worse. But no. He slid to his haunches, unable to lift his head, hopeless. The feeling had been severed. He would not be able to stand over his city men with only thin air below his knees. He would not be able to look them in the eye.

Leaving the city, it was surprisingly easy to locate the track that had first brought him west. With the river behind him he left the towering buildings, the suburbs, the fields, walked on towards the sunrise, setting his feet where they had passed only once before. Nearly twenty years ago he washed up at the One Bar None all green and hungry, just a kid with more body than he knew what to do with, a soul like blocks in a sack, bits all jumbled and sharp and tumbling over each other. He carried internal radar that could spot trouble a week away, eyes in the back of his head and no idea where to look or what to do. Among men who paid out respect for competence he learned how to set his backside in a saddle, hold his spine and balance his body to read the horse beneath him. He learned how to hinge open his mind to encompass what a horse can know, how to create a new beast of horse and man together. Cass added his weight, his hands, his direction, to a creature with more strength and power and different senses than a man can own. He learned the minds of cattle and how to follow them where trucks could not go, down steep banks of sluices through the aspen and poplar to the rivers below, through deeply rolling hills of native grasses beneath the wall of mountain rising in the west. They herded cattle through space so vast it took a dam of rock as high as heaven to contain it. No other space, inside or out, could muster significance beneath this ocean of sky. That boy that had been was left behind. The man, Cass Hutt, began there.

Cass became a deft hand with a rope, and the boss, an old rodeo man, wanted to see him competing for the ranch. Cass roped calves but tried his hand at other events. His size and strength best suited him to steer wrestling, but in the end it was bull riding that won out. He towered over the other bull riders, who tended to be quick and tough and compact like Lionel, but Cass persevered and eventually excelled. When he won enough to be eligible for the professional rodeo association Lionel presented him with the completed forms. The boss hounded him to sign on the line. The official success made Cass uneasy, brought with it a sense of impending loss. Cass tucked his membership card into his wallet next to his driver's license and his birth certificate. He left the One Bar None and moved further north. When they met up at rodeos Lionel greeted him like a brother.

After a couple of years Cass, unsure now why he had left, returned to the One Bar None, settled into a shimmering knowable space where predictability inched beyond the routine of daily chores and peeked at life itself. That winter Lionel hauled him along on the American tour. They rode the rodeo in the States, won enough money to keep them going, enough injuries to keep them smiling at the sight of the morning sun. Cass set his trophies on the bunkhouse shelf, stowed his buckles in a cardboard box under his bed. His bunk developed a Cass-shaped hollow where he slept. One day a bull would take him, the cardboard box would be sent to the dump, the story would be over. He could live with that.

But he could not live without it.

Cass walked. Towns came and went: Vivian, Elma, Rennie. On the third day out of Winnipeg he crossed into Ontario, a land of scrub and scrawny softwoods that cut up sky and ground, constricting the path ahead of him into a corridor. He bought coffee in a Styrofoam cup in Hawk Lake and sat on the curb to drink it. By Dryden he was simply too tired to go on. Rather than interrupt his progress he left the tracks and crossed to the Trans-Canada Highway, where a trucker picked him up. Cass rode in the cab of the rig, resting his legs and watching the road disappear too fast behind him.

"That's quite the belt buckle you got there," the trucker said.

The ride would cost him a story, he knew, so he tried to make a decent shift of the year he made the Wrangler tour finals in Las Vegas. People loved to hear about big winnings, spectacular losses, they loved a long list of injuries. They loved to hear the names of bulls— Mean Street, Hammertime, Shaken Not Stirred. Eight seconds, they loved. Not a penny's worth of time yet all that money for it. As though the money made the ride. Cass listened to his voice telling one tale while his imagination relived another. His last ride, only last month, seemed so long ago, impossibly distant, as though it had all happened to some other man. And yet the details sat so crisp and clear with him. After Lionel's funeral Cass had climbed back in his truck and headed south again, to Tacoma, where he had registered to ride. What else was there to do? There he watched steers being unloaded from trucks, their hooves heavy on the metal ramps. Calves swarmed in pens. He could have scissored his long legs over the pen rails and waded through their warm innocent bodies, lifted a calf into the air and stashed it here or there before it knew its pretty hooves had left the straw. He had often hoisted to his shoulders the still-slick bodies of newborn calves and carried them to safety, the weight of their fresh lives bearing snug against the back of his neck. The penned calves romped with slender delicacy. Soft hair curled at the tops of their heads. Here they would run, feel the jerk of the rope on their necks, the slam on the earth, be tied and released. For them there were no reasons.

Likewise for the bulls. Their brutal bulk shoved and kicked in the chutes, pawing and snorting and slamming. Born to perform, they danced for the crowd, then returned to their stalls and milled as docile as sheep. Cass had absorbed their smell, the bullying of their muscle against wood and metal. Their horns he knew well enough. They could splinter wood, crack bone, rip through flesh like a hand through water. He had counted on their solidity, believed in them, trusted them to make an ending for him. For fifteen years—not this ride maybe but surely the next would take him. They kept his life a fleeting thing, light enough to carry in his pocket.

Since the funeral Cass had kept a bottle always with him and he seldom felt his extremities. He had nipped a shot of rye, then another, just before his ride. One of the pickup men had sniffed and frowned but said nothing. The bull slammed against the chute and Cass tucked his long legs in like a grasshopper, holding himself above the bulk. Cass stared at his gloved hand as he made his wrap. It looked as though it belonged to someone else, as though his arm stopped at the elbow and part of someone else tied him to the bull.

*Cass Hutt is six foot two. They grow 'em big in Cotton Creek Alberta way up in Canada. This cowboy's got himself a sack full of buckles back home, folks. And I guess he would by now cuz I got a bottle of extra-old premium bourbon at home that was corn when this fellow started to ride. In the school of hard knocks this man majors in holding on ...*

Cass watched the bull rope snake over, around, through the fingers and back. He pounded his grip into place, the leather of glove melding into the hide beneath it. He pulled breath into his lungs, down through the bull and out those mighty black nostrils snorting up terrified eddies of dust. The bull clanged the bars just below his boot. Foreign arms steadied him. He felt his head nod the signal, the chute gate flew open. All on its own his body remembered the bull, bent to him, crouched and stretched, gripping, reading the pump of the muscle beneath him, on and on, the full eight seconds to the buzzer. Then run like hell. His legs picked him up and delivered him over the boards. A foggy distance, perhaps the distance of several slugs of rye, hazed the atmosphere around him and he had to be prodded at the end, made to understand that he had won the day money—to understand that he would not be taken, now or ever. Not if he rode for another twenty years. Abandoned. He wandered out to the stage to collect his check, slept in his truck, a bottle in hand and another beneath the seat.

At the next go-round they told him he couldn't ride—in no condition, they said. He couldn't argue with that. He climbed back into his truck and headed north, back to the One Bar None for spring calving. But even when he set the bottle aside and turned his head to his work it was no use at all. What is lost is lost.

When the trucker stopped at a diner Cass fumbled to the bottom of his pack for the Scotch River document, slid it across the table, his eyes fixed on the glass silo-shaped sugar dispenser, his voice low with shame. "I figured out some of this but I read better if, you know, if someone tells me what it says."

"It's the deed to a piece of property," the trucker said. "In Nova Scotia." Cass listened to the trucker read the entire deed word for word while they waited for their steaks and fries.

Cass left the trucker at Marathon, Ontario, reverted to the railway tracks and walked, his feet yawning beneath him, east and south. For a week he walked through desolate, scraggy land, followed a thin line of towns that had been sparse enough twenty years ago and were sparser now. Missanabie, Chapleau, Pogamasing. Then Sudbury where he had passed a dirty winter so long ago, and then North Bay. Trees and more trees everywhere blocked his view. They grew tall here, huge hardwoods with spreading limbs and leaves as big as footprints. Another day's walk took him to Mattawa where he followed the Ottawa Valley down through Pembroke and Arnprior. He kept the river, broad and magnificent, swollen with springtime, on his left. There were so many people now. The ruckus and confusion of Ottawa city rose and fell around him as he walked on. When a car stopped for him outside Vankleek Hill he accepted a ride into Montreal. The driver spoke French at first, then a heavily accented English. It had been twenty years since this language had startled Cass's ears. Cass answered the man's questions. "Heading down east. On the train tracks," he said.

"Ah, le train. I go to Montréal right now. Good, eh? At Place Ville-Marie. I take you dare, okay?"

Once in the city, Cass hovered by the station watching hordes of delicate people in pretty shoes and clean breezy jackets. Exhaustion overtook him and he stepped into the current of people, carried along at the edge of the flow. He emptied his pockets at the Via Rail counter. "East," he said.

He let the train carry him through the night, swaying, rocking, as far as his money would take him. He stretched out his legs and slept, his head lolling against the window glass. In the black before dawn a conductor roused him. "Thirty minutes, sir."

From Matapédia on the Gaspé Peninsula he continued on foot, following the railway tracks south and east, down through New Brunswick. He seldom paused in the towns or villages. When nights were clear and starry he slept in the spruce and fir woods that lined much of the route. If rain threatened he kept an eye out for an abandoned barn or old shed with its back to the track. The humidity in the ocean air often made his shoulder ache, carried the faint taste of salt to his lips. From time to time the trees parted and the land opened up before him. Time shifted with space, jumbled up as though it were a bedroll once spread out wide and open on the prairie, now bunched and bundled, folded back over itself into a space too small to contain it. The ludicrous smallness of everything, the miniature clearings, all the spaces hemmed in, chopped up, shaded with trees, could hide a boy behind a bush, in a gully, by an old barn. His memory, small and fuzzy and deliberately left to die in the back of his head, shook itself, bristling like a porcupine. He removed his hat and rubbed the back of his skull. Everywhere he was threatened with a glimpse of the self he had abandoned. The thin green corridor drew him along, offering the false certainty of a single path, as though the railbed itself had decided there was to be a destination, that leaving must be reshaped into arriving, that a journey must have two ends.

By the Nova Scotia border, near Amherst, he left the tracks for the empty railbed. Twenty years ago there had been steel rails and freight trains, and ties that spaced his stride on his way west. There had been a cabin by here where he had hidden through a long night. Yes, the remnants of the shack still stood. He jimmied open the door, curled into a corner and slept. The next morning he ate the last of his provisions and pushed on. He walked through the day and most of the night, into the dawn, felt the sun warm the air around him. His canteen needed replenishing. The trees opened up where the railbed met the road at Randal's Crossing, three miles outside Scotch River. The white barn with the green star painted on the gable end stood as a landmark. Unchanged. Time swirled inside him, his knees quaking from exhaustion. Tall and broad across the shoulders, a wide but shallow rib cage, so when underfed he flattened out like he had been run over by a cartoon steamroller. Big, but just a boy hiding, waiting for his sixteenth birthday. He wasn't free and clear until eighteen, but at sixteen he had a chance. With no more truant officers there wasn't much they could do to him if he didn't break the law. Hitchhiking north from Dartmouth with a hunger in his belly and fifty bucks in his wallet. And a plastic birth certificate card. Born: Scotch River, Nova Scotia. Lying low and waiting for his October birthday.

Cass continued past the Crossing, the trees closing him in again.

# CHAPTER TWO

PAST RANDAL'S CROSSING, Cass walked on. Another mile along and the bush-wall fell away on his left, exposing the back fields of the farm where he had made hay twenty years ago, the barn where he had stowed it and the house where he had eaten and slept. He crossed the land, now a single consolidated field, picking out the old fenceline that had once divided hayfield from pasture. Silage, he guessed, watching the clipped grasses bend beneath his boots.

Mister ... Mister and Missus High-something? He recognized the path leading from the old barn to the kitchen door at the back of the house, recognized the color of the door's paint. Wipe your boots, Cass. Wipe your boots. He pulled the hat off his head. One long summer and into the fall, working, hiding, poised to run. He shifted the weight of his pack, raised his hand and knocked. An old man answered the door. Cass wiped the sweat off his forehead, looked into the old man's eyes. Yes, it was him. A sudden tingling itched in his big toe.

"Mr. High, uh, Mr. Heighton. I don't suppose you need any help with the hay this summer?" He jutted his head towards the land he had just crossed. "It's been a while, I guess, since we hayed."

The old man's face cracked into a smile, surprised and grateful. "Cass Hutt. Come in. You just missed Effie."

Cass, standing on the doorstep, hat in hand, tried to answer Jack Heighton's smile. Sure, it said, sure it's twenty years ago. Time slides like space and land and limbs and nothing is constant. The world seemed suddenly translucent, taffy-colored, its surface too glassy smooth to hold.

16

Jack motioned Cass inside, indicated a kitchen chair. "You just missed Effie," he said as though she had driven off to a church meeting. "Can I get you something? How about tea? Lemonade? Oh, there's a couple of beer here. Left over, I guess."

Cass accepted the beer, sat and stretched his long legs far out in front of him, wiped his mouth with a dirty sleeve. "Thank you, Mr. Heighton. I been dreaming of this beer since Campbellton."

They regarded each other. Yes, yes, this is the person, the house, we are the same, there is agreement. This could be now, or then.

"A good worker. A good worker and a good eater. Effie loved that." Jack had picked a few odd bits out of the fridge, ketchup and cheese and a couple of oranges. Now he regarded them as though someone else had left them there on the table. "It will be three weeks tomorrow."

Cass tilted back the beer, watched Jack turn away into time, into some previous place. Cass fought to straighten up. "I was wondering, could I rest awhile, maybe spend the night …?"

"Sure, sure. Of course. It was good of you to come. You remember your old bedroom."

Remember. Queasy from hunger and exhaustion, Cass wobbled when he stood, stared at the kitchen chair as if it had caused his unsteadiness. "Please and thank you," Cass said into the air.

Jack leaned forward in his rocker, examining his entwined fingers. "You just missed Effie. She would have liked to see you. Oh yes. Cass. The young man hired on for the summer."

Cass unscrewed the cap from the second beer and drank deeply. He picked up his pack, tipped off balance by its heft. He did not remember exactly where his room had been but walked through the house and up the stairs, following his legs. He recognized the little slanted-ceiling bedroom right away, the gray-painted floorboards, the heavy bureau. The chocolate-brown bedstead with iron piping arching at the head and foot sat precisely where it had sat for twenty years, during which time he had not once thought of it. The same dark tartan blanket with the fringe covered the bed now as it had then.

When he gripped the iron arc at its foot, déjà vu nauseated him. He released his hold. Right now there existed a bunk on the other side of the country, a bunk he had come to view as his own, that by now would have another man stretched out on it. He raised his hand and rested it on the wall angle formed by the dormer window where he had hit his head time and time again that summer. He leaned into the dormer, gazed out over the land. Have I arrived? The question lowered itself into his mind whole. He sat, pried off his boots, the room swimming and ducking beneath him as he sank back on the rough wool. His feet stuck through the iron bars. He slept.

CASS WOKE WITH WOODEN LIMBS that had not stirred or twitched in fourteen hours. He closed his fists, scrunching handfuls of the tartan blanket then releasing it. A water stain darkened the ceiling tiles at the corner of the dormer. He turned his head, let his mind lie white and pulled his body into itself, curled over onto his side and stared at the pink and orange spot where two faded petals met on the wallpaper. His bladder ached with the pressure of the long-ago beer. A sudden and complete memory enveloped him—warm wet release and a consuming desperate sadness, the lonely but reassuring smell of a yellow blanket in a nest around him.

Cass pushed himself upright, let his hobbled legs find the bathroom across the hall. After relieving himself Cass drew a hot bath, sank into the tub, the smell of his journey already dissipating into the vapors.

What Cass remembered was a bathtub, white with amber stains where water leaked from the tap and sometimes a pale blue halo around the drain hole. He remembered the moment the last bit of water disappeared down the drain in a spinning rush with a terrifying sucking snort and how he always thought of that moment all night long, how his body clung to the feeling of finality it gave.

He remembered the cold of the empty tub against his bare feet, the navy blue of a pajama stripe, the stark un-giving chill of the metal. He had to sleep in the tub because he was dirty. They were fed up with his dirtiness. So night after night he tried to curl into the metal. He clutched his skinny pillow and a yellow blanket stiff and redolent with the calming smell of his own urine. He could no longer stay. It was the end of the road for him. When a person got to be too dirty and too stupid, then it was the end of the road for that person, for the little boy called Casper.

"Fuck." Cass slid down in the tub, pulled his whole head underwater. "Fuck fuck fuck." He gurgled, snorted water up his nose, splashed suds in his eyes, came up choking, eyes stinging, and shook his head like a dog, splashing water everywhere. "Excuse me," he said to no one. He had not been expecting fear. He had neglected to expect anything at all. This problem of being alive would follow you everywhere. Always this little trail, scratched by a nail into the brain, even when the wind blew your footprints into the air, blew new dust where your tracks had been; still some realness existed in the brain. There was no such thing as nothing at all.

Downstairs, Jack creaked away in the kitchen rocker and talked. His stories had been wandering through his grief, Effie here and Effie there. Once he looked up at Cass in bafflement, in suspicion even, but immediately his gaze retreated and he resumed his rambles. Cass returned to his stack of toast. Why wouldn't he be here? What difference could it make? People came and people went. These two, these Jack and Effie, had been great talkers, always talking, and leaving things around in the open, taking people in. It was a miracle they hadn't been robbed blind, murdered in their beds and the house burned to ashes. He tried to remember Effie's face but drew a blank.

"You had a dog," Cass said.

"Of course you remember old Tig. You taught him that little dance and Effie laughed and laughed."

Something like that, some trick with the dog. A black and white dog? The space in the kitchen fractured, shards lying over each other. In a slice Cass could not see, Effie was laughing so hard she had to dab at her eyes with the corner of her apron. He could see Jack listening to her laugh, though. Cass ate toast, folded over, four bites per slice. This boy had been him or the thing that predated him, and he had liked the dog or hated it or simply found it here.

"And the cows." Not beef cattle but milking Holsteins. He glanced out the window at the empty barn across the yard. The village of Scotch River lay a couple of miles further along the road or the railbed. The railbed paralleled the road, curved before an iron bridge crossed high above the Scotch River gorge. The miracle of this knowledge, retained and useless in his brain for twenty years, teased some great longing that had not yet taken shape in him. And fear. Some longing so wrapped in fear they grew and wove together like burlap forgotten in the tall grass. It seemed a great shame all of a sudden that he had never feared a bull, never had to summon courage for the chute, for practice. He lowered his head and gulped through two more slices of toast.

Jack's prattling continued. "Now I'd forgotten this, but looking at you, I remember. You left so sudden—too sudden. You had pay owing. Effie fretted about that, and you know, she kept that money in a can in the pantry, handy in case you dropped by. For five years. Now that was Effie all over, right there."

Cass kept getting lost, starting a thought then tipping off track, and when he picked himself up finding himself between slices of time. He looked around the kitchen. There were geese in blue bonnets painted everywhere, a train of them on a strip of wallpaper marching

around the walls, blue checked curtains and little blue checked hats on
the bottles lining the shelves. An old man rocked in the chair by the
window. Have I arrived? Today he would not be walking, moving
forward, leaving. The puzzle of the deed fluttered through his mind.

"Mr. Heighton."

"Oh, call me Jack. No one calls anyone mister or missus anymore."

"Jack. I have no money."

He chuckled. "Me too. I had no money. I wanted to take Effie out,
get a date with her, you know. But I figured, well, how would I do
that with no money, eh? Why would she even look at me? And she
was such a smart girl, always bright as a penny. So I stewed about this
for a while and I thought, well, I'll ask my sister …"

Cass watched him rocking back and forth, fingers intertwined, the
soft rolling of the wooden rockers on the tiles, daylight blue in the
window behind him. Contained. Cass left the kitchen and wandered
outside, no pack weighing him down, no corridor pointing the way.
Space existed in all directions—Jack's, Scotch River, railbed, highway,
iron bridge. He could walk anywhere or nowhere. Born: Scotch River,
Nova Scotia. Cass had known this fact since when? He had no memory
of its discovery, only of the fact itself, there on the birth certificate. The
plastic birth certificate card itself was the same—he had no memory of
its arrival. Likely issued to him by some social worker. Scotch River. He
had had to ask around. Head north from Dartmouth, past Truro,
north to the coast.

Across from Jack's sat a huge modern farm with a barn like an arena.
It had not been there twenty years ago, but what had been there he
could not recall. He wandered down Jack's lane to the road, where he
stood facing east, terribly still, while time shifted and settled and
shifted again. He stepped forward, into the distance between himself
and the village a couple of miles away. As he walked he studied the land
to either side of him, searching out the familiar. Every few minutes he

passed some particular oddment or landmark that had settled on his fifteen-year-old eye: the house with the heart shapes cut into its wooden shutters, the miniature lighthouse painted white and red and marooned on a sea of lawn, the shed by the road with its windows set at angles to form diamonds. These specks of reality made up his memory. See, they said, you were here. All the rest was painted in. He pushed himself to remember, not just recognize. There had been more farms then, more herds pastured by the road, he was fairly sure. Had it been so silent then? He didn't remember the silence.

Somewhere along here had been an old bus—swirled up with all kinds of colors—set off the road in a field backing on the water. More than the bus itself he remembered imagining living in that bus even though it was obvious that someone owned it, had bought it and the land it sat on, set it up there for a cottage, cut the grass and paid the taxes. Nothing is free. That's what he really remembered— rolling the idea of ownership and permanence around in his mind, setting his young self there in that bus, pretending, his boyish innocence playing under the roof of his real, more adult understanding. Not yet sixteen.

There was the spot. Although the bus was gone he was fairly certain this had been the property. An orange trailer sat there now, grass ragged and weedy around a derelict step. If he had not been staring, poking at his memory, he would not have seen the beer bottle hurtle through the air. Its natural arc bent nearly straight by the force of its launch, it smashed against the remnants of an old brick barbecue pit and shattered. Cass searched for the source, spied a sneakered foot and a denim pant leg high in the branches of the tree beside the trailer. A second bottle followed with a whistle and smash, splintering onto the bricks with angry pointless power. A rustle of branches, then all returned to silence.

Cass neared the village. The mouth of the Scotch River estuary sparkled wide and blue to his left, the houses came closer and closer together on his right. He passed the first of the village churches and the liquor store. An ancient man hobbled from an old Dodge pickup towards the liquor store punching his cane into the air. When he reached the door he called out like a crow—whether in greeting or curse was not clear. The building swallowed his words and then the man himself. Cass passed the post office, the bank. Before the bridge, at the junction of the highway and the Station Road that marked the heart of the village, stood the Co-op, the hardware store, the drugstore. Still. Everything looked older, smaller, grayer, emptier than he remembered.

In the Co-op parking lot a white-haired granny tottered, leaning on the open door of a big boat of a Chrysler, her eyes darting like hummingbirds. They lit on Cass, hovered while she frowned, swooped off and back around. She called out to a figure half hiding among the plants in the garden display, "Oh Eleanor!" Then a rattle of busyness, a gush of sentences. An old but elegant woman emerged from the garden center foliage, crossed the lot and answered her in a low purr of words. She watched the other woman with eyes that skimmed the surface, held back, waited. When she continued on her way she passed within three feet of Cass and although she looked directly at him her eyes passed over him, equally aloof.

The old ice cream stand was gone, Cass noted, and several other storefronts stood empty. A new convenience store had taken the place of … he could not think what. The ATV dealership was new. A little further along the road would be the Legion. Nestled between the Station Road and the riverbank lay the park much as he remembered it: a few flower beds, picnic tables in the same spots, a flagpole, the same little wooden bandstand that would have been hard pressed to accommodate more than a trio.

Cass veered off along the narrow cinder path through the park behind the few trees by the riverbank. The Scotch River was a tidal river, wide at the mouth then narrowing as it snaked its way inland, twisting east then doubling back west. Because of this pattern the iron railway bridge was not visible from the village although it was not more than a mile inland. That long-ago summer he had carried his pay in his pocket along the railroad tracks and over that iron bridge. He had come down through the village and sat on this picnic table by the road, his feet on this bench seat, and eaten Kit Kats and ice cream cones, searching the faces of everyone who passed by. If anyone asks, he had thought, I'll say my aunt and uncle have a cottage on the shore. But no one had ever asked. The innocence of it embarrassed him now, pressed on his heart until it felt tender with bruising. As though he would find her here waiting, as though he would know her by sight, or she him.

A child's voice pierced his quiet. "Look, Mom, a cowboy!"

Cass turned from the river to see a small boy pointing at him and hanging off his mother's arm.

"Get in the car," she said, curt and distracted, her voice laden with hundreds of repetitions of that order.

Across the street on the drugstore steps a line of idle fellows sat just as they had twenty years ago. Perhaps even the same men. The guy with the beard—was he the same? The youngest, not much under sixty, hollered at him, "Hey, the parade's not till next month!" Great guffaws. Cass regarded them, touched the brim of his Stetson and nodded. They quieted then, afraid that something might be required of them. Cass turned away and headed off across the bridge feeling the row of eyes following him.

A restaurant, several sparse blocks of houses, three more churches, the RCMP detachment, and Nelson's Shell Station made up the east side of the village. At the gas station Cass stopped and gazed across the road at the head of the trail, still prominent, perhaps more prominent, after twenty years. He knew it led off through a ragged wood then met up with the railbed at the iron bridge that had once carried the trains across the Scotch River. He recalled how, near the tracks, the land swooped suddenly upwards to the plateau of the railbed, revealing the gorge below and the sky all around. What he remembered was a vast space, the sudden opening up and the terrible, tumbling distance from bridge deck to water. That was not all he remembered. Air riffled in his lungs, an image flashed, here then gone.

He took several steps towards the trail then stopped, uncertain. Best if he concentrated on solid things, real things, focused on things he could touch. Like the package with the deed and the pages of handwriting tucked beside his bedroll in the bottom of his kit. Probably some kind of mistake, but there it sat. And its hiding there among his possessions was like owning an idea: an idea of a destination, of a specific spot quite different from this or that arbitrary patch of ground, an idea of belonging to.

He turned around and for just a second there was Lionel coming out of the gas station and heading towards the Bronco parked at the pumps, a bouquet of chocolate bars in his hand. No. Of course it wasn't Lionel. It was just the way the man had tossed his head, throwing a parting shot over his shoulder, the fluid confidence of a man who belongs. This man was not short enough to be Lionel; his hair brown, not red; nothing like Lionel in fact.

Cass turned his back on the path and headed back through the village the way he had come. Scotch River. Nothing here, but nowhere else to go. If he moved on he would be running forever. He needed time and enough food to put some distance between his spine and his belt buckle. Maybe then he could think. In the meantime he had to attach himself to something normal. Do something normal.

# CHAPTER THREE

A COUPLE OF MILES along the railbed, just beyond the Randal's Crossing intersection, Pipe Holmes spotted the walker, a mere squiggle in the distance ahead. All-terrain vehicles, or ATVs, were the norm on the railbed, bicycles unusual, walkers very rare. As she closed the gap between them she could see he was heading east as she was, a tall man with a pack on his back and what looked like a cowboy hat on his head. His stride long, steady, timeless. He had not yet heard her and she did not care to puncture her delicate peace with human contact, so she dismounted from her bicycle and pushed it the last few hundred feet. The man ahead walked on, oblivious.

Pipe skittered down the slope off the railbed to join a footpath no bigger than a deer track. Pulling her bike in tight to her body she slipped through a collar of scarcely restrained undergrowth that soon dissipated to reveal the spacious moss-covered floor of a mature forest. Sturdy hardwoods and softwoods, their foliage and needles spreading out to gather the sun, left the soil rich and springy underfoot, the air cool with shade and redolent with spruce gum and damp earth and a sugary springtime smell. She slowed her pace, almost to a halt sometimes, and stretched her lungs with the dew-laden air. At the far end of the woods young spruce and fir, greedy for light, crowded their way into the path, the occasional branch strumming the bicycle's spokes like a harp as she passed.

Pipe emerged into a clearing, a hole in the woods with a small house and a fenced-in garden. Alders had colonized the ruins of an old barn that lay defeated and rotting in a heap. They threatened the silvered shed with the board door slightly askew, encroached upon the red-painted outhouse standing like a sentry in the yard. They sent their suckers into the ragged grasses, the vetch and daisies growing in a pool around the little house, pushed through the earth beside the packed soil of the once-graveled lane leading out to the Scotch River Road.

A German shepherd bounded forward to meet her. Pipe leaned her bike up against the bare and cracked clapboards of the house, patted the dog. Her eyes scanned her garden: a modest patch, fresh life laid out in rows and clumps, protected by a droopy chicken-wire fence. She ducked under the clothesline strung across the yard and tugged open the shed door, releasing two pairs of geese that rushed past her flapping their wings in defiance of their night's captivity. From the hand pump in the yard she drew fresh water for the hens, scooped a can of oat siftings into their feeder and checked the nesting boxes, pocketing two warm brown eggs. Mindful of the eggs, she gathered up an armload of firewood and went inside.

Pipe laid a fire in the firebox of the ancient cookstove and set her porridge on to boil. With the thrum of the gristmill still in her bones she circled the interior of her house taking in the scenes, the story, what she had completed and where she had yet to go. The main floor of the little house was a single room. A brick chimney rose through the center. A narrow staircase huddled into one wall, cricking around the corner to accommodate its first few steps. Besides the stalwart stove and an iron sink with a square of counter to one side the only furnishings were the wooden table and two chairs, and the sawhorses with planks seconded to hold cans of paint and trays and brushes and rags; sketchbooks, pads of oversized newsprint, shingles and slabs and aluminum pie pans muddy with color. Dominating half of the house, on the opposite side of the chimney from the stove, like a counterweight, sat a granite millstone. Four feet across and almost a foot thick with a central hole the size of a wagon hub. Only the millstone with its handsome quarter-arm pattern remained uncluttered with painting detritus, and it was here Pipe sat with her porridge plate balanced on her knee as she spooned her breakfast into her mouth. She always made more oatmeal than she needed and scraped the leftovers into a pan for the dog.

Pipe set out her paint and brushes and the assortment of bowls and tins she used to mix her colors—set them out then touched them all again, patting the paint cans into a perfect line. When she was ready she shook out her arms, stretched her fingers back, felt the shimmering in her nerves ebb and surge. The butterflies in her stomach fluttered. Always there was the vastness of the project to walk through to get to the specifics of line, texture and color, the delicacy of the curve of an eyebrow, the shading of an eye. It was as though she must spin a cocoon of silence, of time, of reverence around herself. And then within this safety of her own making her heart leaned into the work, transporting her. *Transcendent* was the word she had heard, but really it was the opposite. *Descendent.* Down into. A part of. What comes of. On a good day the subject rose to help, just a little, to leave her with an effect slightly greater than her skill. The tiny miracles of art layered one upon another, building. The effect encircled her and carried her out of this world and into another, not yet created, where possibility sweetened the air and she breathed more lightly.

She mixed a brown and then another, darker, more brown, then less brown. Red brown, yellow brown, pine, hemlock. All brown, a family of browns, finally one adequate to begin the creation of an adze-polished beam. She worked amid a silence that reached back into another time. She worked until the morning bled into the afternoon and the afternoon nodded at evening. She worked until her arms felt heavy as water, the dog paced by his dish and her stomach ached from growling.

The fire in the cookstove had long since cooled to ash. When she raised the stovetop to rekindle the flame, the iron clanged in her ears making her wince and warning her to soften her motions. Once she set the water on to boil for her evening oatmeal and her tea, she wandered outside where she examined her garden and plucked a fistful of the largest spinach leaves. The greens'll keep your feet on the ground, her Nan used to tell her, and though she hated it she ate a handful of lettuce or spinach every day for as long as she could keep it growing.

Back in the house she checked the jar of free restaurant food on the shelf. Still lots of salt and pepper, a few packets of sugar and a dozen soy sauce, but the ketchup was gone. One mustard left. No relish. There was still tea, thank God. She was careful with her supply—three goes at each teabag. She scrambled up that morning's eggs and divided them between her plate and the dog dish. Likewise with the oatmeal. She cooled the dog's dinner with a little well water then poured the last of the rationed dog food, about a quarter of a cup with the last remaining crumbs, over the mixture in the bowl. *Just enough left for flavor, Blackwood,* she signed, avoiding denting her precious silence with speech.

Of course she would have to visit her grandmother. Of course she knew that. Her money was gone, but she needed so much more time. She patted her millstone, the stone she had tracked down and bought. She had bought jack posts and reinforced the floor, suffered the indignity of hired help, a tractor and four men to transport it and roll it inside, set it in place in the middle of the floor.

What do you want a millstone in the house for?

Oh, just crazy, you know.

That shut him up. Looking off all embarrassed as though that's not what he thought in the first place, as though they hadn't all been laughing about it together on the way over. They didn't all get the message, though. The youngest of the group, the one she had gone to school with, had lagged behind at the end, leaned in surreptitiously, close enough to show off his bad skin and leave the furry-teeth smell of his breath in her nostrils. He leered and made the air-circles-beside-the-head symbol for crazy, as though they were still ten years old.

She remembered the old gut-punch feeling, the pain, the fury, and the effort of consciously drawing back from it. She remembered the bitterness in her wordless answer, the detailed and eloquent signing, proof that, unlike him, she had been elsewhere, understood things he could not see from under the bill of his ball cap. *I won't confine my expression to your capacity to understand.* A lonely victory.

They had told their tales all over the village of course. For months afterwards people would ask at the Co-op or the bank, "Are you setting up a gristmill out there, or what? Carrying on the family tradition?" Flimsy smiles. Family tradition. Are you mad? Are you dangerous? Are you like her? And at the hardware store, "That's an awful lot of paint. That house is going to be pretty colorful, isn't it?" Meaning what are you up to? You're not normal. Do you need to be watched?

"Maybe," she wanted to tell them. She didn't want them reassured. She didn't want her Uncle Ben nosing around and reporting back to everyone that she was harmless, she was doing well, that she had come through hard times unscathed, that she was just like them. And then she *did* want that. A huge part of her wanted desperately to let it all go, shake it loose and let it fall away and just be normal. Don't get angry, don't sign at people, don't push people away, don't do anything weird. Don't be like her. Cut her loose.

Sometimes she thought it was possible. During her Halifax years, the years she spent getting her degree at the Nova Scotia College of Art and Design, she used to force herself across the harbor on the ferry, out to the sprawling grounds of the psychiatric hospital. The N.S. as they call it. The disease was drugged into oblivion and her mother with it. Lucy. Still breathing but with her life shrunk and pickled like a specimen in a bottle and shoved to the back of a shelf out of sight. The frequency of Pipe's visits had thinned to a trickle and she tried to believe the story was over, but she couldn't let go entirely. There was a phantom fist living at the back of her head that held on so tight she could sometimes feel it squeezing her brain stem. This isn't over, it said. Nothing's ever over.

The gristmill bypassed the problem, bridged the broken link and connected her back to a line of strong determined women, to a long-ago family insulated with time and silence. Day after day, week after week, Pipe returned to the mill. She couldn't work without it. Nan would have understood. When Pipe was little and Nan brought her to the mill, Nan would steer her away from any official interpretation, guides or tours or pamphlets. Look, she would say, this is where Grandmother bagged the oats. See there where Grandmother attached that belt. Later, at Nan's, they would snuggle up together on the wide old couch and Nan would tuck the crocheted blanket around them, enveloping them in hundreds of little orange and brown and yellow doily-like stars looped together with yarn. Pipe remembered how she used to thread her fingers through the crochet holes and wiggle them as she huddled into her Nan, listening to her stories, absorbing them.

As a girl, Pipe had been both attracted and repelled by the rumbling power of the mill, thrilled by its size and its danger. Now the mill appeared smaller than it had been in her memory, more manageable, more understandable. What had once seemed to her immensely complicated was now elegantly simple. She could see with her practical imagination how her great-great-grandmother Penelope had lived there and toiled there, suffered, thrived, grew old and died there with the rhythm of the waterwheel always in her bones.

Pipe rubbed the grooves of the millstone with the heel of her hand. The money she had saved had got her this far, but now it was gone and here was her work so far along and yet so far from done. She would need another month at least, maybe two. Who knew? She could not stop now, let it all fall away and evaporate into nothing while she went off to scratch through some wretched stupid job. Everything would be ruined.

When she finished her dinner she made her tea and carried the mug outside, tapped a scant measure of sugar out of a packet and watched the crystals trail through the steam and dissipate. She would have to go tomorrow, face her living, breathing grandmother, her father's mother, Eleanor Holmes. No way around it. A sick feeling gurgled through the egg in her stomach. Nothing's ever over.

# CHAPTER FOUR

"Let's move it, man. I got shit to do."

"Yeah, that's what you got to do all right—shit," Earl mumbled into the drone of the diesel engine. The winch swung the lobster box up to the wharf where it was lowered onto a neat stack. Earl glanced towards the wheelhouse where Johnny Everett was lighting a cigarette, flicking out his lit match with one hand, tugging the denim at his crotch with the other, sucking smoke into his lungs. Yeah, that's the boss—both hands and the mouth going and somebody else doing all the work. Earl caught the cable, affixed the last crate and stood back out of the way. Decent catch anyway. They waved the okay from the wharf and Johnny eased the boat away from the loading berth towards his mooring, where Earl leapt out with the rope to make her fast and then just kept going.

"See you tomorrow," he called over his shoulder.

"Yeah."

Unease accompanied Earl Holmes to the parking lot. As soon as the newspaper hit the streets everybody always ran for the obits and the court notes, nosy bastards. Never failed. Sure enough there was one coming now, making a beeline towards him—Chester with his sorry-assed crewman cousin in tow.

"Hey Earl, I see the family name in the paper again. You must be proud."

Pain winked in a little spasm just above Earl's left eye. He commanded his muscles to relax. "I'm surprised to hear you say that,

Chester. I didn't know you could read." Earl stashed his gear in his truck and headed back towards the wharf.

The cousin stepped out practically into his path, his apologetic puppy eyes bigger than ever. "You getting a good catch, Earl? How's it going?"

"Not bad."

"They're getting a lot of little ones up by the Landing."

"Is that a fact? Well, I'll see you around, eh?" It's bad when the likes of that starts feeling sorry for you, he thought.

Earl strode towards his own lobster boat, the *Best Chance,* moored at her berth. He jumped down onto her deck and ducked into the cover of the wheelhouse. He selected a cigarette and folded the pack into the sleeve of his T-shirt. This business with his oldest son Wayne needed some serious mulling over. He paced back and forth across the deck a few times before he managed to get himself settled down. Although it was barely June the morning sun had warmed the decking, warmed the fishy salt air in that brazen way that promised the damp chilliness of spring was banished forever. Finally, leaning back in his white plastic lawn chair from Wal-Mart, with his feet up on a fish tub and a beer in his hand, he began to feel more himself. He had always done his best thinking on his boat and this was hardly the worst scrape he'd seen.

Wayne was a good kid, essentially. A bit screwed up is all. A court appearance isn't the end of the world. It's not great, having a criminal record, but when you look at the problem head-on, look it right in the eyes, bottom line is the boy wasn't going to be a banker or an international diplomat or anything anyway. A few drugs, a little B and E, anybody's kid can get into a bit of that. But this other thing, Jesus Christ! He could slap him. Earl tried to swallow this sudden barb of anger with his beer, finished off one bottle and started in on the next. Roughing up old people. The moment the word was out, people's eyes started to slide off him in embarrassment as though it was Earl himself who had done it, or had sent Wayne off to do it. Right, sure. Here's an idea, Wayne, go off and find some old guy living by himself, push him around, kick him over and walk off with a cheap twenty-year-old TV set you couldn't pay someone to take.

Okay, bottom line, absolute bottom line, he had to get the boy settled into something, get him away from that friggin' crowd of losers he was running with. Get a bit of pride into him. That was the thing. When he was Wayne's age, no, way before that—God, he loved those days. They would be on the water when the sun rose. They would see it coming up big and beautiful and spilling that strip of silver across the water towards them like God's finger. Earl and his Dad side by side hauling lobster pots. Boys will be boys. It wasn't like he had been any kind of angel himself. Out there on the water, though, that would straighten a man out—that was what it always came back to. There was no way his father had meant for things to go the way they had. He was probably up there in heaven right now looking down and wringing his hands, maybe wringing his wings, over the whole fiasco.

The thing was to fix it, though. The lobster license was gone and that was another story, never mind about that now. Licenses came up for sale and bottom line was getting the cash together, getting a loan, getting the money together to snag one. Once he got Wayne out on the boat—that would be the magic bullet there. For sure.

He felt himself drifting, easing into those days, the weight of his father's arm across his shoulders, a glow of resolution, satisfaction, completeness. He pulled himself back. What needed the hard thinking was the money business. The trouble was he had trod these paths so often, money money money. You gotta think outside the box here, Earl. He shifted down a bit in his seat and let his head fall back, his eyes lifted to the clear sky above him. He needed liquid assets. But there was not one thing that he owned that he wanted to sell. In fact there were a good many things he did not own that he wanted to buy.

His wife owned nothing worth selling. He would love to have that woodlot to sell off. But he had sold it off years ago for a truck that only ended up in the knacker's yard anyway. His mother, well, she could help him of course but she wasn't going to since she was the cause of the problem in the first place. And with his brother Ben there was simply no point. Every time he wanted to talk money with Ben, Ben only wanted to talk about what Earl owed him already. You've been around this mulberry bush a thousand times, Earl. Let's find some new territory.

His Dad never meant for him to be left without the license. Jesus Christ! Here I am, a lobster fisherman with traps and all the gear and the *Best Chance* tied up at the wharf, ready to go, and I'm crewing on some-bloody-else's boat. Crewman. Taking orders from Johnny Everett. Getting my goddamned hours from Johnny Everett! Then pissing around with herring and groundfish and fucking rock crab.

Earl opened another beer, lit another cigarette. His Dad felt so close his heart hurt. The day after he finished high school, the *day after graduation,* he was on the boat. He had leaned in the doorway of the wheelhouse looking out at all that blue ocean, looking at the back of his father's brown plaid shirt, the brown curls bundling out beneath his grease-streaked cap, the engine roaring away and the tubs full to bursting with lobsters.

"Your brother Murray never wanted to fish," his father had shouted over the engine, still looking straight ahead. There was something about the noise and the work, looking away, shouting to be heard, being all alone together in the middle of the strait, that brought them together. Working out there together, there was stuff you felt but nobody ever said, that you didn't *need* to say, that you just wouldn't. That made it more true, not less. "Your brother Murray could have been some help, eh, back then," his Dad had shouted. "He could've helped bait traps for Chrissake. I could've used the help but Murray wouldn't do it. Didn't like the water. Afraid, he said. I could cure that. One day I got fed up. All the other guys there with their sons—Jesus. I got fed up and I just picked him up, an arm around the waist, and hauled him on board. Well, Murray started screaming like a girl, kicking the air like I was bloody murdering him. I locked him in the cabin to shut him up, but there he stood, palms pushing into the glass, bawling and pleading, tears running down his face—I don't want to go, Dad! Christ. I figured he'd be all right once we got out, away from shore, but all he did was snivel and cry and cling to anything he could wrap his white knuckles around. I gave him a couple of hearty slaps but it never did any good. He was useless. Scrunched there in the corner of the wheelhouse the whole trip, shaking. The second we touched the wharf he was up over the side like a rat on the run. Ran all the way home to his Mommy. The other guys on the wharf all staring at us. Smirking. It was the most humiliating day of my life." Earl drank deeply reliving the story, heard his father's voice again over the engine. "Ben could bait a trawl but he never liked to, never liked the wharf at all. You know that yourself, eh? Your brother Ben's no fisherman. Always wrinkling his nose and wiping his hands."

Only Earl was a fisherman. Only Earl had what it took to make it in the business. "Here, you take her into the wharf," his dad had said. Over twenty-five years ago and he could still remember his father's hand on the back of his neck and the graveled voice in his ear. "We'll make a go of 'er, eh, Earl-boy? We'll make a go of 'er."

Poor Murray. He hadn't thought about that story in ages. A fisherman's son afraid of the water. Every story about poor Murray ended or started with "poor Murray." Nobody wants to think about their own brother as a loser, but jeez. Don't speak ill of the dead now, Earl. Poor Murray would have been glad to help him out of a fix, but what good would it do when he never had one goddamned thing to give? He gave away faster than he ever got. He never owned anything. Earl frowned.

Earl had been so young when Murray left home. There had been an argument, but then there had been so many arguments. What difference did it make? Murray was banished and out of the house and living in that hovel on that scrubby patch of dirt.

Earl took a good long draft of beer, his brain snagged on the thought. It was funny it had never occurred to him until this very moment to wonder about that land. Murray had lived there from the day he left home as a teenager to the day he died. How come there had never been any kind of will or anything? How could the land go to Murray's widow if she's locked in a padded cell chewing on raw mouse carcasses? Honestly now, who paid the taxes on the place? Funny it never came up for tax sale. Twenty years and it never came up for tax sale? Nobody can tell me his loopy daughter paid twenty years of taxes. Well, she was just a kid then anyway. Never thought of it at the time. Well hell, your brother dies, who's going to think of money at a time like that? He should ask Mom about that. Murray had heirs, after all. A daughter yeah, but brothers too. Twenty years—it was possible that there might be a decent stand of trees on that land by now. The thought glowed in his chest; first hope then a calm confidence that blossomed into certainty.

Earl drove his Bronco to Nelson's garage and filled the tank with premium. Inside the gas station he paused over the chocolate bars. He couldn't remember if it was Aero or Mr. Big the boys fought over. He loved the way their eyes lit up when he brought them something— the way they'd laugh and jump for treats he held high above his head, the twins' joyful scrabbling, climbing up his body like little coons up a tree. Laughing. Dad, hey Dad. Even Brad, who was nearly fourteen and suddenly too cool to care, reverted to boyhood in the face of candy or toys. Aero or Mr. Big? He bought both for each of them—six bars and a tank of gas. He could take a run out to Wayne's trailer right now, see how his oldest son was getting on.

He caught Bob Nelson's banter and batted it back as he left—a running joke about the TV set up in the back room. There was a guy in a Calgary hat across the road, just standing there, staring down the ATV trail towards the iron bridge. The guy turned as though unsure, looked straight at him then away but said nothing. It was still a little early for tourists—the cold shoulder season. Earl started the Bronco, idled for a moment of indecision, realizing he hadn't bought any chocolate bars for Wayne. He eased the pickup out onto the highway and turned east, away from Wayne's trailer and towards home for a shower and lunch.

## CHAPTER FIVE

Cass's second morning in Scotch River began the same as his first—Jack rambling on in the rocker by the kitchen window, Cass with his pile of toast. But this morning the comfort of necessity sat with him.

"Who farms this land now?" Cass asked.

"What? Oh, Hans Weidermann. Just across the road there. It's some operation: a thousand acres, zero grazing, milks three times a day. The way of the future. We sold everything but this couple of acres we're sitting on—house and barn. Who knows, he may get that too when we're done with it. When *I'm* done with it. Tear it all down, likely."

"You suppose he needs a cattleman?"

Jack crinkled his forehead and tapped an index finger on the rocker's wooden armrest. "Well now, I don't know. An awful lot of work goes on over there. I suppose it's worth asking."

Hans Weidermann's main barn, broad and shiny as a new hockey arena, stood in a yard the size of a parking lot. On one end of the lot a many-bayed machine shed housed a combine and an idle tractor. Forage wagons lined up beside it. A faint growl of machinery emanated from the adjacent field. At the opposite end of the yard sat a large glistening white house with copious thermal-paned windows. The tang of cow manure struck him as slightly foreign, sharper than he was used to. And he smelled horses.

He rubbed his nose. He followed the barn wall. Even before he stepped around the corner the soft thudding of hooves on dirt whispered to him of the corral. He clapped a palm to his chest, felt the thump against his rib cage. The shape of his dislocation twisted, balancing this carry-over from one life to the other. Four of them. Good feet on all of them, straight legs. The two geldings milled about, a huge black one and a smaller roan. A full-grown colt skittered and ran along the rails. A chestnut mare pricked up her ears and trotted a few paces, whinnied and galloped around the edges of her confines. Beautiful feet on her and strong legs, broad healthy chest, straight back. The mare danced up close to him, bobbed her head over the top rail of the corral and nickered. He felt air on his teeth. When he approached, she threw her head. One of the geldings then the other trotted over. He stroked their noses, slapped their necks. "Hey boy," he murmured. The colt bullied up looking for treats. Cass grabbed for its mouth. Three years old, more or less. They hadn't done a thing with him he guessed from the way he tossed his head and pranced.

The corral was attached to an old-fashioned barn, high and hip-roofed, hidden behind the new barn. He leaned on the fence railing, watching the horses, spacing his breath, waiting for someone to notice him. When a teenaged girl wandered across the farmyard in a halter top, shorts and flip-flops drinking canned Pepsi through a straw, he approached her asking after Weidermann but she just smirked, shrugged and sauntered on towards the house.

A few minutes later a metallic-green Silverado with a deluxe chrome grille and running boards drove into the yard and headed towards him, parked by the corral rail. A large tawny-haired man stepped out, a man who held himself upright, as tall as Cass but three times as thick. His eyes, startling for the density of their blue, focused forward, landing on a series of individual targets with confidence and expectation. This was the sort of man who stood in the middle of things while people walked around him, the kind of man who was always thinking.

"Hello?"

"I'm looking for Hans Weidermann."

"Yes, I am Weidermann. And you are …?" His German accent, thick as his tawny eyebrows, stabbed *V*s through his *W*s, *Z*s into his *Th*s.

"Cass Hutt. I'm looking for work. I'm a cattleman, eh? Horseman too."

"Looking for work." *Verk.*

Cass nodded.

"Cattleman, horseman, you know everything then?" *Every-sing zen.*

Cass said nothing.

"You have been doing this farming work for how long?" *Haf been doing zis.*

"Long time. Twenty years, I guess, on and off."

"On? Or off?"

Cass watched him, uncertain. "A long time."

"Ah yes? And we have pigs also. You also are a pig man?"

"No sir." When Weidermann didn't respond he continued, "I've heard they're pink."

"Yes. You have the theory then, but not the practice." He did not smile but his eyes sparkled. "You were admiring the horses, yes?"

"Yessir. You got some fine-looking animals. You use them much?"

"These are the big pets. They don't get out as often as they should, you know, we are busy. My daughter, once it's all horse-horse-horse, then like this"—he snapped his fingers—"it's only boys-boys-boys. This black gelding I like. I want for him to be in the parade this year."

"You started working with the colt?"

"Not yet. But it is time, I know. We must start with him. There is no excuse. So you are a horseman." Weidermann ducked through the rails into the corral, cocking his head for Cass to follow. He talked about his horses, where they came from, what they cost, their papers and lineage, all the time watching how Cass filled his hands with the smell and weight and muscle of them, pressing into their coats, looking into their eyes.

"The mare has spirit." Cass had her by the halter and stroked her neck, ran his hand over her back. She tried to dodge his attentions.

"She has spirit. Perhaps too much."

"Could get up and give her a try."

Weidermann smiled now, a leer really. "See if you are a horseman, on or off? You have the hat after all, like the rodeo cowboys."

Cass shrugged. With men like this, you never knew. "I done some rodeo, yeah. Some broncs, years ago, but bulls mostly. Just bull riding at the end."

"Is that a fact? You are not from here, then? You are coming from the Wild West." He chuckled.

The vilde vest. "Been out west, yeah. Working a cow-calf operation near Cotton Creek. Alberta, eh? But I'm here now."

"Well-well-well. I watch all the time the rodeo on the TV. The Pro Rodeo is very good, yes? We have no bulls here, I am sorry to disappoint. So really you are a horseman. A cowboy. And you think you can ride this mare?"

"Could give her a try."

Weidermann leaned back a little, his gaze shifting to the horizon as Cass watched him balance prudence and desire. "Okay, you can saddle her up."

The German led the mare into the barn and snapped her halter into a ring in the stall. He watched Cass move around the animal with confidence and grace. The mare balked at the bit then took it. He set the saddle and tightened the cinch. The German had beautiful tack, beautiful stalls. Back in the corral Cass swung up into the saddle. The confidence of familiarity flowed through him. The mare danced to the right, balked, took a few steps then stopped. Cass pressed her forward. She trotted twenty feet then bucked and stepped to the right, bucked again. Cass straightened her out. Three more times she tried her trick, right and left. She tried ducking and weaving. He stuck with her. Once she found her gait she moved with the strength and fluidity Cass had predicted. He would have loved to take off into that perfect field of grass behind the barn.

He rode her up to where Weidermann stood leaning on the fence, examining him. "She's a bit of a joker, I guess," Cass said, a tiny smile bending the corners of his mouth.

"Now, Cass Hutt, you are looking for work."

Cass bobbed his head.

"And you know cows also?"

"I worked cattle, yeah."

"Working in the night shift—this is possible for you? You work steady in the night?"

"Night, sure. Don't see why not. Day or night." He shrugged.

"Well. Perhaps you come up to see the main barn with me now. See what you think of the cows. It's the cows that put the money in the bank. Horses only take it out, heh?"

PIPE'S BIKE TIRES CRUNCHED over patches of loose gravel on the packed earth of the railbed. She listened to the purr of the bike chain, the ever-whispering poplar leaves overhead, birdsong. She had never learned which bird was which; one had four notes in a row then stop and start again, one had an airy twitter, there were several of the same species with a musical chatter, then the crow's caw. All this, lace hemming a silence the color of the sun and the size of emptiness. Sound. She hoarded it and drew it close with the tenacity of a child who knows she is about to have her security blanket yanked away.

Pipe pedaled onwards towards her grandmother. Most of all she needed dog food, but there were other things too, if not today then soon. Need stretched out in front of her as sure as this path through the trees, stretching on beyond her vision. The humiliation of it blew on the coals of anger.

Up ahead the railbed curved and narrowed onto the iron bridge. Pipe stopped and dismounted, staring immobile at the point where the trail disappeared. The vague light-headedness that always met her here shimmered through her. Her neck tensed. As always, she turned away and pushed her bike off the railbed and onto the path that wound through the woods, along the edge of a hayfield, detoured around a marsh and deposited her on the highway just outside the village. It was a longer route and so rough she had to push her bike over much of the path, but it avoided the iron bridge. The soundscape tipped, a pickup passed her as she remounted her bike, the roar of a lawn mower bloomed in her ear, two kids called to each other. She pedaled along the highway, following the shore, and crossed the village bridge to her grandmother's bright blue house trimmed everywhere with flowers.

Pipe propped her bike against the house and continued around to the backyard, where she spotted Granny Eleanor crouching over a perennial garden. She approached without a sound, stood several feet behind her, watching her weed, watching her pluck delicate green shoots from the bed with an efficient gloved hand. Elegant was the word most often used in association with her grandmother. Elegant Eleanor. She wore her old cotton slacks and work shirt, like a gown. Most people didn't know Eleanor like Pipe did. Steely was more like it. An overseer. Slim and supple, all will and resolve and bullying domination. And tight.

The golden retriever beneath the tree looked up and jumped to her feet, literally caught napping. She trotted over, wagging, alerting Eleanor.

"In some parts of the country we say hello or good morning or perhaps how-do-you-do." Over five decades in the country and still Eleanor's lilting English accent clung to her voice with tenacity. Pipe tried not to listen. She watched her grandmother slip the gardening gloves off her hands, revealing long slender fingers with tidy, utilitarian nails. Wrinkled and liver-spotted, worn but strong; the dirt from the gloves did not stick to those hands as she folded the gloves across her palm.

"I'm due for a cup of tea. You might as well come in."

Wordlessly Pipe followed her grandmother and the dog into the house, bright and clean and spare. She slumped into the closest kitchen chair, a teenager once again, splayed her hands on the table in front of her. They were a mass of dirty mixed paint smudges, streaks up her arms to the elbow, her nails chewed to the quick.

"Dog food" she wanted—and did not want—to say, with equal desperation. She tapped her thigh and pulled her fingers towards her mouth in the dog food sign. Forget everything else, she thought. Get the dog food and get out. She imagined the wealth inside the fridge, the cupboards, the purse on the sideboard, the bank accounts. Anger bolstered her when it seemed she had nothing else. And so she fed it.

Eleanor had been busy by the stove. She set several digestive biscuits on a saucer and placed them on the table beside the teapot. She brought matching mugs to the table.

"You may pour, Pipe. I hear the fish plant is having a hard time getting a second shift together. Are you looking for work? I'm imagining you must be starting to wear your resources thin."

Pipe filled her grandmother's mug then her own. She double-scooped sugar into her tea and stirred it fast enough to create a vortex and slosh a little over the lip of the cup.

"I worked many a shift at that fish plant myself over the years."

Pipe broke pieces off her biscuit to keep herself from wolfing it. Six pieces, she decided. Two, then a sip of tea. No more than two at once. The tea was strong and fresh and sweet.

"MacLeod's will be opening their strawberry fields soon. I was speaking to Eileen the other day and she says they will be looking for pickers again."

Pipe looked out the window. She listened to herself slurping tea. A lovely great slurp.

"The lobsters are plentiful this year. Your Uncle Earl says the price is up, too. He claims to be doing well. He's with Johnny Everett this year, did you know? Kyle's gone out west apparently. Fortunately for Earl."

Pipe eyed a second cookie. *Uncle Earl, what a prince.*

"I believe I've mentioned before that sign language, unfortunately, is beyond my ken. Perhaps you could use your voice when participating in conversation."

*Ken,* she finger-spelled. *It's beyond my kin,* she signed. She gave a lopsided smirk and a snort. She felt so much stronger now, ludicrously so. She sat up straighter, although not straight certainly, and poured herself another cup of tea.

"Is your mother as well as can be expected? Have you been to see her?"

Pipe shifted sideways in her chair and snapped her fingers to call the retriever over, ruffled her head, let her smell her jeans for traces of Blackwood. The way she had visualized it as a teenager was two windows, one at each ear. Each window had four panes. The crosspieces and sash often were bright colors, red or blue or green, but sometimes a creamy off-white. And the trim usually white. She imagined black paint, imagined watching the brush, a big ugly four-inch brush dripping with black paint (sometimes a deep burgundy or charcoal gray), slap against the panes, spattering paint over the glass and trim indiscriminately. Drip and splat until the windows were entirely swiped, opaque. In the worst-case scenarios it was tar, not paint, smeared everywhere.

She ruffled the dog and petted her coat smooth, ruffled and smoothed, smiled into the adoring chocolate dog-eyes. She snapped her fingers again and gave the sit sign, which she had taught her, lie down, roll over. She never missed a chance to demonstrate that *dogs* had no trouble with sign language.

Pipe waited until the buzz of her grandmother's talk-noise had faded, waited until her mug was drained dry and the last cookie tucked into her shirt pocket. She stood up and moved towards the broom closet where the dog food was kept. "Could I have some dog food? For Blackwood," she said in voice. "Please."

Eleanor placed her hands on her hips. "Are you asking for a loan until your next paycheck? Are you working somewhere? Your Uncle Ben has some chores you could do for a bit of money if you can't manage anything else. Wayne was going to do them and hasn't, of course." She waited in the silence for an answer. "Why are we expected to do everything for you? Can you answer me that?"

Pipe shook her head and shrugged. No, that question she could not answer.

"I suppose the dog shouldn't have to suffer. Why people have animals they can't look after is beyond me. Go ahead."

"Thanks." In faux gratitude she signed, *If your lips were pursed any tighter I'd mistake them for your asshole.* Pipe turned and opened the broom closet, found a brand-new bag of dog food beside one nearly empty. Behind her she could hear her grandmother snapping open a plastic bag, opening the fridge. The kitchen air crackled with hostility. Pipe hoisted the heavy bag to her shoulder.

"Here." Her grandmother shoved a Sobeys bag at her.

Pipe could see bread, the outline of a liter of milk. The weight of the dog food pressed on her. She averted her eyes, accepted the bag with a muttered "thanks" and scuttled out to her bike.

You'd think they were the only ones to ever suffer! You'd think they were the only ones anything ever happened to! Eleanor wiped her clean counter cleaner. She inspected the tabletop where the girl had been sitting, where her hands had touched the wood, her forearms had met the edge of the table, checking for paint smudges. Those hands— covered in paint. Covered! What did she think when she left the house looking like that? To think she was supposed to take pity on that. Her Murray was never like that. Never. God knows she'd searched for him in her. Tirelessly, endlessly. But honestly, what was the point? Whatever Murray had given Pipe had been utterly overwhelmed by Lucy's influence. Eleanor wrung the dishcloth out under the hot water tap twice, letting the water run until it nearly scalded her.

Won't lift a finger to help herself. Oh! The frustration cut through her. And I suppose she's starving herself now. Like the girls do nowadays. As though the world isn't crawling with people who'd love the chance of a square meal. As though it's some kind of recreation—being hungry. Too lazy to work, too stubborn to work. Would rather starve. Let her, then! It's beyond belief. With opportunity everywhere. Everywhere!

The ringing of the telephone interrupted her sputtering. She straightened her back and smoothed her clothes. She touched her hair, patting it into place, and breathed deeply twice before picking up the receiver.

"Hello.

"—Yes of course, Thelma. Before Monday I should think. Then we can put the packages together on Wednesday evening. You'll have to make sure Shirley buys the envelopes; we don't want to be left sitting there like last year." With the phone chucked up against her shoulder Eleanor added an entry on her to-do list in her rigidly neat handwriting.

"—Of course, yes.—Oh yes?—Lovely.—Is that so?—Yes, fine. I must run. Goodbye."

She hung up the phone and switched off her answering machine. "No trouble at all. Financial report for the annual general meeting, squares for the lunch. I'll knit up a boxful of socks for the boys at the

front as well, shall I, before I get out to my garden? Come, Belle." The
dog trotted at her heels back to the garden.

At noon Eleanor returned inside, set aside her gloves and punched
her middle son's number into the telephone.

"Hello, Ben. Pipe was here this morning."

"Oh, yes. How is she?"

"Beggared by the look of her. Sullen. Haughty, but not too proud to
beg a bag of food for her dog. So in short, much the same."

"Does she need food for herself?"

"She didn't say."

"Mom."

"Don't 'Mom' me. She doesn't look well. She ought to be seen to.
You know what I mean."

"Does she look physically healthy?"

"She looks able enough. A bit ashen perhaps."

"Did you encourage her to see a doctor?"

"I might as well encourage the toaster, as you well know."

"Did you give her money? I told you I'd reimburse you."

"I told her you had chores she could do. You can't, Ben, be giving
handouts. It's not right."

"You said you thought she might be ill."

"I *said* she looks able."

"I don't know what more I can do, Mom. Is there something I can
do that I haven't tried?"

Eleanor clicked her tongue. "You saw the *Advocate,* I assume. I don't
need to tell you that anyone who hadn't heard about Wayne before has
heard now."

"Yes."

"What do you suppose we are to say about that?"

"His court date has been set for September. Nothing happens until
then."

"If we're lucky. The phone's been ringing since last night. Eileen called me up and essentially said the boy should have been drowned at birth. You know she's been waiting years for someone to act up worse than that one of hers. And Thelma called me about church business and circled so far out of her way to avoid the subject, I thought we were going to wind up in Truro."

"How's the weeding going, Mom?"

"Quite well, thank you. You know the lovely thing about gardens, you give them what they need and they pretty much do as they ought."

"Good, Mom. I'll drop over later, after school, shall I?"

"Suit yourself."

BEN HUNG UP THE PHONE and set his bowl of soup in the microwave. At this time of the year he liked to slip home from school for lunch, for a sliver of peace in the middle of the day. There were four children who needed to be held back this year and eight more in need of serious intervention. Already he knew the script. He would set up parent confer-ences and Donna Markham would spend the entire time complaining of her boy's behavior as though it had nothing to do with her. Chloe Nelson would agree to a meeting and simply not show up. She would repeat this pattern through twenty rescheduled appointments if she had to. The MacRaes would not respond at all. The list went on.

Ben arranged a handful of saltines on a plate and warmed his teapot with a splash of hot water. Twice since the incident with Wayne he had been out to his nephew's trailer and found the music at full volume and nobody home. He saw Wayne every day, though, in the face of the Markham boy—him and half a dozen others. Nobody should be surprised by Wayne's actions, but everyone would be asking why some-thing hadn't been done sooner. Why indeed.

The microwave timer buzzed and Ben settled in to his lunch, sighing deeply over his steaming bowl.

In the middle of the day with Judy at work and the boys in school Earl felt uneasy in the silence. The house harbored a mildly traitorous quiet as though it were sneering at him behind his back. Earl cranked up the volume on the radio and carried his sandwich and a couple of beer out onto the porch. He chewed too fast and kept checking his watch, staring up the road towards the rise where the mail car would appear. At the sight of it he abandoned the remnants of his sandwich and escaped into his Bronco, checked the mailbox at the end of his driveway and continued on to Scotch River. He stopped by his Mom's bright blue house, like he often did, on his way into or out of the village.

"Hi, Mom, what's the news?"

"Hello, Earl. The last of my tulips is finished. Even the late ones."

"Jeez, did you phone the obits in to the *Advocate*?"

"Speaking of the *Advocate* ..."

"Don't start, Mom."

Eleanor folded her hands in a moment of silence where Wayne hovered, bidden and waiting, then ignored. Then she continued, "Pipe was by earlier."

"Oh yeah? Stopped by for a session of witty banter?"

"Scrounging for food. Imagine! Streaked up with paint like a Red Indian so we'll all know she's a starving artist."

"Pretty desperate, is she?"

"She's as desperate as she wants to be. There's jobs going begging."

"So did you give her anything?"

"What?"

"Did you give Pipe any money or anything?"

"Dog food is what she wanted. She cleaned all the biscuits off the plate, I'll tell you. Probably hasn't had a decent meal since who knows when. Lots of money for paint, it appears. Throwing money away on foolishness all last winter from what I hear." Her hands were shaking slightly now, like they always did when she got upset and was trying not to show the extent of her emotion.

"Ah well, eh Mom? Maybe she'll sell some masterpiece and get rich and famous."

Eleanor only looked away.

"How does she keep that place up, Mom, if she has no money?"

"Well, it wouldn't necessarily be hers, would it? It's likely her mother's—Lucy would have inherited it when Murray died. And anyway I don't think she *does* keep it up."

"But taxes, though. How would her mother pay taxes? All those years?"

"I imagine they have people at that hospital who look to things like that. I don't know. Maybe it was held in trust. I really don't know, Earl. No one ever consulted me on the matter."

"Good, well, I better get going. Stuff to do! See you, Mom."

Earl drove out to his dead brother's old place by Randal's Crossing, slowed right down so he could take stock of the growth there. A little bit scrubby, sure, but there was lots worse than that sold for pulp. Lots worse. How many acres was that? Man, he knew nothing about the place. He turned left at the intersection and then, after slowing and checking no one was around to see, turned left again onto the old railbed. He didn't know if the property ran back this far, didn't know if he would recognize it, but then saw the signs: No Trespassing, Beware of the Dog. This was it. There seemed more hardwood than softwood here.

He climbed out of the truck and slipped down over the bank of the railbed. No trace of the dog. He beat his way through thickets of undergrowth, his pulse quickening. Standing now on the moss floor of the mature woods, he set his hand against the trunk of a pine tree so big around he knew his hands would not meet on the other side if he tried to encompass it. Maple after maple with trunks two feet in diameter. An oak. "Jesus!" Three feet across. Minimum. That tree itself would be worth what? Hundreds. A thousand maybe. And there was another almost as big. And there. He moved from one to another touching his fingers to the bark and, staring up, trailing his hand around the trunk. Acres and acres of them. They seemed to go on indefinitely.

Behind him a clipped questioning bark broke the silence of the woods, then suddenly a string of harsh barks heading his way. Earl sprinted for the truck and had himself safely tucked in behind the wheel before the shepherd appeared at the edge of the property snapping and barking like a demon in some horror show. Earl backed the Bronco all the way out along the narrow track until he reached the road again.

Well, well, well, he kept saying to himself all the way home. Well, well, well.

## CHAPTER SIX

CASS SHOWED UP at Weidermann's barn for the morning shift as arranged. The sickly smell of warm milk and pungent snap of disinfectant set him back in Jack's barn of twenty years ago.

"You the new guy? How ya doing? Hey, great hat." A man waddled in, snickered and poked at the brim of Cass's Stetson expecting to dislodge it, but it did not budge. Cass stepped back.

The fellow seemed to be spilling out of himself. His ball cap at one end of him and rubber boots at the other contrived to keep him together, but between these two points his hair spilled out from under the cap, his chins wagged from beneath his jaw, his shirttail escaped from his pants, belly from his shirt. When he smiled even his teeth seemed on the verge of wandering off in different directions.

"Just kiddin' ya. Now, where do *you* live? Big operation here—thousand acres. How 'bout that for a farm? Bet you never seen a milking parlor like this one, eh?"

The man did not pause in his patter but led Cass through the milk room and down a short ladder into a concrete pit three feet deep and about the size of Jack's kitchen. Along both sides of the pit were stations with giant jars to collect the milk and meter boxes hooked up with an arrangement of cords and plastic piping. A young man with shoulder-length hair descended from the computer room above and began fitting in suction cups at the milking stations.

The talker pointed with his chins. "That's Gord. You know when you're coming along the new road and you pass MacIntyre Road there on your left? Well, the next place on your right, back in, well that's where Gord used to live, eh Gord?"

Gord looked over and, when the older man turned away, rolled his eyes for Cass's benefit.

"These readouts all come out in that computer up there, but don't worry about that, it's all automatic. You want to know about computers and whatnot you ask Gord there. My God, there's not much they don't know about every single cow here. Read it right off the tag on their collar. Now, here's the disinfectant here …"

Without warning, Gord clanged open a gate and a flood of cows surged forward, shoving up against each other. But almost instantly the mayhem sorted itself into a single file as the beasts surged into a narrow chute ending in a kind of angle parking arrangement above and to either side of them. Eight per side, sixteen udders, waiting. Once all the places were taken, Gord shut the gate behind the cows and wordlessly began affixing suction cups on teats.

Cass watched milk pulsing into the rows of clear plastic canisters. When the first cow finished he raised an eyebrow in surprise as the suction cups flicked back to their hook, the vacuum having been automatically cut. Numbers flickered on a meter before the milk flowed into a pipeline and off, he assumed, to a bulk tank. But despite the technology, the essence of the job had not changed. There was no more bending under cows, no lugging milk pails, and they no longer stripped the udders to get the last drop as Jack had taught him, but a motor still powered a compressor to produce the vacuum that seesawed in the steady rhythm of the machines. Jets of milk still hit the sides of containers with satisfying twacks.

An electronic trill sounded over the hum and pump of the system, and Gord, who had finished hooking up his eight cows before the talker had done six, pulled a cell phone from inside his jacket pocket and unfolded it. He spoke into it, shook his head in mock disbelief and held it out from his body as though offering it to a cow's hind end. He tilted the device in Cass's direction. "My girlfriend wants to see the cows. Christ! You just press that there, see, and line up your picture like this. Send anything, just like that. Text message, digital pictures, e-mail, whatever you want." Gord's last cow finished and he clanged open the heavy metal gate in front of the lead cow, releasing them all into the corridor that circled them back to the herd. In less than a minute his alley was filled up with eight more and the process began again.

"You ready to start?" Gord asked.

"Yeah."

"I'll be back in a minute." He handed Cass the udder cloth and was gone.

An hour later when Cass was certain he had heard of every possible complication that could arise in the talking guy's imagination, if not in the job itself, Gord reappeared in a flurry, grabbed the cloth from Cass and busied himself. An instant later Weidermann appeared.

"So! You have met Hank and Gord." The German beamed and rubbed his hands together. "Everything is going off wonderful? Soon you will be ready for nights, yes? The night milker, she says always oh tonight is not good, the baby is sick, I have to go here and there, my back is sore. Before this I have a man who thinks nighttime is only for drinking. My son—I hear this summer he is too busy, yes? Sixteen years old and already too busy to help his father. So how much money for this big house here and I am half the nights in the barn, milking, waiting for a calf? This is what happens when you are the boss. You work here now, Cass Hutt, and we see what is harder—to ride a bull or to milk a cow, heh?"

Cass nodded. "Yessir."

Back at Jack's, Cass retreated to his little room under the eave. In this room he had lived a season, from spring to fall, a short time yet a long time. He tried to fix facts around him, but the trouble was these facts were not hard like pebbles but oozing and amorphous like handfuls of mud. Lionel used to bring him to his family's palatial home in Lethbridge for holidays. Cass had watched the brothers and sisters banter over memories. The picnic had been in this year because so-and-so had his first girlfriend there, but no it was right after Lionel's twelfth birthday because he wore his new spurs, but it couldn't have been then because they drove the van and they had not purchased the van until the following year. There were photographs everywhere and scrapbooks. They leaned over childhood pictures, peered into them, and Cass watched them soaking in the information they mistook for memory. This is what I looked like, this is how my father held me, this is what was real on the day I remember only the joy of beating my older brother in a footrace. Cass remembered the collection of snow globes that was integrated into the extravagant Christmas decorations throughout the house and how he had wandered from windowsill to mantel to bookshelf studying each frozen moment of bubbled perfection, complete and separate. He had shaken the globes and watched the snow fall on the castle or the snowball fight, the city street or the lone cowboy in the hills.

Cass rummaged in his knapsack, tossing the illegible bundle of notebook paper aside, and spread his deed open on his knees, where he followed the words with his finger. He patched his memory of the trucker's reading to the typing, and wrung what meaning he could from it. He picked up a pencil with fingers like carrots and pressed an uncertain line under the names of the two people involved in the sale: Catherine Taylor and Angus MacCarron. He could see where the borders of the property were set out, locate the words *north, south, east* and *west*. Fifty acres more or less. Bordered on the north by the Scotch River Road and on the south by the rail line. To the west, something Randal—the old farm at the Crossing. It wasn't far.

Several times he walked up the road and down the railbed pacing out distances until he was sure of the site. There was a stretch of trees along the east edge of the old Randal's Crossing farm. At the back of the property, off the railbed, grew a patch of big trees marked by signs—something "the Dog." "Beware" probably. At the front, off the road, the trees were smaller, scragglier, and a narrow lane led up through the center of the scrub. By the Crossing the original farm had been subdivided into lots that sprouted bungalows and split-levels with riding-mower lawns. But that little stretch of trees—that was the place.

The first time he tried to walk up the lane that bisected the property he was met by a German shepherd with a rumble in his throat. He retreated, did not press the issue. The second time he made it all the way up the lane with no sign of the dog. This time four white geese, spitting and hissing, met him at the edge of a little clearing with a house, shed and garden. He stood stock-still with his arms folded across his chest, staring down the geese. He advanced one step at a time, the geese running at him, circling, flapping and hissing. One nipped at his booted ankle, one at his calf. No one came. He did not approach the little silvered, paint-peeled house but hovered at the edge of the clearing taking in the shed, the chickens, the pump and the pails, the garden, the red outhouse. He kicked at the ground until he loosened a stone the size of a horse's eye, flicked the dirt off it and slipped it into his pocket, feeling nothing but a confused buzzing of shame. The deed was a mistake. This property belonged to someone else. But still, someone had sent him that deed, a real true thing you could hold in your hand.

Cass found Jack, as usual, in his chair by the kitchen window.

"You know the place up the road there, Jack? Just this side of the Crossing? About half a mile up where there's all the trees, before you get to those new houses."

"Where's that now?"

"Nearly to the Crossing. There's a long lane up through trees. There's some guy lives there with geese and a dog."

Jack sighed so deeply Cass wondered if in the time it took for him to fill his lungs and then empty them again he had forgotten the question. When Cass peered at him he saw him struggling to set his mind on such a specific question, to figure out what was now and what living person might be nested in this pocket of time.

"Oh yes. Murray Holmes's daughter."

"Does she own the place?"

"I expect so. Or well no, perhaps Murray's widow does. I guess that's more likely. Sad place." Cass thought he might say what was sad about the property, but he didn't, just rocked back in his chair and stroked his chin with his thumb.

"That was once part of the Randal farm. You know … that original Randal had a shipyard just about where the post office is now. Well in those days I guess they were everywhere—seven big yards in the mouth of the estuary. Oh yes, Scotch River was big news then—built ships that sailed all over the world. Most of those shipbuilding families came and went with the age of sail, took their money elsewhere when steam came along, but Randal's son married a local girl, you see, and she made him promise they would never leave …"

Murray Holmes's daughter. A girl. Cass tried to carry the thought forward but there was nowhere for it to go. Across the room Jack was in full flight. "… ten daughters and not a single one ever lived to bear a child. They say there was seven full years with not a heifer calf born on the place. Every one a bull calf. Twice the rams and half the ewes of any other farm …"

The kitchen clock ticked soft and steady in the background.

WAYNE PUNCHED AT THE AIR. Clifford hadn't been by for ages, hadn't brought his truck around. What was he supposed to do, all by himself with no wheels? Fuck it. He walked all the way, blackflies and every-thing, miles inland along the River Road. Trees and trees and more trees. Nobody stopped to give him a lift. Clifford was home all right, his pickup parked in the driveway. Wayne climbed the porch steps and tugged at the door but found only resistance. He rattled the knob, gave it a good yank, then another one, as hard as he could.

"Jeez." He rapped on the door.

"What do you want?" Clifford stood in the half-opened doorway, blocking it.

"What's going on?"

No answer.

"You got a beer in there by any chance?"

"Hold on." Clifford shut the door in Wayne's face, slid the deadbolt back in place, and Wayne felt the click of the metal between his ribs. A minute later Clifford returned and passed a bottle of Keith's across the threshold through a slit of an opening.

"Hey, come on. We got business to discuss." Wayne's smile drooped, too heavy to hold in place.

"I don't see no business."

"Come on, ya chicken shit. Open up." Wayne leaned into the door but Clifford's foot held it firm and when Wayne looked into his face he found it locked as tight as the door had been. Wayne blinked, looked away, sick.

Clifford pointed a finger at him. "Look, I don't know nothing about your business. The cops've already been around here once and I told them your business is your business. Got nothing to do with me. You keep my name out of it. Christ, how do you think I feel? You pushing an old man around, breaking his friggin' bones, for Chrissake, for a few bucks and an old TV set. Then the cops come after *me*?"

Inside, the television blared, and Wayne, for a second, was there with Clifford and the others and he had the best chair, the blue one with the tip-out footstool and everybody talking and joking and a case of beer open on the floor and a bit of hash and some pills around maybe. Music on loud and some girls getting drunk. Sally Nelson getting drunk and looking at him, putting her hand on his leg.

Clifford opened the flat little tin he sometimes carried in the breast pocket of his shirt and pulled out a Baggie with a few tiny white pills. "I've got a few of these ones you like. Take 'em."

Wayne barely had time to grab the bag before Clifford slammed and locked the door.

"Asshole." Wayne shoved the pills deep into the pocket of his jeans, plunked down onto the porch steps, unscrewed the beer and tipped it to his lips. He emptied the bottle and tossed it onto the lawn. On the way down the driveway he flailed a kick at Clifford's truck tires, scooped a fist-sized rock from the driveway and hurled it at Clifford's front window. The stone bounced off a trim board and fell into the grass. "Shit."

Wayne walked all the way back through the village and on out to his father's house. His feet hurt from all the walking. As soon as he opened the door the smell of something frying made him almost dizzy with hunger, led him through the house to the kitchen where Judy, his father's second wife, stood at the stove.

"Earl's down at the wharf," she said when she looked up to see him standing in the kitchen doorway.

Wayne shrugged. "Anything to eat here?"

"Well, I was making myself a grilled cheese. I suppose you want one."

Wayne tipped back in a kitchen chair, leaning against the wall, and picked at the scabs on his fingertips with his teeth. Judy said nothing to him until she set the plate in front of him, two sandwiches stacked up golden and crispy.

"Beat up any old people today?"

Wayne ate his sandwiches, the hot margarine burning the wounds on the ends of his fingers. He followed the pain up to his elbows, where it swelled and sat. He followed the warmth of the sandwiches to his insides.

"Well, you got your court date anyway. That's something."

"Can I watch TV?"

"Yes you may. Until two-thirty."

He wiped his greasy hands on his jeans and shifted to the couch in the living room, the remote control in his fist, and sat while melodramas filled the space around him. Before he left he checked the bathroom, but pickings were slim in the medicine cabinet. He pocketed the bottle of Tylenol 3s.

Wayne wandered back through the village and out the road to his trailer with the dented orange siding, jumped the ditch into his yard. His Air Patrol CD had been on continuous play since he got up that morning. He heard it from the road, felt the pounding bass track vibrating through the ground by the trailer steps. It blasted forth when he opened the door. People used to come around when his pal Darryl had shared the trailer with him, they used to come and talk and drink, and he did some business for Clifford. And girls would come too. One time with just him and Darryl there were two girls and they each fucked one and then they changed and did the other. But after that one time the girls didn't want to do it again and everybody got mad and that was the end of it. Not long after that Darryl said he was sick of frigging around wasting his life and he went up north to get a job. He had a brother up there who said there was tons of work, thirty, forty bucks an hour, no problem. People hardly ever came around the trailer now.

He dug in his pocket for the pills Clifford had given him, crushed them with the back of a dirty spoon and snorted them off the countertop and into his bloodstream. He climbed over his kitchen table and swung out the back window onto the trailer roof, where he hopped from one foot to the other playing air guitar and singing at the top of his voice. He jumped up to grab the limb of the tree that grew out over the roof and pulled himself into the branches, shimmied up the tree as far as he could go, until the limb he clung to swayed and sagged with his weight. And now, at last, with his blood popping, sparking, sizzling inside him, he laughed like he knew he would, swinging from a twig, light as a bird.

## CHAPTER SEVEN

THE DEALS WERE STRUCK one week from Cass's arrival. Cass would milk the night shift, Tuesday nights off. Seven bucks an hour. In return for exercising the horses and working with the colt in the mornings he had the use of the mare. Jack would be his landlord: fifty bucks a week, full use of the kitchen. Weidermann wanted a cheap reliable cattleman for the night shift and free help with his ponies. Jack wanted company; no matter that Cass seldom heard what he said. There was nothing complicated about that. What Cass wanted, he could not say. His feet back on the earth, perhaps, and something in the empty space behind him.

Every couple of days Cass read over his deed, practicing the words the trucker had read to him, ensuring he would not forget them. The fact of the deed, though, had taken up as much space as it could, lying there in his pack, in his brain, waiting. The problem was he wanted a few clean answers with no questions attached; he wanted to ride into the mess and cut out one or two facts. He needed to figure out what he could *do*, what action he could take. He ran his finger under the names on the deed: Angus MacCarron to Catherine Taylor. At a propitious break in one of Jack's ramblings he asked, "You know a person called Catherine Taylor?"

"Taylor? No, I don't believe I know any Taylors at all. Why?"

"You ever hear of a guy named MacCarron, Angus or something like that?"

"Angus MacCarron. Sure. Lives just in the back road there, just this side of the village. Quite the character."

"Must be old, is he?"

"Oh Lord, yes. Still gets around though. What did you want him for?"

Cass shrugged. "Just heard people at work talking about him. Which place is his, did you say?"

THE OLD FARMHOUSE had been the object of a holding action for many years. Shrubbery and weeds had grown in around the rotting front porch. White paint flaked from the clapboards but the roofline remained true, the structure stood solid enough. An ancient Dodge pickup sat in the driveway. Cass swung down off the mare and looped her reins around the truck's surprisingly strong bumper. A well-worn path ran to a sturdy step by the kitchen door. The remains of last winter's woodpile lay scattered under a shed roof. He knocked. A radio or TV blared inside. He hammered. Eventually the door opened and an old man, leaning on a cane, peered at him with curiosity.

"Angus MacCarron?"

"Hold it a minute, now. Just a minute." The old guy tottered across the room to turn off the television. As Cass had surmised, the old man had abandoned the main house and had moved, bed and all, into the kitchen. The air was close, heavy with the smell of stale bacon grease and liniment and old laundry. A film of neglect coated the windows, the floor, the furniture. Dusty barn clothes still hung from pegs behind the door.

"Who are *you,* now? Do I know you?" He swung his cane out in front of him like Zorro and stabbed it into the air towards a kitchen chair in invitation. They both sat. "Cass Hutt is my name. I got this deed." He unfolded it and held it out to the old man. "I wanted to know who you sold this place to."

"I'm ninety-two years old. Got my own teeth. Here, look. I had them carve my initials right into them." He took the teeth out of his mouth and pointed to the inside of the back molars. "They're mine all right. Look."

Cass looked.

Angus squinted at the deed in his hand. "What's this, now? Who'd you say you were?"

"Cass Hutt. Hutt," he yelled.

"Hunt? Who's your father?"

"Don't know." Cass shrugged.

Angus erupted in a braying laugh. "You're not the first one around here with that story! There's enough with that complaint, eh?" Another laugh then a sudden sobering, "You're not blaming me, are you?"

Cass shook his head. He pointed to the deed, to where he had underlined her name. "Do you remember her?"

Angus pushed himself to his feet again and tottered off across the room. "I'm ninety-two this year." He scooped up his eyeglasses and a newspaper off the little table by his armchair and hobbled back, shaking the newspaper. "Look at this! This is what they call news these days. 'Rural Services Eroding.' Who doesn't know that, for the love of God!" He settled back at the table. "The bootlegger's gone sober. Jackson Bigney. He's given up the business altogether. The nearest fellow now is way up the shore, I'd say twelve, fifteen miles anyway. They don't think about the old folks when they start eroding their rural services. Well, I think about these things. I'll be old soon myself. Would you like a cup of tea there, young fellow?"

Cass shook his head, picked up the deed again and pointed. "Do you remember selling this land?"

"I know. A man can have too much tea." He pulled a flask out of the front pocket of his baggy trousers, took a swig and handed it across the table. "You say your name is Hunt?" Angus picked up the deed, put on his glasses, leaned back in his chair resting his chin on his chest and appeared to doze off. Cass sighed and drank deeply from the flask.

Cass twitched in surprise when the old man shook the deed and spoke. "This is the east field of the old Randal's Crossing place. Fifty acres, long skinny piece, front thirty acres in hay. Seeded it in '56—clover and timothy. Back twenty acres had a nice stand of trees. Ready to go. Old house there too, I think. Nineteen sixty-three it says here, and that's right. I was cutting back the herd some that year. That's a bit of a distance to go for a couple of loads of hay, eh? So I sold that piece."

"The strip with the young trees this side of the Crossing farm?"

"Oh, it's all grown over now. Nobody bothers with work nowadays."

"Do you remember her? The woman who bought it?"

"When you're milking a herd of cows, you're working every day. *Every* day, mind."

"Who was she? Who was the woman who bought it?" Cass roared at him, trying to make himself heard.

"Who was she? Nobody. Came to the door, just like you. Paid in cash. Packed up and drove off before the spring came. Well, what does a girl want with a square of land?"

"Who did she sell the land to?"

"Then those years later came that crowd that bought that old swamp from Willis Henderson. Hippies, eh? Going to live on goat milk and buckwheat. They had some good ideas, though, like the women going around with no underclothes. I was ready to go join them." He brayed again. "Those fellows couldn't grow nothing but their hair."

"The woman? Catherine Taylor?" Cass poked at her name on the paper.

Angus stared at Cass and Cass stared back. Finally Angus shuffled to his feet and headed back to his armchair. "I'll tell you who was getting a piece of that one, though, and who ended up with the place. That Holmes boy. Peter Holmes's boy. You know Peter who fished—Ronald's son. Well, that boy of Peter's, not the ones that's his brothers now, but the other one."

Holmes. "Who?"

"That one who died. Hit his head on a rock, swimming. Some say. His mother's just there in the village. Eleanor. Christ, I used to go to the Anglican Church strawberry tea just to watch the legs on that one. If she wanted more than them three lads she had, she could have asked me the favor." He sank into his armchair, grinned and poured another shot of rum down his throat. "I wouldn't have minded the bother." Another great laugh.

"Eleanor Holmes?"

"Right in the village, across the bridge there. Blue house. Big flowers. I never lost a hair on my head till I turned eighty. Not a word of lie. I'm ninety-two years old this year. Now what did you say your name was again?"

But Cass had slipped out the door.

CASS TURNED THE MARE towards the village and clicked her into a trot then into a gallop down the dirt road, giving her her head, letting her blow off steam before they reached the pavement. She loved the outside world and the farther he ventured with her the more she gave. And the more she asked of him. He had ridden her among people and animals and roaring machines, weaved her in and out of all manner of distractions, but he had not brought her this far before. She required strength and confidence from him in the village and for this he was grateful. Once they reached the paved highway Cass reined her in and they trotted along the verge.

Almost every house in the village was painted white—white with white trim or white with black or red or blue trim. Some were covered over with an off-white shade of vinyl siding. A few venerable old homes favored a jersey cream yellow with ocher or green highlights. Third place past the bridge the single bright blue house stood out as Angus had intimated.

From the road he saw her, kneeling by a flower bed beside the blue house, her back towards him. When she looked up at the clop of the horseshoes on the driveway gravel he dismounted and led the horse forward, drawn on by the shelter of a large tree. He nodded in greeting.

Tall and slender, fine-boned with bright active eyes, she rose with more grace and less effort than her age would have predicted. Sprigs of pure white hair poked out beneath her straw sun hat. She plucked off a gardening glove and pushed the brim of her sun hat up, tilting it back where it formed almost an aura around her face. Cass was struck, as he often was when he came across women, by her physical delicacy, her tiny hands and feet. Women presented a kind of physical surprise to Cass. Their voices occupied a foreign register, their hands and feet and muscles were of insufficient size to operate tools, lift and carry ordinary things, as though they had been pulled from a manufacturing process before completion or thrown together at the end of the day when materials had run low. He didn't like to get too close to women, afraid he might break them. Then there would be trouble.

"Good day," she said. Her English accent floated out to him as soft and pliable as he imagined her aged flesh. "Can I help you?"

"I guess you're Eleanor Holmes?"

"I am indeed Eleanor Holmes, and who might you be?"

"Cass Hutt. I heard you might know about this piece of land here." He picked the deed out of his pocket and unfolded it for her, steeling himself in a sudden gale of vulnerability. It's only paper, a few sheets folded together. "It's that place out the Scotch River Road, near Randal's Crossing but not quite that far. Backs on the railbed. Somebody lives there now, with a big dog and geese. Named Holmes, like you. I been to see this guy here"—he pointed to the name underlined on the deed—"Angus MacCarron, and he said you might know what happened, like who bought it or whatever. 'Cause of your son or something? Maybe he knew this one here?" Cass pointed to the other name. "Catherine Taylor."

She frowned and shifted her gaze to the horse, looking her up and down, saying nothing.

"It's the property with … it's got softwood by the road and a path up through, and it's next to—well, a house with a big rig cab there sometimes …"

"Yes, I know where you mean. My son Murray lived there before he died. But that was years ago. Where did you get this deed?"

"Came across it, you know."

"No, I'm afraid I don't know."

"Murray Holmes? So he bought the place from this one here?" He pointed back to her name.

"Catherine Taylor. Good heavens. I don't know about that. I don't know about this. I believe the land registry in Pictou keeps track of that sort of thing. I really don't know what you're asking. Why would—"

A golden dog bounded over to them and dropped a rock at Eleanor's feet. "Oh, for heaven's sake! I want you to cut that out! No!" She tapped the dog's snout with her forefinger. "Ridiculous carry-on!"

When she picked up the stone and petted it, Cass leaned towards her and saw it was not a stone at all but a turtle tucked into its shell. "He keeps carting poor Mr. Eyebrows about the place. He never seems to do him any damage, but it must be most disconcerting, if you're a turtle, to be forever being picked up and carted off somewhere. It would be like always waking up in someone else's bed, I would think. Not to mention all the bumping and thumping going on."

Cass reached out to touch the colorfully patterned shell. "Is it real?"

"Oh yes, but I …"

She stopped speaking suddenly and when he turned he found her staring into his eyes, something like fear draining the color from her face.

"Who are you?" she asked, her voice a whisper.

"Cass Hutt."

"Where are you from? You never told me where that old deed came from."

Cass tucked the deed away and bent to ruffle the ears of the retriever sniffing his boots. "I don't know. They say I'm from here," he said. He swung up into the saddle and nodded at her. "The land registry in Pictou."

Cass rode back the way he came. When he turned into the Co-op store the front-step idlers busied themselves talking and carrying on with each other. Two little girls lolling about the Co-op parking lot eating Cheezies laughed and pointed in delight when he tied the mare's reins to the guardrail.

"Hey, a horse!"

"What's its name?" the braver girl asked. "How old is it?"

"Mare," said Cass. "Eight. Leave her alone."

"Can I feed it a Cheezie?"

"If you want her to bite you."

What Cass needed was something for that dog up the road. He found a package of wieners and a box of Milk-Bone.

"That's quite the horse you got there," the woman at the cash said and got no response. "Is it yours?"

"No. She's a rental."

"Looks like one of Hans Weidermann's."

He nodded.

"Are you working for him? With his horses?"

"Just milking."

"Saw you over at Eleanor's just now."

No comment.

"Not often we see horses in the village."

"Yeah, car's handier."

"I haven't seen you around before. Are you a friend of Eleanor's?"
He shrugged, picked up his purchases and left.

How odd. "How odd, Belle." Eleanor stroked the silken hair on the
retriever's forehead. But it was beyond odd. Fear tingled at the outer
reaches of her radar. There were things she did not wish to remember.
Yet she knew there was no real forgetting. What is gone one day is back
the next. No ocean is wide enough. She tried to dismiss the interchange, divert her attention from the conversation by concentrating on
the horse and on the strange habits of the man with the pervasive barny
odor. "What a rude man!" she said out loud to the dog. "He never said
where he got that deed although I asked him point-blank. And I don't
imagine shod horses' hooves do a lawn much good. Not that he seemed
concerned in the least."

As the afternoon wore on, her mind wandered off the paved road
she had set out for it. She found herself counting back. How old would
that horseman be? A young man, but everyone looked young to her
now. It would be twenty years this fall since Murray's death. There was
no help for a sadness like that. Eleanor set her hoe aside and retired to
her bench under the tree, where she sat with her hands clasped in her
lap. Her son Murray, such a gentle soul. A handsome boy, oh yes, and
kind. It seemed to her even then before events unfolded that he was the
fountain of all the gentleness, all the kindness that had ever touched
her life. What patience she mustered for her two younger sons came
directly from Murray, she had felt it even at the time. Her fondest
memories of motherhood put her and Murray side by side in the
garden for hours on end, neither wanting to be called away; Murray
tending to the sick and maimed, birds with broken wings, stray cats,
any hobbling or homeless beast. Murray softened her, required her to
grow within herself a tenderness not native to her spirit. The day he left
home she thought would be the saddest of her life, but it had not been.

The loss of him sat with her now as fresh as on the day they pulled his body from the river.

A plot of land deeded to Catherine Taylor! What was that supposed to mean? Why was the horseman asking *her*? He never said what he was doing with that deed anyway. Completely ridiculous! He must have found it in an attic somewhere. How could a person begin to imagine how he would come by something so outrageous?

# CHAPTER EIGHT

THE DECK ROLLED GENTLY beneath Earl's tipped-back chair. He lit a smoke, closed his eyes and listened to the water lapping against the side of his boat. The lobster season was three-quarters over and soon he would be free to delve into his new project full-time. Even now, though, he could lay out the groundwork, get everything thought through. No big deal with the acreage out front. Obviously he would be entitled to a fee for arranging the pulpwood contractor. But those trees out back, man, the quality of lumber in those babies! They could split the take on those. Partners. What was crucial to negotiations, to making the pitch, was whether the land belonged to Pipe or to Pipe's crazy mother. It would affect the slant of the partnership. Probably better for him if the crazy lady owned it, keep Pipe from getting too full of herself. But on the other hand, if Pipe had clear title they could look at other options, more intensive development. No need to stop at just stripping the trees. But the deal might be a harder sell if Pipe herself were the legal owner. She came into a bit of money when her other grandmother died; suppose she had bought her mother out. Suppose the land had been left to her in trust. It didn't seem likely, but it unsettled him that his mother didn't know this information. Eleanor usually stayed on top of this kind of stuff. Earl glanced at his watch, stretched and got to his feet.

Earl stopped by to check his mailbox on the way to the village, where he ordered a medium pizza with the works. He would bring a few groceries too, maybe ten bucks' worth, bulky stuff to fill out the bag:

hotdogs and buns, a loaf of bread, chips. The remnants of a six-pack nestled on the seat of his truck.

Pipe met him in the yard with her arms crossed over her chest and a scowl that would scare a goat.

"Hey, Pipe. Mom said you were looking hungry. I brought lunch. With a little barley soda." When he stepped out of the truck the geese rushed towards him and he involuntarily took a step back. "Christ, do they bite?"

"That's their job, yeah."

The dog at her side flattened its ears when he glanced at it, looked ready to pounce any second. It was a good sign that she was talking, though. "Can we go in?"

"Nah, here's good." She took the pizza from him and he could see he had hit the nail on the head. She lowered the tailgate, perched on it with her feet dangling and dove in. The dog kept to her side but never took its eyes off him. Earl jumped into the truck bed and out of the line of fire of those teeth, trying to appear as casual as possible. He handed her a beer, helped himself to a slice of pizza.

"Yeah, Mom was kinda worried I guess." She's going after that pizza like a religious experience, Earl thought. She's forgotten I'm here. "She was afraid you might be a little short."

"I'll bet."

"Look, I hear ya. I mean, fuck, tell me about it. It's not like it would kill her to help out a bit. Christ, you living here like this, you could live for a year on what she's rolling up in her coin jar. I'm serious. You know what she told me, eh? When she sold the lobster license? I ever tell you that?"

No response. She put back half a beer in one go.

"She told me she bought that house in the village with the money. Well, sor-ry, that bungalow ain't worth near what she got for that license. Not when you subtract what she must have got for the

Crooked Harbour house. And anyway she could've paid cash for that bungalow. On the barrelhead. No prob."

Pipe handed a couple of inches of crust to the dog, tossed another bit towards the gaggle of geese. She pulled a second slice out of the box.

"Christ, don't hurt yourself with that. Her sitting there on all that money and you living way out here, starving. The thing is, you know what, eh? Bottom line? It's family." He could have been talking to the goddamned geese for all the attention she paid him. Wayne was the same. Sit there while you talked—could be a hundred miles away, could get up in the middle of a sentence and walk off. You never knew if they were even listening. "I've been thinking about this for a while. Probably should have come sooner, but you know, I've been thinking for quite a while, it's all right for Mom and Ben, they're sitting pretty. But not everybody has it so good. You and me, we've had our tough times. I mean, take you, eh? You're—what?—eight years old when your Dad—"

"Hey! What do you want?" The words exploded from her and her hands flashed angry signs.

"Take it easy!" Silence bristled between them. "I'm saying I'm your uncle. It kills me to think of you out here starving to death and me not able to do fuck all about it, while those that can help a bit don't give a rat's ass. You know what I'm saying?"

She had him fixed with that same withering stare that Wayne would give him sometimes, like he was some kind of moron. He was only trying to help.

"Look, I'm only trying to help out here. I was just thinking, that's all, thinking what we could do. We're both in a bit of a jam, financially speaking, a bit of a crunch, and I think we could help each other out. Have another piece of this. It'll be cold soon." He pushed the pizza box a little closer to her, slurped back a long draft of beer.

She had slowed down now. She chose a slim slice from the box and laid it on top of the cardboard, pulled the cheese off a triangle at the bottom of the slice and picked at it, plucking peppers and mushrooms into her mouth. Finally she pulled the cheese apart in bite-sized pieces, eating as she went.

"I was thinking we could work something out. I know you must need stuff."

*So pay my power bill.* "I need my power bill paid."

"Well, there you are. That's what I'm talking about. Okay, power bill's paid in full. Bingo, like that—I'll take care of it. But that's the thing, see—we need some money coming in for stuff like that. And food, you know, that's pretty basic, and you've got that dog to look after—that must be a worry. He could need a vet." Earl took another swig. He might need to get someone's ankle splinters removed from his gums or something, he thought, and smiled at her. "And taxes, I suppose. Or does your mother pay those?"

No response except the moron look again.

"Look, I know a few people. I've got connections. There's things we could get done around this place. We could be looking at some serious money."

Pipe slid off the tailgate, called her dog with a pat on her thigh and started towards the house as though Earl were not there.

"Hey wait, I brought you a few groceries. You can keep the rest of that pizza too. It's good cold for breakfast. Might as well take this last beer too. There's more where that came from, eh?"

She returned to accept the proffered gifts and without a word turned back to the house.

"Hey, wait! I'm talking to a few friends. I'm getting some ideas together. Things are going to change around here." He had to shout the last bit, just got it out before the door slammed. "Hey, you're welcome. Just trying to help out, you know." Christ! No matter what people said about Wayne, at least he was goddamned normal. At least he wasn't as bad as this one. Loopy as a ball of knitting.

Pipe inspected the bag of groceries, set it aside and turned back to work. *There, Blackwood,* she signed, *goes a true patron of the arts.*

Earl hummed nervously and bounced his palm off his steering wheel all the way back to the village. Four-thirty. His brother Ben might be home by now. He turned in Ben's drive and caught sight of him approaching across the back parking lot on his way home from the school, his briefcase swinging at the end of his arm. Suddenly Earl wished he hadn't given that last beer away. He climbed down from the truck and leaned against it watching his brother approach, watching his brother watch him, wave to him. He waved back.

"Hi, Earl."

"Hey, Ben. You got a minute?" Earl, frowning in concern, related his story. "Things are desperate, boy. I brought her a few groceries, a pizza. Set me back forty bucks." In fact it had been closer to twenty-five.

"What does she need?"

"Everything. She's got no money for her power bill. They're going to cut her off, for godsake. She doesn't hardly use anything but her lights and she's going to lose that! She needs more food, stuff for the dog ..." Earl trailed off looking pained.

Ben pulled two twenties out of his wallet and handed them over. "That's for the groceries. I'll pay the power bill. Don't tell Mom."

"Mum's the word." Earl pocketed Ben's twenties and held his hand out again. "You can just give the power bill money to me. I'm going in to pay my own anyway."

"No, I'll take care of it." Ben looked off into the trees so he wouldn't have to watch his brother draw his hand back and stuff it in his pocket. "How's the fishing going, Earl?"

"Good. We're getting some pretty lobsters out there this year."

"That's great. Say hi to Judy and the boys for me. We'll have a barbecue or something after school's out, when the lobster's over."

"Sure. Sure, Ben."

THE SUDDEN INFUSION of the heavy, greasy pizza slowed Pipe to a languid pace and after a while she set down her brushes and wandered back outside to sit in the sunshine. She flipped a bucket upside down for a seat and leaned back against the yard pump. It occurred to her for the first time that it might be nice to rig up a hammock between a couple of trees. Blackwood dropped a stick at her feet and she tossed it for him.

Her Uncle Earl had no interest in her. He was quick with the hearty how-are-you-nows but he'd greet a turnip if he thought he could squeeze a beer or a buck out of it. In fact the last time he had shown any sustained interest in her was when she came of age and inherited the little stash of money her Nan had left her, mostly money from the sale of her wee house. Art college was not what Earl had had in mind, and he didn't try to hide his disdain. It cut her even now to remember the vehemence, the personal attacks. What in hell do you want to throw your money away on that for? You'd have to be bone stupid, or something else like it, to be suckered into dead-end shit like that. What that sounds like to me is some cock-eyed scheme your Uncle Ben would try to screw into your head. That's just the kind of thing he'd love to see you frigged up in, like he hasn't got you frigged up enough as it is. He knew it would burn her ass to hear she was doing what her Uncle Ben wanted, to insinuate she was under his thumb or even on his side. And it had kind of worked, too. Almost worked. She had put off her application a year in indecision.

What scared her about Earl was that his false friendliness might catch her at her weakest. And she so often felt at her weakest that how could she resist proffered friendship from any quarter? She had to be so vigilant. Whatever Earl was up to had everything to do with her land and her trees and nothing to do with her.

Blackwood dropped his now spit-shiny fetch stick at her feet for the twentieth time and panted in anticipation. She ran her hands along his back, looked into his eyes and almost cried. Then she tossed the stick again.

Nothing had been completely right except her days with Nan. Even before the accident Pipe had spent a lot of time at Nan's, especially when her mother was not well. Not well. Like the day her mother ripped the phone cord out of the wall, screaming, "They listen to you, they come down the wire!" Or the time she and Daddy had to collect up all the knives and hide them at Nan's house, or the day her mother dropped Pipe's open lunch can, wailing, "She brings these things into the house! She's horrible!" and her Daddy wrapped her mother in his arms and talked softly, like Pipe was on one side of the fight and both of them were on the other. As though imaginary bugs crawling out of her lunch can were her fault. There had been brilliant times too, like the summer day her mother had tossed buckets of cold well water into the air, the sun glinting off the tumbling water and the butterfly scarf flitting out behind as they ran and twirled through sudden drenchings. But too soon innocence evaporated and Pipe understood even the few shining days were also tainted with sickness.

What did it matter anyway, after the accident? She found herself staring hard into the woods behind the house. Her father had painted her a sign—Forest Studio—and hung it with a rope between two trees like a doorway to the little clearing. She did not know what ever became of that sign. In the clearing buffered by mature conifers, amid the silence of the woods, she remembered the softness of the forest floor on her bare knees and on her palms as she patted the ground, smoothed out the earth for her canvas. She remembered the slant of light through overhead branches as she swept away spent needles to expose shallow earth. She hoarded collected stones as tiny as sparrows' beaks and as big as apples, flat like coins and smooth as eggs and craggy as a can of bolts. Sorted in piles and in innumerable plastic containers were every kind of seashell hauled up from the beach; acorns, pine and spruce cones, maple keys from the forest floor; lichens, mosses, stacks of dried leaves in red, orange, yellow, brown. She remembered the delicious order of it and how the concentration transported her. That day she chose orange and yellow leaves with a sand dollar center for the sun, blue mussel shells for waves, dried spruce needles for sand.

WHEN HANS WEIDERMANN CAME in for his usual Mars bar and pack of chewing gum the woman at the Co-op was ready for him.

"We had a visit from one of your horses, Hans. Are we going to have to get a hitching post for the parking lot? Who was the fellow riding? A big guy with a Calgary hat."

"Ah, Cass Hutt. A smart man with horses and with cows too," Weidermann said. "From out in Alberta. A rodeo man, this is true, no joking. All kinds of rodeo and bull riding especially. That's not something you see every day."

Cass Hutt. The name was floated a few times—the guy in the cowboy hat who had ridden into the village on a horse, milking at Weidermann's, Cass Hutt, something Hutt. Rodeo, imagine! A cowboy in this day and age! A rancher. Alberta. And staying with Jack Heighton, Hans had said. Why would Jack be taking in a stranger? Does Jack's daughter know about this? For a few days the name was bandied around, tossed in the air like a ball waiting for someone to catch it, place it in context, find a place in a family, a property, a memory. If none was found, the name would simply be dropped and roll off out of sight, replaced again by "the cowboy."

When Earl walked into the gas station and leaned against the counter, he heard the name like everyone else, repeated it and shook his head.

"Don't think I've heard that name before. What do we know about him?"

"Not much, I guess. Except he was a rodeo cowboy."

"Go on!"

"No, really. Came from out west."

"On the horse?"

Everyone laughed. "How did Johnny do on the lobsters?"

"Good. The season was half decent for a change."

A gray-haired man frowned and shook his head. "Yeah, you can't win. If the numbers are up the price is down, if the price is up the traps are empty."

"Life's a bugger, b'y." Earl paid for his gas on the Visa and headed back to the wharf.

ELEANOR PRESSED her coolest cotton dress for church. She would love to slip in late and out early and avoid all the senseless yakking but this was hardly possible. Since the incident with Wayne it seemed to her that every comment had some hidden meaning. Even with the conversation focused elsewhere she felt people avoiding the subject. The man he had beaten was a Catholic living way out towards the point and not particularly well known in the village, thank God for small mercies. People had learned not to ask after Pipe. They all knew far too much about her eccentricities as far as Eleanor was concerned. She felt herself puttering, buffing shoes already polished to perfection. The kitchen clock read four minutes to ten before she set her hat in place and set off up the street to the Anglican church. She slid into her regular pew beside Ben just as the processional began. Ben patted her leg and smiled. She straightened her dress.

There was no avoiding the congregation of ladies outside the church after the service.

"Oh Eleanor, tell us, who is this mysterious cowboy?"

"What do you mean?"

"The man who rode through the village on a horse. I understand he stopped at your house for a chat."

"Oh. He only wanted directions, saw me in the yard, I suppose."

"That's one way to beat the price of gas, I guess."

"I hope he's cleaning up after that animal."

Some laughed, some didn't.

"What could he possibly want directions to?"

"Marnie at the Co-op says he works at the Weidermanns'. I don't know which brother, though."

"Hans, I think. It's Hans's horse anyway. Or that's what Marnie said. He stays across the road with Jack Heighton, they say."

"With Jack."

Silence held Jack's name in the air.

"How is Jack getting along?"

"Well, he misses Effie, you know."

"He does, of course."


BLACKWOOD DANCED beside Pipe as she made her way through her morning chores and took a couple of playful runs at the chickens, barking. She frowned at him. *You're full of beans this morning,* she signed, and he wagged his tail. As she did from time to time, she decided to take him with her along the railbed that morning. Together they set off through the woods, and once they met the railbed and Pipe mounted her bike she and the shepherd raced off at a great pace. At the top of the hill overlooking the mill, just off museum property, she left him guarding her bike and continued on alone.

Pipe descended into the mill basement where the workings, the giant spur wheel and the stone nuts, engaged, where shafts drove the power to pulleys and belts and gears. She tucked herself as best she could into a corner and set her eyes on the wooden gear teeth where the sunlight from the window hit them and turned the wood tawny. A maple brace met the trunk of the spur wheel at a handsome angle, causing the faintest of shadows. She set her pencil to paper.

Her first sketches were no good. They seldom were. Too much fussing. Look, she told herself. She forced her eye to hold the line, followed the curve along the blank page with her pencil. Slow down. Slowly. There was a bevel gear way in the back of the mill that she was trying to capture. It was a beautiful thing but so far from the barrier she strained to see it properly. She collected the curves, the lines and their junctions that formed shapes without names. Spaces and negative spaces. Seemingly random lines crossed and recrossed in her sketchbook but she did not look down. Holding her eye steady, she felt a delicate peace slip in under her skin. She hadn't felt it arrive, but when she finally stood and shook the chill out of her legs, stowed her pencils in her case, she found herself in that silent, woolen space where anger and fear and loneliness did not live. If she could carry this home with her she could set it on her walls, on her floor and ceiling, where she could keep it forever.

WAYNE DIDN'T KNOW what to do with himself now that Clifford wouldn't even talk to him. Everybody had gone crazy since the thing with the old man. If he could get a little stash of toys together, though, then Clifford would *have* to talk to him. Clifford wouldn't want to miss out on the profit. But Wayne had no car and anyway he couldn't think of doing anything more like that without seeing that ugly cop's face so close he could smell the recent tuna sandwich on his breath. Jail, the cop kept saying. Violent crime, he kept saying, as though Wayne were some kind of maniac. Jail. And he really needed some kind of pills or smoke or something, anything. He wandered across the road and over a field into the woods.

Wayne came upon the place from behind, by accident really, but once he realized where he was it struck him that family couldn't call the cops. No matter what. He cut in off the railbed, through a stand of huge trees and into a clearing, his heart ticking with anticipation.

There was no sign of anyone so he edged towards the stark little house. A hissing like a gas leak then a rumpled sound like someone shaking out a blanket alerted him. Four geese rounded the corner of the house, racing towards him, their necks craned forward, spitting rage, beating their wings. He froze more in surprise than fear but then they were upon him, swarming him, lunging at his chest, their wings pounding, slapping at his face, arms, shoulders, sucking his oxygen.

"Jesus Christ!" He struck out against the air, kicked blind and kicked again, screaming at the nip to his calf, his thigh. One had hold of his pant leg. He flailed his arms, desperate to fight through the blizzard of their wing-beats. He couldn't see. One squawked as it took a kick. It was nothing like fighting a human. There was nothing solid to punch. He took a heavy blow to the side of the head, landed another good kick, felt the weight against his foot. Shielding his face, swatting, cursing and kicking, he lunged for the house. He pawed at the storm-door latch, felt it lift, screamed at the tearing of flesh on his left leg, punched the air, a goose, the air, and squeezed himself in through the door, fighting to keep his attackers at bay. Half caught in the door, they screamed in pain and hissed their rage as he slammed the door repeatedly on a foot, a wing, finally a neck. He banged and banged against the last caught goose, kicking at its head. It looked up at him with cold black desperation forcing a gurgling hiss before Wayne finally pushed it away and pulled the door tight. He sank to his knees panting, trembling, rested his forehead against the door. Both his legs below the knees, his right wrist, his left shoulder, his head, all hurt. The familiarity of pain centered him. He did not inspect his wounds. He stood, cracked his knuckles and looked around.

He snorted, laughed to cover his unease. "What the fuck is this?" The little entryway in which he stood was … what? All around him, every square inch of wall and floor and ceiling had been painted in a tableau of an old-fashioned schoolhouse. There were three children with slates and old desks, a little girl with long braids and a pinafore, a boy with heavy boots and suspenders. There was a floor-to-ceiling bookshelf and a potbellied stove and a chalkboard where one of the boys worked a sum. The door to the main house was painted with a young woman in an ankle-length dress, her expression more hopeful than happy, reaching for the doorknob but looking back over her shoulder, her attention focused on the room. Unnerved, Wayne reached for the doorknob, apparently grabbing it from the woman. "This is pathetic!" He yanked at the knob but was careful not to touch the door or walls lest their oddness contaminate him.

Tensed to brittleness, he edged inside. Like the entry, the walls here, floor, ceiling, were being consumed by paint. The story spread out across the floor into one corner then up over the walls, out in all directions, growing across the ceiling. It was overtaking the entire space, wrapping around the windows. Where the work stood out rich and deep Wayne recoiled, afraid of being grabbed and drawn in, swallowed. Some areas had figures in great detail with no background; in some places outlines like ghosts or shadows foretold images to come. On the ceiling a huge wheel, a gear with wooden teeth, encircled the chimney. Smaller gears engaged at the corners, mysterious bits of machinery seemed to rumble and spew dust, and there by the stairs water splashed over a waterwheel and down the steps. He braved a touch of one of the huge beams with double angle braces held in place with wooden spikes, found them to be painted, not real. Seasons bloomed out of the corners, the heart of the color shooting upwards and dispersing into the mural, one in gold with a hint of a woman and a workhorse, this one here in silver-white and gray sucking the heat from his body. And the woman there, what was it? Was that a child? He tore his eyes away, tried to look without seeing the colors and forms.

In front of him, in the middle of what should have been the living room, sat a flat, doughnut-shaped stone about four feet across with diagonal patterns cut into it. A millstone. He had seen them before, set up in people's yards for decoration, as if there were something nice about them, ordinary gray-white rock. The place was a mess of paints, pails, brushes stuck in cans and bottles, rags. There was no stereo here, no TV, VCR, computer, no appliances of any kind. Not even a phone. He checked the only shelf—dishes, utensils, a few scant groceries. No liquor. Not so much as a jar of pennies.

He bounded up the stairs, unnerved by the painted water flowing under his shoes. Upstairs was a single steep-walled loft with a window in each end. No painted walls here, only a nest of sheets and blankets on a mattress on the floor and a stack of milk crates holding paint-smeared clothes. He rummaged through them. Nothing. A bunch of old paintings and stupid drawings leaned against the walls. There was a stack of books he pushed over and a cheap hardware-store wristwatch he tossed in disgust.

"Loony. Goddamned loony!"

He pelted down the stairs, trying to keep his eyes averted, to block his sight before it reached the walls. This place infuriated him, set his stomach on edge. It was the fight with the geese that made his knees weak, that hauled the strength from his legs. He stumbled off balance, bumped into a wall and caught himself against the ashen face of lone-liness. He grabbed one of the chairs and smashed it hard into the painted woman's face, the endless hollows of her eyes. Outside, a dog barked then barked again, very close.

THE FIRST THING Pipe saw was a goose struggling to walk, falling over and flapping in the dirt, blood shining and terrible against the white feathers; the other geese milling, nervous and distracted, by the back door. She ran to the wounded animal, stroked its grossly crooked neck, the feathers sleek and soft like fine white flour. The bird gurgled, tried to right itself and flopped over again. Pipe picked up her ax from the woodpile beyond the back porch. The dog barked and pawed at the back door, insisting. Pipe opened the porch door, saw the main door open and followed the dog as he bounded into the house. Wild-eyed and backed up against the stairs, Wayne screamed, "You're fucking crazy, Pipe! Everybody knows that! Call off your fucking dog, ya crazy! Call off your dog!"

Pipe advanced towards her cousin and curled her fingers around the dog's collar. The dog flattened his ears and continued growling like a diesel. Sweat stung Wayne's eyes, blurring his vision, his skin aflame with fear. "Keep that dog away from me!"

Pipe forced her voice out of the pit of her stomach hard and sharp. "Just. Get. Out. Wayne." Each word strafed her eardrums.

He shuffled his way along the wall towards the door. "I wouldn't come back here if you paid me!"

Almost to the entryway now he turned and ran, the three mobile geese at his heels. Pipe gave him a little head start then released the dog just to make sure he kept his pace up. Even when he had reached the railbed, ran beyond the property lines, left the dog barking behind him, he wanted to throw back his head and scream. He bled, shook, cursed all the way home, the scream trapped at the top of his skull.

Fierce with the violation, Pipe followed her walls, looking for damage to her work. He had been everywhere, touched her dishes and food and sink and doors and windows. No one, not one other person, had seen her work here and the first set of eyes to take it in had to be her brain-dead cousin who wouldn't know art from a flattened toad. A chair lay in splinters. She picked up the pieces, used the ax to complete the job and tossed the bits into the kindling box. She ran her fingers over the indentation in the wall where the chair had made its impact, examined the damage to the paint. She would be able to fix it. She would not be able to fix the gander that lay outside her door.

She carried her ax back to the wounded beast. Wayne had destroyed his neck, broken a wing. He flapped intermittently at the ground, his eyes dulled with pain and confusion. Pipe gathered him in her arms, absorbing the little resistance the bird had left, and carried him to the chopping block. It took three blows to completely sever the head. She picked the head off the ground, its proud whiteness now ridiculous, the perfect black-bead eyes, the orange beak now unnatural as plastic. She threw it with all her strength, high and long into the bush, where it lodged in the branches of a tree to await the crows.

She wanted to grab her cousin by the shirt and shake him. She fetched her knife, twine, a feed bag and basins. She arranged the decapitated body on the grass, slit it open and plunged her hand into the warm cavity, releasing a nasty acidic pong. She scooped the innards into the pan at her feet, where they flopped with a slosh. The dead stink of offal billowed into the morning air, sickening the sunshine. Her fingers bumped over the inside of the goose skeleton scraping blood, lung, organ, intestine, clearing the cavity, leaving her arm bloody and slimy to the elbow. The little bastard. The gander's mate kept circling the house, calling. Calling.

She rinsed the cavity, tied the feet of the goose with twine and hung the limp, swaying body from the corner of the shed. She tore handfuls of white feathers from the carcass, dozens of tiny explosions, tiny cries telegraphed through her fingertips with every grab and pull, until the naked body hung yellow-pink and exposed. Goose flesh. He had no business around here—she had nothing for him. She set the bird in a washbasin by the well and covered it with cool water, sloshed water up and down her arms, cleansing herself. She left the body to chill and returned to the house, stood hands on her hips, staring down at the marred image.

Loneliness saturated her muscles, pulled at Pipe's bones. Desperately she blew on the coals of her anger, dying now, nearing ash. The tears she could not abide. Wayne. Just a little guy. Your mother's a loony. Your mother kill anyone lately? You could see he didn't care at first, didn't really understand, just did it because someone dared him to. Later, after his own mother left, he took it on for real. She felt badly for him, pitied him. She knew that was why he tried to make her hate him. The little fucker. Even when she was way too old for taunting he could drag her into it. All the Holmeses could. Where's *your* mother, Wayne? Then she had felt so bad for him she wanted to punch his snotty face, wanted to shove his face into the snowbank, accidentally into a ragged chunk of ice. Don't listen, don't talk back. Ignore them. Nan couldn't cope with fighting. Just ignore them, be nice. There might have been a time when she could have helped him. Maybe. Maybe not. Paint, she told herself. Paint.

# CHAPTER NINE

CASS WAITED until his day off. He waited because every time he stepped towards the problem, trepidation pushed him back. He hated buildings with offices and signs and clean smart people who looked up at him with a kind of impatient sympathy. But it was more than that. Somewhere there existed information he once would have run through fire to get at. Somewhere there was a loneliness that he had left long ago and did not want to meet again. He soaked half an hour in the tub, put on clean clothes, planted his hat on his head and started for Pictou. A long-haired fellow in a Japanese pickup gave him a lift, dropped him off at the registry and pointed to the door. Cass shrank from the clack of his boot soles on the tiled floor. A blonde woman with hoop earrings and an efficient smile said good morning. She looked clever and smelled crisp as rhubarb.

Cass passed his deed over the counter. "I want to check who owns this land here. I don't know, like, is that a true deed and all? Legal?" His fingers drummed on the countertop in nervousness. He drew his hand back, tucked his hands into his armpits to hold them still, then, certain he looked stupid, shoved them into his pockets.

The woman's smile softened. "Let's just see," she said, and turned to a computer on a desk behind her. When she returned to him she flattened the deed out with her hand while she spoke. "Yes. As it says here, Catherine Taylor of Scotch River bought this property from Angus MacCarron in 1963. The taxes have been paid by a law firm in Ontario, most recently Goodrich, Delaney and Associates of Toronto.

The land was left in Catherine Taylor's estate, which they handled, to Casper Hutt of Cotton Creek, Alberta. Are you Casper Hutt?"

"Cass Hutt, yeah. So it was hers, now it's mine, for sure?"

"Yes, everything seems to be in order. The land is registered in your name. Taxes are all up to date, up to this year anyway, and those aren't due for another month."

"And Catherine Taylor? Is there an address or anything about her?"

"No. Obviously she died, but we don't have anything except the law firm's information. I can give you that if you like. Was she a distant relative?"

"Pretty distant."

"Do you have a new address, Mr. Hutt? If you're no longer in Cotton Creek we might as well update our records, since you're here."

Cass lay on his bed staring at the angles in the sloped ceiling, waiting for sleep, the summer sun so bright it penetrated the dangerous edges of everything. A woman named Catherine Taylor, a woman he had never met, never heard of, had owned the land until she died then willed it to him. Owned the land and had the taxes paid. Keeping it for him.

Cass had not known at first. Who was there to tell him? There are real children and there are adopted children. Real children cannot be made unreal but adopted children can be un-adopted. He remembered such a scrambled mess of things, he could not sort it out. There were boys, brothers. One bigger than him who said Cass had no mother, said she was dead. The brothers had a mother, the big one said, but not Casper. Casper. What he remembered was how fear funneled into a point, excluding everything, how the struggle consumed all. There were two brothers and because of this number they could hold him down on the ground. They forced open his jaw and stuffed crawly things in his mouth. A centipede he realized now and it had crawled across his tongue, running like a drumroll for the darkness inside him. The brothers themselves disappeared in his fear, reduced to the force and weight of their arms and legs, reduced to their actions. He could not remember their faces or names or the pain or pressure of their bodies but he remembered his helpless entrapment and the hundred tiny legs of the bug. He remembered the two-ness of them. *We* have a mother, they said. When he choked and puked they pushed his face into the puddle of gooey slime. It was soft and foul-smelling like all the dirt inside him.

Hidden in the pack under his bed the folded-over pages of inscrutable handwriting lay stuffed in an envelope. A fear as cold and tight as wire gripped him. He reined his mind around and galloped in the opposite direction.

ELEANOR RETURNED HOME with a couple of scruffy pages of three-ring-binder paper folded together. There was no reason in the world why the minister shouldn't be printing up the church bulletin himself, but she just couldn't bear the sight of it with its punctuation spattered around, apostrophes abandoned in ludicrous spots, dashes and dots in chaos. His spelling made the skin crawl and any word with a homonym was doomed. When she first offered to type it up she wondered if he had noticed the slipped-in corrections, but of course he would never be left to notice on his own. "Oh yes she does," she'd overheard from around the corner in the church kitchen. "She goes over the whole thing with a red pen just like a teacher. As though the man can't list his own hymns. Good thing it's not me, I'll tell you that!" She'd held her tongue of course; slipped off like a thief, as though it were her fault the man could not compose a sentence. Never let on you know the right way to do something. But they were happy enough to have her whenever there was work to be done. You bet. Eleanor can take care of it!

She sat at the table and smoothed the pages before her, but almost instantly her mind wandered off. No, not wandered, more like it was abducted. Not a day went by that she did not worry over the horseman. Not a day went by that she did not relive the moment of his peering at her turtle, the question on his face, those eyes. Catherine Taylor. My oh my. There were not enough cups of tea in the world to settle her nerves. And yet why would she waste time trying to settle nerves when the whole thing was preposterous? Ridiculous! Utterly unfounded. Half the day she spent upbraiding herself for the most ludicrous of notions and the other half of the day she was lost in them. She would call the registry and put the entire matter to rest. That was that.

"Casper Hutt," the woman at the land registry said. "From the estate of Catherine Taylor. Handled through a lawyer in Toronto."

"Well," Eleanor told the woman, "that is ridiculous. Perhaps you'd best give me the name of the law office. You must have an address for them, and a telephone number."

It took several days for Eleanor to shift her gaze from the land registry to the Ontario lawyers. The protracted effort required left her strangely achy and tired as though it were a stone wall she was moving and not just her attention. Perhaps she would not phone at all. Each time she poked at the question, now bruised from rough handling, each time her eyes strayed towards the phone, her heart skidded. Catherine Taylor indeed. Eleanor's misery wriggled sideways and emerged at the day her son Murray was banished from her home, his home. That was the day she ceased thinking of Peter Holmes as her husband. Nowadays people just divorce and have done with it, but then it was "marry in haste, repent at leisure." You made your bed and you lay in it. Peter had no interest in babies. Well, men are like that. But even as Murray grew to a boy and then a young man Peter was always picking, always finding fault, bullying. He followed Murray around, criticizing his little garden, his kittens or some wounded thing he'd found and was nursing back to health. Peter knew the best way to get to her was through Murray. He wasn't so bad with the next two boys. With Ben he seemed to negotiate a grudging standoff. With Earl, well, Earl was the boy he wanted. Thick as thieves, those two. Whatever became of Earl, that was Peter's doing. But Murray he dogged, Murray his pawn, his whipping boy. The bastard. Never mind, never mind, Eleanor tried to prod herself back to the present, blinking away the final scene. Peter with the crowbar, smashing the kitchen table in two, his bellow shaking the house. What madness to hurl all this at gentle Murray. And for the likes of Catherine Taylor! Long long before the day of banishment she had thought she had resigned herself to Peter Holmes, but from that day forward she resigned herself to disgust.

She remembered almost nothing of what must have been their courtship in wartime England. There are all kinds of war. After all that had happened, Peter seemed so inconsequential as to be harmless. What she married was a steamship ticket to Canada. To anywhere would have done—away, was the point. He was always on about home and Nova Scotia and Canada, and after everything she heard she thought she was prepared for the vastness of this new country. What she was not prepared for was the smallness of her new life: rocks, trees, fish guts and sparse half-educated neighbors. Ah, but she had her Murray. Until Catherine Taylor.

She could say nothing to anyone. So she phoned her second son, Ben.

"I suppose there will be reporters and such at Wayne's trial?" she said to him.

"Yes, Mom, there will be. He's not a minor."

"There should be some kind of dispensation for people like him."

"What do you mean, 'like him'?"

"Well he's not all there, really. He has problems."

"His intelligence is within the range of normal, if that's what you mean. Almost everyone who finds themselves in conflict with the law has other personal problems."

"If you're about to quote me statistics, don't."

"Well, it's true. I wish you wouldn't stew over it. There's nothing we can do until the trial except offer support."

"Why? So he can go out and rough up more old people? That man will probably never walk again. Older people don't heal up like younger ones. There's been more than one carried off to the grave with less than a broken hip. If he dies I suppose Wayne's charges will be upgraded to manslaughter."

"Two things, Mom. One, I was in to see Mr. Forbes and he was looking quite well considering everything. The fracture is relatively minor, a crack really, and his recovery is coming along. They are expecting to release him shortly. Two, Wayne needs to know he has family he can count on, even when he makes a mistake, but this is primarily Earl's call. Earl is his father. I've stopped by Wayne's trailer a few times but he hasn't been there. I'll try again when I get the chance."

"Well, I guess everything is fine then. We'll all just be supportive. And here's another thing: I don't want Pipe going back to the welfare office. I can't stand it. It's not right. There's no need of it. She can work. There's no reason in the world why she can't."

"Good, Mom. I'll see you soon. School is always really busy at the end of June, as you know. I've got to dash. I'll be by later."

"No, don't bother. I won't keep you."

The relief of fretting over the shortcomings of her grandchildren was disappointingly short-lived. She climbed the stairs to her bedroom and although she was completely alone in the house she locked the bedroom door behind her. She sat on the edge of her bed, buried her face in her hands and wept like she had not wept in twenty years.

EARL SMILED and leaned across the counter towards the woman at the registry desk. He knew how to manage these situations, no problem. Girls loved guys like him, loved getting a bit of attention. He set his hand on her computer monitor. "You gonna show me what you got in your little box?"

"Can I help you, sir?"

Earl winked and set out his request.

"Casper Hutt," he repeated, trying to place the name. Then, teasingly to hide his surprise, "Go on, it's not! You got the wrong place."

"Casper Hutt, 1842 Scotch River Road," she replied, matter-of-fact, turned the monitor so he could see for himself while she stepped away to answer a phone on the desk behind her.

Frowning on the way back to his truck, Earl struggled to make sense of the information. Casper Hutt. Hutt. Not that guy on the horse? Cards shuffled madly in his head, desperate not to have his perfect plan slip away. And before that, Taylor. So his brother Murray had never owned the land! So Pipe's mother never owned it. So Pipe didn't own it. Murray only rented. All those years, all his mucking around there, and he never even owned the place! And Pipe was renting it from this Taylor woman and then, when she died, from Casper Hutt. So suppose the guy is away, being a cowboy or whatever, then he gets word that he's inherited this place and he decides, what the hell, I'll go see it. Well, it's a dump, so he thinks I'll keep renting it out for now since it's a miracle I got a tenant nuts enough to want it; maybe sell it later or something. I'll wait for some good opportunity to come along. Earl could still manage this—the trees were still there, the land was still there. This was good news, really. Now he didn't need to deal with Pipe. He just needed to get to this Hutt guy before anyone else did. Absolutely! This plan would be even better than the last one. Before the summer was out he and Wayne would be fishing. Side by side.

NIGHT WORK LEFT Cass alone in the stillness of the barn with the snuffle and heft of cows' bodies, each beast singular in the night. They chewed and shat and shifted their weight. The steam off their backs knitted with the smell of green feed and sweet molasses, creating a tanginess in the air. Yet beneath this, the warm and homey cloud of barn smell, of manure, reassured him. The cows pressed themselves, eight at a time, into the milking parlor stalls, were milked then released to rejoin their herd. Row by row, he milked one line and replenished the other; back and forth, the process took Cass through the darkest hours. He worked away, the squish-squash heartbeat of the vacuum, the hum of the motor and lights, the smell of warm milk and disinfectant lulling him into an easy rhythm. Over the clang of metal, the click of suction cups knocking against each other, he moved, efficient but detached, always surprised with progress.

The ribs of these beasts insulted him. No meat. Of course they were supposed to have no meat other than the muscle it took to keep them standing for the milking and the heart to keep them in calf and keep the milk flowing. Divorced from all natural knowing, abandoned to the stupidity of staring at food on concrete, they didn't know the difference between night and day, grass and ground, coyotes and kittens. Cows as tall as horses, great spindly beasts stretched over massive frames with bloated distended udders bound up under their hind ends like some failed experiment, swinging between their legs when they walked. Sleek-coated, they had none of the wooly hardiness, the compact thickness of the Herefords and Limousins he had been accustomed to, had taken for granted—animals bred for bulk of muscle, beef. He could not lay a hand on these stingy hides without a physical memory that he had lived among those other cattle, had been there and was now here. The same man, same body, same mind.

After milking, Cass shut off the fluorescent lights in the milking parlor and wandered outside into the night. Two streetlights lit the yard, but if he rounded the north end of the barn he could escape the worst of it, rest his eyes in the darkness, sometimes see the stars. Often he sat on his haunches half an hour, waiting to dematerialize. But he did not, and so stood up and returned to the barn.

The main section of the barn was free stall, a huge single pen serviced by concrete mangers, automatic waterers, surveillance cameras and a computerized grain dispenser that read the tags around the cows' necks and rationed out their grain. At one end of the barn was the milking parlor and above it the glassed-in control room. Walled off at the other end were the birthing stalls and the calf pens.

Every two or three days a calf was born and separated from its mother. This night all the birthing stalls were occupied, with two cows recently calved and one about to give birth. Once the main herd had been milked he led the newly fresh cows across the barn to the machines, where he milked out their orangey colostrum. The milk produced in the first three days after birth was thick with antibodies and essential for calves but could not be shipped. Cass filled plastic nipple bottles for the newborns and poured the overflow milk into a barrel destined for Hans's brother's pigs. The little ones were kept behind a solid wall, out of sight of their mothers. They butted at Cass, at the air, at the bottles, desperate for the comfort of the milk. They sucked the bottles dry in no time and butted for more.

The cow due to freshen stomped her foot and fidgeted, restless and uncomfortable. As Cass replenished the drinking pails from the tap on the wall and cleaned out the stalls he watched her closely, saw her push unsuccessfully a few times. He soaped his arm and let himself into her pen. He sunk his arm into the cow, feeling around for the magic triangle of nose and two little front hooves. The nose was there and one of the hooves. "Two out of three, missus." The cow danced when he pushed his arm further in, almost up to his shoulder. She let out a startled moo. "Quit complaining. Who do you think's having fun here?" He worked the calf's second foot forward to join its mate and pulled his aching arm free. By the time Cass found a rope and got back to her he could see she had made progress. The hooves lay well along the birth canal. He slipped the noose over them and when the cow pushed he leaned his weight into the effort with her. Several heaves later the slimy black and white fish slid out and into his arms. He helped it flop to the straw, watched the eyes flutter open and the lungs fill. He pulled at the mucus over its nose and mouth. "Here ya go, ma'am. Good work." He released the cow from her halter and smiled as she nuzzled and licked her prize clean.

Within a couple of minutes Weidermann appeared. Clearly the boss had been watching from the much-rumored computer monitor in the house.

"There was some trouble, yes?"

"Not that much. Right leg bent back at the knee is all."

"If there is any bad trouble you call me. I get the vet. These are valuable animals. One of the most valuable herds in Nova Scotia. This is true."

Cass washed himself off at the tap and reached for his shirt.

"Still, it's not so much trouble, heh? One little hoof? What did we get?"

"Heifer."

"Ahh, I am now a happy man. We call her Cassandra because she is the first one you help. Yes. And for me, I do not even miss my breakfast." The German set himself between the calf and her mother and, using his body as a gate, corralled her around the barrier to her own pen, where she set to bawling.

Cass crossed the road for breakfast at Jack's before he started in at the horse barn. He poured milk over his Shreddies and sat in to the table. But then he couldn't lower his spoon. It hovered in the air six inches above the bowl. This was not the cereal bowl he had used before. This one was an awkward shade of green that reminded him of a child's plastic bowl and made his stomach lurch. He set his spoon down on the table and sat staring at the cereal, the milk bright against the woven checks of wheat. His forehead crinkled in a frown so deep it hurt. His burly finger lowered to the lip of the bowl and slowly pressed downwards, tilting the bowl until the milk met the edge of the rim, seeped over, dribbled, flowed. His brain kept telling him to stop. Stop. But his eyes were riveted on the controlled tip, on the descent of the finger, the roll of the dish. When the bowl clattered to the floor Cass jumped up and back from the table, half dodging the stream of spilt milk. Jack stopped his rambling, turned from arranging and rearranging boxes of strawberries covering half the kitchen counter, and stared at him.

"S-sorry." Cass swept at his jeans as though he could dust the spilled milk off his pant leg, fetched a dishcloth. Once there had been yelling, a commotion and bare skin in the morning cold. Once there had been fear. Once, not now. I don't have to put up with this, he thought, dumping the mess into the sink.

"I can't think what Effie did with all these berries," Jack said. "She used them all, though, I know that much. Jam, I guess. She was always carting bottles of jam off to people. Always." Jack wrapped his arms around himself, helpless.

"Yeah, strawberries. Remember that, eh, Jack?" Cass struggled to bring himself to the present. Here and now, focus on now, on the strawberries. He plucked a box off the counter, grabbed a large berry off the top and popped it in his mouth, sucking the fruit off its stem. The juice bled over his fingers. Think about the property. The property is mine, he told himself, drawing the meaning of the words towards him, but just as he approached an understanding of the words they veered off and galloped into the woods. Fry bacon, he told himself. You like bacon. Cass lifted the cast-iron frying pan off its hook and held it a moment, pinging at it with his thumb and forefinger.

Cass iron, he thought for no reason, and set the pan on a burner. He practiced holding his mind still, sensing without reasons, following motion as though it had no purpose. He watched his fingers pinching each slice of bacon from its package and laying them in a tight row across the bottom of the pan. The bacon sizzled around the edges, began crimping into ridges.

Okay, now the property. A stranger was living there, a girl. She had obviously been there for some time, with a dog and geese and hens, planted a garden. Perhaps this was all explained in the pages he had quarantined in his kit bag. His mind twisted so suddenly from the idea of the package it felt like a physical jerk. Once he had stood on a scuffed hardwood floor in jeans stiff with newness. Before him stretched a line of drawings of sticks and bumps that went every which way and there were about a hundred different ones. Everybody else knew the name of each letter, everybody else knew a song that started "ai-bee-seedy." He did not remember the words spoken but he remembered the flush of shame, sudden and overpowering then dripping, oozing shame. A puddle at his feet. No. Think of now! The colt had been making good progress but yesterday balked, threw his head around, ran against the lunge line and kicked out as though he had never seen leather before. Cass speared his bacon strips and lifted them out of the pan one at a time, piling them onto a slice of bread. When droplets of fat spit up and landed on the back of his hand he did not wipe them away but watched them burn red pinholes in his skin.

# CHAPTER TEN

THE GEESE were more surprised than the horse. The mare paused as she entered the clearing, stood her ground as they flapped and hissed around her. Cass urged the mare forward into the backyard, where chickens scratched, where the little garden grew behind sagging wire. Two pails lay by the well, an ax by the woodpile. A bike leaned against the house. Cass patted his supply of Milk-Bone in his breast pocket but saw no sign of the dog. If the house were at all grand, if it were brick or vinyl-sided or split-level or if it were sprawling and gregarious or shiny or stately or tall, surrounded by fence or lawn or neighborhoods, he would not have felt a thing, knowing such a building could have nothing to do with him. This house was small enough, shaggy enough, to fit into his understanding of "house," and yet within that definition it pushed at the edges. It looked so solid, so real, with an upstairs and a good brick chimney and an entry like an extra little room built just for the back door. It had windows with trim boards, weathered but reasonably tight-looking shingles, a cut-stone foundation. The house was close enough to him to frighten him with its promise. He *could* own such a place. It was possible, and the possibility terrified him.

A ripple of black appeared at a window. Then the shepherd rose up to fill the bottom pane, his front paws propped on the inside windowsill. Cass watched his head snap, his jaws clap, in one sharp bark.

Inside, Pipe started at the bark, her concentration tipped and shattered like a teacup falling from a shelf. She climbed down from her chair frowning and crossed the room to her dog. His hair prickled on his neck, a rumble rose from his throat, hovering like an aura. Through the window she saw a cowboy on a horse, and a flash of fear split her as always when she saw or heard the illogical. She touched her dog, drew reassurance from his vigilance. The cowboy was real. The geese pressed together watching him, six black beads trained on his every move. They shifted their huddle each time the horse stepped. The cowboy looked around the yard then at the door a number of times, not afraid but uncertain.

She crossed through the back entry and out the door, Blackwood at her side. Cass glanced at the dog and swung down off the saddle, kept close enough to the mare to feel her warmth on his arm. Murray Holmes's daughter. He took off his hat and hooked it over the saddle horn, wiped his brow with his forearm. He bobbed his head. "Cass Hutt," he said.

Pipe looked him in the eye, felt her heart hiccup unaccountably and slid her gaze to his horse. She took in its fine chestnut coat, the endearing white blaze that brightened its face, the eyelashes as long as cats' whiskers. The mare twitched an ear and tossed her head slightly to one side as though indicating Cass was the one she ought to be addressing. Pipe made her name sign, a short rightward jolt ending in a fist. She never knew, sometimes not until the last fraction of a second, whether she would speak or sign, whether she would thrust her voice forward into the delicate nosegay of sound that surrounded her. She never knew if maintaining her silence would be more trouble than it was worth. But this was her house and she should be able to do what she wanted.

Cass watched. When she said nothing he returned her sign although he did not know what it meant.

Hearing people never returned signs. They usually tried to stifle the alarm in their eyes then searched for exits. She reached towards the horse and stroked its nose. "Pipe," she whispered. "Pipe Holmes." She needed a horse. Her summer wall, her green wall, her growth and sweat and strength and determination wall, had a horse, but her first attempt was awkward and ungainly and she had not yet returned to the challenge. Pipe stared at the length of the horse's ears, the dimensions of its nostrils, trying to absorb everything at once.

"I, uh—you know who owns this place?" Cass asked.

*Yeah. I do. Why?*

She signed something short and uninviting, starting with a finger pointed towards herself and ending with a question. What had he expected? If she thought she owned the place, what could he possibly be doing here? Here he stood abandoned by facts and without a plan.

"I thought maybe I was born here. Somebody said this place … maybe it was here. This is a nice place. You like horses? She's a good horse. You ride?"

Her eyebrows knit in suspicion. *Born here.* "Born here?" She spoke barely audibly and signed simultaneously giving him the impression that he understood her gesticulations when in truth it was only the words he understood. Born. He made the sign back, one palm rising from the abdomen and landing in the other. Why did he say that? Why would he say such a ridiculous thing? Now he was stuck with it.

"I heard once Catherine Taylor had this place," he said.

She shook her head, looked back at the horse. Cass stepped aside still holding the reins but giving her clear access to the mare, courting her grace. She looked like she could go either way, like she could just as easily turn back to the house and leave him alone to deal with the dog. Cass crouched on his haunches making himself as small as he could. He moved slowly, set a biscuit on the grass for the dog.

"Never heard of her. You got the wrong spot. My father owned this place." She was speaking now, had her hands busy, one stroking the mare's neck, the other seeming to follow the line of the horse's back despite the disruption of the saddle. She didn't have a horseman's touch.

"Never heard the name?"

She shook her head no. He searched her features. If she was a liar, she was a good one.

Pipe rolled the name around in her head, Catherine Taylor, Cathy Taylor, Kate Taylor, Catherine Taylor. Nope. The trouble she had had before, in her early attempt to capture the horse, was the chest muscles and the point where the front legs met the body. She could see now how mistaken she had been, how poorly she had rendered it. The line of the head as well, she'd got the curve wrong. Pipe followed the line now taking in the horse's profile, following the line down through the reins to the resting cowboy crouching as though he would be comfortable there for hours. Tranquil. Patient. Beautifully silent. Beautiful. Again something tweaked in her chest opening a small scratch across her heart.

She had never heard of anyone called Cass Hutt.

Pipe hovered a second in indecision then held up a wait-a-minute finger to the cowboy and ducked inside the house. She returned a moment later with her sketchbook. She just wanted to catch the horse's chest muscles, just wanted to make a few notes on the eye, couldn't turn her back on such a windfall of luck. She squatted much like Cass but leaning back against the wall and set to work with quick, deft strokes of her pencil. Cass watched, saying nothing.

It was Pipe that eventually broke the silence. "What are you doing way up here with cookies for my dog?"

"I wanted to know about Catherine Taylor. I—"

"There's no such person. Not who lived here anyway."

He didn't argue, just kept sitting there holding the reins while she drew. Since he made no move to leave she kept at her work, and since she seemed content to let him sit there Cass did just that, taking in the clearing, the woods, the section of the house in front of him, the wreckage of the derelict barn. He passed another biscuit to the dog.

Finally Pipe stood and spoke. "I've already had one break-in here and I don't need another. I've got nothing to steal. And look, an artist's rendering of the suspect." She tilted the sketchbook so he could see her last drawing: a sketch not just of a man crouching with reins but of *him*. Absolutely and unmistakably him. Cass gawked. She might as well have pulled a live dove out of his ear. He stood and stepped towards the drawing, reaching out to it. He stared at her then back at the picture.

"Th-that's me."

She laughed a delighted tinkling laugh, a woman's laugh, at his amazement and when he looked back into her eyes he found himself smiling at the magic of it. When he tried to touch the page she snapped the book shut. She signed something brief into the air and laughed again. *That's for the police.* The next time she signed she whispered along.

"You from around here?"

Cass jutted his chin towards Jack's. "I stay at Jack Heighton's. The mare is Hans Weidermann's. I wouldn't steal anything here. I don't steal." The last sentence caught him up. He had never said such a sentence before and it sounded embarrassingly unconvincing to him. False even. Taken over a lifetime, it *was* false. He tried to think of what else to say to reassure her. "I was here one summer, twenty years ago, at Jack's—practically next door. Spent the whole summer here."

"You were a kid then," she said. *You were a kid then.* She squiggled her forefinger under her nose, looked at him with a question in her eyes.

"Kid," he said, signing it back, grinning. "I guess so. Nearly sixteen. Big, though, full-grown." With "big" he gestured tall and wide, an attempt at a sign.

She laughed and gave him the sign, a pointed forefinger sliding up an open palm. *Tall.*

"You living here then? Twenty years ago?"

He watched her toss her head and stare into the trees. When she looked back she nodded, leery.

*Kid*, he signed. "How old?"

She pointed a sign at him.

"What's that?"

She held her hand palm out with fingers spread until he followed suit. "Five," she whispered. He followed her as she tucked her little finger in under her thumb. "Six." She released the little finger and tucked the next finger.

"Seven," said Cass. He moved up another finger reproducing her original sign. "Eight."

*Eight.* Nod.

"You were eight. Living with your folks? Your parents? What were their names?" Cass's heart beat faster in spite of himself.

*What's with the third degree, buddy?*

When she signed this time she gave no interpretation. The words did not look inviting so he circled back, lightened his voice and changed the subject. "It was a good summer, that one. Sunny. Good for hay. There were train tracks on the railbed then, remember? I used to lie in the river to cool off. I couldn't swim though. Did you swim?"

She nodded tentatively and Cass plowed on, unsure, but loath to let the contact end. He searched his memory for something in that summer besides the Heightons' hay and the picnic-table vigils in the park. "There was a funny thing that summer. There was a crazy lady on the tracks. You ever see her? She was pretty funny, flying down the tracks with this scarf sailing out behind her like wings. All colors. Then stop and pick up garbage and put it in her pocket. She yelled stuff. You ever see her?"

Pipe did not move, did not blink. In a moment of confusion he wondered if she really was deaf—but no, she heard him speak.

He persisted. "You must've seen her. She'd make ya laugh. Crazy, gee—she shakes this Coke can at me, 'This is the word of God,' she says. I called her Crazybird—'cause of the wings."

Still she did not move. When she finally spoke it was with no signing at all, her voice clear and icy. "That was my mother. Her name is *Lucy*."

"Oh."

She stood then and turned to return inside but paused at the door, her sketchbook folded to her chest, and waited, watching him mount. "Where you from, Cass Hutt?"

"Out west. Alberta. Cotton Creek. That's southwest, in the foothills."

"Before that?"

"Here."

She held cupped hands out and dipped them back and forth. *Here.* He returned the sign and nodded goodbye.

Once inside, Pipe scrambled upstairs, peeked through the little gable window where she watched the man in the cowboy hat click his horse into a trot and disappear down the lane. She frowned in confusion but managed to set her sketchbook aside and pull herself back to work.

Pipe stopped for a supper of her first tiny new peas and another great feed of the goose she had roasted. The meat would not keep much longer. She carried her plate outdoors, settled on a tree-stump seat. She opened her sketchbook and gazed again at the image of the cowboy. Cass Hutt. She printed his name beneath the line portrait.

After supper Pipe struggled to focus her mind back on her work, kept at her brushes and paint late into the night. Her concentration did not fail her, not exactly. Her work progressed well enough and yet that thicket of protection, that buffering of her from the world, never appeared. She felt vulnerable, as though she were painting exposed in the village park. That fellow had cut into her solitude like an apple, exposing it to air and turning it brown with loneliness. His eyes were dark and made darker by the way his eyebrows bunched a bit, locking his face in a perpetual determined calm. His jawline arced gracefully giving him a gentle, heart-shaped face. Perhaps his rough shave was supposed to combat the softness of the line. One great thing about living alone, being alone, is that you can cry whenever you want, as long and hard as you want.

IT WAS NEARLY NOON when Wayne heard the roar of a mufflerless truck turn into his yard. He rubbed the sleep out of his eyes, pulled on his jeans and sauntered out of his trailer letting the aluminum door flop behind him. It was Clifford's old truck, the Dakota with the tinted windows. You never knew who would be driving the Dakota; it was always out jobbing around.

Roger rolled down the window. Roger could always be counted on for a toke; he grew the best bud around except for Jackson Bigney, who had got out of it now anyway. Roger didn't really look at him but he nodded in his general direction, lit a smoke and propped his elbow out the window. Next to him sat a girl Wayne had seen before at Clifford's, but he did not know her name or who she was supposed to be going with. Wayne leaned against the hood by the driver's door.

"Clifford's pissed," Roger said after a while.

"So?"

"So. Yeah." Roger scratched his nose, noncommittal.

The girl leaned over, her face pushed out with indignation. "So, *yeah*! Clifford's like totally upset. That was so mean, beating up that poor old man. That's like hitting, like, you know, like your *grand*father or something. You are such a loser—you know that? Clifford is, like, *embarrassed,* to even know you."

Both men looked at her, as though momentarily curious as to the source of the noise, then Roger pulled the keys from the ignition, slid out of the truck and slammed the door without looking back. They rounded the truck and Roger dropped the tailgate, where he sat swinging his legs. Neither spoke. After a while the girl pounded a couple of impatient blasts on the horn.

Roger hollered over his shoulder, "You wanna go? Go."

"I got beer," Wayne said.

Roger smiled and hopped off the tailgate. He gave the briefest of nods towards the bed of the truck where several cardboard boxes huddled. "Clifford's got a few things you could keep an eye on."

Silently they carried the boxes into Wayne's trailer.

Roger tidied the boxes into the cupboard beneath the counter. "Wanna smoke a joint?"

"Yeah." Wayne felt better than he had in weeks.

ELEANOR KNEW IT was Ben who kept batting these things her way—a call from this one or that one about doing something for the children, something for the kids. Those words were supposed to open every door, silence any protestation. This clamoring from the school's "Village Garden" and the 4-H garden club made her crazy. Today it was Mary Jean with the CGIT girls. "The girls would love a tour of your garden." They didn't of course. Running here and there, asking inane questions, none of which had the slightest relevance to the plant world. All the while she had to maintain the demeanor of an indulgent aunt. Murray had been selling his own strawberries by the time he was their age. He had built a rock garden and established perennials for the sheer love of it. One of the girls kept inching closer and closer to the edge of the pond, just dying to "fall" in. After the ordeal was over with, when they had finally all been rounded up and bundled back into vans, after she had waved to them valiantly from the driveway, Eleanor slipped into her kitchen and dribbled a thimbleful of gin into her lemonade. Then she returned to her garden to survey the damage.

Belle met her with a wag and set the turtle gently at her feet. "Oh now stop! I thought we were through with this. You leave him be for years and now every time I turn around you're trotting him here and there until he gets no peace at all." She picked up the poor turtle and tapped the dog's snout with her index finger in chastisement. "No." She sat on the bench by the pond nestling the turtle into her lap, unconsciously petting its shell. When she closed her eyes Murray was so close—off in the village perhaps, on his way to see her. It made her desperate all the time, grief melted into anticipation, the most incongruous of emotions mixing in a slurry of confusion until she was sure she could not abide another minute.

So much is taken and so little left in its place. Every night when Eleanor slid into sleep Murray was waiting and trying to give her something, but Eleanor did not believe in dreams. Important things happen in the daytime when you can do something about them. She had got on all right before the horseman had shown up, before she had been forced to make inquiries, before everything turned back to Murray Murray Murray. As raw as it had ever been. As though it had all happened yesterday. There was no going on like this. Every time she turned the soil, passed a framed photograph, touched her heart, there he was. The phone stared at her, taunting, smirking with truths. It would drive her mad knowing the man was right there on the other side of the village, that something of her Murray could be touched, held, spoken to, here in this life. Certain facts must be made clear to Casper Hutt. And, as always, there were things best left unsaid.

CASS WAS NOT SURPRISED when Eleanor Holmes phoned Jack's house and asked to speak to him. If people knew where he worked it would be easy enough to learn where he slept. He was not surprised when she asked him to return to her bright blue house in the village.

She was looking for someone to mow her lawn she said and she needed someone to help her with a few chores around her greenhouse. Her voice was clipped and brittle as though she were holding herself above him, away from him. She is afraid, he thought. Cass knew that certain facts lined up, certain facts were waiting for him to turn his head and look. He had lived in a room once, with three gray shelves that ran the entire width of the room. He used to trail his palm across the empty space. The bottom shelf sat only a couple of inches off the floor, so he duckwalked along the shelves with his arm trailing, back he went in a bent-over position to stroke the middle shelf, then upright for the top one. Every day the same, left to right, bottom to top. He wanted to keep the shelves completely bare. There was something about the empty space that reflected him. It was hard to keep them empty. People were always piling things there. Every day he had to guard those gray shelves, clear things off them. Murray Holmes lived on Catherine Taylor's land that now belongs to Cass Hutt. If you consider a thing the way a horse sees it there's no need for *why*, just *is*.

Cass rode the mare along the railbed, veering off before the iron bridge and skirting the marsh and the field. He had once owned a most handsome saddle, won it in a competition. He tried to recall each design tooled into the leather, each intricate rose and swirl, keeping his mind busy all the way to Eleanor's.

Cass could see Eleanor Holmes wanted to grab his jaw and examine his teeth, take hold of his head between her hands and stare into his eyes, check his profile, run her fingers over his shoulders and his chest. She frowned as she spoke, wanted him to cart a stack of old windows from this place to that place, bang in a few nails along a board in the greenhouse, mow a patch of lawn so short he could barely see where the mower had passed. The place was so neat and tidy she must have had to dig deep to find these few chores. She followed his stride, watching his legs as he mowed. He wondered if she could see the space between his feet and the ground. And then she called him over, waving above the roar of the mower.

"I need to speak to you."

He should not have come. He should not have come to the blue house; he should not have come to Scotch River. A sudden breathlessness opened in front of him as though oxygen had been seared from the air in some invisible explosion. His lungs would not take in air. He recoiled, releasing the lawn mower, and the abrupt silence engulfed him. In this sudden bubble Cass was making his wrap, leather on leather. The rider does not control the bull, he controls himself, keeps himself in line with the bull's back, heels down then tucked, never letting go, anticipating from the muscle. He wasn't ready. The bull was twisting in the chute beneath him and his wrap was wrong, flapping loose. Hold it—hold it.

"Never mind that," she was saying to him. "Come over here. I must speak to you."

He shook his head no, afraid his voice might have abandoned him.

"Really, I must insist." She moved towards him and he turned, almost lunged for the mare, but Eleanor persisted, backing him into the horse's flank, would not let him be.

"It must be said. There simply isn't any easy way. You belong to my son Murray. I spoke … I checked … I know, well, there simply isn't any doubt. My Murray was your father. Murray Holmes."

There now. A few small simple words. There he stood with a hand on the saddle horn and the other pressed against the cantle. Words said and heard.

"I recognized that look, that dark gentleness in your eyes. Just like him when you looked at that turtle. This is not easy for me. It is quite a shock, as you can imagine."

"Yes ma'am."

Her voice fell to a whisper and lost its declaratory tone as though she had come to the end of her prepared speech and was now abandoned onstage, left to her own devices. "Do you understand what I am saying to you?"

"Yes ma'am. Murray Holmes. He lived on that property. I showed you the deed."

"Yes. You must come into the house. There is no need to have the neighbors gawking. There are aspects of ... I can show you ... This must be our secret for the moment." She reached out her hands to him, her small age-softened hands, and he watched them approach, aimed first at his elbows then at his shoulders, closer. She advanced on him, froze a moment before contact, and in that crystal moment Cass found the stirrup and swung himself into the saddle.

"'Fraid I won't be able to get that lawn done there."

"Casper Hutt. This is our secret."

Casper. "Yes ma'am. Secret."

Cass did not look back, he did not turn his head towards the village park as he rode past, did not pause when a voice sung out to him on the road. He turned back onto the trail beyond the school, trotted to the railbed, and from there he let the mare fly, wide open, to the Crossing. To hell with Eleanor Holmes, he thought. You can lead a horse to water but you can't make him think. No, it's drink. Can't make him drink.

PIPE WHISTLED for the dog and headed for the narrow path she had hacked around the perimeter of her property. Here she ran most days to keep her body fluid and to impress upon Blackwood the dimensions and limits of his kingdom. Along the path through the scraggly young woods at the front of the property Blackwood caught the scent of a rabbit and flushed it from the insufficient cover of an alder thicket. Alight with fright it bounded in front of her with the dog in ecstatic pursuit. The dog pounced. There was a sickening high-pitched squeal and a desperate wriggling. Blackwood lifted his head and shook with magnificent joyful force. When he trotted back to Pipe the rabbit dripped, lifeless, from his jaws, its head swinging pitifully from its limp body. The word heartsick came to her and she signed it just to feel her limbs move in this sudden lacuna made by death. Pipe had skittered through the underbrush all her life too it seemed, from one clump of sparse cover to another. Bolting was dangerous, especially if you had no firm idea of where you were headed, but staying put could destroy you too.

The furry sack that had been a rabbit up until thirty seconds ago lay flopped at Blackwood's feet. Pipe breathed deeply and forced herself to praise the dog. The meat he caught would save on store-bought dog food, and rabbits, if their populations reached significant numbers, would wriggle under the chicken wire that protected her garden. *Good boy*, she signed. *Good boy*.

PIPE DID NOT HAVE the two dollars she needed for the bag of cheap scratch she usually bought at the mill for her hens and geese. Could she face Eleanor again? Or a day at the berry patch picking for two bits a box? She wouldn't give her grandmother the satisfaction! She would love to go back to welfare to see her grandmother squirm again. It almost gave her a coronary the last time—family at the welfare office! It was almost worth it, but not quite. She remembered how the plastic upholstery of the waiting-area chairs squeaked with every movement. Light gray walls stretching out, interrupted by a row of closed doors, the receptionist protected by a wide plastic-smooth counter that curved around her territory like a moat. On the walls, Government of Canada posters featured an industrious multiracial citizenry with responsible and reassuring smiles. Pipe had tried to soothe her nerves by devising slogans for the posters. "We treat poverty like a business," or "Working for a better class of poor." The place smelled sanitized. Sitting across from her a thin man tried to hide behind his ball cap, folded one leg over the other and bounced it in quick jerks. Pipe watched his hands shake as he repeatedly touched the cigarette pack in his shirt pocket. A deeply furrowed woman spoke too loudly to the large meek woman beside her: "… they can't move him in his condition. They've got tubes hooked up, my God you should see some of the stuff that comes out of him!" The dread when Pipe heard her name called. No she wasn't going back there.

There was always Uncle Ben, but she would ten times rather face her grandmother's self-righteousness than Ben's solicitous caring, his phony "faith in her," his programs and options. His unbearable forgiveness. It embarrassed her to think of how far she might have gone as a teenager to get her own way, to make it clear to him that she did not need him or want him. Ben could not be raised to anger. He could not be approached without contrition. If she stopped eating the eggs, collected up a dozen, she might be able to trade them to the miller for a bag of scratch. That was what she would do. Most of all she didn't want to leave her work. It was going so well. Even at her most pessimistic she felt the flow carrying her along. There was some kind of sin in letting the fleeting present interrupt the permanent past.

Today she was working on the image of the workhorse. It seemed an omen to have been handed the model, to have a horse ridden right to her door. Of course her horse needed to be a bit bulkier, more broken down, more resigned, but this was the challenge of her craft.

She worked the rest of the day at her sketchbook and easel.

# CHAPTER ELEVEN

CASS CHECKED all the horses' feet, lifting their hooves from an angle that purposefully teased the ache in his shoulder, reminded him of the truth of his body. Murray Holmes was the one who died. Dead. That's all there was to know about Murray Holmes. Weidermann joined him for a while in the corral but thankfully was called away to deal with some problem with a forage wagon. Murray Holmes. Pipe's father. Ryan was the name his brain supplied so quick and clear Cass was not sure if he had spoken the name or merely thought it. There had been a camping trip once. No, more than once, but the trips had melted together, now indistinguishable in a single memory, a single moment really. What Cass remembered was heaving a canoe onto shore. It was a red canoe trimmed and ribbed with light-colored wood that curved upwards in a graceful wooden smile. Cass remembered tugging at the weight of it, again and again, gaining an inch and then another. What Cass remembered was the dark brown of the soil beneath his sneakers and the way the tree roots laced up and down into the earth and how a root offered a perfect foothold to brace against. He remembered the heaviness of the canoe against his straining and the moment, in mid-tug, when that weight dissipated, the canoe lifting and heaving forward on a magic wave of air. Dad-Ryan behind him, smiling, lifting with a great sweeping strength. He remembered a kindness the color of the sun, a voice but no face. Even the size and shape of the man's body was lost, diluted and altered in the memory of the boy left behind. Dad-Ryan. He remembered with utter clarity the words "my lad" pronounced as though they were a single word, as though that word were Cass's name. He remembered a moment when he silently, privately, secretly took the name into himself. Millad. It would be his secret Indian canoe name. It referred to the moment weight was lifted.

"Millad," he whispered in the mare's ear as he rubbed her down. The mare had a German name Cass could neither pronounce nor remember.

When Cass came home for lunch he found Jack behind the house crouching in a patch of green, a brimming flat of strawberries on the ground beside him.

"Jack."

"Oh my," Jack said, standing. Such despair radiated from his eyes, as though each berry were a tiny corpse, as though he had been sent to pick and box these corpses from some tragedy. "Oh my."

Cass bent over, slipped a finger under one of the red tentacles spreading out from the plants like spider legs, connecting them.

"They're tied together. With these little ropes," Cass said.

Jack looked at Cass, startled. "Of course. Those are runners. That's how they grow. The first plant sends out runners to start the next ones and so on like that. A lady phoned for you. She wouldn't leave her name but I'd say it was Eleanor Holmes."

Cass shrugged and left Jack to his business. The kitchen table was half covered in warm, slowly rotting strawberries. A puff of fruit flies dispersed when Cass picked a berry off the top of a box. He pulled a chilled six-pack out of the fridge with one hand, grabbed a loaf of bread in the other and carried them outside, settled himself on one of the broad wooden front porch chairs. He plucked a slice of bread out of the bag and rolled it into a cigar, bit the end off it and chewed slowly. He pried off his boots using the edge of the porch deck as a bootjack, let them tumble to the grass. He stretched out and tilted his Stetson forward over his eyes trying to keep his mind on the colt. Cass chewed through his bread cigars, washing every few bites down with beer. The colt had been so much better today, perfect really. He would start him on the lead lines tomorrow—not too much longer before he would be ready to mount. He closed his eyes and opened them again, started another beer.

A black Ford Bronco turned into the yard and a shortish fellow with snappy eyes and dark curly hair climbed out. It was, he realized, the guy he had briefly mistaken for Lionel in the village. The man looked about forty-five. Most of Jack's visitors were old, moved slowly and balanced cardboard boxes or grocery bags on their way to the door. Most of them nodded, tight-lipped, and looked him up and down with suspicion.

"Jack's out back," Cass said as he approached.

"You Casper Hutt?"

Casper? He pushed his hat back and sat up slightly. "*Cass* Hutt."

"Earl Holmes," he said, stretching out his hand, grinning.

Cass shook hands saying nothing. Another Holmes.

"Say, you don't mind if I have a seat here, buddy? Oh, look at this." He lifted a beer out of the box at his feet and cocked his head at Cass, his eyes dancing. Cass nodded. The guy twisted off the cap and winked. "You're new around here, I guess. Thought I'd stop by and say welcome. So what brings you to Scotch River?"

"Oh, you know." Cass shrugged.

"You got business here? Family?"

"I work for Weidermann." This man, Earl Holmes, almost certainly knew this already.

"Yeah, I hear you like horses and that. People seen you riding in the village, eh? So you been in Alberta."

"What makes you think that?"

"The hat?" Earl flicked the brim of Cass's Stetson and laughed. "You were, though, right?"

"Yeah."

"I know lots of guys out there. Big money out there. Oh yeah, big money. So you in the oil patch or what?"

"No, a cow-calf operation. Pretty big spread."

"Lots of money in that?"

"A bit for the boss if prices are up."

"Fort McMurray—that's the place. They can't get enough guys there. I'm serious. Thirty, forty bucks an hour—just to start. It's hard to find a place to live up there because they pay so much at the refineries nobody's left to build houses."

"I weren't ever up there."

"You have a house out there in Alberta? Land or anything? Stock?"

"No shortage of land out there." Then he added, though unsure why, "I had a truck once."

"I hear ya, buddy. I used to have one sonofabitch of a truck, a real bruiser. Goddamned insurance companies though, they don't give half what the thing's worth. Yeah, but land, eh? If you've got the vision, if you've got the connections, if you've got the expertise with this kind of thing, that's where you can make a bit of money. If you're looking to the future."

The cadence in Earl's voice, that stop-and-rush thing, brought him back to Randy with a dip-in-the-road suddenness. He remembered the way Randy's bangs fell over his eyes but not the eyes themselves or any of his other features. It was Randy who had set him free. Lots of opportunity for a growing boy. Cass remembered Randy's wink, the connection it implied, remembered his own stirrings of hope. Earl was still talking.

"Hutt—now, I don't know that name at all."

Cass started on his second beer. Earl knocked his empty bottle into the side of the six-pack so the bottles rattled. "Can you spare another one of these clinkers?"

"I guess."

"Thing is, I think we may have business to discuss, Casper."

Cass's voice snapped sharp, "Cass. It's *Cass* Hutt."

"Cass. Right. There's this land you got here, eh?"

"Who's talking about land?"

"Well, word gets around you know. In selected circles." Earl shrugged in sympathy as though they were both victims of this malicious gossip. "All I'm saying is you look like a serious man, a smart man. A workingman. Opportunity is what I'm saying. Potential."

Earl cocked his head and winked just like Randy. Randy had brought him to a steep lean house across the harbor where Cass carried sixty sheets of Gyproc up three flights of stairs. When he was done the boss handed cash to Randy, who slapped the boss on the shoulder, peeled off a bill for Cass and folded the rest into the front pocket of his jeans. Randy bought them both burgers and fries. Cass rubbed his nose, suddenly full of the aroma of grease, hamburgers and fries and the sweet tang of shiny green relish. He used to slip fistfuls of the packets into his pocket. Later he would pull them out and rub their slippery smoothness between his fingers, suck the relish out of them slowly between his teeth to assuage the near-constant drive to fuel the body bursting its boyhood. Cass made his way home, fell into bed and slept knowing he would wake hungry but with money in his pocket. This was how it was done. There were holes that could be filled and those that could not be.

Earl had pulled a photo out of his wallet and was waving it under his nose. "There she is—the *Best Chance*. A real beaut. All mine, free and clear. A stake in the future."

Cass had not been paying attention. "So you, um, fish?"

"Yup. Herring. Groundfish."

Cass did not know what this meant. How can a fish live on the ground? Or maybe ground fish like ground beef? He said nothing.

"I fished out of here my whole life—since I was twelve. On the boat every chance I got. Soon as I graduated high school I started on with

Dad. Full partners for over twenty years. That's a fuck of a long time to stand beside a man.

"Lobster's the big thing. We did other stuff too: mackerel, herring, fucking rock crab. No goddamned money in rock crab." Earl stopped talking, looked off across the road. He set his features dark and still.

"Now listen, I'll tell you what happened. Six years ago, well, it was choppy as hell that day. I told Dad not to bother, to save the gas, but he was a stubborn bugger. He went out alone. John Everett saw the boat tossing around, waves smashing up over the sides of her, listing like grandad's pecker, got to her before she swamped completely. When he climbed aboard her, there was Dad in the wheelhouse. Dead as a stick. Massive heart attack." Earl tossed the bottle cap he had been worrying onto the lawn. "Anyway, anyway, after everything, you know, I hauled the boat up and got her sound again. Not easy, not cheap either, but I got her going. Then it turns out the lobster license is in Dad's name. Well, it would be, wouldn't it? So I'm left with no license. Lobster is where the money is, buddy, in case you didn't know. So now lobster season I gotta crew on other boats. Fucking crewman, while my own boat sits there."

"What happened to the license?"

"My mother sold it out from under me and bought herself that house in the village. Spends her days planting pretty flowers."

"Holmes. The blue house."

He tipped back his beer, drained it. "Yup, that's her. She's sitting pretty. Drink up there, Cass."

"Can't you get your own license?"

"Sure, but the thing is you're talking a significant little packet of money there, investment in a profitable business. These licenses go in the neighborhood of eighty to a hundred thousand."

"Dollars?"

"Yeah. Now listen to me, buddy. You and me got business in the public house. You come with me. It's gotta be done!" Randy would flip him that smile, here's your business, Cassie-doodle. You come with me. Cass pulled on his boots and followed Earl across the lawn to the driveway just as he had followed Randy.

Earl's Bronco had black metallic paint, four-wheel drive, air conditioning, a CD player and four speakers. It had power windows and cruise control. Keeping up his stream of patter, Earl drove them through the village. When they passed a tidy house with a bright red door Earl honked and waved at the pudgy guy heading down the paved driveway.

"That's my brother Ben. He's principal of the school here. You got any principal questions, he's your man. Anything else—useless. Tits on a bull."

"How many brothers are there? There's you, there was Murray. Now Ben."

"Oh, you knew Murray? You're a friend of the family then! Fantastic. There was just the three of us. But don't worry about Ben. Like I said—bull boobs."

Earl parked in front of the Legion and led the way into the hall and down the stairs into a small bar with a dark basement smell.

"You sit in there, Cass, I'll get us a couple." Earl plucked the cap off his head and dropped it onto the seat he chose for himself, one with a slight angle to the door where he would be able to keep track of who came and left but not have to look at them head-on. Cass was practiced at picking out such seats himself.

"Now you and me, Cass buddy, we're a perfect combination and I'll tell you why. You don't want to be working for that old Kraut any longer than you have to, and I got that boat just sitting there, waiting. I know this guy in Pictou, got no more land than you got right there, and he made a fortune on that. Like I'm talking serious money here. An old piece of farmland, just like you got, and he developed 'er up, cut 'er into lots, sold every piece for fifteen thou. The guy had twenty lots going there. Now I know that piece of land you got there. You got all that out front, that's good for pulp—cash on the barrelhead. I know a guy who'd take that down for you tomorrow. And I'm talking cash up front before you even *start*."

"Who told you about the land?"

"Well, it's yours, ain't it? I know a guy with a bulldozer. That's the first thing—a decent road up the middle." Earl nabbed a darts score pencil and smoothed a napkin flat to draw on.

Here's your business, Randy used to say. The warmth of it was what Cass remembered. The warmth and security of an arm over his shoulder and a voice in his ear. Cass must have smiled, because when he glanced up at Earl, Earl grinned back.

"Look," Earl said, "it's a good thing, you coming home when you did. I been making a few calls. The answer, buddy, is this—the answer is *incorporation*. Here's the way it goes. The debt is carried by the corporation that is defined by the officers: president, vice-president and so on. Three guys'll do it—you and me and don't worry about the other guy, you don't need to do anything about it. I've got a son Wayne, twenty-one years old. You're going to meet him. Land and Sea Incorporated, we can call it whatever we want. Thing is, all your gas, your gear, truck, everything, that all goes down as business expense. The license is a joke. I'm serious."

Cass rubbed his bad shoulder where the humidity had settled into his joint.

"You ever get a day off from that salt mine?"

"Tuesdays."

"Tuesday." Earl glanced at his watch. "That's the fifteenth. Perfect. Absolutely perfect. That's the day you and me are going for a little cruise. I'll pick you up at Jack's. Two o'clock. It's all arranged."

Cass drained his beer, nodded and stood to leave, suddenly exhausted. Earl called after him, "I'll hammer this out. I know people I can call …"

In the stairwell Cass flattened himself against the wall to make way for an old man hobbling his way down to the bar—the old man who told him about the deed, Cass realized. Angus MacCarron. He nodded but the old man seemed not to recognize him.

Cass walked the railbed home, comforted by the walls of trees that guided him. Guys like Earl were seldom dangerous. They stirred things up into a froth and kept themselves afloat on the bubbles.

ELEANOR SMACKED HER SACK of groceries onto the table and yanked the hat off her head. The old fool! "Now I heard ..." he says to me. Sure, I'll bet. What's the last thing Angus MacCarron ever heard? That the Americans were withdrawing from Vietnam maybe. Deaf as a wheel of cheese. But that doesn't stop him from poking his nose in everyone else's business. And we're all lucky, I suppose, that it's only his nose at this point. All his stumbling about—"that young fellow, you know the one. The one with the horse but he didn't have the horse you know, wants to know about you and what was the name of that one of yours who died?" Honestly, going on like it was Earl and Casper at the Legion! What business would Earl have with Casper? Earl wouldn't know Casper from a hole in the fence.

Her hands shook as she unpacked her groceries. Even trying to busy her eyes elsewhere it was impossible not to see the box of Bran Flakes quaking, hear the slender flakes rustling inside. She set the box on the counter and pressed her arms tight to her sides to still them. How could things slip out of her control so fast? She stepped out of her kitchen and into her garden, strode towards the pond hoping to calm herself. The golden retriever trotted to her immediately, her flag of a tail flying, to set the turtle at her feet.

ELEANOR USED HER LITTLE HONDA CIVIC so rarely the steering wheel felt odd beneath her fingers. Jack and Effie Heighton. She hadn't seen

Jack since Effie's funeral, hoped he would not present a burden, an obstacle. She despised public grief and he was just the type to wear it on his sleeve.

She drove to his house and marched up to his door. It took longer than necessary, she thought, for Jack to answer her knock. "Hello, Jack, I'm looking for Casper Hutt."

"Oh. Cass. Yes. Oh dear. Cass is, yes, Cass is staying here. Eleanor Holmes."

"I hope you're well. We're all very sorry for your loss, of course." Eleanor stepped past him into the kitchen, sized up the room and peered around the corner into the adjacent rooms. Effie's absence was obvious enough. Those were Casper's boots by the door, his hat on the peg, but there was no further sign of him.

"Effie—yes, come in, come in. Effie was very fond of Cass, you know."

Eleanor whipped her head around. "When did Effie know Casper? Surely he hasn't been here that long."

"Now you remember the summer Cass was with us. Or perhaps not. We still had the herd then. Time is a blink."

She hovered over this, considered pressing him, but spotted Cass through the back window, crouching and frowning in a patch of garden. "There he is, Jack, never mind. I'll just go through, shall I?" She did not wait for an answer.

"Casper," she said and he raised his head at an angle to look at her. A perfect angle, a perfect positioning of eyebrow and shoulder, that nearly broke her heart.

"It's Cass. I'm out of the lawn-mowing business."

"I'm not here about mowing lawns. I suspect you know that."

"What happens to these plants?"

"I beg your pardon?"

"Look. Jack said these ropes, these, ah, uhm, *runners* start the little ones, so then what happens? Are you supposed to pull them out?"

"No. Well, you can start with pulling those weeds. Good heavens. Poor Effie. Then you need to select which daughters you are going to keep and which ones to pull. You'll need a few bales of straw for mulch."

"What?"

"You see what that strawberry plant looks like—pull out everything else. Everything. Get the weeds and you can worry about the daughters later." Murray the child gardener, ever curious. "Never mind about this now. Come home with me, Casper."

"It's *Cass.*"

He stood up his full six foot two, tucked his hands up into his armpits and turned from her. It was astonishing how much of him disappeared. Side-on he flattened out into a narrow target indeed. His feet were bare.

"You know who my mother was," he said staring off at some invisible line, the junction of the lawn and the Heightons' cut-stone foundation.

"Yes." Tight-lipped, she did not go on.

"She was this Catherine Taylor, I guess."

"Yes. But the point is my Murray was your father, as I've told you, and—"

"Who was she?"

"Catherine Taylor? There is very little to tell about her. I'm sorry about that, I suppose it is understandable you might want to know. She was here today and gone tomorrow. She was not the sort of girl to take responsibility."

"You didn't like her, I guess."

Eleanor sighed. Her own Murray's son asking about a mother he never knew. She tried to soften her voice although this usually just made her sound phony.

"I'm afraid I barely knew her. She arrived in June, left in March. She was disinclined to confide in me. I only had what you could rightfully call a conversation with her once in that time. I can say she was a spoiled selfish girl on the run from some undisclosed mess of her own making. But Murray wouldn't hear a thing against her. He believed any syllable she'd take it into her head to utter. I'm sorry about your mother but the main thing is you are Murray's son. Your father Murray was a wonderful man. Kind to a fault. It was his own heroic faults that killed him in the end." Her voice cracked and she abruptly stopped speaking.

You saw her, he thought, touched her, heard her voice. "You know something. You know where she went, what she looked like." And why ... His brain refused to string the words of the question together. That question that had snapped like a bone within him long ago in another life, jagged, it had pierced muscle, nerve, skin, bled through him and out of him and finally healed over, cauterized and encased. He grew up and out and around it. The question. Stop. Stop!

"You're all I have left of him. You must come with me."

A buzz rose in Cass's ears drowning out Eleanor's speech. What he could hear was the breath entering and exiting his lungs. His eyes blinked hard, again and again, although he had no tears. She was still speaking. "—he was my first son, you understand, not much beyond a boy ... he was lost in it all. Of course I feared for him—"

Tumbling, he fought to control his fall, avoid the horns. "She bought that land?"

"Apparently. There was a terrible row between Murray and his father, you see. They hadn't seen eye to eye for years, so different they were. And that fight, over *her* as a matter of fact, was the end of it. Murray was gone. Just like that. Left home to be with the likes of her. Out to the Crossing, fixing up that run-down old house. Quaint, my eye! A haven for coons was all it was. So there was Murray tending to her all day, and all night too I suppose. It wasn't right and I won't pretend it was. Murray slipped out to the Crooked Harbour house to see me from time to time when my husband was fishing ..."

"She …"

"She was a bit of a scandal, but then it doesn't take much to get yourself talked about around here. No one saw her leave so don't even ask about it. No one knew anything about any baby. And she didn't care about anyone but herself. I'm sorry but that's the truth. That's all there is to say about her. Nonetheless, who knows what gossip and fabrications other people will come up with."

Silence froze the space between them, each unable to pry their eyes off the other. Cass's chest ached with the pounding of his heart and sweat soaked his back.

"My grandson. A natural gardener, a horseman. Kind to animals just like my Murray. Casper."

"Don't say that name. It's *Cass*. Cass Hutt." The syllables came out hard and square. He would have loved to pick the words up and hold them in his hands, rough and heavy and substantial like concrete blocks. "Cass Hutt," he repeated, patting himself several times on the chest like someone searching his pockets for cigarettes. "I got to go to work." He headed for the back door, forcing himself not to run. He couldn't have managed it in any case with his legs numb from the soles of his feet up to the knees.

He passed through Jack's house collecting his boots and hat and kept right on going over the road, drawn to the shelter of Weidermann's horse barn. The shattered parts of himself leaned closer together as he approached the beasts and he could not wait to flatten his palms against their necks or withers, breathing in the proof of his own existence.

Cass knew what remained of him was the man sitting in the saddle. Nothing's changed, he told himself. A mother's name. A string of sounds. What's changed? Nothing. He clipped the colt on the lunge line and led him out into the corral. Across the road was Jack's house with his dormer window room. He imagined everything inside that room that had been sitting there for twenty years. No, much longer than that. He imagined all the things that belonged to Cass Hutt under that bed. Nothing had been added or subtracted. Nothing had changed. When he finished with the colt he would move on to the mare.

"What has changed? Nothing," he said out loud. "Earl is coming tomorrow." Every trivial thing was the same.

ELEANOR SAT OVER her teapot, warming her hands on its round belly, breathing in the aroma in the escaping steam, no matter that the summer sun had pushed the temperature to the upper edge of the comfort zone. She was supposed to chair a meeting of the horticultural society tonight and she simply could not face it. Her poor Murray, there wasn't a thing you could say to him. The young are irredeemably foolish. Her and that ludicrous yellow car. No job, mind you, but drove her own car. She came from money all right—used to getting what she wanted.

Ontario plates on the car and no more specific than that. What does that tell you? But you couldn't get Murray to open his eyes. He wouldn't hear a word against her. Completely infatuated. She took advantage. A year or two older than him and an old hand at every manipulation suspected by man—and well known to woman. She tortured him. There's no other word for it. Eleanor slid backwards into the quagmire of that long-ago summer, dismayed at the vividness of her recollections, the appalling detail.

Murray met Catherine at the Crooked Harbour beach. She used to swim interminably. Out as far as she could, then turn and see if she could make it back to land. Murray begged her to swim parallel to the shore. But she loved to see him suffer. He would pace back and forth on the sand, back and forth with binoculars trained, sweating a blue river and yammering away. Beside himself with worry. Eleanor had seen it with her own eyes. Then when she came ashore she would laugh, taunt him. Stretching out her body, flaunting herself in a black and violet bathing suit just this side of legal and a long way from decent. Murray, fetch me this and get me that. Toying with him was a game to her. Flouncy little harlot was what she was.

But she was all he could talk about and when a person could no longer bear to hear it he would not talk at all, would shut himself away completely. Oh yes, Miss Taylor had some long tale of woe, had been awfully ill-used according to her telling of it, and Murray lapped it up. Well, he was always such a kind-hearted soul, always giving more credit than was due.

One real conversation, she had told Casper. Yes, just the one. If that girl thought I would swallow that ridiculous "simple life" pap she found out differently that day. There's nothing simple about it. And I was in a position to know—I made sure she knew what I was talking about. I painted a picture for her that day. Oh yes. There would be no one here interested in listening to long sagas from Miss Catherine Taylor. "Where are you from?"—that was the one and only question ever asked me in all my time here. And the answer is "England." Don't bother elaborating because it's all just "England" to them. Tinker, tailor, soldier, sailor, it's all the same to them. They'll be only too happy to talk about their own lives though, you can be sure of that: the berries, the fish and the weather, and now, thanks to modern communications, the most god-awful television programs and that monstrous tripe from Hollywood. Show up at church or the school or the Women's Institute or the fire department auxiliary and they are always ready to instruct you in the one proper way of doing things. Since you're obviously too deprived to know. A holiday at the seaside is one thing, real life is another. If you think you know what the word "alone" means I can assure you that within a year you will have a considerably deeper understanding. Yes, she had made it clear enough what Miss Catherine would be making the best of. Well, what little missy scoffed at in September she understood by February. That was for sure. But by then it was too late. Apparently.

The headache that began as a dull squeezing pain when Cass had turned his back on her and walked away had escalated into hot needles piercing her frontal lobe. Even her stomach was beginning to feel queasy with the pain. She would take an aspirin with her cup of tea and lie down awhile.

# CHAPTER TWELVE

EARL WAS ALREADY PRATTLING as Cass swung up into the cab. "Yeah, Wayne's a great kid. Great kid. It's his birthday today—did I tell you? Twenty-one years old. He got himself a little screwed up here lately, running with a bad crowd. We're just getting him squared around now. He's had some rough patches, eh? His Mom walked out on him when he was small. Seven years old and she buggers off, just like that. Bitch. Wayne's my oldest kid, eh? Then I got three more boys. Like, I married again, to Judy, and we've got three boys. Brad's fourteen then the twins are ten, no, eleven now. But yeah, Wayne's twenty-one. Hard to believe when you got a kid twenty-one years old. Hard to believe. Say, you got any kids, Cass? It's quite the thing I'll tell you that. You never know what's going to happen. He's a great kid though, Wayne."

Cass relaxed into the Randy-patter. Nothing had changed. Earl knew nothing about him, was not interested in him. Everything would be fine.

"You're going to love the boat," Earl said. "You been out on a boat much?"

"We're going out on the boat?"

"Ye-es. I only told you a hundred times! Bit of a birthday party you might say."

In no time at all they turned off the Scotch River Road into the yard of the orangey trailer, the yard where the painted bus had once stood. Cass's eyes were automatically drawn to the old barbecue pit where sunlight played off a heap of brown glass shards. Old barrels were scattered in the unmown grass, their insides blackened by fire. He kicked at the remnants of a demolished picnic table that were strewn about. The wooden steps to the trailer door wobbled, the aluminum storm door no longer latched except with a loop of string that wrapped around a nail. Its bottom panel was twisted into boot-kick ridges. When Earl pushed the door open a residual tang of urine and vomit that underlay the smells of old food and motor oil made their noses twitch. Traces of marijuana smoke offered what relief was to be had in the atmosphere.

"Wayne!" Earl bellowed, shook his head in disgust and heaved open a window. "Wayne!"

A scuttling overhead then the thud of a landing and a moment later Wayne leaned in the doorway.

"Why don't you clean this place up for godsake? What a Christly mess! This is Cass, the guy I was telling you about. Cass, Wayne."

Cass nodded. The boy's eyes skittered, darted in and away, reminding Cass of rats. Wayne could have passed for sixteen. Everything about him was ragged and greasy and abandoned, the hair that straggled down to meet his shoulders, the haphazard clothes, the rangy limbs. There were sores on the ends of his fingers.

"Judy sent ya a card, here, look." Earl started pulling things out of the white plastic grocery bag in his hand. The boy rubbed his nose with the back of his arm. He accepted the envelope, checked it for money and tossed it on top of a stack of pizza boxes by the sink.

"Look, you got candles here, a cake, everything." Earl stacked a McCain's chocolate cake and a new box of children's birthday candles on the table, upsetting the jumble of clothes and dishes and cans and piles of unopened junk mail. A slice of the mountain avalanched to the floor where Earl kicked at it. "For fuck sake, Wayne!"

The boy shrugged.

"So, twenty-one years old, eh buddy! How does it feel?" Earl grabbed his son by the shoulder, clamped his arm around him, patted his chest, shook his chin until Wayne showed his crooked teeth in a shy child smile. "How does it feel?"

"The same I guess."

"Are you ready to go?"

"Sure." Wayne looked around, uncertain. "Where are we going?"

"Out on the boat! Like we talked about. Remember?" Every second sentence of Earl's cracked with irritation like he was walking on crusty snow, his foot falling through the delicate ice every few steps.

"Oh yeah."

"I guess, oh yeah! You, me and Cass. Just like I said. Let's go then. Birthday cruise." The three of them piled into the Bronco, Wayne propped up in the center like a rat on its hind legs, grinning.

At the wharf Earl hauled a metal toolbox out of the back of his pickup and strolled towards the boat, shouting out to the only two other men they saw. He waved Wayne into the boat and handed down a dozen beer barely camouflaged in a canvas bag and the clanking toolbox of wrenches and bars.

"Way you go there, Cass. Hop in."

Cass eased over the gunnels, took two steps towards the wheelhouse where he clung onto a railing and did not move. Around him Earl stashed and stowed and bustled just as though he were on solid earth. Cass stared at his feet, at the bottom of the boat, which might be maybe an inch thick he figured. Then nothing. Even if he could feel his feet there was nothing beneath them but what? Not wood. Some kind of plastic? And then sea all the way down, as far down as the sky was up.

"What's the boat made of?" Cass asked.

"What? Oh, fiberglass. I'll just stow this stuff then we'll cast off there, Wayne." Earl started the engine.

Wayne looked around, seemed to have to think the whole casting-off process through but then scuttled up to the wharf again, untied the

boat and leapt back to the deck with an impressive fluidity of movement. Earl eased them away from the dock and out into the strait.

Wayne, in a pair of ridiculously puffy sneakers, stepped onto the
stern as though he were going to walk out on the water but he turned
like a dancer and strolled along the gunnels, his arms out slightly from
his sides to help him balance. He barely wobbled as he mounted the
incline and stepped easily onto the roof of the wheelhouse. Standing
like a small-town war memorial, a man-boy with his feet apart, his
mind on something higher than the mud he marched through, he
faced backwards where the wake combed through the water and shores
widened. Cass clung.

Earl talked into the wail of the engine. Every now and then an "Eh,
buddy?" floated back over his shoulder through the hum. The ocean
was everywhere now, dry land growing impossibly distant. Cass sucked
air deep into his lungs, tried to feel the breadth and height of his body.
Stand, he told himself, it'll be like riding a bull, a quiet one. Maybe it
will even be like riding a horse. Let go of the railing. He did. It was not.
When a man is riding a bull there is a great deal beneath him, a couple
of thousand pounds of solid muscle and bone and beneath the animal
is firm, hard earth. Even if you can't feel the earth you know it's there.
It will catch you, hold you, and if you die it will bury you. Earth
seemed a miracle from here, a blessed miracle that he had taken for
granted all his life, but at this moment he loved it like he never had
before. Earth, land, dirt, ground, soil, rock. Land. One slender sheet
of ... of fiberglass, then a real never-ending nothing. He did not
really know what fiberglass was exactly, now that he thought of it.
They sometimes made box liners out of it. So he was bobbing around
the ocean in a big box liner, which was pretty close to nothing. His
knuckles turned white clutching the shiny bar screwed into a piece of
almost nothing floating on absolutely nothing.

Earl stuck his head out of the wheelhouse.

"Lots of fresh air out here," Cass said.

"You bet, buddy. Can't beat it. Wayne! Where the fuck is he? Get to hell down from there. I want you to take 'er now." The boy pounced from the roof to the gunnels and into the center of the boat like a cat. He took the wheel while Earl rummaged through the canvas bag and tossed a can of beer to his son, tucked one under his arm and opened another and held it out to Cass. This meant Cass had to release one hand from the railing to accept it. Earl set the plastic chair next to him.

"Don't squeeze the aluminum out of that rail, buddy. Have a seat."

Cass eyed the chair. Now that he had one hand occupied with the beer he would have to let go of the railing altogether to grab hold of the chair. He focused, released his grip, grabbed the chair back and with one great leap of faith landed his backside into the seat. Now he had four points of contact with the boat instead of two but the contact was, if possible, flimsier. His right hand clamped onto the chair arm and he turned his focus to the beer, to getting a swallow of it to his mouth.

With Wayne at the helm Earl leaned against the wheelhouse doorway. "How old were you, Wayne-buddy, when you first come out on the boat, eh? Remember you used to come out with Dad and me? Baiting the pots, Jesus yes."

"When I'd have to go hide in the wheelhouse?"

"What hiding in the wheelhouse?"

"When I got in the way and that. Or when the winch broke that time."

Earl snorted and waved the air like someone had farted. "I was thinking, you know, buddy, it's time to get this business going again. Not frigging around. Serious. I mean, you're twenty-one. We're all men here now. We'll really get this off the ground now."

Cass inclined his beer in Earl's direction. "Off the ground," he repeated and poured a cold stream down his throat where it immediately chopped into beery little whitecaps sloshing around his stomach.

"You got it, Cass. Hear that, Wayne? Cass is ready to go. Forget all this bullshit with the police and that. This thing coming up, never mind about that, we'll get through that. Then you'll be okay. Nobody expects you to be an angel. Nobody gives a shit if you smoke a couple of joints or stuff like that, you just got to learn to be a little more discreet." Earl's eyes twinkled. "Discretion, they say, is the better part of keeping your ass clean." He laughed here like they were pulling one over on the world. "Set her off to port there, Wayne, we're taking a little toddle off towards the cove."

The boy yanked the wheel to the left jarring the boat into a wave and sending Earl lurching off balance and grabbing for the wheelhouse door frame. Cass's chair hopped, skittered a foot across the deck and stuck. The beer can flew. The chair's plastic arms had welded themselves to the skin of his palms, bit into his fingers. A yellow liquid lapped at the toe of his boot. I hope that's beer, he thought, checked himself, heard the emptying can wobbling across the deck. It was.

"Fuck!" Earl grabbed the wheel from his son, shouldering him out of the way. "It's a fucking *boat*, you dickhead!" Earl steadied the vessel saying nothing for a few minutes while the boy crouched outside the wheelhouse, his forearms on his knees and his hands hanging limp in front of him. Cass found himself panting. He caught a breath and held it for three beats before letting it out, tried not to gasp for his next, slowing down. Now, once he got the breathing settled down, he would wipe the sweat off his forehead then try to move his chair back against the wheelhouse. He started uncurling the fingers of his right hand.

When Earl spoke again it was as though nothing had happened. "Root around in that bag there Wayne and haul out the sardines."

Wayne hunched his shoulders forward and rummaged in the canvas bag. Eventually he pulled out the sardine tin, held its rounded squareness between his palms. He pulled back the ring and stretched the cover off with a yawn and a pop.

"We're going to idle her down just over there. I gotta take a look at the engine." He winked at Cass. The boy was busy holding a sardine over his upturned mouth and dropping it in like a baby bird being fed by its mother.

"Leave some of those, eh? You know we need them. What's Johnny Everett doing out here? The fucker. If he's into my trap I'll beat the crap out of him. The sonofabitch. Where's he going?" Earl followed Johnny's boat with his chin more than his eyes then turned to Wayne, waiting for an answer. Finally, when the other boat had almost disappeared around the head, Earl scratched his ear. "Well, we'll see, won't we?" He doubled back and after a couple of minutes cut the engine.

"Hey, who's the dirty bastard that tossed a used condom off their boat?" Earl was all smiles now as he hooked the white squiggle from the top of the waves and drew it towards him. The condom covered a tiny float attached to a string tied to the rope that Earl pulled in, hand over hand, until a lobster trap broke the surface with a sigh. Earl looked around again, jerked the trap over the side and shoved it into the corner of the boat.

Wayne picked up the float, laughing and fingering the condom like he had just understood his first dirty joke. "A fucking rubber!"

"Hey! Look at these beauties. Bring me the pliers and those bands there, Wayne. What have we got here now? Look at this, looks like five, no, six. Quit playing with the condom, for frig sake. Are you bringing the fucking pliers or what?"

Wayne bobbed into the wheelhouse and returned with the tool. He held it out to his father along with a fistful of elastics that he dropped on the deck.

"What in Christ's shitty hole are you doing, Wayne? Hand me those one at a goddamned time would ya, eh? And hold the bag open. Cass'll help you hold the bag open. Cass!"

Cass eased himself off his chair and slid one foot forward across the deck, then the other. He had to let go and stand without support. He managed to shuffle across the deck and held out his hand for the bag.

Earl lifted a waving, grappling bug into the air. Cass jumped back with an agility that stunned him, backpedaled until his shoulder blades were pushed up against the wheelhouse wall. He had never seen a beast so ugly—like a huge scorpion crossed with some wicked double-armed cockroach. Its great spider legs knitting and unknitting, antennae long enough to reach out and grab the hat off your head. And the claws on it! They could slice you like a slab of baloney. "Christ, that thing looks dangerous!" he croaked.

"Oh yeah, they'll take your finger off," Earl said, pressing the banding pliers to expand the elastic and slip it over one claw. He repeated the procedure for the second. "They'll take a good chunk of you home for lunch if you let 'em. Here, though, this one's trussed up good." Juggling the pliers and the banded lobster and the plastic bag Earl managed to stuff the lobster into its new white world then held the bag out to Cass. "Here Cass, my man, hold this."

Here's your business, Cassie-doodle. Cass watched himself from above, imagining he was Earl, moving like him, stepping forward across the deck, grasping the bag like Earl would, watching the lobsters be rendered harmless by the bands and curl into themselves in captivity. One at a time Earl held the lobsters aloft, banded their claws then stuffed them home. Cass stood with his feet apart balancing in midair as though he were hanging from a bridge by a cord. An antenna waved up out of the top of the bag, brushing his hand. His stomach slid sideways but he held fast.

"Big-time money in lobster," Earl said.

There'd *have* to be a fuck of a lot, Cass thought.

Earl had the trap baited again with sardines and over the side in a flash. He stowed the banding pliers away in the wheelhouse and packed the poached lobsters in the bottom of his toolbox, settling the trays of sprockets and wrenches over the bags. Wayne leaned against the wheelhouse chewing on his fingertips.

Earl crowed with success. "Discretion, boys. Discretion and a single condom will save a man a lot of trouble in a wide variety of circumstances. So keep your mouths shut or we'll have every maggoty faggot in the cove hauling our trap. There's not one of them that's above it, I'll tell you that for free." He ducked into the wheelhouse and rummaged for more beer.

"Bring that chair in here, Cass. Come on in here, Wayne." Although the wheelhouse was cramped with the three of them Cass found it a slight improvement with at least the illusion of walls all around. As soon as Cass was settled Earl put the engine in gear and they were off.

"Oh yeah, eh boys? We get that license and we're back in business. What do you think of that? Land and Sea Incorporated."

"Land's good," said Cass.

"What? You're not feeling a bit Nancy, are ya? Don't worry about that. It's your first time. Christ, a couple more times out and you'll be bobbing around like the seals."

"Yeah, I wouldn't be surprised." For a minute or two anyway. Cass wondered if he could get a mouthful of beer down to his stomach without it meeting the last mouthful coming up.

"What do you think, Wayne?" Earl's enthusiasm bubbled over.

Wayne scratched his underarm, slid down the door frame into a squat, chugging his beer. "Why don't you take Brad on to help you?"

"What? He's just a kid. He's not old enough."

"He'll grow."

"So what? Jesus *Christ!*" Blood rose up in Earl's cheeks in two red branches and lit up his ears. "I'm asking *you.* You're my oldest son. Is that such a big goddamned deal? A man can't take his own son on to fish?"

Wayne blushed the barest pink and cracked his knuckles. He stared off to the stern and Earl finished his beer in silence. When he spoke again it was with determined cheerfulness.

"Me and my Dad were partners since I could poke a bit of herring on a spike. Come fish with your old man, eh? Sure. Yeah, why not? I got it all figured out, buddy-boy. You know, the thing is, we've both been fucked over pretty bad, one way or another. It's either bad luck or women. Or both. You too, I suppose, Cass. Like I don't know but I bet you know what I'm talking about, eh? Well, that's the thing, you know. They think they can get you, but there's more than one way around a tree. With the three of us here now, we got everything we need.

"Yes b'ys, it's time to get the friggin' license back where it belongs. Lobsters love us, as you can see. Everything's going to be turning around for us now, buddy-boys. Eh?" Earl laughed and shook Wayne by the shoulder until he looked up. "Right?"

"Sure. You getting me something for my birthday?"

"I might. You never know. I might get you something real good. You might be surprised."

"Yeah? Like what?"

"Like guess. You'll never guess."

Wayne stared off to sea, silent, bewildered.

"Come on, guess. What's good?" Earl persisted.

"Weed?"

"No. Jeez."

"I don't know."

"Well, you'll just have to wait till we get in then."

"So are we going in now?" Wayne asked.

Cass pricked up his ears. That he could develop such a yearning love for something as simple as land he could never have predicted.

"Yeah." Earl turned his attention to the wheel. Wayne wandered outside, tossed his empty beer can into the ocean, skipped along the gunnels and back onto the wheelhouse roof. Earl rambled on but Cass could concentrate on nothing but keeping his stomach contents where they were. As the wharf came into view he locked his eyes on it as though his line of vision were attached to a come-along and a cable, as though his will could pull them closer, faster, to shore.

Earl's change in voice jolted him. "Get to fuck down out of there! We're headed into the wharf. People can see you. You look like a retard for Chrissake. Snaky as your fucking cousin."

Cass reeled onto the dock, trying to right himself by setting his legs out straight under him and locking his knees. He set a hand on his stomach. Might as well eat a spider, a cockroach, a water bug, as one of those things.

"I'm going home," Cass told Earl when they were all settled back in the truck.

"Go on! We just started here! You're not going back yet."

"Yeah, I am. I just remembered something I gotta do."

"Do it later. This is serious. This is a party."

Earl cursed and cajoled but Cass was sick of him. He was just plain sick. Say Uncle. If Earl was his father's brother then Earl was his *uncle*. And this rat-boy beside him was … was … He couldn't be bothered figuring it out. "Drop me at the Crossing," he said.

As soon as Earl was out of sight Cass crawled into the cover of the trees and let go. He puked. And once he got started he couldn't stop. He puked up half a can of beer and then his breakfast, his body shaking. He puked up Eleanor's assertions, his mother's name, his father's name, Earl's blindness and foolhardy confidence and rat-boy's stupid misery. A grandmother and an uncle. He hurled some greenish slime onto the ground. That boy. On his hands and knees in the woods by the track he leaned his body against a tree trunk for support and retched dry heaves until he thought his stomach would come up through his mouth. He crawled further into the undergrowth, pulled himself out of sight behind a rock outcropping and curled into sleep, the hard, unyielding, blessed earth solid beneath him.

WHEN EARL AND WAYNE PULLED in at Wayne's trailer a ten-year-old Nissan pickup with a king cab and dented tailgate sat in the yard.

"Whose truck is that?" Earl asked.

"I don't know. Nobody comes around no more since Darryl moved up north. Girls never come around no more."

"Ah, come on. People come by. I come by. Who else comes by?"

"Clifford."

"Oh, that asshole. I don't want him around here. I'm not kidding. You got a problem, you come to me. I don't want you messed up with him. I'm going to have a chat with him as a matter of a fact. Soon. So whose truck is that?"

Wayne shrugged. They pulled up beside it.

"Look inside and see."

Wayne pulled open the driver's door. A small green bow barely clung to the steering wheel, its sticky-back faltering, a tag hanging down with a key and the letters W-A-Y-N-E.

"Happy birthday."

"Seriously?"

"From your Dad. Did I tell ya you were going to love it?"

"No shit."

"What do you think of this baby, eh? You'll need a truck if you're going to be a lobsterman."

"Cool." Wayne slid in behind the wheel and started up the engine while his father stood beside him, holding the driver's door open. "Let's go. I'm driving."

"No, look now. You just put back—what?—three beer and you got no dinner in your belly. There's no insurance on this truck. That's where you start having problems, see? So okay—so let's cook these lobsters, get a bit of food in you. Then we'll take 'er for a little spin. Just careful on the back roads till you get the insurance on 'er. Understand?" Earl hooked his arm over his son's shoulders, around his neck, almost like a wrestling hold. "You like the truck your old man got you?"

"Yeah."

"Yeah?"

"Yeah."

They tugged and poked at each other on the way to the trailer, Earl drawing out the boy's smile for as long as he could. Everything would work out perfectly.

Earl flicked on the kitchen tap and bent to open the cupboard under the counter. "Where's that big pot I gave you?" He had not expected the cupboard to be as neat or organized as it was, nor had he expected the tidy stack of four VCRs, five CD players and a radio. "What ta fuck is this?"

Wayne rolled one shoulder back an inch or two. His neck twinged. "Some stuff I got."

"What is this crap? What are you doing with a stash of hot stuff in your trailer? We are just getting this thing together, getting stuff sorted out. You are coming fishing with me! You have a truck! You'll have money! Didn't you tell me this crap was done with? What are you, a complete fucking moron?"

Earl was advancing now, fury overtaking him. Wayne backed up, shrank even further behind his skin. "You told me you were finished with this shit. You want to end up in jail? We have been through this one hundred fucking times! We're going to get through this thing that's hanging over you right now and then that's *it*. You are going before that judge as a fisherman, ready to start a new life."

Wayne lifted his eyes, lifted his hands.

"Why are you doing this? Moron! Retard! Fucking stupid fucking moron!" Earl's arm flew out to grab his son, his fist bunched the material at the neck of his T-shirt and his hand twisted, bringing the boy's face close to his own. The boy could have been ten years old.

"D-d-dad."

Earl shoved him back out of the way and almost in the same motion smashed his own fist into the wall. His breath came to him heavy and fast. Slowly Earl shook his hand loose, watching his errant limb emerge from the hole in the trailer's cheap paneling. He stretched his fingers and rubbed his knuckles. Earl's mouth moved but nothing came out. It was Wayne who spoke first.

"Good thing you missed the studs. It really hurts if you hit a stud."

Most of the holes in the walls were at kick level. A few at punch level.

"I'm going home," said Earl.

Earl drove home and tossed the bag of lobsters into the sink. "Hey Jude, love bugs for my lover," he said to his wife because this was what he said every time he brought home lobsters. Every time for the past fourteen years. He left the kitchen immediately and hid in the shed, crouched behind the workbench where he could pretend to be working if he was discovered.

Wayne flopped in front of his TV. He had smoked his last joint but still had a couple of codeine pills. He swallowed the tablets. When the drug kicked in and some distance began to open up between himself and the world he gnawed the scab off the tip of his most chewed-up finger and with his eyeteeth peeled off the fingerprint, watched the blood rise to the surface beneath the too-thin translucence of his innermost skin.

# CHAPTER THIRTEEN

PIPE HAD NOT BEEN to the mill in a week. Even with the false summer gaiety and the annoying cluck of guides and tourists, still she needed the solid hemlock beams and the soothingly endless rumbling of the gears to bring Nan's stories to life. She packed her book and pencils and the dozen eggs she had saved up to barter for a bag of oat scratch in her bike carrier and set out for the mill. Now she could eat eggs again. Her body reached out to the protein but it longed for fat, for cheese and butter and a juicy hamburger. Junk food was what she really wanted, bars and cookies and deep-fried bobo balls in plastic red sauce. She thought of Earl's pizza with an almost romantic nostalgia. Whatever plans Earl had been cooking up must have fallen through. Someone else would be suffering his charity by now.

At the mill, people hovered around like blackflies. It took forever for Pipe to settle down and when she did she found herself frustratingly far from where she needed to be. A barrier built from two-by-fours blocked off two-thirds of the basement, preventing public access. "Staff only" in the kiln, "staff only" around the moving machinery. Her angles were dreadfully restricted by the few places she could crouch with any degree of privacy. Nevertheless, she closed her ears and worked with what she had.

At noon the mill shut down as usual, the wooden gearing slowed, its momentum dragging, slow, slower, stop. The miller went to lunch and half the tour guides with him leaving a lone guide on the main floor, another in the shop up the hill. The only remaining clutch of tourists in the mill strolled off to buy cheap souvenirs, and silence descended. They had forgotten about her. Quick before she lost her nerve, before she lost any time, she hugged her sketchbook and tiptoed to the barrier gate, flipped the butterfly toggle and let herself in under the giant resting spur wheel, where she stood surrounded by the workings. She could put an arm out in any direction and touch a belt or pulley or gear. The main drive belt threaded between her legs like a giant game of Chinese skipping, her elbow hooked around the main shaft. Here she, like her grandmother and great-great-grandmother before her, became part of the machinery. Her shoulder muscles twitched in a memory that never was, in a lost anticipation of the weight of the stone nuts. With the length of log resting at her feet the miller would pry these heavy cogs up or down along their shafts to engage or disengage the stones. She imagined the weight against Penelope's shoulder, the power in her great-great-grandmother's arms. She felt the swish of her long skirts at her ankles, the determination in her heart. Pipe squatted, leaning behind the main shaft, and slapped open her sketchbook, throwing her head back to see the overhead gears. She rushed to capture the points of intersection where wooden gear tooth met wooden gear tooth. All maple teeth, some chipped from accident, all worn and wise-looking. Her neck ached then cramped. Quick, quick. Her drive for intimate knowledge of the wood grain fought with her need for efficiency. Her pencil lead flew across one page after another.

Finally, rubbing her neck, Pipe stood and picked her way over the motionless main belt to the very back of the mill, to a metal bevel gear about the size of a dog dish. The teeth were cast to meet at forty-five-degree angles to drive power from a horizontal shaft to a vertical one. The gear was set off the floor about hip height. Or shoulder height for a small child. One particular small child. Pipe closed her eyes and Nan's voice poured through her. The child, Penelope's first to survive infancy, had been called Daisy and had wandered in, her mother preoccupied with the business of milling. Pipe's pencil recorded the space between the teeth, the way they zippered together chewing space to nothing; she drew the terror of their impassivity. The piercing scream, the dangling mass of bloody tissue, the days of praying by the bedside and the tiny grave she did not sketch. Beside her the main drive pulley, wood worn shiny as satin by the years, called to her. She could capture the texture in the light if she could just have a little time with it. But she was not done with the angles and darkness inside the bevel gear.

Pipe didn't hear him in his steel-toed sneakers until the bottom step creaked. Her head shot up and they stared at each other, both frozen in surprise. The miller was a small intense man in his late forties, a wiry fellow with long artistic-looking fingers that he would drum on his teeth while thinking. His rapidly graying hair forever looked as though it needed a trim. To the world he showed only two aspects: "concerned" or "contented." His features plunged into cavernous thought and hopped back out again, seemingly at the flick of a switch.

"Oh dear," the miller said, his eyebrows pinched. "You're not allowed back there. We can't have this. Really, we can't."

Caught halfway between the past and the present, Pipe could not grab hold of anything real.

"There are questions of safety, of security, of insurance. Only staff is permitted behind the barriers. The signs are quite clear." The miller toyed with his hands, quick slender movements as though he were trying a ring on each of his fingers in turn.

There was no way out but to maneuver her legs around the belts and gears and scurry as best she could towards the gate. Struggling to maintain her dignity she scuttled past him on the way to the stairs, dropping the curtest of nods in his direction. Behind her the miller's voice trailed away, "From now on you must be accompanied by a tour guide at all times in the mill. *All* times. I must insist—I just don't see any other …"

Damn, damn, damn. As though things were not bad enough already. Damn!

IT RAINED in the nighttime. It poured steadily while Cass milked the main herd then fed the calves. He ran his hand along the flank of the only cow due to freshen, feeling for the calf beneath her hide. She was still carrying low; there would be no birth this morning. He listened to the pelting of drops on the barn roof and he felt dry. Dry was a very easy thing to feel. He could imagine himself out in a snow squall or blizzard searching for some calf, the weather whipping through him, but here he was, warm and dry in a barn. A man with no relatives— dry. A man with dead parents and living uncles and a grandmother— just as dry. Related to some lost rat-eyed kid. How do you feel, Cass? Dry.

She came in summer and left in winter. People didn't take as long as horses, he knew. They were the same as cows—nine months. She left pregnant, went away, gave the baby up for adoption. But maybe not right away. Maybe she kept him awhile until she—until maybe—until the baby was too dirty and stupid. Stop. You feel *dry*, Cass. He hugged himself, concentrating on the sound of the rain pelting on the steel roof above him. In his back pocket his wallet harbored his crumbling birth certificate. Born Scotch River, Nova Scotia. In October. How could that be? She didn't go away? Dry, Cass, warm, dry, sheltered.

WEIDERMANN ALWAYS TRIED, and sometimes managed, to drop by the horse barn in the morning to see how the colt was progressing and to watch Cass move in and around the horses. Cass felt him approach with his wide confident stride and hearty voice, felt both his admiration and his authority.

"Ah, good morning, Cass!"

"Morning."

"Were you watching the Pro Rodeo last night?"

Cass shook his head and fetched the saddle for the mare, bracing himself against his boss's expansiveness.

"Ty Murray was on the TV. A great bull rider. Did you ever meet this guy, Ty Murray?"

"Yeah. A few times. He's a good rider."

"He makes the big money." Weidermann stretched his arms along the top board of the stall, encompassing nearly the length of it. "You ever make the big money?"

Cass shrugged. "Enough."

"But enough for what?"

At first there was so little money it was a struggle to meet expenses. But after he settled into bull riding and started to win more often, there were times he made more than he could spend on boots and gas and steak. Sometimes, more often than not, there were thousands of dollars too much. But there were always kids, often Indian kids. Always kids. He didn't want to think about this, about picking out some tough-looking young one with a hollowness behind dark eyes, hungry, dirty jackets and torn jeans, taking the boy aside.

"Well, one year I won big—bought a new truck. Another time I got a big-screen TV for the bunkhouse. I don't know what else." Cass threw a saddle blanket across the mare's back, eyeing escape.

"Why did you start in this bull riding? It's a funny thing to start, eh?"

He did not want to tell Weidermann about the concentration that takes a man out of himself to where nothing matters but the thudding flesh beneath you, or tell him how the world stopped with the clang of a chute gate, how riding created a pocket of pure freedom. He did not want to tell him about fate's broken promises.

"Ah, now I get a visitor."

A bus-sized silver trailer looped into the yard, the truck wheezing to a stop in front of the horse barn. Weidermann grinned and waved.

"Ah, come, Cass. You will meet my friend Harry. Harry the horse trader."

"I'm taking the mare out."

"No. For just a minute. Come."

Cass followed him into the sunshine, watched Harry the horse trader climb out of the cab and shake hands with the German. There were pleasantries, then, "I hear you have a new man for the horses."

"No, no. For the milking. But a very good horseman. Cass, come here."

Cass nodded and the men shook hands. The horse trader drew Weidermann into the trailer. Cass could hear them through the trailer windows.

"Look at this, Hans. Can you believe this? I could've fucking shot the guy, you know. There's no excuse."

"This is not right."

"Then he says, five hundred bucks 'cause she's a little lame. So I say, here's a counter-offer for you, man: we get that horse on that trailer right now and in return I don't phone the SPCA and have you charged, and if you ever do that to a horse again I'll do it to you."

Their voices dipped, then the horse trader said, "I'm full up at my place. The wife says if one more comes in, I'm going out." More murmuring.

When they led the miserable creature down the ramp and into the barn Cass shuddered. Disgust nearly turned his stomach. The breathing of the rescued horse, the wounded horse, the foster horse, filled the entire barn. Its head hung with the weight of stone, nearly dragging on the floor, ribs like giant fingers of a grapnel clutching its dregs of flesh, holding the beast upright. Its eyes were nothing but hollows. The smell of festering wounds overpowered the aroma of horses and sawdust. The leather instantly absorbed the smell of leftover life. Horses and dogs remember all their lives. Do they remember their wounds or their wounders? He spat into the gutter but there was no rinsing the taste of filth out of his mouth. It would only take a second to pump a bullet into that pathetic skull. He finished saddling the mare as quickly as he could and trotted off to the railbed without looking back.

All day it bothered him, left him too fired up to sleep; he wasted his evening sleeping hours staring at the splotchy wallpaper by his bed, listening to his heartbeat. Without a wink of rest he rose for his night shift as usual. After milking, as soon as he was done feeding the calves, just as dawn was breaking, he headed for the horse barn and for the rounded-edge shovel that was kept there. Behind the horse barn he was hidden from view, and although he understood he could be discovered, he did not plan for discovery. After a couple of hours of digging he heard the morning milking shift arrive. No one interrupted his progress. He worked on undetected. Finally satisfied, he climbed up out of his hole and crossed the road to Jack's. Three guns lay across the rifle rack nailed to the hall wall at Jack's. Cass lifted down the .22. As he had guessed, the shells were tucked into the drawer of the little table in the corner.

The wounded beast barely turned its head towards Cass when he entered the stall. It allowed itself to be led, shuffling, around to the back of the barn and stopped where Cass left it beside the grave, did not stir when Cass lifted the rifle.

The dead thing's tumble into the grave was not graceful but at least it fell inward and he did not have to harness another horse to pull the corpse over the lip. He climbed down into the hole and arranged the body the best he could. By the time Weidermann arrived, breathless, searching for the source of the gunshot, Cass had re-emerged from the grave and was shoveling dirt onto the lifeless form. A scoopful hit a glassy eye, a clump of earth ran down the neck and fell to the bottom of the grave. Weidermann waved his arms.

"What in hell do you think you are doing?"

Cass did not answer. In his opinion the response was clear enough to see.

"There was hope for that horse. The vet was coming to see that horse today."

Cass listened to everything Weidermann said over the rhythmic scrape and toss of his shovel. He listened to see if he would be fired but most of the speech had to do with Weidermann being boss, the one in charge, the one who gave orders. Uncertainty clouded his voice, and his heavy German accent thickened when he came to the subject of the horse itself. Cass listened to him steer away from the subject almost as soon as he introduced it. After a while his rant petered out. "You think that horse should be put down, you can tell me, yes? You can speak?"

This was not unreasonable but Cass could not say why it was impossible.

"The tractor blade will not be used for this. You kill my horse on my time and you can bury it on your own time."

"You think I owe you something, sir, you can take it out of my wages," Cass said.

Weidermann turned and left him.

From way off up the road, before he could actually see the red metal flag lying prone on his mailbox, Earl felt a little ping in his stomach. He drew up to his laneway. Shit. His wife's Chevette sat in the driveway and there was Judy herself, sitting on the porch step in her pinky-salmon uniform and her pink nylon sport shoes staring at a sheet of paper she held in her lap. Earl checked the empty mailbox anyway, vainly, checked his watch as though giving the world a final chance to right its wrongness. It did not. Of all the goddamned fucking luck. The one day I don't make it home in time. Shit! *She's* never late though, not a fucking hope in hell. Not a chance. Not her. He drove in and parked the Bronco. She stood as he approached, sending the collection of envelopes in her lap fluttering to the ground at her feet. Silent tears rolled down her face.

"Ah jeez, what now?"

"What now?" She sounded like she really wanted to know, her voice lonely and punched in as though someone had died. "Exactly. What are we supposed to do now?"

"What've you got there?" Earl yanked the bill from her. Dalton's Used Cars. Figures it would be the worst one. "Oh, that. Don't worry about that, it's covered. It's paid for."

"If it's paid for why am I looking at the bill? If I call them up right now are they going to say it's paid for? Twenty-eight hundred dollars. Two thousand eight hundred dollars. I don't even care what it's for."

"You don't even have to think about that. It's part of a deal. It doesn't mean anything."

"Part of a deal? Don't tell me. Somebody, for no apparent reason, will give you something of theirs, you double the money, which is an easy thing to do, and buy back your lobster license. Spare me the details. Surprise me!"

"Now, come on!" He had been prepared to be patient but now she had made him mad.

"How much do you think I earn?" Her voice sharpened to meet his.

"Christ, Judy! I told you, if you'd listen to me, I got a big project on the go here. You got nothing to worry about. Twenty-eight hundred lousy bucks is nothing to get—"

"How much do I earn? Fifty-two dollars a shift, that's what. Minus the four dollars' worth of gas to get there and back, minus tax, minus CPP, minus the EI deduction. We just got hold of it, Earl. We've made one payment on the consolidated loan. *One!* Twenty-eight hundred dollars! Where is this supposed to come from?" She shook the bill at him. "And that's not counting every other goddamned thing that needs to be paid, and you know as well as I do what those things are." She picked up a baseball bat lying at her feet and threw it onto the wooden porch with a clatter. First one then two faces peered out through the screen door, the twins pulled from the couch in front of the TV by the racket and the anger in their mother's voice. Their older brother pushed past them onto the porch, swaggering. He leaned against the railing uneasy and grinning, straining to appear casual, like this was a great show watching the old woman blow her stack again. The other boys slunk after him, slightly more curious than scared.

"I didn't hear you complain when I bought you that new TV! What about that new fridge I bought you?"

"Yes. What about it, Earl? Picking out stuff in a store and bringing home the ho-ho-ho, that's easy. Who's going to pay for it? Who?" She kicked her way up the steps sending a baseball glove into the peonies, an in-line roller skate onto the lawn. "You boys want new stuff, no problem, Dad is frigging Santa Claus, get you whatever you want. You go to your father, new bloody anything-you-want." She bent and picked up a skateboard and sent it hurling through the air into the driveway. "I've had it! You're bound and determined we're going under? *Fine!* Fine. But I'm through busting my ass for nothing. What I earn is nothing anyway, a lousy ten thousand bucks a year. Chicken feed! Nothing! So why bother? I quit."

Judy whipped her uniform dress off over her head in a single stroke of fury revealing her dingy brassiere and heart-speckled underwear. Her white ankle socks and sneakers made her feet look comically large, especially when she stamped her foot on the porch boards. Judy tossed the balled-up uniform in Earl's face with impotent rage. "I totally and absolutely quit! I quit my job, I quit trying to make something out of nothing, I quit trying to get you to act like an adult." She stomped, nearly naked, past her sons into the house, the screen door slamming behind her. Their teenaged son's face burned so red, raindrops would have sizzled on his cheeks. The younger boys gawked.

"Hey, I'm the one that makes the big money around here and I'll spend it however I want! Judy! Judy, don't be ridiculous." He called after her but did not follow.

One of the twins, the chunky one, scampered down the porch steps and collected playthings in his arms, chucked them into the garage, hiding the guilty objects, harboring them. On his way back up the steps he had to dodge his father who continued to stand exactly where Judy had left him. The boy paused before his mother's discarded dress, a sickly pool of flesh-colored polyester like some superfluous skin shed on the porch floor. He tiptoed around it.

Earl felt his sons' eyes on him, expectant. "Women! Take notes, boys. This is your future." He turned on his heel, jumped back into the Bronco and sped off.

By the time he returned, later that afternoon, after he had given her a chance to calm down, she met him with that soft aren't-we-crazy-to-fight smile that he loved. He gave her his sheepish grin then beamed at her in return. Everything was fine.

She took both his hands in hers and kissed him. "I called in to work—no more shifts for me. Quit. Man, that was exhausting. Funny eh, how it's the fear and not the thing itself that takes it out of you?"

He blinked, unsure of what she was saying. She kissed him again. "But here we are. We'll probably have to declare bankruptcy but, you know, so what? So what? No more bills and they'll abolish your credit. That's not a problem, that's a solution."

Earl's stomach dropped to someplace it hadn't been in years and the smile drained from his face. "Jeez, you didn't really quit. You didn't quit your *job*. Look, there's no need to get excited. I'll tell you if you want to know. I was waiting till I had the money. I'm working on this project—"

"Like I said, save it. Surprise me. All these years of worrying, working like a slave for nothing. We're probably going bankrupt and I'm going to watch from right here in this kitchen. I mean, what can they do to us? Worst comes to worst, we can go on welfare. You know, I don't care. I can honestly say I don't care."

"What are you talking about? We're not going bankrupt. We sure as fucking hell aren't going on fucking welfare! I'm a fisherman and by next spring I'll be a lobsterman again. Guaranteed."

"That's great. I'd prefer that, of course. I'm just saying I'm not worrying about bills anymore and I'm not busting my hump for money anymore. Whatever happens, whatever's repossessed, whatever's canceled, turned down, cut up, I'm ready."

"I'm telling you I have got this covered! But you still have to work for Chrissake."

"No need to shout. It's too late anyway. I've quit and I'm not going back."

She couldn't be serious. With this sudden headache he really couldn't think. "I'm going to bed. Have we got any aspirin?"

"Not if Wayne's been here lately."

Earl curled into himself under the light summer blanket on their bed. Below him, through the heat vent, he listened to snippets of his wife complaining about him on the phone to one of her friends. How was a man supposed to get to sleep when he had to listen to shit like this? From his own wife? Her voice faded in and out. "… so I work and work and plan to get us a bit above water … not his fault but … my self-esteem is just shot, you know? I mean seriously, it's in the toilet … just a big kid …"

Wait till he and Cass started pulling in the money. Then see what she had to say to her friends! He pulled the blanket over his head. It was all a matter of timing. As long as he could keep things rolling, keep one step ahead, everything would work out brilliantly. It was important to get things moving. And why not? There was nothing standing in his way. Cass was hot for the project. Didn't he come out on the boat and everything?

THERE WAS A PACK of playing cards on the table in the corner of the bulk tank room. Cass sat and shuffled the deck mindlessly. He fanned them out and tucked them back into a tight pile, shuffled again, then with deliberation spread them out in a broad arc across the table and picked out three kings: Murray, Ben, Earl. He set them in a line and above the line he placed a queen: Eleanor. He tucked the fourth king behind the queen for her dead husband, Earl's father the fisherman. He did not remember this man's name. Behind the Murray card he tucked two queens. To one he dealt the ace of spades, to the other, the deuce of hearts. He tucked a queen behind the Earl card. But Earl had had kids with two wives: Wayne (Jack of clubs) with the first then later on three more kids (ace, two, three of diamonds) with the second. Already he was short of cards and had to use a joker instead of a queen for Earl's second wife. Ben he didn't know anything about. Nor his grandparents, who may have had brothers and sisters and they could have sons and daughters. He could see how eventually every card could fan off into an infinite number, out of control.

Suddenly Cass remembered stacking gravel in little piles beside a driveway. For each stone he pedaled a bike down a long packed-dirt driveway all the way to the road, picked up a stone, then pedaled back to the house. One pebble per trip, back and forth until he had collected ten. He hunched his collection into a pile hidden in the grass beside the driveway then searched for twigs and set them around his pile, penning in his stones. Then he started on his second set of ten. Anyone who did not know their one-to-ten was very, very stupid. Well, he practiced and practiced and *he* knew his one-to-ten. Back and forth he rode until his legs ached then trembled from exertion. Two piles of ten and three more pebbles made twenty-three trips. That was how it worked! All numbers were piles of ten plus leftovers. Twenty, thirty, forty, fifty up to one hundred and then on forever. He could make any number at all. The elation of discovery gave him the strength to go on until seven piles plus four equaled seventy-four trips and he had to stop.

Later there had been a lawn mower that scattered his piles of stones and some yelling and hauling and a switch. Casper had sat in a corner listening to the red lines of pain crisscrossing the backs of his legs. He didn't care. One-two-three-four-five-six-seven-eight-nine-ten. One-two-three-four-five-six-seven-eight-nine-ten chased itself around his elated head.

After dawn he stepped outside to watch the rain come down, leaned against the barn, snugged up under the eave, the drip line a few inches beyond the toe of his boot. Rain ran in rivulets across the yard and rested in puddles, puffed the air into pillow softness, dispatched its weight into the jagged joint of Cass's left shoulder. The fibers in his clothes swelled with humidity and grew heavy. He breathed in the rainy smell of the land and waited.

Before the morning milkers arrived Weidermann emerged from his house, stood on his porch and surveyed the sodden yard. He planted his cap on his head and ducked forward into the rain, making a beeline for Cass and his sheltered spot.

"Good rain, heh? Good for the grass," Weidermann said in greeting. Cass could hear him struggling to put the sick horse incident behind him.

"Payday's always a good day." One of the guys at the One Bar None had said this every single payday and Cass listened to his own voice carrying the sentence, familiar and strange at the same time in this new place. Weidermann handed him his pay envelope.

Cass discovered Jack in the parlor, surrounded by photographs, crying silent easy tears. He sat down on the soft chair opposite Jack and set two twenties and a ten on the coffee table between them. There were photographs everywhere, all over the table, in books and in picture frames, single ones and collections.

"Cass," Jack said as though this sorrow were a shared thing. Lionel had cried too, quietly like this, over the lifeless body of his first horse. But what was the point? Cass picked up one of the framed photographs and studied it. Yes, he did sort of remember Effie he supposed, enough to say he thought she must be this one here.

"I never had one," Cass said.

"Oh, you should really. A man needs a wife. I don't know what a man does without a wife. I honestly don't know."

Cass meant a photograph, not a wife, but decided not to say so.

"That's Effie and my daughter there. My daughter's in Saint John, did I tell you that? She was just here—when was that?"

"The pictures are nice. That's the rent money there. You going into the village later?"

"Oh. I don't know. Do you think I should?"

"Sure, Jack. You get paid, you should go to town."

Cass spent half his wages on new jeans and socks and underwear and T-shirts in the clothes corner of the hardware store. Replacing his boots was another matter. Nothing on offer here would do. He picked up a sturdy-looking jackknife and measured the heft of it in his hand. Catherine Taylor. Cass let the name enter his mind, close and controlled like a calf through a chute, in and out. Murray Holmes. He picked up a ball cap and turned it over in his hands, his forehead crinkling in annoyance at its flimsiness, its uselessness. For $5.50 he could look just like everybody else. He set it back on the shelf. Murray Holmes.

The rain had stopped, leaving puddles everywhere and leaves shimmering. Cass leaned against the outside brick wall of the Co-op store for several minutes considering what he should do. Finally he headed off on foot through the village. At the garage he turned onto the trail towards the railbed where he picked his way over ground slick with mud, emerging not far from the iron bridge. It was funny how different the bridge looked after twenty years. The train tracks were gone of course and the bridge had been properly decked and a railing built, but it wasn't that. The span, the river below, the rocks, all these things were obviously unchanged by two decades of time, but his memory had been twisted by every other rail bridge he had seen since then, every other river, every other space and hole and void and stretch of sky. Everything looked smaller than he had remembered it, and more— what? Just different. He would never have guessed this was the place if he did not know it for a fact. He knew this was the spot where he had been standing that day. He knew it but he did not *feel* it.

# CHAPTER FOURTEEN

EARL HAD CALLED Weidermann's and left a message for Cass. He had called Jack's twice but in vain. An unstamped letter appeared in Jack's mailbox addressed to Cass, and Jack told him it was a little red Civic that had dropped it there. Cass stared at the envelope on the table and backed away.

"Eleanor Holmes, I'd say it was," said Jack. "The Holmeses want to get a hold of you, I guess. Effie used to say the Holmeses are a real box lot; you never know what's going to come out of that family. Well, you know Eleanor. And you knew Peter Holmes, did you? He once wore his rubber boots to a funeral. I remember that because the minister then—oh, what was his name?—said why would Peter know any better because he hadn't been in a church since Noah was building the ark and then rubbers seemed like a good idea.

"They married overseas, during the war. A lot of people did, I guess. Effie said— Now don't be telling this or we'll all be in trouble for sure." He chuckled, rocking back into another time. "Effie once said Eleanor Holmes came to Canada because there wasn't room for two queens in England. Don't you repeat that now! Effie would just die if she knew I told that story on her." Jack chuckled until his eyes shone, focused off somewhere in his bubble of time.

Cass raised a booted foot onto the seat of a kitchen chair and crossed his arms, leaning forward onto his leg, resting. He did not know which way to turn so remained exactly where he stood. The present was too skittery to trap, the past too slippery to grab hold of.

Twenty years ago Randy wore a black leather jacket. Cass remembered when Randy took him along that first time because Daddy-O paid extra for someone just to stand there and watch. You don't have to do a thing, Randy said, it's me that gets all the exercise. Keep your eyes peeled, you might learn something. There had been a room some-where, high-ceilinged, dark in places then busy with mirrored light. Perhaps he had gone a number of times, watching. Probably. He didn't remember. What Cass remembered with stunning clarity was how the man stopped him on the way out by placing a hand on his cheek, so soft Cass wondered did he feel the skin of the palm at all? The man leaned forward and kissed him on the cheek, touched his face and kissed him. A thing so intensely shared for a single moment that he knew this was the reason for all the rest. No matter what else is true, the touch said, you and I, without names or pasts or futures or circumstances, are both true right now.

Randy was annoyed and never brought Cass to the house again. But he never had to. Daddy-O stepped in front of him on the street. "Come," he said. All Cass did was go, all he did was give the man what he wanted, what he was willing to pay for, just like Randy said. All he did was draw the pain out of the man's eyes, wind it up for him, hold it for a while. All he did was reach in to touch, just for a second, that diamond hole in the center of the man, hold up the bead of solitude and slip a thread through the center of it, tying it to his own.

Daddy-O said to call him Bill. Bill always had a present for him, new jeans or a T-shirt. One day an expensive pair of high polished boots. Cass wore these all the time, looked down at them marveling at the size of them, how far they seemed from him, the extraordinary length of the legs that rose above the feet. When he walked he felt the length of his stride, the heft of his footfall on the pavement. Bill gave him a leather jacket similar to the one Randy wore. Cass felt the proud weight of it settle on his shoulders. He watched himself in store windows, glaring at the reflection that glared back, taking in the image of the ominous man who had grown around him. The dirty stupid boy who lived inside him slumped in relief.

Cass slipped his arms and feet into sheaths of black leather every day. Randy's eyes narrowed and Cass did his best to stay out of his way. Randy saw him getting out of a cab downtown. Cass walked in the opposite direction though avoidance was pointless. He slipped into the recessed storefront of an abandoned business. Plate glass formed two walls of the angled little corridor reflecting Cass back to himself on both sides. He pressed his back against the door, half hiding, half waiting. He did not care what happened. He watched his reflection, watched Randy's reflection as he appeared and strode towards him as though this meeting had been arranged. No, as though Randy had maneuvered Cass here, trapped him. Cass tried not to look at him, to follow only the reflections where Randy seemed so much smaller, the two of them like the big dog–little dog sketch on *Bugs Bunny*.

"Where's my money, Dogshit?"

"What money's that, Randy?"

"Listen you stupid piece of dog shit! I know who's sending you downtown in a goddamned taxi! I know what he pays! What's a dirty little prick like you doing cutting me out of my own business? Did I tell you not to fuck me over? Did I?"

"He wanted me, Randy."

"Shut up! You fucking dickhead. If that pathetic little queer wants you to tie him to a pole and bang his arse in a parade from here to Toronto, I don't give a shit. But you bring your fairy-gold back and slap it into my palm. *I* decide what's your cut, Dogshit. *I* decide! In case you got a problem with that I got about three hundred B and E's with your prints all over them. I've got guys willing to put the finger on you for things you couldn't even think up."

"You can have your Daddy-O back."

"Listen here! I'm the one who tells you what you can and can't have. Because I am the one who can think, and without this precious baby here"—he tapped his skull—"you would have starved to death long ago."

Randy was right. But as he watched him yip-yipping in the glass it was clear enough to Cass how unimportant this was. Randy couldn't blow the whistle on him without upsetting his own applecart. Cass didn't want to be there. He wanted to get his teeth into about a pound of hamburger and then find a place to sleep. He could deck Randy if he had to, if it came to that.

"I'm heading out, Randy." He had not known this before he said it, stared at the man in the reflection to confirm it. Yes, the reflection said, yes, you're heading out.

"You got money belonging to me!"

Cass had no recollection of what had happened next. Had Randy tried to stop him? Had Cass flattened him, sent him sprawling? Maybe he had given him the money. Perhaps they had made some deal about Cass's foster money. Randy. Cass tried hard to recall the features of Randy's face but nothing came and the loss nearly sickened him. I would never have made it without you, Randy.

All he remembered for sure was that he had walked out of the city and stuck out his thumb, headed north on the highway. Scotch River was no accident. It was right there on his birth certificate. Where you headed, boy? Scotch River. Jack and Effie Heighton's farm was an accident, Jack taking him on to help with the hay like he did. That summer he had loved the clunking and banging of Jack's old square baler, loved how the rhythm of it stitched one moment to the next, loved tossing bales high into the air building the load on the wagon. But back then there was no deed, no property, nothing to point to Murray Holmes or Catherine Taylor or a grandmother or uncles and such. Not a clue.

CASS COULD SEE Weidermann thinking, could see it in the way he started his conversations with open-ended questions, in the way he deferred to Cass without relinquishing his superior position, encouraged Cass to speculate despite his reticence.

"You will be settled now here? You like this place here, yes? You think people like horses here?" Then always some small practical question that Cass could not avoid answering. "How many stalls we can build along this wall here, heh?" Sometimes these questions made Weidermann look a little stupid and because this was so far from the truth Cass kept a close eye on him.

The colt was smart but spoiled. Because he had been fussed over, if not worked with, for three years he was accustomed to the flapping and snapping of tack and blankets, to bodies busy around and behind him, so sacking out moved quickly. The next step was to get him out on the road, get him used to space and traffic. And load was a new thing. Every time Cass set something on the colt's back—the blanket, the saddle, a sack of oats, his own hanging weight—he repeated to himself, "My land." The weight of the idea pressed down on him, compacted, solidified and constrained. For several days in a row the colt had taken the empty saddle without complaint. Cass tightened the cinch and led the colt out of the corral, then out of the yard, then walked him along the verge of the road. And this was how Cass happened to see the bulldozer on the flatbed pull over and set its hazard lights blinking at the foot of the lane to the property. His property.

"My land." He turned and walked the colt back to the corral, taking time to consider what he had seen. Where's Earl, he wondered? He thought briefly of those unanswered phone calls. He returned on foot and by this time the dozer driver had backed the machine off the flatbed and was headed up the lane. Cass loped alongside waving his arms. When the dozer stopped he climbed up to the cab and the two men hollered over the roar of the engine. The minute Cass hopped down the dozer driver guided the machine back down the lane. Once the roar of the dozer began to fade he could make out yelling up by the house. Earl. The dog had not trotted down the lane to investigate his intrusion and when Cass reached the top of the lane he saw why.

Trapped in the bed of his pickup, Earl paced back and forth, the German shepherd following him step for step on the ground, his teeth bared, sharp barks spiked from his steady throat growl like barbs on a fenceline. Every time Earl made a move to jump down out of the truck bed the dog lunged at him.

"Tie up this goddamned dog. You never really had a right to this place, you know. Call off this goddamned dog. We're going to make something of this place, something besides a—"

Earl and Pipe spotted Cass at the same moment. "Cass! I got the dozer here. Where the fuck is he? He was coming up the lane."

"Yeah. He went home." Cass and Earl called to each other across the yard.

"What did you say to him, Cass? Get him back here, let me talk to him!"

"I told him he wasn't going to get paid."

"He'll get paid! There's tons of money here for Chrissake. He doesn't have to worry about that. What did you tell him that for? Hey, I explained all this. Cass, buddy, we need to get some proper machinery in here. We got pulp cutters coming! Don't you want to see some money out of this place?"

"Nope."

"What?"

"It's not happening, Earl." He caught Pipe's eye but she turned away from him.

Pipe fixed her uncle in a cold glare, signed with clear angry gestures accompanied by staccato speech. *Get off my land.* "Get lost, Earl." When he did not comply she set off across the yard. She bent over the pump handle, its muted donkey bray pulsing gushes into two tin pails. Up and down, oblivious to Earl screaming at her from thirty feet away, her ears painted shut against his voice. She hauled the water over to Earl's truck, set the pails on the ground, put her hands on her hips and looked around. Earl's rant continued unattended. Then she picked up one of the pails and let fly a dousing of water so cold Earl gasped, stunned momentarily into an incredulous silence. Water dripped off his hair, off his nose and chin, off his arms outstretched in mid-gesture. A flutter in Cass's diaphragm broke free and rose in a chortle that tumbled into a laugh startling every muscle in his chest and face, startling his ears that had not heard the sound in three seasons, startling his memory.

Pipe stared at Earl and jerked her thumb towards the lane.

"I'm not going anywhere, girl. You're the one who's on the way out—"

Calmly, she opened the driver's door of the pickup and emptied the second pail of water onto the seat of the truck, watched the gray upholstery darken in a great swimming stain, the water running down between the seat and the back, cascading onto the floor, splashing over the pedals and trickling out the door onto the ground. Drip dripping everywhere.

"Jesus fucking Christ, what are you doing? Get away from my truck. This truck is a lease, you know. I'm calling the cops."

Pipe leaned over the drenched seat, picked up a cell phone and handed the dripping little box up to Earl. When he unfolded it water dribbled out onto his shoe. Water oozed up from the plastic buttons when he punched in numbers. He cursed and tossed the thing into the truck bed. Again Pipe indicated the laneway.

Cass approached, now within fifteen feet of the truck. Pipe betrayed only the barest hint of a smirk.

"This isn't funny! I'm telling you, Cass, she's a loony. I could tell you a story, buddy, that would change your mind. Couldn't I? Oh yes.

Things are going to be a little different around here now. You bet your sweet ass. Tell her, Cass. Who owns the place?"

Pipe left him cursing and pacing and disappeared into the house. She returned a moment later shaking a paint can in front of her, a screwdriver clamped between her teeth. She set the can down on the grass and began prying at the lid.

"What color you got there?" Cass asked.

She surveyed Cass, unsure, then jerked the index finger of her right hand down from her bottom lip. The paint can opened with a little creak and a stretch. Cass started to chuckle again, couldn't help himself.

"Red," he said. He tapped the truck's shiny black metallic paint. "That'll go good."

"Ah fuck to Jesus no. This is a lease. Don't you dare. This is— Don't— Get in the truck, Cass. For Chrissake …" Pipe drew the can of paint back in a threat. Dog or no dog Earl bounded out of the truck bed and into the cab in one magical, gravity-defying leap. An audible squish rose from the sodden seat when his backside hit it. Earl spun forward, turned in a tight three-point turn and charged past Pipe, tires spitting gravel, down the lane. As he passed she sloshed a tiny slurp of red into the lane behind him, a few giddy drops finding their way to his tailgate.

Cass hugged himself, felt the laughter bubbling silently beneath his lungs. When the geese swarmed him, one pecking at his knee, he stood his ground. Pipe grabbed a stick and shooed them away. Chuckling quietly, she fit the top back on the paint can. The dog lurked.

"That was a good one. Red," he said, making the sign. *Red*. He crossed to the water pump and drew enough to splash his face and slurp back a few handfuls. He wiped his hands on his jeans. My land. My water. She had not moved but remained by the laneway, regarding him. My property. My house. When she turned away to examine the spill of paint on the ground Cass walked towards the back door of the house.

Cass stepped into the house as he had stepped onto the rolling prairie. Up over the crest of a ravine or out of a patch of cottonwoods and there with the suddenness of awe was every living thing. The inside-out feeling of knowing everything and nothing all at once, of certainty and insignificance, swept over him. It had been so long since he had felt it, this cherry stone, this marble in his palm, the air stilled in his lungs. Not since before the bulls had left him and taken Lionel, not since his feet refused to meet the ground, had he known this thing he could not rope with a word. Cass pulled the hat off his head in reverence. Images loomed and retreated, perspective altered with each step, this bit clear and perfect from here, slippery and off-kilter from there. What was it? He knew only that it was wondrous. The work surrounded him, ceiling, walls, floor, engulfed him and drew him in, making him a part of the melee. He followed the walls around, his footfalls electric on the animate floor. A tree root that grew into a grave. Is that what it was? One image melted into another. He did not attempt to sort them out at first for fear they would shed their power. Such a naked yearning splashed across him and he thought, for just a flash, of the city men he had known and their crystal desire.

He heard her come in, heard the clicking of the dog's toenails on the floor. He turned to her, knew his heart hung open before him, desperate. Across the room they stared at each other.

*What are you doing in my house?* "What are you doing in my house?" As direct and angry as her exchange with Earl.

"How can you make this feel?" he asked, just above a whisper, and knew the question made no sense but did not know how to alter it.

Between the toes of his boots spread a puddle of red barely brighter than the dirt colors around it. He followed the red up the wall where it flowered in the starkness of a snowbank, blood seeping from a spilled bag of unshelled oats. How could she paint anything as delicate as oats, blood-soaked oats? He crouched by the bleeding bag, leaned into the wall. Momentarily confused, was it him bleeding here? No, of course not.

He waved towards the wall. "It's ..." There was no word. He crossed his arms and held them to his chest as though in one of her signs but he could no more make an unknown sign than he could find an unknown word. "Good," he said, looking away, knowing he did not have it right. "No."

Anger had washed off her features leaving nothing Cass could read.

Above her sink sat a jar with restaurant packets of free food: salt, pepper, sugar, ketchup and mustard. A nearly empty sack of something, flour perhaps, slouched between the jar and a tea tin. Then empty shelf. He blinked back a pain, looked to see if he had given himself away, but she averted her own eyes as soon as he raised his. "Beautiful," he said, but that was no closer to what he wanted to say. A tiny smile pried at the corners of her lips. She spread her fingers and circled her palm in front of her face. *Beautiful.*

The painting revolved around some sort of old-fashioned factory. Despite its complexity he felt as though, if he stared long enough, he could grasp the truth in it. He knelt by the doughnut-shaped stone dominating one-half of the house, running his fingers along its cut-in grooves, searching his memory. He had come across these stones before, these stones like the eye of some great stone god. Millstones. A flour mill. In the center was—a tree? No. Well, it was really the chimney, rising through the middle of the house, but she had faced the brick with bark slabs until it resembled a tree growing up, evolving into a shaft, spreading out in six great limbs that became wooden spokes supporting a huge cartwheel gear. On the ceiling above him the gear's wooden teeth, all worn to an irresistible smoothness, meshed with those of smaller cogs. He reached over his head and touched the paint to prove to his eyes that the teeth were painted on, an image sitting flat against the ceiling.

On one wall a tired old workhorse leaned into its collar, and behind, a woman's face echoed exhaustion strained through fear. Harvesting, he thought, no, haying, with everything so green. Details blurred, giving the essence of the work without the work itself. A woman working, hefting, grinding. Mostly women. But then this face, this partial face, all eyes and forehead, this was a man. And another one over here, familiar but muted with darkness and stretched into the background of the wall golden to bronze with grains and heavy with something more he couldn't set a name to. And here the coming of winter with crisp colors taken by brutal cold and ice encroaching on the bottom stair of tumbling water. Everything moved. But of course it did not. It was him that moved, drawn from image to image by a subtle tug of season, a greater passage of time, in an almost irresistible path around the central chimney, following counterclockwise the circumference of the giant ring gear overhead.

He absorbed the images, let them rain around him. She had lined all this up, pulled it together close enough to see all at once, to puzzle over. She had painted herself a chance to search for a bit of sense in it all. The answer slid in under his skin and waited. The woman behind the horse, at the hopper full of grain, bent under the weight of a sack. She was the main one. But there were others—a girl ground up and spit out? Could that be true? Another girl looking to a blank corner of the house. The work was not yet finished. This painter girl, Murray Holmes's girl, was younger than him, could never have seen these people, but something in her made a single thing, a life, of all this … A word shimmered just beyond his reach. He started another tour of the work.

Story. She found the *story* in it.

A weak thing inside him quivered, and he let it. He tumbled from her world to his, a chaos of another color. With bits of homes and feelings and other people's lives no one held his story. His past twenty years he had hung on the peg of cattle and horses and rodeo, but before that, nothing. Now, although bombarded by flashes of memory, pattern and meaning eluded him. Once he had sat at a school desk kicking his legs, worried. He had picked the white ring of congealed glue off the nozzle top of a plastic glue bottle and chewed its tanginess. He was supposed to be making a picture but had been given only a sheet of thin cardboard and a pile of pale macaroni elbows—a thousand indistinguishable pieces.

"These people—are they real, were they real?"

She nodded, signed, then stopped, dropping her hands to her sides like laying aside useless tools, and she spoke. "My Nan's nan. She ran MacLaughlin Mills. You know where that is—the museum. That's true—all that story."

Cass could see how speaking could annoy her, why she wanted only silence. He could see how this work needed its own air. He thought of the gentle seesaw of the milkers at the barn and how the silence of the night let in a world covered by the noise of the day shift. They should not be speaking here. He held a hand out in front of him like a piece of paper and waved the other across it. *Draw me.* He squiggled his forefinger under his nose. *Kid.*

She cocked her head. An amused smile began at the ends of her mouth and grew inward. "You better speak."

He had done it all wrong, of course. His signs were no good and she was laughing at him. He pointed to the main figure, the woman who appeared older on every wall. "That one there. You drew her young and old. You drew me before. You could draw me being a kid."

*What?* "What?"

"Come on. Draw me. How much? I can pay. You could do it right now." He pulled his wallet out and thrust forty dollars towards her.

Gingerly she reached out for the bills. *Draw. You have a photograph?* "Do you have a photograph of you as a boy?" She whispered as she had done before, translating her signs, which she made slow and deliberate.

She knows I'm stupid, Cass thought, and tried to ignore his rising shame. He shook his head.

She set the chair in front of him and indicated he should sit, pulled her easel towards her, positioning it. She scrutinized his face, her frown of concentration deepened as she noted lines, shapes. Distractedly she reached out to turn his chin but then, just before contact, snapped her hand back as though she had been burned. Cass waited. She had a collection of pencils, or things like pencils, and kept changing, using one then sticking it behind her ear, another between her teeth. Finally she tore the oversized newsprint sheet off the pad on her easel. She studied it and him, made a bit of a face and a shrug as though she was not exactly satisfied.

Cass stepped forward to see and again could not believe her magic. "But as a boy," he said, unsure if she had understood.

She left the drawing clipped to her easel and beckoned him outside. *We'll see.* "I'll see what I can do from the drawing. It's hard without …" The curved fingers of one hand she set against the upright palm of the other.

"A photograph," Cass supplied.

"Why does Earl think he owns this place all of a sudden?"

"He doesn't. He thinks I do. Earl's full of shit." As he spoke Cass noted the truth of each sentence on its own and the lie of all of them together.

*That Earl's full of shit isn't news. But forty bucks is news.* She signed something silently with no translation then let her hand fall to the dog's head.

"Like what I must have looked like when I was a kid. You understand?"

"Yeah, I get it already." Her smile was friendlier now but Cass suddenly, desperately needed to escape. He felt her eyes follow him down the laneway.

He couldn't risk returning to Jack's for fear of a visit from Earl or Eleanor. Not now, not yet, not today. He slipped into Weidermann's horse barn and climbed into the mow. Thank God the air was as oppressive, hot and oxygen-poor as he had anticipated, desperate enough to contain this irrational elation, this horrible dangerous hope. The feeling was round and as big as the world and fear cut into it like wire. Cass closed his eyes and breathed in the stale, dry, too-warm air, his heart beating too strong, jolting the pain in his head in a steady rhythm. Draw me as a boy. Casper Hutt.

What had he done?

# CHAPTER FIFTEEN

PIPE DID NOT INTEND to think of Cass but repeatedly found him with her as she emerged from unguarded moments. There was such self-containment about him. He rode a horse as though it were a part of him, and wore that hat as though it were the normal thing to be moseying around like a movie cowboy. He wasn't flaunting his difference, it was as though he hadn't really noticed it. He dismissed her uncle with a single deed instead of endless circles of argument. True, he had walked into her house without invitation when her back was turned. True, it was a brazen act and he had no right and he simply disregarded her property and her privacy. It was important to remember this and to remember how her anger had flared when she realized he had disappeared from her yard. But the awe in his face, the wonder in his eyes—like a child mesmerized by a magician—the undisguised adoration of her work had brought her up short. She could have easily run him out of there; it was only her hand upon Blackwood's head that had kept the dog restrained by her side. Cass was the first person to step into the work, to truly see it and understand the magnitude of it, even with it incomplete and strands of story hanging loose. Wayne had seen it of course, but Wayne had no idea what he was looking at and didn't care.

She had not admitted to herself until she saw the amazement on Cass's face how much she yearned for approbation. It made her cringe in embarrassment but she could not deny it. And there was the crux of the thing right there. She was dependent on the opinions of others and he was not. He seemed to have achieved perfect solitude, not plagued by anger or loneliness or isolation as she was. He was not without uncertainty, not fearless. In fact she had seen the lightning flash of fear in his eyes before he asked her to draw him. It had startled her, alarmed her, made her momentarily afraid herself, before she realized the source of the fear lay inside him and was not anything that could touch her.

There it was again—she was too much affected by those around her: see fear, be afraid. She was too much wounded by what was said, spent too much energy running for cover. The world was full of people with knives drawn on her, but whenever she grabbed for a weapon herself she caught the blade and not the handle. Every refuge twisted into an isolation chamber. No solitary without confinement.

Her American Sign Language was a perfect example. She had been just a kid then—fifteen years old. Long after the accident. Forced into another help-the-troubled-teens camp weekend by her Uncle Ben, Pipe had been hiding out in a cabin when a square silent girl walked in and pulled something off her head, something from her ears, attached to some small packet. She faced Pipe with defiance, making a sign like a slam, one open hand dropping to meet the other like a wall closing between them. "Hut-ta." Pipe watched in confusion as the girl whipped her hands around a bit then folded her arms across her chest. She was deaf! She had taken off her hearing aids. "Hut-ta." Shut up. Pipe repeated the gesture over and over, her eyebrows knit with anger. Such a satisfying thing to do this shouting out in silence. She was seized with envy that this girl could pull off her ears and fling them in a bag. Never have to listen to anything anyone said. Never have to hear gossip or taunts or nasty opinions. This would be the perfect world. Here was a girl hollering at the top of her hands and those around her powerless in the face of her anger. Pipe had mimed plucking the ears off her head and dropping them into an imaginary garbage can while the girl laughed. It turned out that there were sign language lessons at the community college in the evenings. With these and her new friend to show her the way Pipe entered the world of this beautiful silent language.

Now she could weave a voiceless space around herself, a nest of breezes and birdsong, twigs and leaves and the whisper of far-off automobiles. She could rest in the soft cloister of a language without the clatter of speech. But she knew this was only half the story. At the thought of locking horns with her Granny Eleanor or Earl or any of them she would revert to the hostile genesis of her attraction to the language. She would become angry and sullen and helpless in the face of it. A teenager again and forever. Well, Eleanor hated Pipe's mother. Eleanor would scrape Lucy right out of her if she could, make her Murray's daughter. Only. Lucy never existed—didn't exist now as far as Eleanor was concerned. They all hated Lucy. Pipe would not leave her mother—leave her mother to … But Pipe had not been to see her mother in nearly two years. She slammed that door in her brain, turned back to Eleanor.

No, never mind Eleanor. Never mind what other people think. She had her art, the most powerful refuge of all. But even this turned on her. Let them all think you're crazy. *Make* them think it! There were times she believed they were right, that she *was* crazy. Who knew what they said at the mill about her and her sketchbook and pencils and her crouching in a corner—nothing good, that was for sure. And now she wasn't even allowed to sit in a corner without them standing over her, gawking and breathing down her neck. Fuck 'em!

She remembered, shortly after she had begun her degree at the art college, the day she huddled, unsure, on the outside of a ring of students. There had been some opening in the conversation, someone talking about small towns and small minds, and she had complained bitterly about her family, about her village. A girl with a brilliant green streak through her hair just shrugged. "Why don't you leave Nova

Scotia then? Why come to NSCAD? It's a big country. You could go to Emily Carr. That's why I came here—I wasn't staying within a thousand miles of Powell River, that's for sure." She always hated that girl after that. And she hated that question. She just couldn't leave. It was all she could do to get as far as Halifax. There was something about what really was, what really had been, that she could not relinquish. Like she was standing guard over all that had happened or might have happened. The Truth. The Holmeses would love to erase her and her mother, and the museum would love to erase her Nan and Penelope MacLaughlin and all the women who were not what they were supposed to be, all the things that never should have happened. That's why they didn't want her there. That's why the Holmeses didn't want her at all. She could work herself into a fury but then tumble into uncertainty. What truth, exactly? What exactly disappeared without her?

Cass wasn't trapped like her. Solitary is not necessarily isolated. He paid attention, understood things, returned her signs. He could be a part and be apart. Pipe spread her pencils out in front of her, settled in front of her easel and stared at the sketch she had made of him. Draw him as a boy. He hadn't said what age. It was hard to say what he had looked like, mostly guesswork, but what did he expect? She moved him back maybe ten years, erasing the wear on his face, softening the lines. She tried to work without being drawn in, without absorption, treat it as a simple mechanical task. She drew and crossed out and started anew with mounting frustration. It was the distance, she knew, and, against her will and judgment both, softened the wall between the subject and the object, let herself slide. She moved closer into her drawings. The sketches became more and more intricate. Such an ache overtook her. She stalled, studying her work, frowning, clutching at the edge of something. She wandered to the window and stared into space. When she returned to her easel the answer shone out at her as plain as the nose on his face.

The packet of photographs Pipe fetched from upstairs surprised her with their banality. She examined them one by one, flipping through them, waiting for some monumental emotional response. As a teenager she had fought with Granny Eleanor over these pictures, repeatedly drawing out the battle, thrusting their clash forward at every opportunity. Now the box drooped in her hand, one corner crushed and hanging like a tongue from the impact when she had driven it across her grandmother's floor, spurting tiny faces everywhere. Other things had hit the floor too, glass smashing, bits of figurines. Smithereens. Later Uncle Ben had engineered mediation, cornered her with resolution.

Inside the sagging box the photographs were rigidly contained, zipped into a modern black nylon case lined with some specialized material, all Uncle Ben's work. Since he had returned the photos to her after making copies she had never glanced at them. Not in all those years. She worked her way through the color snaps, most of them sloppy and indistinct. Behind these, set in (no doubt acid-free) sleeves, were displayed the more formal black-and-white portraits of her father as a boy, first alone then with little brother Ben then with baby Earl added. Three brothers. But always more of Murray alone, the special one. She chose several portraits of him, child, boy, teen, and packed the rest away.

With that glistening darkness in the eyes, the way the ears stuck out a little, the line of the face, the new model was totally convincing. The sketches practically drew themselves. Presto, Cass as a boy. The naked admiration she had seen in his eyes, the wonder and awe, came back to her in her own anticipation. It wouldn't take that long to do one little painted portrait, she thought. A rough one. Outside, from her collection behind the chicken house, she chose a length of planed one-by-eight and sawed a foot off the end of it. She sanded the butt ends smooth and primed the board well.

A PACKAGE with the simple label "Cass" appeared in Jack Heighton's mailbox. Paper, those same large sheets of newsprint, was folded around and around, wrapping something of more substantial weight and form. A thin string circled the package's width and length, keeping it together. With his heart beating in anticipation and trepidation, Cass tucked the package under his arm and carried it across the road and up to his room. Once you've seen something there is no way to un-see it. A flash of Lionel falling through the air so slowly now it seemed possible for Cass to hop over the rails and snatch the body, replace it with his own, before it landed on the bull's horns. He bit the string through with his teeth and unwound the many layers of newsprint carefully. He uncovered the weight at the center of the package, exposing it gingerly—a piece of pine board, one-inch stock but the true inch of older lumber. With the final turn of wrapping he stared at the painting in his hands.

A lad of about ten looked out at him, asking with his eyes. Cass's diaphragm constricted. Afraid he would drop the painting he set it on the bed in front of him and let gravity ease his body onto the floor where he knelt, elbows propped on the mattress, his eyes never leaving the painted boy. There was no doubt. This was definitely him here in colors arranged on a scrap of board. Eventually Cass turned away and sitting now on the bedroom floor he rubbed his feet until his palms hurt.

With the exception of the very outside layer, the newsprint wrapping was covered in drawings, not just the one she had done that day but others, lots of them, at every age, boys everywhere, almost like practice, but all perfect. It would take him days to properly look at them all, to sort them into ages so he could see himself growing up. He didn't know she would draw so many. He hadn't paid for all these, surely, not with forty lousy bucks.

And the painting. He clutched the painting to his chest. A drawing was not a painting. Before seeing both together he would never have considered the difference although it was clear enough. Nowhere on the work or on any of the papers had she marked the value of this thing she had made, these magical colors of paint on wood, these colors all his own. He had not known that a person could own a thing like this.

ELEANOR REPEATEDLY FOUND herself kneeling in her garden perfectly still. Thinking about him, about anything connected with him, about all that was connected with him, immobilized her. She could be weeding or pruning or fertilizing, then as imperceptibly as falling asleep she was encased in a bubble of herself as though she were the film in a child's bubble stick, the breeze blowing through her, stretching her insides out through her bones in a thin membrane that ballooned to encase her and hold her. Frozen in place, caught, haunted. Murray with his wheelbarrow, carting fieldstone for a rock garden. Murray's eyes glistening with a childish ardor, oblivious to the terrifying cost of spilt love. She would come to, blinking at the tactile world, embarrassed and afraid, adrift in a pool of frighteningly polished moments.

Annoyance still had the power to rescue her, provide distraction if not refuge. Now that Ben's time was no longer consumed by his school year she could be equally annoyed with his visiting her and his not visiting her. When she looked up to see him approaching across the back lawn she sent him in for ice tea while she recovered herself.

By the time Ben returned Eleanor had settled into one of the white-painted wrought iron garden chairs that sat by a matching table overlooking the pond. She admired the amber tea in the pitcher foggy with sweat, absorbed the faint cleansing lemon scent, imagined it wafting upwards through her hair.

Eleanor passed her eyes over her son. "What's Earl up to? He's looking like the cat that ate the canary these days."

"I don't know," Ben replied. "The suspense is killing me though. He was out to see Pipe a couple of times. You'd think he had enough to occupy himself with all he's got on his plate."

"He had Wayne out on the boat for his twenty-first. He said it went well, whatever that means. I wasn't entirely convinced, I'll tell you that."

"I was looking into a project the federal government is designing for youth in conflict with the law."

"Well, good. Maybe there's some sort of package deal we can get for the family, is there?"

"Now, Mom, come on. If you mean Pipe, she's never done anything that could even remotely be considered illegal. She just baits you because you rise to it."

"Thank you very much for clearing that up. I got a call from Jim MacGillivray, who claims to be representing Wayne. I didn't know Wayne had such a fancy lawyer. Who's paying for that?"

"I am. With his previous drug charges Wayne needs a good lawyer. People can have a very negative attitude about home invasions. Especially when an elderly person is hurt."

"Oddly."

"He had a hard start, as you know, Mom. There's a lot can be said in his defense and I think it's important that it gets said."

"There's lots worse off than him." Eleanor set her chin and Ben looked away.

"How old is that turtle, Mom? You brought it out from Crooked Harbour didn't you? That's not the same turtle Murray had?"

"Of course not. His was a *woods* turtle. Murray picked berries and caught insects, dug worms for that turtle every day. This is a *painted* turtle, not a *woods* turtle. I certainly hope you don't have yourself in charge of teaching biology."

A twitch flickered on Ben's forehead above the eyebrow. He tried to fight down the hurt, tried to catch it before it spilled all over everything again. A lifetime of cardboard smiles and forced moments of feigned interest then back to Murray. That was the best he could hope for from his mother. And from his father, only the repeated backhander, "Well, that'll please your mother." School play, science fair, 4-H, public speaking, university degrees, advancements and promotions—all the same. He should be used to it by now. But he knew no one ever got used to a wound by poking it with a stick every day. Ben swished the tea around in his glass, listened to the ice cubes tinkle. I will not, he told himself, succumb to self-pity. It was the most loathsome of emotions.

CASS SHOWED UP at the main barn during morning milking. He climbed down where Hank was working one side of the pit and Gord the other.

"You guys know of some old-fashioned mill around here, like a grain mill?"

"Oh yes, sure, yes!" said Hank bobbing his earnest head. "The old gristmill, sure. That place is haunted, you know. Ghosts. When they were fixing it up, you know fixing it up for a museum—man they could hardly get anybody to work on it 'cause of the chains rattling all the time and tools would move around. Like you put your hammer down here and then when you came back after break it would be over there. Stuff disappeared."

"They got the mill fixed up though?"

"Oh yeah. After a while."

"Ghosts still there?"

"Oh no, I don't think so. After they opened up and started charging admission they all went somewhere else."

Cass stared at the guy, sure he must be kidding him, but Hank looked lost in the terrible mystery of it all.

Gord snorted and strolled over like this one was going to be too good to miss. "Ghosts went somewhere cheaper, I guess."

The sarcasm was lost on Hank. Cass watched him soak up the attention of an audience. "Oh, it's true! My uncle worked there. Ages ago now. I was just a kid then. My uncle, he quit 'cause the ghosts were all the time swirling around and you couldn't get no peace."

"Christ, Hank!" Gord shook his head in delighted disbelief.

"Oh yes, he used to tell us all the time about the ghosts. They chased him right out of there! He said he wasn't going back there no more."

"Chains rattling? What chains? Give me a break, Hank! Ever think more likely your uncle was fired? Maybe something to do with all those tools that kept disappearing whenever anybody turned their back? Nobody else ever heard of any ghosts."

Hank stepped back, stung. Then he stuck out his jaw, clinging to his story. "He wasn't fired. I know what I know."

Gord returned to his cows' udders. "Moron," he muttered under his breath. Then to Cass, "MacLaughlin's Mill—used to take us off to old shit like that on school trips. It's a couple of miles from here. Not far."

"East or west?"

"That way. I'll show you on my GPS, look." Gord pulled his phone out of his breast pocket and began poking at buttons. "This is brilliant, look."

"Nah, that's okay." Cass left them to it.

It wasn't hard to find the mill; he simply headed west, turned off the railbed at the first stream and followed the road. He rode the mare down past the main door and off by the millpond where he tied her beneath a tree. He took off his hat, wiped his forehead and headed for the mill door.

A young bright-eyed guide met him halfway. "Wow, a horse! There's hitching rings up here," she offered. "I don't think anybody's ever tied a horse to them before, though. Well, not since—you know, the old days."

"She's better off out of the way a bit."

"Is she tame?"

"Well, she might bother you if you bother her."

The girl frowned, disconcerted, and Cass disappeared into the mill before she decided what to say. He declined the offer of a tour and set out on his own. At first he wondered if he had come to the right place. The main floor was roomy and bright and held little of the sense of Pipe's house. His house. Mostly there were wooden hoppers and sacks of grain. But once he descended the stairs recognition enveloped him. There, above his head, the giant wheel turned, rumbling and squeaking. There were the gears, the beams, the sense of enclosure, almost entrapment. All that his half sister had painted lay before him.

It seemed impossible that a living person could have all of this left to them: family born, lived, died and passed down all of this. He lifted his arm and pressed his palm into the hemlock beam above his head, leaned into the cut-stone wall of the kiln, pushed his weight against its solidity, followed with his index finger the initials the builder had cut into the stone 125 years ago. *EML.* All this sturdy existence tumbling back and back seemingly to the beginning of time. Stone and lumber, intricately fashioned wooden gearing, shafts and belts, all this rumble and smell and taste. All this proof.

Half sister. The half connected to him was not the same half connected to all this. He paced through it in his mind to keep it straight: this was not Murray's family, not Catherine Taylor's, but another woman's. Pipe's mother, this crazy lady, this Lucy—her mother and her mother and her mother, however far back it went. Not his people. But he could hold out his arm and reach across a narrow ditch of circumstance and touch the person who owned all this past, all this truth, who was rooted down through the earth here in this place. The proximity to such permanence was almost dizzying. Like the deed stashed under his bed, it did not make him a part of something significant—it offered a point of contact, a grip. Once again he was crouched in the chute over the bull making his wrap, lacing glove to bull rope, with the loudspeaker in his ears. "We got two thousand pounds of glory here ladies and gentlemen, and a cowboy hanging on to him with a pretty little braided rope." The bull rope around and back and between his fingers, pounded tight.

Cass tucked his long arms around himself and stepped up to the barrier where he could examine the workings of the mill. He followed the power train along, belt to shaft to gear, melting the mystery into simple mechanics. The stones, he realized, must be on the floor above and he had somehow overlooked them. The only natural light pushed its way in through two small flour-fogged windows. Overhead the spur wheel growled and oat dust began to tickle his throat. What he owned was memory, a thing less than air, less than a bump under his skin, waiting to be made solid. And his sister, his half sister, could do this. He willed his memory forward, braced himself for the fear, steadied himself against a century-old wall. What Cass remembered was a cardboard box with all the things he would need for his life, his yellow blanket, his lucky cap, his plastic soldiers collected in a bread bag and closed with a twist tie. When a boy gets too dirty and too stupid it is the end of the road for that boy. Cass remembered driving off in the backseat of a car, hugging the box on his lap, the feel of the rough woven upholstery on bare legs. The end of the seat was shiny, cold and smooth where he touched it. Off to the end of the road for the little boy called Casper.

The chipper young guide materialized at his elbow. "How are you getting on? Did you have any questions at all?"

"Pipe Holmes comes here," he said. This was not a question but the girl had startled him, caught him in his pain, embarrassed him, and he wondered now how his half sister with her quiet language could tolerate all these yakking interruptions.

"Oh yeah, all the time. Her grandmother had, um ... her husband ... no, wait. Her grandmother's father, I think ... yeah. He was the miller, you know. So yeah, I know her. She's kind of … Her mother's … You know Pipe?"

"Yeah." Cass escaped up the stairs and back to the mare, uncertain as to what to do next. Laden with that heavy feeling like he had just won a large sum of money and the wealth was bearing down on him, constricting his airway. He had to think. All that mill, all those drawings by his bed, the painting. He swung up into the saddle and headed for the railbed. And Earl would still be looking for him after the scene with the bulldozer. He was leaving messages again. Overwhelmed, Cass pounced upon this diversion like ducking behind a rock for cover—Earl and Randy and "Here's your business." Both of them all plans and orders and full steam ahead.

"You do as I say, Dogshit. I go out on a limb for you, vouch for you, I give you every opportunity, and you can't wait to fuck me over. Is that it?" Had he decked Randy in the end? Or had Randy simply let him walk by, walk out of the city? Such tiny details for such a large betrayal. The whole thing was such a perfect plan for Earl: step in and pull half the profits from someone else's land, buy a license in his own name and half the loan to pay for it in someone else's. What money he couldn't skim off the top he would see invested in a business for which he was entitled to half the profits. Such a brilliant plan Cass didn't want to be the one to foil it.

Randy used to bring home sacks of groceries. When the foster checks came in, all of them, the foster mother and all the boys, would troop off to the grocery store and load up a shopping cart to overflowing. Then they'd hit the McDonald's and everyone could have whatever they wanted that night, but two weeks later both money and food were only memories. Randy's bed was only intermittently slept in but soon Cass and the younger boys would take to checking it several times a day, staring at it, willing Randy to appear. And he would. Any time of the day or night he might burst in, singing and calling out to them, loaded down with food. He would keep them all busy with his tales and his boasts while a huge feed was spread out, no matter the time of day. That boy eating there at that table was living now on a sheet of paper under the blanket on his bed. Him and the one before him and the one before that. And the one after that with eyes that scanned the horizon and the heart that believed in death, like Earl's son on the boat—all of these evaporated boys were waiting for him.

He would pay for the painting. This was a thing he could do right now to stop the mash and jumble in his head. Cass rode back to the property, the land where Pipe lived, but she was not there. With the help of his Milk-Bone and the mare's dauntless courage he managed to make it across the yard, but the shepherd barked and growled and flattened his ears when Cass dismounted and approached the house. He set his sleek body between Cass and the door, his bark sharp with purpose.

"Yeah, okay, pal, I get your point."

Cass looked around. A clothesline ran between the back porch and a tree. He emptied his wallet, nearly a hundred dollars, and pegged the bills in a neat row, like waving leaves, green, purple and blue, by the door. Before the dog became any more agitated Cass retreated.

It was mid-afternoon now and hot. Cass followed the railbed east, facts, notions and images dashing and fluttering around his head. If he had held a few bucks back he could have ridden into the village for a cool beer to settle his thoughts. As it was he continued on to the iron bridge, past the spot where the ATV track veered off, and up to the bridge itself. He dismounted and tied the mare back from the bridge, as horses could be sensitive to this sort of thing. Here was a separate and specific part of the whole that he could focus his mind on. His boots spoke each step across the wooden decking of the bridge. So high up was he that Weidermann's corral could have fit in the space between his feet and the river. The height made him part of the sky rather than a creature of the land.

He stopped in the middle of the bridge and gazed upriver where trees in their full greenery lined the slopes down to the banks, where the river wound off around the point and folded out of view. The blue of the sky reflected in the water, lighting it to a powerful blue and gilding its ripples with silver. Cass turned and leaned back against the railing, his arms crossed over his chest and one leg crossed lightly over the other. Downriver the view was similar except the watercourse bent to the west instead of the east. Deep blue. From here the river looked as deep as the ocean had from the boat, water all the way down to the center of the earth. The sun drew sweat up through his shirt dampening his back and armpits, his jeans held heat close to his skin, his forehead moistened beneath his hatband.

Cass stood up straight and continued across the span, slipped down the bank at the far end into the sparse band of shade the bridge offered, and he peeled off his boots, his shirt and his hat. He hiked his jeans up to his knees and inched out into the cool river water. He knew the stones underfoot were awkward and uncomfortable, but though he tried he could not feel pain. Cool water soothed his calves and he leaned over and splashed his face and chest. With cupped hands he drizzled water over his hair, felt it trickle down his back. Looking up, he followed the long iron legs of the bridge, great straight spider legs, up out of the impossible blue to the metal structure arching above him, up beyond into the blue globe of sky.

This was the beginning. Heading backwards, from now to then—no, from twenty years ago to all that came before, this was the start. The end of Scotch River for him then and the beginning now—the midpoint perhaps, the linchpin holding that life to the man he was now. Yes, there were many reasons to talk to Pipe Holmes, but this one thing he needed to get straight.

PIPE BUNDLED UP her sketchbook and pencils and headed off. Since the incident behind the barrier the guides gave her no peace and she couldn't sit anywhere without their eyes upon her, looking at her like she was a cholera blanket heaped in a corner.

Pipe hesitated at the corner of the museum property, crouched by a slender maple tree on the steep slope above the mill. The mill's ocher-painted shingles weaved sunlight with lines of shadow. The millpond reflected a flat glassy light that sparkled when the occasional crane fly or frog disturbed its patina. Motionless and silent as the pond itself, she watched people come and go. When finally she descended to the mill a guide greeted her warily. She pulled herself together in determined friendliness and nodded, her facial muscles caught in a grimace, her teeth ragged like gravel stones in her mouth. Inside the mill she climbed the stairs and crossed to the back window where she stuck out her head and watched the water tip over the dam and plunge into the gorge forty feet below, spilling white froth across the rocks. A family pelted up the stairs and filled the air with their footfalls and calling out. They were all around her then, bumping her elbow, a head popping out the window so close to her it made her stomach lurch, a foreign arm pressing into hers. "—Jason, wait now—what's this, Dad—don't bump the lady—Mom, look—can we make the winch go …"

Pipe backed away and headed directly for the top of the stairs. When she glanced over her shoulder she was amazed to see there were only four of them, not the dozen she had supposed. Down she went, two floors to the basement, and here a group of adults were laughing with a guide, listening to a description of the mill workings that in Pipe's opinion was worthy of a seven-year-old. Pipe squeezed up against the far wall, closed her eyes and soaked in the vibrations that hummed through the floorboards. She's over there in the corner—well, watch her—don't let her sneak in behind that barrier. Don't hear them, she ordered herself, but if she painted her ears shut she could hardly make out the rumble of the spur wheel and the water never mind the stamp of hooves on the dirt outside and the creak of wagon axles. Never mind the low voices of men, the swish of a long skirt. This is where we light the fire for the kiln—how much would one of those stones weigh—do you want to go upstairs—oh, I don't know. Pipe scooted further into the corner and scrunched down, opened her book. Concentrate. Concentrate! But she could not smell the leathery sweat of horseflesh or hear the harness buckles clink. Dust did not catch in her throat as palms slapped flour from layers of cotton clothes.

The idea, when it descended, had the solidity and shape of an apple and it came to her full and ripe as though it had fallen from a tree into her outstretched palm. It was sharp and sweet and perfect. There was no problem at all in executing the initial necessary act. It was nothing to bundle herself into a tour, to pause on the stairs, reach up and rest her hands on the window sash. It was nothing to ease the one common nail that served as a "lock" out of the hole where it nested above the sash and slide it into her pocket. She slipped out quickly and quietly, elation quivering all about her.

When she arrived home, there hanging by her back door was a line of what appeared to be freshly laundered money. She unclipped the bills and counted them out. Ninety-five dollars. In addition to the previous forty bucks, that made a hundred and thirty-five dollars for a few sketches and a rough painting that had taken her a couple of hours. *Blackwood,* she signed. *This guy should be on the Canada Council.* Giddy with her plan and her good luck, Pipe tore for the village and its bounties.

Once back on the railbed, her bicycle basket laden, she did not mount her bike but walked it along, guiding it with one hand, and with the other dug around and pulled out a liter of thick dark chocolate milk so sweet it made her blink then laugh out loud. Recklessness and courage played together beneath her heart. Her plan was brilliant.

Releasing her voice like a toy snake coiled in a can, she let out a whoop of excitement, a wild startling whoop that did not recognize fences and rules and prohibitions, that leapt into the air trailing like paper streamers bits of herself she had not used in ages. Daring. She would succeed. She would finish her work and it would be true and clear and brave and everlasting. From behind her on the trail an answering voice called out piercing her with sudden self-consciousness and quashing her abandon.

CASS, STILL GLISTENING with river water, his jeans rolled up, boots strapped behind the cantle on his saddle and his T-shirt dangling out of his back pocket, rounded the corner of the railbed leading his horse to see her walking, pushing her bike up ahead. As unlikely as it seemed, the whoop must have come from her, his silent half sister. "Hey! You get the money?"

Startled, she whipped her head around, then, recognizing him, stopped to wait. She was drinking chocolate milk from a carton and balancing her bike with her free hand. As he approached she held the carton out to him. Her eyes glistened with a secret and for a second panic buzzed around him like a wasp—what does she know?—then flew off.

"Yeah, I got the money, see?" She was smiling.

Cass fell into step beside her and accepted a slug from the carton, the chalky paper spout precarious on his lower lip. He remembered settling on the guardrail of a parking lot and tipping milk cartons back, white and chocolate indiscriminately, unwrapping premade sandwiches from their clear plastic bundles. There had been bags of cheap doughnuts, molded see-through packages of baloney with slices that peeled away one at a time to be rolled up and dropped into his mouth. The chocolate milk was smooth going down and sweeter than he remembered. She was stroking the mare's neck when he handed the carton back.

"That painting is really good. I got it sat up in my room."

"That painting is bullshit."

"No. It's real, it's true."

She shrugged but looked pleased all the same and they walked on together in silence, Cass mute with indecision. It was all so complicated and everything he needed from her so crucial. If he scared her off he would never learn anything.

"How much to paint me growing?" Cass asked finally.

"What?"

"How much money? How much to paint a story like you got in the house? It don't have to be as big as that. Smaller. I don't know how big. As big as a door. A story of me."

She laughed. "The story of your life? How modest of you."

"Just the boy. There's stuff I know, like is on your walls there, but it's all out of order and I don't know … I don't know what *happened*."

"You don't know your own life?"

"I was just a kid. I forgot a lot. When you're a kid it ain't like being grown up. I don't know why. Like when you see people carrying little kids around, it ain't just their bodies they got there, it's all the stuff you can't see. Little kids can't keep hold of nothing but today and yesterday and tomorrow. They got to have somebody carrying all the big stuff around for them, keeping it straight—first this, then that, then later on something else. Sure we know one little flash of time, but that don't mean nothing. You got to put all the flashes in order to know what happened. You're on a train track here, you're on a train track there, and then one time gets mixed up with all the other times till you don't know what's true. But that picture you're doing on your walls, on the walls of the house—that's true, ain't it?"

She stopped and set the milk back in the basket to free her hand and nodded.

"You paint me like that wall there—I'll pay you. Really."

"I can't now. Later. I'm just about to ..." *The whole thing will come alive tonight. I'm on the brink. I've got this plan—it's brilliant. You bet the story's true, and it's going to get truer.*

Excited signs danced in the air between them. For a moment, as they stood looking into each other's faces, he thought she might translate the secrets but the moment passed and all that remained was his inexcusable ignorance. He did not understand and nothing could be done about it.

Still, he pushed. "Later. When?"

She shrugged and straddled her bike. He needed to know when, needed to ask her about the bridge, about his father, about everything. Don't go, he thought, and the words, even unformed, unspoken, unheard, dizzied him and stirred a woozy gurgle in his stomach. Stall her.

"Earl ain't been back?"

"No. Good old Uncle Earl. That's my loving family for you."

Keep her here. "Uncle, what's the sign for that?"

She wiggled a two-finger salute downwards from her temple. Cass followed her, repeating the word to himself. *Uncle.*

"Aunt?"

A fist with a thumb up she wiggled similarly at her chin.

"Sister."

*Sister.*

"Father."

*Father.*

"Brother."

*Brother.*

"Half sister."

*Half sister.*

"Mother."

*Mother.*

Cass replayed them all in his head. She continued unbidden. "This is grandmother." *Grandmother.* "Grandfather." *Grandfather.* "This is how you spell Cass Hutt, by the way." Her hand twisted almost quicker than you'd notice then bobbed in the air like someone knocking at an invisible door, twisted and knocked again.

"That's your name. You can shorten it, change it any way you want for a name sign. For, like, a short form."

"I like the knocking."

"Try this then. Nice and easy. You'll get quick later." She spelled out a short form slowly, with exaggerated movements so he would notice how to position his thumb, how to use a steady beat. *C-S-S.* A curved hand and two knocks.

Cass signed his name sign over and over, spoke over his hands. "Your father have any other kids?"

"No."

"I heard he was a nice guy."

*What's it to you?* "What's it to you?"

"Was he a nice guy, your father?"

Something shut behind her eyes like a pane of glass. She was still there, he could still see her, but from a further distance. She set her hands on the handlebars and searched out the bike's pedal with her foot. When she spoke, brusqueness replaced her easy signing.

"Depends who's asking. He was nice enough, I guess, but he wasn't a goddamned saint. I don't know what he thought he was doing. My mother was sick, is sick. What kind of ice did he think *nice* was going to cut? She needed treatment."

"You remember him pretty good?"

"Not really. He'd take in any stray, people say—that bit is true."

"Wait. That day on the bridge. I guess I got to know. You and Murray Holmes and—"

"You want that mural, you should think about what you know, make some notes. I gotta go—big night tonight!" She leaned her weight onto the pedal and glided away. In a minute she was nothing more than a speck in the green corridor in front of him. Shit!

With leaden arms he tugged on his boots. Putting one foot in front of the other seemed an awful effort but so did hoisting himself into the saddle, so he rested awhile, leaning into the mare. Think about what you know, she said. That was all he did these days. Think about the boy he had been, not the bridge, not Eleanor or Murray or Catherine. The last place before Jack and Effie's, just beyond the end of the Dartmouth city bus run, was tucked away, not really in the city or outside it. A small house with flaking turquoise paint, a path of cracked cement to the front door. Out back, dog kennels filled with jumping, barking strays lined the yard. German shepherds at one end, lapdogs at the other and every other shaggy or short-haired mutt in between, all desperate and clamoring all the time, all bunched together. She claimed she loved them, thought she was doing them a favor by taking them in and locking them in there. It made him sick to look at them. Cass was supposed to clean up the dog shit in the kennels and in the yard but there were too many dogs yelping and howling and producing more shit than anyone could ever pick up. The smell of it clung to his clothes, worked into his skin. That was why, Cass remembered now, they called him Dogshit.

That foster mother, what was her name? He remembered hair red and gray, cigarette smoke, orders, called assignments, given out but never checked. She pretended everything was in perfect order but the place was chaos. Don't bring me any trouble home. Yes, there had been a truant officer. I don't want trouble at my door. Waiting for the Children's Aid check, he remembered, and a slant-ceilinged room with walls the color of watered-down Kraft Dinner and beds crammed in like toes in a Sunday shoe. Mostly what he remembered was Randy. You come with me, do what I say, Cassie-doodle. Fair and square, my Cassie-boy. But you try messing me around I'll fuck you for free. You understand?

He could stretch out and fall asleep right here on the railbed the air hung so heavy around him. Cass rubbed his head to feel the last of the river dampness in his hair. *Uncle,* he signed, the weight of his arms making the word onerous. *Sister, half sister, brother, mother, father, grandmother.* I wonder what's the sign for "my land." The land, fifty acres, he set it out in his mind, the thirty acres out front, a hay field only thirty-five years ago, now grown over. My land. A yard, a pretty house, tight and sound, a well, a woodlot. My land. More than a woodlot, a forest, nearly twenty acres of trees, some so old they were tall before anyone now living was born. How beautifully simple that would be, to stand and watch things, animals, people, come and go and nothing mattered at all. My trees. All legal, aboveboard, a legacy from his mother. *Mother,* he signed. "My land," he said again.

# CHAPTER SIXTEEN

PIPE COULD HAVE laid out her plan before him. She knew this as they walked along, him disarming in his bare feet, his long man-feet fresh from the river, long fine bones fanning out to slender toes. Him leading his horse, never mind the stones, like a kid toughened by shoeless months of summer, but him on feet so elegant. He carried himself the same way, no idea at all of his beauty, a guy who measured himself by his use. A guy who thought beauty came from away, from somewhere outside. Him with his height and breadth, all that maleness. She hardly knew this man and yet she knew she could have told him all about her plan for the night ahead, and this knowledge lightened her spirit with an odd, amorphous hope. Of course trust could be easily misplaced, set it down here just for a second, just for a moment, to rest your weary loneliness and look back to find it smashed or stolen. Betrayed. It wasn't so much that the cowboy was trustworthy, it was his sense of solitude. He was an island. He would keep a secret without even being asked. But then he starts in with the business about Murray and wrecks it all. And the bridge. She tossed her head like a horse, deflecting.

At the first hint of dusk Pipe set off up the railbed. By the time she wrestled her bike into its hiding place in the brush the sky had sunk to a rich river blue and distant trees had flattened to black silhouettes. She crouched on the trail waiting and watching light being pulled from the sky. Once darkness had obliterated the daylight she double-checked the kitchen knife in her back pocket beside her pencil case, stuck her flashlight into the waistband of her jeans and pulled a purple sweatshirt over the top of her T-shirt. She clutched a sketchbook and set off on foot, her skin prickly with adventure, the darkness and daring of it. Above her a fingernail moon touched the edges of the trees.

It wasn't hard. She eased upward pressure against the windowpane, took it slow and easy, finessed the sash up far enough to slip the knife blade under it and finagled enough of a crack to wriggle her fingers into the slot. Then it was an easy matter to lift the sash all the way up. She passed her few possessions over the sill then eased herself through the opening, clinging to the sill as she lowered her weight safely to the solid treads of the stairs below. She closed the window behind her and looked around. The mill was hers.

EARL'S BRAIN REVVED and spun and spit rocks and got nowhere. The bulldozer driver would not listen to reason, claimed he didn't want to find himself in the middle of any property squabbles, and no matter how long and sweet Earl talked, the guy would not budge without proof of land ownership. Cass was avoiding him—that was for sure. The bastard could not be found, not at work, not at home, not in the village. Jack Heighton didn't know where *Jack* was, never mind where *Cass* was. The more Earl thought of it, the two of them, Cass and Pipe, standing side by side in the yard, the more he was convinced they were in cahoots. Cass had stolen his idea and was planning to go into business with Pipe. The thought of it drove him nearly demented. The thing was to get to Cass soon before he got in too deep. If he could just talk to him he could warn him away, tell him the truth about certain matters that she might have forgot to mention. He would have Cass back in the fold in no time—if he could only find the bugger.

Bottom line, the guy had to show up for work. Earl would have preferred to catch him elsewhere, somewhere they could talk at length, but Cass had forced his hand. Midnight shift Cass had said, so sometime after midnight Earl would head over to Weidermann's. In the meantime there was no need to waste energy trying to chase him down, and as it happened Earl had developed a deep longing for a few cool jars of suds and a bit of the camaraderie such as he could expect to find at the Legion.

Time slid by in the Legion bar, dusk disappearing into dark as one beer chased another. Earl cocked his head at the sound of an engine revving in the parking lot outside, a door slam and a bellow. The floor wavered slightly under his foot when he stood, when he stepped away from the table to take a leak and a precautionary glance outside.

Earl climbed the stairs to the main room with a line of windows overlooking the parking lot. He eased back a corner of a curtain and peered down on several young men converging, starting the ritual stances and jeers, foreplay to the brisk, thrilling violence of direction-less youth. And there was Wayne, bold as fucking brass, lit right up under the streetlight. "Goddamn it!" Earl lurched down the stairs and pitched himself against the crash bar of the Legion's steel door, strode out across the parking lot, gravel shifting beneath his soles. He came upon his son from behind.

"Wayne! Get your ass home. Get on out of this before there's trouble."

Wayne turned to face him, fuzzing in from somewhere far away. "Fuck off, Dad."

"Don't fucking talk to me like that. You got enough goddamned trouble already without this fucking useless crowd handing you theirs. Christ, your eyes are like two piss holes in a snowbank. Get in the truck. We're outta here."

Wayne blinked and turned his back, no more concerned than if Earl were an old barn cat strolling by. A normal kid would get in the car to avoid a scene, never allow a public dressing-down, but not Wayne.

"Jesus Christ! Get in the goddamned truck! You got a place of your own, a truck and everything. A lobster license practically. You don't want to hang around with these losers. Get in the truck. We're going home." Earl lunged for him, grabbed at his shoulder but caught only a handful of shirt and, with all the evening's beer, was tipped off balance. Wayne literally shrugged him off, broke contact, stepped away, not even embarrassed, not even trying to shut him up. By the time Earl found his feet again Wayne had shinnied up the light pole, laughing. The youngest Everett kid leaned on the hood of a nearby car, his face ugly with a lopsided sneer. He looked Earl up and down and snorted. Earl could have smacked the face right off him.

"What am I supposed to do, just leave you here? Fine. You're worthless anyway, you know that? You don't even know what you got when somebody lays it right in your lap. You're fucking pathetic. You know that?" But he might as well have been yelling at the street lamp. He wheeled around and headed for his Bronco, slammed the door and spun out. In the rearview mirror he saw the eddy of young men beginning to roil, tension swirling upwards. Forget Cass for tonight, he was going home.

THE HAIR on Wayne's arms spiked. The new pills he'd come across pumped fresh cold air under his skin in a rush. He slid down the pole and strolled towards the growing knot of young fellows, his feet and hands glowing with energy. Clarity, confidence, focus, filled his body, not vanquishing fear but shaking it, turning it inside out, standing it up so it felt nothing like the fear in his ordinary life. Strength and possibility pumped through him. He hung back, glowing with energy, letting others shove and shout. He liked to fire his first punch hard to the face, feel his strength brought to bear, the crack of broken resistance, the pure success he knew nowhere else in his life. Outside the circle, the world shrank and blew away.

His first punch loosed a spurt of blood. Quick, quick now he followed with a knee and a kick, the face of fear and pain groping from the gravel. He could have placed a name on the face the way he could have named a car or a tree. Could have. He saw his boot heading for that face but then a blur and blow to his gut grabbed his breath. He grasped at what he could not see. His fists found hair, yanked hard then pummeled brutal and fast on the closest flesh. Curses, the slide of boot on gravel, smack on flesh, a satisfying grunt, Wayne heard the whiz of limbs through air and felt the kiss of sudden pain. Thrashing like a madman he connected again and again, direct cause and effect. He could go on like this forever. Flying.

Blue lights flashed.

"Fucking cops!"

Everyone scattered. Wayne held his ground, king of the Legion parking lot now that all the rats had scurried off. He stood, breathing hard in the aura of the streetlight. The Mountie climbed out and Wayne started towards him, head up, eyes alert, arms swinging loosely at his sides. There they were, two guys walking towards each other in a parking lot. If he could have frozen this fearless moment of confidence he could have fashioned a lifetime around it. They would shake hands and call each other by name. Wayne admired this ritual, men clasping hands, smiling but not too much. Sometimes men would slap each other lightly on the shoulder with their free hands. Ordinary men. Here he was walking, ten feet from the Mountie, both of them yellow in the street light. Eight feet. Six.

The cop carried his cap in his hand. "You're not fighting, now, are you, Wayne?"

Wayne looped his right fist into the Mountie's jaw, sent him staggering backwards in surprise, tipping almost slow motion to the gravel where he landed, legs splayed in front of him, one arm propping him up, one hand to his chin. The police cap lay upside down in the dirt several feet away, its lining catching the light.

Constable Townsend recovered himself, let out a string of curses and jumped to his feet. "Up against the car! Hands on the fucking car!"

All Wayne had been a moment before popped like a balloon. He shriveled into his real self, felt the sides of a box close around him. He shuffled to the cruiser and set his hands on the cool rounded edge of its roof. His head hung between his shoulders. Townsend grabbed his wrists and twisted them around to the small of his back, snapped the cuffs into place. He pushed him down into the backseat of the patrol car.

Townsend retrieved his cap from the dirt then took his place behind the wheel. He sat awhile, massaging his jaw, not speaking. Finally he picked up his radio.

"I've got Wayne Holmes here on a 270."

"You okay? Hope you're okay because we're short staffed already, as you know."

"Yeah, I'm all right. Just a sucker punch. No damage. Five minutes into my shift. Fucking little pecker-head. I'm bringing him in."

"Okay."

After a minute Townsend started the car and pulled out of the parking lot. In the rearview mirror he searched out Wayne's eyes. "What did you punch me for? Everybody else runs off and you just stand there. But you can't just stand there even, you've got to puck me one. What's the point? Now you've got assault of a police officer and breach of probation on top of everything else. What's the point? Can you tell me that?"

Abandoned by adrenaline, the pain from Wayne's wounds bloomed and overran his body. He turned away, said nothing.

"Apparently not."

At the station Townsend checked himself in the mirror, watching the glossy bruise settle against his cheekbone. Another cop appeared and clapped him on the back. "Whoa, Trevor. What's the other guy look like?"

Townsend hunched over and fixed his hands behind his back. The man laughed and strode over to the cell where Wayne had curled himself into a ball at the far end of the cot.

"Now, *Mis*-ter Holmes. I just don't know what we're going to do about you. We don't want you taking up valuable space in the lockup. We may need it later for some deserving felon. You are the cause of a great deal of unnecessary paperwork you know."

He turned to Townsend and continued, "You going to do him up and take him home?"

"Yeah."

WAYNE LAY ON HIS BACK behind his trailer and howled with fear. The neighbor's dog started it. Yip yip ya-hoo. Wayne answered, nipping bites out of the night. The dog caught the response, howled again. Wayne pushed himself up on one elbow long enough to gulp a swig from his bottle. He dropped back into the grass and keened his loneliness into the dark. The echo looped around and met the next wail. He howled until he was hoarse, until his bottle lay empty on the ground beside him. If anyone comes, he thought, I'll beat the crap out of them. Then he fell asleep.

PIPE WANDERED among the stones, trailed her hands along the tops of the wooden grain hoppers, sinking her hands up to the elbows in the soft rolling liquid of the wheat kernels. She reached for a small handful of wheat, guided the raw seeds into her mouth, chewing carefully until the gluten balled into gum. She stood at the window staring at the millpond, centering herself, waiting for the noise of her illegal entry to settle and her heart rate to return to normal.

She descended to the basement waving the flashlight beam before her until she found the light switch. The basement's dusty windows pointed into the gorge, so she could light this floor with no risk of detection. The two upper floors would have to remain dark. When her eyes adjusted to the light she pushed open the forbidden gate and walked in under the giant spur wheel. She climbed up its trunk, curling her foot into one of the huge angular braces and hoisting herself onto the top of the wheel. Dust as thick as a snowfall clung to her sweatshirt or drifted and fell. She crawled her way along the top of the spur wheel and stretched out along its arc like a cougar on a tree branch, one arm dangling. After a while Pipe swung her weight off the spur wheel and onto the bridging tree that supported one of the stone nuts. She wrapped her body around the wooden cog, leaning into the belt that transferred the power from the gear to the buckwheat sifter. She climbed over and under the belts, crawled from one stone nut to the other, hunched over, snaking through the headspace between the top of the spur wheel and the ceiling, like climbing around inside an enormous watch.

When she jumped down bending her knees and landing in a squat on the floor, she studied the dust at her feet and the boards beneath. She wandered, sank her hands deep into bags of flour, buckwheat bran and shells, rubbing everything between her palms, holding it on her tongue. She scooped up a handful of oat shells and blew them away into the air. The oat dust tingled and itched on her skin. She drank in the essence of everything, reveling in what she knew by smell, by taste, by sight, by touch, by heart.

Next Pipe mounted the stairs to the main floor, her flashlight beam guiding her. The kiln door was held shut with a simple iron hook. When Pipe pushed it open she found oats strewn over the cast-iron tiles in preparation for next week's drying. She stepped into the kiln and nestled into the oats, squirming into a ridge here, a valley there. One hundred and twenty-five years of wood smoke blackened the inside walls of the kiln, which held the aroma in its cells. Pipe closed her eyes, worked her palms down through the oats to the cool iron floor beneath, felt the grains prodding their form into her skin. She lay on her back and flailed her arms and legs to make an oat angel, cast-iron black when she stood up to admire it. Water spilled over the dam, hit the rocks fifteen feet below, an eternal backdrop of white noise that could be subsumed by the sound of one's own breath, noticeable only in its absence.

When she had finished with the kiln she climbed the stairs to the upper story and pressed herself against the window forty feet above the waterwheel. In the dark only a dim reflection of moonlight and the faint glow of the basement light illuminated the water as it spilled over the dam. The wheel turned, its thumping pale and rhythmic.

Pipe had watched the miller at work time and time again, had heard him describe the details to tourists, had thought it through. The stream no longer contained enough water throughout the summer tourist season to be counted on for power, so the water-wheel had been disconnected and now turned without purpose beyond the aesthetic. A ten-horsepower motor had been installed to power the wooden gears. There was nothing to it: Pipe pushed the button to start the motor then gradually lowered the clutch lever that engaged the main belt. For a long while Pipe listened to the rumbling of the gears.

When she was ready she interrupted the power long enough to engage the burr stone. No problem. She cranked its adjuster a quarter turn as she had seen the miller do and heard the timbre of the stones alter as the runner stone was lowered to within a hair's breadth of its mate. When she released the wheat from the shoe it tumbled into the eye and fanned out between the stones in a thundering, heart-trembling rush. Pipe gripped the wooden vat that enveloped the stones, held it until the grinding settled into a constant growl, until her blood stopped pulsing at her temples and her hands could be trusted not to shake. She set her flashlight on end like a candle and sat in ancient gloom, with water, wood and stone. Grinding grain. She swayed, imagining lantern light twisting shadows across the walls, playing the dark against the darker. Grinding flour.

Two sets of trapdoors, one directly above the other, were built into the floors. With the doors open a winch-powered rope elevator could hoist a sack the full height of the mill. From the basement Pipe looped the end of the rope around the half bag of flour she had ground and hauled it up to the main floor. She untied the bag then worked her foot into the loop at the end of the rope. The elevator pulled her upwards to the top floor. It was not a fast ride but an inexorable one. The winch creaked softly as it worked. Upstairs she disengaged the elevator and returned to the main floor where she sat, her head resting on her drawn-up knees, her arms wrapped around her. The rolling clatter of the mill soothed her to drowsiness. The flashlight beam had worn now to a thin brave light. A mouse skittered by. When her light melted to nothing Pipe retrieved her sketchbook and made her way back down to the lighted basement.

WAYNE WOKE AFRAID, as he did every time he didn't wake drunk or drugged. If he had aspirin or sleeping pills or antibiotics or antihistamines he would take them before bed. Without them now he rarely slept through the night. He woke cold, even in summer, even when the air around him stunk hot and stale, cloying and stubborn, still a silver core of chill, like shaved icicles, mixed with the marrow of his bone.

Soon he would be going to jail, of this he was certain. There lurked a vague relief at having at least one concrete cause for his fear, something anyone could understand. Mostly his insides shivered simply because they always had.

He grabbed a Pepsi for his hand and another for his pocket and took off into the darkness, headed up the road to nowhere in particular. The sparse moon reflected enough light to keep him on the road, enough so he could make out the pavement and the gravel shoulder, enough to walk into blindness. If anyone had come by he would have hitched a ride as far as they were going then hitched another ride back, but no one passed on the road. Behind him daylight's forerunners edged the horizon, draining black from the rim of the world, at first stretching visibility ahead of him from six feet to ten to twelve, then easing silhouettes from the darkness, cutout figures of trees, telephone poles, the house to his left and the barn beyond. A dog saw or smelled him and set off a frenzy of barking. Wayne walked on. The silhouettes rounded in advancing light, with colors emerging from gray. He turned off into the museum park, avoided the public entry and cut into the woods that surrounded the old gristmill. The light had penetrated deep enough to illuminate his footing on the forest trail. He shoved his hands into his pockets. A bag of Ritalin pills crinkled against his fingertips and he pulled it out, suddenly elated. He had entirely forgotten them. Well, there had been the fight. A good fight. He shook his swollen knuckles in remembrance.

Wayne searched the forest floor, found himself two rocks, one flat, one jagged. He pulled a large maple leaf off the tree beside him, crouched there on the path with the concentration of one building a fire without a match. He hunched over his rocks, meticulously placing each tiny pill in turn in the center of the flat rock, twisting the jagged one with his wrist and crushing the pill to powder with slow, deliberate strength, felt its integrity give way between the stones. With a finger he swept the powder onto the leaf. When he had crushed all sixteen pills, counting as he went, he licked the stone clean smacking the pills' bitterness against the roof of his mouth. He crouched on the balls of his feet admiring the snowy mound of dust then ever so carefully lifted the laden leaf as though it were a golden platter. He snorted as much as he could up one nostril, then the other. He licked the leaf clean, crumpled it and dropped it at his feet. The calm before the high was almost as good as the high itself—the promise of a happy future; he was inevitably, inexorably headed towards a few really first-class moments and nothing could interfere with this.

Wayne followed the path along the top of the gorge, the land falling away abruptly to his left, the woods to his right, continued upstream to where the path joined the main tourist trail, graveled and sign-posted, which guided the visitors from the parking lot to the gristmill. Here stairs built into the hillside descended to the walkway over the dam. He stopped at the head of the stairs looking out over the scene, waiting. Already faint tinglings of the drug had aroused his blood. The millpond below lay smooth as skin, luminescent now with morning sun, displaying the mill upside down in the world below the water. How quickly the light had consumed his darkness. He felt its heat melting into his arms. He stepped forward into the sky that spread out before him. The step below reached out and caught his foot, cradled it and held him in midair. He stepped out with the other foot. The next step caught him. He laughed, held his arms out to either side like a tightrope walker and descended as though on clouds to the walkway over the dam.

To his right the millpond hovered, perfect below his feet, to the left the edge of the world. He felt the newborn daylight silky on his palms as he held them up to the sky, he wanted to be lifted again, carried on the air. There was so much sky, so much awesome wonderful sky that spread over everything, hugging the whole world, holding it all together. Railings ran along each side of the walkway, a fence of a pleasant height to rest your arms on, lean over and gaze down into the gorge, watch the water flowing over the dam and through the flume where it turned the wheel. The rumbling of the mill, like a lion's purr, filled the gorge with an ambience both soothing and exciting. Wayne hoisted himself onto the fence, onto the top rail, a bar four or five inches in diameter. With his arms out and his eyes straight ahead he walked the rail, his sneakers gripping the wooden railing, his hands holding on to the sky. He tottered slightly, straightened, laughed, took another step. He no longer saw the walkway three feet below him to one side; he was walking over the waterfall almost directly beneath him. The water slid to the edge of the dam in a single slippery sheet then tipped over, all at once, tipped over and broke into a million bits, a happy clatter of cutlery, tumbling, tumbling to the rocks below. Tumbling the height of three men, of six children, of twelve big dogs, of three dozen cats, of thousands of birds tumbling a foot or two then catching the air with fluttering white feathers and never, never coming down. The water spilled beneath him, cracked open, hatched and flew off. The spray pattered on his eardrums. Wayne walked the rail with fearless freedom brushing his skin, his eyes full of sky, his ears catching and holding every sound, laying each in a bed, one on top of the other in luscious layers that could never reach a top—every sound of the water, the first chirpings of the birds who never fell, the creak of the wheel, the rumble of it turning on its axle, the slap of water on wood, the laughing of the water as it rode in the buckets to the rock beneath then scurried to join the stream again. The mill growled beside him, a deep rolling heft and heave of gears, the crush of stone on stone. Rich white powder.

He reached the other side of the stream. The gorge no longer lay directly beneath him. Now it was the wooden flume, and below it the waterwheel and the rock streambed. He faced the gorge, flapping his arms to keep his balance on the thin rail, tottering a bit. The flume was an inviting size, the approximate dimensions of an open-ended casket. Water frolicked through like a tide of kids headed for a waterslide. It dived off the end of the millrace into the waterwheel buckets and was carried, kicking, splashing and squealing with delight, on its Ferris wheel ride down to rock beneath. In a half jump, half fall, Wayne pitched forward into the flume. The pain of falling nearly six feet, of landing half in and half out of the flume, startled him. The millrace jerked to the side as though someone kicked it. He waited, kneeling in the shallow rushing water. Another kick. Kick. Kick. With every rotation of the wheel the race was jarred slightly. He tried to stand but found the wooden floor slippery so he rolled over and lay in it. The water slowed momentarily, building up depth, but soon found its way around this new obstacle and rushed as fast as ever over his legs, around his arms, into his ears, through his hair, and into the waterwheel buckets once more. Wayne lay there laughing, his eyes full of the blue-yellow sky.

He struggled to his feet, stood in the flume like a pulpit above the gorge. He reached out to touch the water pouring off the dam but it was too far away, a foot or two beyond his grasp. For a little more height he tried to climb up on the sides, managed to get one soggy sneaker on each wall of the millrace and stood there astride the waterway, the gamboling water beneath him, the wheel just in front. Kick. He nearly fell. Kick. He anchored his feet more firmly. Everything was so wonderful, so awesome. But his ankle hurt and the edges of his body were already starting to chill with the shimmer of reality. Still he stared at the airborne water in front of him, felt droplets on his wet face, held on to the roars and growls and splashes stacked in his ears, concentrating on living the high as long as possible.

From behind and above him, somewhere in the mill itself, he was sure of it, came a bang, like a shot, like a crack of wood on wood. He twisted around, upsetting the balance of his body weight. His left foot swung forward to catch him but found no wood. The foot fell into the space at the end of the flume, slid outwards into the waiting bucket of the wheel. All his weight followed it, shoved it deep towards the center of the wheel, where the foot caught and twisted. For just a moment Wayne flew. He reached out and he flew, laughing, like a child being swung by a dad in a backyard. A child swung and then suddenly let go.

The wheel smashed his body, hard, onto the rocks below. Water continued to tumble through the millrace, over the wheel, over the body. Blood found a new route through Wayne's brain and rushed to freedom through the crack in his skull, burbled along joining the water in the stream. Shortly the blood stopped rushing and simply rested where it was, sunk to the bottom of its cavity, its vein, its artery.

WHEN THE NIGHT THINNED, diluted by the first glow of light in the east, Pipe raised her eyes from her work. She uncoiled herself now, her muscles yawning, throwing off the ache of stillness. She must tidy up, erase signs of her visit. She shut off the basement light and headed upstairs. Dawn sparkled on the flour dust in the air. Light eased the world into its parts, each piece of matter, each form and body distinct from all those around it. Morning had arrived, full and uncompromising. The elevator rope she sent back down to its original position in the basement with one quick tug. She tipped the heavy trapdoors shut and they closed with a sharp bang like a shot. A faint thud, an irregular bump in the churning mill sounds, followed the bang. More than a thud, it was a few noises all together like a brief tumbling sound. She cocked her head and listened hard but heard nothing more. She climbed the stairs and shut the upper-level trapdoors. But no errant sounds followed. She shut down the mill bringing the rolling gears to a halt, made sure the burr stone was properly disengaged, raked the oats smooth on the kiln floor.

Pipe opened a bag of wheat and tipped it into the hopper to replace what she had used. The half sack of flour she had ground she slung over her back. Dawn light had bloomed into morning light. She shoved up the window sash and climbed out the way she had come in, easing the window shut behind her. Then she was up over the hill and on her way to the cover of the railbed.

# CHAPTER SEVENTEEN

ELEANOR HOLMES PLUNDERED her hanging baskets of petunias, pinching deadheads with efficient ferocity, jetting them into a plastic yogurt container, bound for the compost. Earl Holmes popped several Advil for his head and took a slug of Pepto-Bismol for his stomach. He leaned in the doorway of the TV room hoping one of his boys would ask for something he could provide, but no eyes left the screen. If he thought he could have withstood the refusal he would have asked who wanted to come to the wharf with him. When he could dredge up no reason to remain, he left for his boat. Ben Holmes took his morning coffee and newspaper into his backyard to work on the crossword. He wondered if the grass had grown sufficiently to withstand a mowing.

At the gristmill the first tour guide to arrive unlocked the door, turned on the lights and began opening windows. She mounted the stairs. When she opened the window above the waterwheel she stuck her head out as she often did in the morning to drink in the view she never tired of. She admired the millpond to her left then bent her head to take in the dam and the waterwheel directly below. She sucked in a gasp, coaxed trembling limbs to carry her down twelve steps to the mill's main floor then outside and down the fifty-two outdoor steps to the young man face down on the rock. She did not scream. She touched him, whimpered and backed away.

Constable Trevor Townsend of the Scotch River detachment of the RCMP caught himself checking his watch again. He frowned and turned back to his computer screen. Then the call came in.

TOWNSEND CHECKED FOR VITAL SIGNS though anyone could see it was pointless. He backed out of the rivulet, shook the water off his boots like a cat shaking her wet paws. Each passing bucket in the waterwheel spat a weak spray of water over the body. "Wayne Holmes." He touched the fresh bruise on his jaw, recalled how Wayne had stood waiting while he groped for his hat and picked himself out of the dirt. He recalled the anger in his own voice, also the satisfaction in twisting the arm behind the back, the slide and bite of the cuffs, the token resistance. Pecker-head, he had called him. Townsend looked around, at the dam and the wheel and, way above, the open window. He called the medical examiner and his corporal. He climbed the fifty-two steps where the miller met him literally wringing his hands, his countenance registering the deepest possible concern.

"Oh my," he said. "Oh my," and waited, it seemed, for an answer.

Townsend fetched his crime tape and started securing the scene.

"There was someone in the mill last night. There's no doubt about it." The miller hugged a dark purple sweatshirt streaked with paint of every color to his chest as though he had lost it long ago and was grateful to be reunited.

"I asked you not to go into the mill, sir, please. Have you been in the mill?"

The miller's eyebrows dug so deeply in the "concerned" position Townsend was sure they must be hurting him.

"Well, yes. I saw the window, the nails … that must be how she got in and out."

"Step over this way please, sir. No one is to go into the mill. Now why would you say *she*?"

The miller held the sweatshirt at arm's length to display the paint stains. "Well, this shirt, the paint, of course I can't swear it belongs to her, but you know Pipe Holmes and paint. I just picked it off the chair inside and I know it wasn't there yesterday because I had feed bags over the back of that chair."

Townsend took the shirt and tried to look stern. "Evidence, sir."

"Oh yes, of course. I'm sorry."

"Now about this Pipe Holmes?"

At last Townsend heard his corporal arriving. He knew he would draw doorstep duty, felt a certain penance in it and was impatient to get on with it.

WHEN HE DIDN'T SEE the Bronco in Earl's yard Townsend continued out to the wharf, parked the cruiser. Every eye followed the gray shirt and the yellow-banded cap along the wharf, watched him pause by Earl's boat and step forward.

"Earl." He caught sight of movement in the wheelhouse, squatted by the boat and removed his cap. "Earl."

Earl folded over a stack of papers and stuffed them in a box. Cops he did not need. His frustration swirled. "What now? And don't tell me any sentence with the name Wayne in it 'cause like I said, he's twenty-one and there's nothing I can do."

"Earl, can I come on board?"

"What for? What do you want?"

"Mr. Holmes ..." Townsend stretched out the silence, waited for the change in address to make an impact. "Can I come aboard, Earl? I have bad news, sad news. I'm sorry."

Earl stared at the Mountie stepping down onto the deck. He motioned him into the wheelhouse that was suddenly way too small.

"There's been an incident, an accident. I'm afraid your son Wayne was involved." Townsend clung to his professionalism. "I'm sorry, Earl. He died. It looks like he fell into the gorge at the gristmill museum. We don't know what happened but he died on the rocks there, probably early this morning. There will be an autopsy and an investigation."

Earl stared, belligerence propped on his features. None of his prepared remarks matched the information making its way through his ears. What the cop was saying, this was not possible because he had spoken to Wayne just last night. Outside the Legion. Wayne was there, alive. "He's not dead. I talked to him last night! What's this bullshit? What did you do to him?"

"There was a bit of a racket at the Legion last night. Everyone else ran away as soon as the police were called of course, but Wayne hung around like he was waiting for us. I don't know why. I would have sent him on his way if he hadn't pucked me one. I've got no choice then, you see." Townsend touched the bruise on his jaw. "I charged him with assaulting a police officer, then drove him home. He was quiet, Earl. I drove him myself, sent him to bed, to tell you the truth. Told him to get some sleep."

"You don't need to tell my kid when to go to bed!" Earl heard his voice crack. Earl did not want Townsend to leave him, he wanted him to stand here and take the blame. All of it. And he knew that, just like everything else, this was not going to happen. That Townsend would turn and walk away and leave everything right in his lap.

"If you could, Earl, we need someone to identify the body."

Earl stared.

Townsend looked down, touched his bruise again. "I'm sorry, Earl."

Cass squeezed the lunge line clip in his hand. The animal was doing well. In mid-session Gord from the day shift jogged over to the rail and waved at him frantically, calling out.

"Hey, did you hear the news? They found Wayne Holmes dead at the gristmill this morning. No shit. Called in the major crime unit and everything. They're there now—from Truro. Looks like Pipe Holmes tossed him out the top-story window. Smashed his skull. I wouldn't doubt it. But you know, there's other fishy stuff too, eh? Last night there was a fight outside the Legion and Wayne decked the cop, Townsend, in the parking lot. I was there. I saw him. That part was pretty funny actually. Set him right on his ass. So Wayne's last seen being driven off in the cop car. Then miraculously a few hours later the same cop finds his dead body in an out-of-the-way place. So I don't know, you tell me, eh? They're doing an autopsy, the whole nine yards. They've got the crime scene taped off, newspapers, reporters, Dan MacIntosh from ATV news is headed this way. My girlfriend's gone over to see what's happening and she phoned me." The fellow pulled his cell phone out of his pocket, checked to make sure it was on. He looked around, impatient. "Christ. I gotta get back to the milking. The guy was no angel but still, eh? That's brutal. It's not right, you know."

Cass kept his eyes on the colt. "Wayne Holmes?"

"You know. He lives in that orange-looking trailer a mile along, on the Scotch River Road. You know Earl Holmes?"

"Yeah, I know him." Some leftover kid—climbing around looking for something to claim him. Cass led the colt back to work in the center of the corral leaving the messenger bouncing his palm off the top rail of the fence, annoyed and restless. He punched a number into his phone.

AGAIN ELEANOR WAS IMMOBILIZED, cradled in the stillness of another time. Ben found her on the bench by the pond, hands folded. Still.

"Mom," he said.

She traveled a long way in the time it took to turn her head towards him. She blinked twice and arrived.

"Good morning, Ben. I was just sitting a spell." Even as she spoke she rose and picked up the gloves she had laid on the bench beside her.

"I thought perhaps you had heard?" Ben spoke tentatively.

"Heard what?"

"About Wayne."

"Oh, what now?" Her voice instantly cross.

"Let's sit down again, Mom." And Ben told her all there was to know.

He fell, or perhaps he had been pushed. Either way he tumbled from a height onto river rocks. And died. Not again, not again! "Wayne," she said and kept repeating to herself. It was her grandson Wayne, that poor waste of a boy, who was dead. But no one died for her that was not Murray. When the world called for her compassion, only Murray's memory answered.

"Oh my," she said, all she knew swirling about her, blinding.

Eleanor needed Murray to stand beside her in the face of loss. When that death had been Murray's, this was when she knew there was no redemption, that she would walk the rest of her days with the wind whistling through the holes inside her. It was people like her, gouged out and drilled through, who had conceived of heaven. Uniting with God, they supposed, but really reuniting with all that had been lost, with all that had been intended. And here it was again, the fall. Leave it to Wayne, his death couldn't have been worse.

"I'm in contact with the police and the morgue, Mom. I'm going over to the funeral home to speak to Lonnie later. Earl is—I'm off to get Earl now. I think you should wait here. Do you want to wait here? I can get someone to stay with you."

Yes, you just organize every little thing, Ben, she thought and managed at least not to say. She could not strain annoyance from her voice though. "I'll stay by myself, thank you. You just get on with it."

There is always the moment of the tearing, when flesh of another ceases to be connected to your own, when your own flesh is no longer yours. Torn and torn again forever. When Eleanor dreamed, it was never of the endless fall. In movies, in the dream sequence, in stories so often reported by dreamers, it was the terrifying fall through the air. For Eleanor it was the moment when fingertip left fingertip, and all was lost. What cry a living thing can make will never approach the truth. A gull in fog, a coyote at night, the various keenings of uncivilized peoples, even a babe torn—the closest yet still as far from the truth as the distance from the brink to the abyss; there is no sound to match the tearing of the heart. The sound of asunder.

Eleanor watched Ben disappear around the corner of the house. She drew her hand to her chest and held it there. No one can feel the beat of a heart beneath the bone. Still we know it is there. It wasn't enough to suffer it once? But this is Wayne, the one so hard to look at. Earl had brought the little boy Wayne to the house, the Crooked Harbour house, the house handy to the wharf as they say here. Almost midnight and there is Earl on the step with his arms full of boy, still in school clothes, still with his little satchel on his back. Earl full of rage but with no clean clothes for the boy, no toothbrush, no pajamas. Tricked, ranting against the woman, his wife, the boy's mother. What kind of a woman leaves her own kid? The bitch the cow the monster the cunt, no matter the boy clinging there, no matter Eleanor herself with her dressing gown and slippers, her graying secrets and worn kitchen tiles. Never mind that he brought it on himself, another woman carrying his unborn child and the scandal all over the village. The boy's mother beat him to it, got out first, left the boy before Earl managed to get around to it. Eleanor took the boy, sent Earl away with a list, stern, demanding his quick return, demanding but knowing all the while that what is lost is lost is lost. There is an indelible stain on the one the mother leaves. Earl, humiliated by his wife's last laugh, wild with his defeat after nearly a decade of their childish tussles, knew nothing of the boy, of the rending and falling and cracking open. Yes, Eleanor thought, falling from that day to this and now broken open upon the rocks. And those left, frayed and jagged, their empty torn hands in the air.

Another one to follow her Murray. No stone is ever left un-tossed. Murray the solid, born quickly into the shadow of the departed, swimming forward and filling the hole. Not filling, no, but Murray the baby, the boy, the young man, compassion walking in solid flesh. Compassion asked to fill the ocean that forgiveness cannot cross. Impossible of course with compassion weak and reedy and no help at all but to sing for courage when all weapons are spent. With Murray fallen and now Wayne. Oh my, oh my, oh my.

Eleanor tumbled too far and could not see her way up. If only she could grab hold of herself, force her legs to carry her to the kitchen, she would boil the kettle and settle herself with a cup of tea. But she had not the strength. Take her, take her, she had said the first time her body had created another. And no, she said also, don't take her. She had no memory of decision. But she had memory of bellowing, war or no war there'll be no bastards in this family, of her body demented with emptiness, grabbing. There would be no filling that void ever. War takes everything. Hope died a miserable squalid death of dysentery. With him. What was left for her then but distance? A Canadian soldier would do for immediate relief, for transport. His name was Peter, a soldier now but really a fisherman. Good enough, she supposed. Soon, but never soon enough, at last, at last, baby Murray. She held him in her arms every waking moment, could not bear to set him down, for when she did, irreparable damage was exposed. Across the Atlantic with a boatload of war brides, of girls, tearful and excited and shy and exuberant. She did not care to share the giggles or the fears, the loneliness or the longing, but passed days on deck in every weather with baby Murray wrapped and tight to her breast and the ocean impossibly vast in every direction.

She could not rest her mind on Wayne. Dirty and desperate, a stranger to the truth, a petty thief, fingers always dirty with scabs, one or two damp with blood. He would leave red-brown fingerprints behind him. It nearly made her stomach heave the day she found a bloody print on a digestive biscuit on a serving plate after he had been there with Earl and his family. He had picked up the biscuit and set it back on the plate with his scabby fingers. Leery even of touching the plate, she had slid the remaining cookies into the compost and sunk the plate into extra-hot wash water. Sometimes she wondered if he could speak at all, then he would explode in some argument with one of Earl's younger sons exposing his limitations to all within hearing range. Wayne had been a baby when Murray died. She remembered so little about that time apart from Murray. And here was Wayne taunting her with his death like that. Not to mention Casper Hutt. Where had he been then? What difference could it make—she knew where he was now. Murray had sent him for her, knowing she would need him, the small remaining part of him. The fall and the water were a sign from him.

EARL IDENTIFIED THE BODY. Yes, he said. As they wheeled it away he identified the sheet and the gurney and the van and the mill and the sky and the laneway. For all the good it did.

Three steps up to the porch at home, TV cartoon voices through the screen door like a speaker, the hall's wooden floorboards squeaked in the two regular places on the way through to the kitchen where Judy, irrepressibly cheerful since quitting her job, was baking gingerbread men. He stood silent at the kitchen door watching her fit currants into half-circle smiles on their faces, buttons down their chests. Worthless, he had shouted at him just last night. A few short hours ago. His throat still scratched from the violence of the last words he'd ever said to him, ever would say. I am going to be sick, he thought, and ducked into the bathroom. He tried to steady himself on the sink but the shaking had taken over not only his fingers but his entire arms. In the end, Judy would not have Wayne. Too hard on the boys, too hard on her, couldn't take it, couldn't do it anymore. And when he played his final trump, if Wayne left he would have to leave too, she had only nodded and started to cry. Yes, she knew, but she was ready, she would live without Earl if she had to but Wayne had to go. Earl was beaten then and that was the only time he had ever truly beaten his son. Sure he cuffed him from time to time, shoved him occasionally, but that one time … His stomach lurched but nothing came up. Sweat beads tingled on his forehead. He splashed his face trying to wash the memory from his skin where it had lodged. The crack of the stick in his hand, the bruises and welts and how he had quivered and pulled Wayne to him and kept him out of school until he healed completely. The terror of it and then the trailer, meant to be theirs.

Earl returned to the kitchen doorway. They all hated Wayne—Judy and the boys too.

Still he had not spoken but Judy was staring at him. The phone rang.

"What's happened?" she asked and moved at the same time towards the receiver.

He could have said let the machine get it, considered saying this, but the job of forming words overwhelmed him. He could have held his hand out to block her progress but he didn't. Let her answer it, he thought. The scanners will have alerted everyone. The details will be well fleshed out by now, everyone will have decided on a story. He hauled a chair out from the kitchen table and steadied himself into it.

"Hello. Good. What's wrong? No." Then he could tell by her voice she had turned and was looking at his back. "Earl isn't home yet." Earl could hear the buzz of the telephone voice talking into her ear. All through her long silence on the phone he felt her eyes on him but he did not lift or turn his head. "No. Thanks. Bye.

"Earl."

Guilt and blame, anger and a dreadful defensiveness bumped around blind and nameless inside him. If she had called to any one of these they would have answered. But she did not. She drew him to her, her hands on his head, and whispered again, "Earl."

He clung to her and cried like a boy.

PIPE JOGGED OVER the path through her woods and burst into her clearing at a run. She swung open the goose shed door, snatched the chicken eggs, dumped a scoop of dog food into Blackwood's bowl, barely pausing to pat his head. Cans of paint were lined up on the sawhorses. She grabbed them one at a time and shook them, her eyes scanning the last corner of the room back and forth, up and down, over the painted-in background, composing and deleting in her mind while her hands pried and popped paint-can lids, stirred, set mixing pans out before her. With the energy of the night burning through her she could work straight through for a week. She met her backdrop with sweeping strokes of the brush, broad strokes, the story flowing through her onto the wall, curling up onto the ceiling and down onto the floor. Up and down off her chair. Even as the broad swipes of form and color met the wall, detail rose in her imagination, latent. Time spun out like a trailing of yarn, a lone filament guiding her between then and now. Hours passed. Then Blackwood was whining and pacing. Perhaps he had been for some time, she didn't know. Someone knocked on the door then the window, rapping and shouting at her and gesturing for her to open the door. A cop. The geese were giving him a very hard time, hissing, lunging, tugging on his pant leg. Good. Really she could not speak to anyone now, let him go somewhere else for whatever he wanted. Keeping her eyes on her corner for as long as she could she sidled to the door to let the dog out and gave him the signal to make the intruder unwelcome then climbed back up on her chair, barely interrupting her thought.

THE ENTIRE MILL had been taped off now, the building, the dam, the entrances to the park. All the staff except the miller and the tour guide who discovered the body had been sent home, each one brimming with unofficial information. One of the guys from major crime stood conferring with the corporal, several more combed the upstairs, a pair prowled the dam. There were several critical questions unanswered.

The dismissed staff did not all feel this paucity of information. Pipe Holmes had broken into the mill and had actually operated it. The audacity of the act was breathtaking. Besides the miller, only the lone male tour guide had ever been entrusted with running the mill. No woman had ever controlled the machinery. Pipe had been there. Her sweatshirt was found on the floor. There was evidence everywhere. The cops were taking fingerprints off the windowpanes. They had gone off to question her. The window high above the waterwheel was open and forty feet below Pipe's cousin Wayne Holmes was found dead on the rocks. Nobody's forgotten twenty years ago. Everybody knows Pipe is as loopy as her mother and she's proud of it. She goes out of her way to make sure you know she is. Not all the staff thought this but those who did relayed what they knew with loud certainty to a population desperate for news.

Townsend returned to the site empty-handed and shaking his head, trying vainly to direct attention away from his torn trouser leg. The corporal frowned. "Christ, Townsend ..."

AN UGLY BLUE FLASHING LIGHT, red, now blue again, bleached through Pipe's paint, distorting the color in spurts like handfuls of disdain. The RCMP Jimmy stopped right outside her back window, had driven beyond the lane and up to the back door. From outside Blackwood barked repeatedly then gave several confused yelps. The entry door slammed followed by pounding on the inside door. Alarmed, she jumped towards the door almost colliding with two Mounties who barged in. They stood by the chimney: one older and puffed out with fat and arrogance, with his arms folded across his chest, the other a younger man, perhaps the one she had glimpsed earlier, unfolding a paper. She could not believe what she had to put up with.

"Penelope Holmes?"

She made for the door to check on Blackwood whom she could hear whining but the cop reached out his hand to stop her. "The dog's fine, we just asked him to let us by. Now leave him out there where he won't get himself in trouble."

Their presence appalled her, the effrontery! Their voices appalled her, raking through her silent world, now perfect in the magic of creation. Their uninvited eyes on her work.

*Where is your warrant,* she signed, wild with insult.

The younger cop handed the paper forward. It *was* a warrant. Could this guy sign? *What do you think you're doing here? I'm busy. I don't have time for you,* she signed in response. The younger one stared at the walls, his mouth practically hanging open.

"Do you need an interpreter?" the constable asked.

*No, I understand you fine. Do* you *need an interpreter?*

"Can you hear?"

*Unfortunately.*

"She's not deaf! Let's dispense with the mime act here. I have a few questions," the older larger cop interjected.

She glared at him.

"Do you visit the gristmill often?"

She nodded, angry.

"Have you ever been inside the mill at a time when it was not open to the public?"

Pipe stared into space.

"Where did you spend last night?"

*In the realm of the imagination. Not a place you're equipped to follow.*

"Look. You were so inhospitable to Constable Townsend earlier this morning that we had to go to all the trouble of getting a warrant, which is ridiculous. A dog that bites a police officer can be ordered destroyed. Did you know that? You have already exhausted what precious patience I have. Now, we can bring you down to the station and find an interpreter and go through every jig and reel. We can keep you for twenty-four hours. Or we can just get this over with here and now and let you get back to your, uh, decorating."

"What?" Pipe tried to force her brain to focus.

"This is spectacular. How long have you been painting?" the one called Townsend asked.

"Is that one of your questions?"

The big one took over again. "Do you know Wayne Holmes?"

"He's my cousin."

"When did you last see him?"

Pipe shrugged. "I never see him."

"That looks like him you have painted on your wall there," Townsend said.

Pipe followed his finger to the face painted up high, almost at the ceiling, ghostly and menacing but distracted, distorted and looking everywhere at once. She squinted, trying to see it through the lens of the here and now, stripping it of its significance. Yes, she could see a resemblance, see how her fury over the goose killing had guided her hand.

"No, that's an artistic composite."

"When and where did you last see Wayne Holmes?" The ugly fellow took over questioning again.

"When he was in my house last month. Illegally." She said this pointedly as though the cops were personally responsible. "I told him to get out."

"Did you report this illegal entry?"

She shook her head.

"Why not?"

"Didn't want cops standing in my house asking me stupid-arse questions."

"Did he steal anything? Touch you? Threaten you?"

"What's to steal? He broke the neck of one of my geese. He wouldn't dare touch me, the little jerk. I'd beat him to death."

"When was this?"

"A while ago. Last month."

"But you've seen him since then."

"No."

"Through a window, far away, up close, you've seen him."

She stared in fury, signed *That is not a question.*

"Have you seen him since?" the old cop bellowed.

"I said no!"

"Do you know where he is now?"

"No. How would I know? I don't know."

"He's dead. We found his body this morning, his skull smashed on the rocks below the gristmill."

Townsend watched her stone face crack with the first flash of— what? Fear? Guilt? Shock?

"Now. We have prints from the window that was jimmied open, shoe tracks in the flour dust and a number of other fairly strong indications of your presence. So why don't you tell us where you were last night?"

After endless questioning the cops left taking with them the sack of flour she had ground at the mill. By the back door a whiff of pepper spray lingered. Blackwood had backed off beyond the goose shed, lain down and kept rubbing his foreleg into his eyes and cool sensitive nose. Bastards. She ran for a pail of water to bathe his head, knelt beside him and stroked his fur. How could it be that Wayne had died right there? While she was inside, they claimed—but how did they know that? Wayne. She knew as well as anyone, better than most, how they had left him. Earl and his bullshit, going on like nobody knew what was really happening. Earl was the only one who didn't know what was happening. Sure, Earl and his boy Wayne living together in the orange trailer. Right. Father and son, very tidy. Except Earl's not there at night or in the afternoon or the evening or the morning. Thirteen years old and in grade nothing. Ben always poking at Earl about Wayne's schooling, Wayne's development, Wayne's care. And Judy, does that one sleep at night? She was the one who kicked the kid out in the first place.

All of a sudden exhaustion fell upon Pipe like a wooden beam. She barely had the strength to stagger into the house and climb the stairs before sleep claimed her. A couple of times she swam close enough to consciousness to be aware of Blackwood's barking and human voices but when they dissipated she returned to the depths of unconsciousness.

Cass DID NOT INTERRUPT the colt's training. He finished his session then rubbed the animal down and turned him back out into the paddock. The mare nudged him when he approached, rubbed her head on his shoulder as he talked softly in her ear. "I had a relation, a nephew or a cousin or something like that, and this guy could walk on a moving boat. Up over the sides and on the roof and everything. Pretty as you ever saw, a trick rider on a boat. He's dead now but that's kind of the way with relatives and that. Sometimes you never see them, sometimes they're just a splash in front of your eyes and they're gone. As dead as if you never had 'em in the first place."

At the house Jack rocked by his window, an oversized scrapbook in his lap and a pile of similar books at his feet. He squinted up at Cass then back at the pages in front of him. "Effie liked to keep up on things, you know. She liked to save anything interesting, you know."

Cass glanced over, put the coffee on and hauled out the frying pan. Wayne. Falling. His legs felt as rubber as they had the day on the boat.

"Effie kept these books all her life. All the old stuff about Scotch River."

"Oh yeah?" Cass was not interested in breakfast but he needed to see his hands busy, something being accomplished. What was odd about the day on the boat was how clear it had been to Cass that Wayne was not going to fish and how blind Earl had been to the fact. It was always like that with people, they could never see what they didn't want to, no matter if it was right in front of their faces.

"See, look here, Cass, this old picture from when the whales came ashore? There were about two hundred and fifty of them I think, great big fellows."

Cass wandered across the room and glanced over the old man's shoulder at an ancient black-and-white photograph of dead whales stretched out across the shore at Scotch River, a phalanx of sleek corpses marooned on the mud. Men and boys stood for the camera with their horses. Four men had climbed up onto the corpse of one of the beasts and posed there, one man in a suit and tie and hat, the rest of the men in overalls or trousers with wide braces and work boots.

"Can you see the fellow standing back in there? The one in behind? My eyes are too old now. There's a head there, see that fellow?" Jack asked.

Cass followed Jack's finger to a youngish man in the background holding a horse.

"That's my father," said Jack.

"Go on."

"Yessir it is. I wasn't even born yet but that's my father and old Prince. Dad used to talk about that time the whales beached up there. It was quite the sight to see. Folks hauled some of the carcasses away for fertilizer but after a while you couldn't go near the place with the smell so bad."

Cass returned to the stove, shoveled his bacon and eggs onto a plate and set it on the table where he promptly abandoned it. He pulled out a kitchen chair, swung it around backwards and sat resting his arms on the back. Raspberries had replaced the strawberries on Jack's table to the delight of generations of fruit flies. Cass tipped half a pint of raspberries into his palm, picked through them, setting aside the moldy ones and eating the others.

"These berries ain't going to last."

"It's such an awful waste, good raspberries. I don't know. It's hard to believe I used to run a farm, isn't it? Looking at me?"

"Ah well, eh Jack?" Again and again he saw Wayne stepping up onto gunnels and twisting perfectly, his sneakers exactly in line with the side of the boat, and him dancing forward with less trouble than if he were balancing on the steel rail of a train track. Up towards the front then a quick bounce and he was on the wheelhouse roof.

"See this page here? Willy DeYoung was the strong man from Scotch River. He worked awhile with a circus, you know, as a strong man. He pulled a truck with his teeth. Just clamped onto the towrope and away he went. He had a car drive up on his chest. I don't know how he did it. The strongest man ever in Scotch River, that's for sure. This picture is of the time he lifted the horse. They had the horse all rigged up with a pulley, see here?"

Cass got up again to look at the old man's picture, a huge workhorse suspended off the ground by a sling rigged around some kind of contraption and a man grimacing from strain. "All that stuff happened around here?"

"Sure. We all knew Willy DeYoung when he was alive. Effie said when Willy was young he was sweet on her Aunt Liza but Liza thought he would be better off lifting furrows with a plow and tossing hay and sheaves into a mow than lifting horses and cars and things. She didn't like people making shows of themselves. Effie collected all the history. Look at this: the Scotch River Foundling." Jack pointed to an item that had a big headline but no picture and Cass returned to his seat where he poked at his eggs. "That was the time they found the baby in the village. Griffin Richards came across it one morning when he was walking his little terrier. All bundled up tight on the step of the little maintenance shed the Lions Club used to have there in the village park. Not a soul around. Griffin said first he thought it was dead, I guess it was none too healthy. Some said it was terrible for someone to leave a baby like that but Effie said it was probably some poor wee girl who just didn't know what to do. Effie said she would have taken that baby in a heartbeat, said …"

Cass blinked his eyes trying to call up the picture of the marooned whales again but they kept melting into human bodies, dead on the rocks. Wayne sprawled out there beneath the dam he had visited just the other day. He kept seeing the body tumbling towards water. Then splat. Wayne Holmes. Jack was still talking. Cass waited for a pause.

"You remember Murray Holmes, Jack? He died by the iron bridge, didn't he? The rail bridge."

"Murray Holmes. Oh, Murray Holmes. In the river down from there, yes. Around there. Drowned. Effie was so upset, my yes, with the little girl and all. And you left so sudden that fall Effie kept your last days' wages in a can in that cupboard for *five years* waiting for you. Now that's Effie all over, that is."

"Funny, things we remember, eh Jack? Know what I remember? I used to have a black leather jacket. Didn't I have a black leather jacket when I come here? What happened to that, Jack? What did I do with that jacket?"

"I don't remember a jacket. I don't know anything about a jacket."

"You don't remember no jacket, eh?"

Jack scratched his head, moving it from side to side.

"Lots of stuff to remember, eh Jack? Remember Effie used to cook pancakes in the shape of a heart, didn't she? Real funny-looking things but she liked 'em like that, didn't she? And blueberries in 'em. Real good."

"Yes she did. She always did it like that from the day we were engaged to be married. Always. That day, that day it was early in the year and I'd been all day boiling sap, you know. I'd been all day in the woods thinking I'll take a jar of this first syrup up to Effie. And there was I all smoky, my boots melting snow all over the mat, and her flying about her mother's kitchen as bright and smart as could be. She never saw me there at first. I came into the kitchen with her brother. I'd met him coming across from the barn. She didn't look up and her brother didn't say anything. It was a joke between us, you see. There I stood, dripping, clutching onto my bottles of syrup, and Effie filling the reservoir in the stove and helping the young maid, her little sister, with her schoolwork, talking over her shoulder. Her cheeks were pink from the heat of the stove and her working. She was the most beautiful … I thought, there looking at her …"

Jack was crying again now and Cass watched him dabbing at his eyes underneath his glasses then taking them off altogether and attacking his face with his handkerchief.

"Say Jack, if your father had a brother, and that brother had a son, what'd that boy be to you? Like what relation I mean?"

"Well, that'd be your cousin."

Cousin, Cass repeated to himself. He did not have the sign for "cousin" and regretted it. He pulled off his boots and padded upstairs leaving Jack weeping and the raspberries rotting. He lay on his bunk trying not to think of his new cousin, Wayne Holmes.

Sometimes, after he started to win the bigger rodeos, he could find himself with way too much money. He spent what he could, stayed in expensive hotels, bought drinks for people, but still he was left with more than he could stand to have. At first he tried to get Lionel to take it, but Lionel wouldn't. Lionel just told him, why don't you buy this or buy that, but what was the point in buying things to stick in a cardboard box under his bunk? It made him edgy, afraid even. All that money in a bank account, it shamed him, made him feel a fake, a liar, a cheat, and made him afraid of discovery and exposure. An imposter. Like he would lose everything he ever had. He could deposit and withdraw from the bank on his own, didn't need Lionel for that.

He didn't want to get caught so he used different cities, big cities. He withdrew stacks of hundred-dollar bills. That was who Wayne reminded him of, one of the kids. More than one of the kids; most were like Wayne, always lots of Indian kids, in the States there were Spanish kids, some black. It filled him with shame to do it but the need outweighed the shame. He closed his eyes now and felt his face burn with embarrassment, him with a wad of bills in the front pocket of his blue jeans wandering through the darkest neighborhoods. Not always kids. From time to time there would be an older woman and he would know the one he wanted when he saw her. They all knew the same thing and you could see it in their eyes. Lionel, the smartest guy Cass had ever known, could have lived to be 110 and he would never have known what these people knew, what that poor little fucker of a cousin of his knew. Again Cass felt the way Wayne's eyes slid off you and onto the ground, the way he leapt from pillar to post, riding the boat roof without the slightest concern. Live or die.

Shame squeezed him. Pick out the kid in the alley, all by himself, alone and up against the wall. Get close enough to see the black in the center of his black eyes, see him trying to judge: danger or opportunity. "I had a bit of luck," was all the explanation Cass could muster. Quick, push a few scrunched-up bills into a pocket, or a hand if he had to. Then get away. Don't run, it will only attract attention. Turn the first corner, keep turning corners, but still he felt their eyes on him long after. Sometimes one would run after him but he couldn't look at them and pushed them away. A shove was nothing to a kid for four or five hundred bucks. Him giving out stuff like he was better than them. And them with nothing to say about it at all. They thought he was better than them. That's what they thought. Not just about him but everyone with money and a good place to be. He couldn't stand it to have them think that but what could he do? The money made him crazy, made him sick. It was never meant to be his.

Cass got up from his bed, picked his painting off the dresser and stared at it. I have to think about the funeral, he told himself. The family will all be at the funeral. I will have to go to his funeral. Yes. My cousin. Family. What he had yearned for. He closed his eyes and set his hands upon his ribs to slow the rate of his fast-beating heart. He pictured the morning sun on the mountains, the sky, the rolling emptiness of a ranch, a horse beneath him. Once, after a spring storm, he had come across a ranch hand, drunk to staggering, who had fallen into a hollow, just a shallow bowl in the land no bigger than the bed of a pickup but low enough to collect the rain and turn the indentation into a muddy wallow. That was not at the One Bar None but a place with several compounds fitted out with electric fence—the first time and only time he had encountered electric fence. The wire ran over the slick and every time the drunk man tried to rise, his backside touched the wire, which jolted him and slid him back into the mud. The fellow was too drunk to think, too drunk to find the dexterity he needed to extract himself, so he kept hefting his ass into the wire, cursing the shock, falling back and heaving up again. Cass had watched in wonderment. Christmases with Lionel's family were like that. Lionel and his brothers and sisters all around a table, all in one room. He couldn't stop looking at how the eyes and the hair and the nose repeated itself over and over, that way they looked up at something always leading with the left eyebrow, that thing they did with their shoulders, their footsteps on the floor. Not everyone the same but all *from* the same, *of* the same. Lionel and the brother closest to him in age, the accountant, hooked their arms over each other. Brothers. Obviously. The current zapped his chest every time he saw Lionel with them but he couldn't stop looking, bumping into the fence wire again and again. These are not your people. You have no people. The truth clacked between his teeth like a bit.

That yearning had been the last thing to leave him. It had also been the first to return, and Cass realized it had never entirely left, only changed its clothes, settled in, settled for. Those electric shocks were to keep it alive, as if he had known he would need the yearning later. It slept in his trust of Lionel, in his love for his city men, in the dark-eyed street kids. His summer in Scotch River had been his last act of boyhood yearning. His mother could have stood before him, she might have seen him, walked up to him and touched his skin and walked away. Of course he would not know. But then, with the boyhood innocence still thrashing around inside the newly grown body, he thought he would recognize her. He didn't know so much as feel that he would see her and their eyes would meet and they would both know. Cass lay back on his bed remembering the fear and the hope and again the physical hunger as his body winced in slits of pain, invisible beneath his skin. He thought of Pipe, his half sister, and her paint, that slash of unearthly green through the figure on the wall, the color of raw grief.

That Jack-and-Effie summer he had mourned the loss of Randy and wished Randy had not been angry and he missed Bill that summer and missed the tiny kiss on his cheek before they began and after they finished with the games Bill paid him for. Daddy loves his little boy, eh? Outside the game like that Cass didn't know which was supposed to be the boy and which the dad. He gave a tiny smile, noncommittal, and got his kiss. That was the summer of missing and yearning and catching up, a season of steady work, regular meals and deep sleep. That summer he stopped growing and finished being a boy. When he left he packed hope away.

The funeral. Think about your cousin and the funeral. Cass Hutt has a grandmother. Living in Scotch River. Eleanor who could tell him all about himself, as if she knew, say everything there was to know and leave him stupid and changed. Steal his only-ness in exchange for dead parents. A sister, really a half sister, who was magic and could draw his life, build his life for him, but he was to steal her land and her home in return. An uncle, two actually, and cousins who die the first time you set eyes on them. A father—same story. A mother who is a name and a couple of pages of ink folded and stashed under the bed.

PIPE WOKE AFTER DARK starving and swirling with emotions she could not sort. She boiled a pot of oatmeal and wolfed it down with milk and sugar thanks to Cass's money. Desperate for escape she set her lights on her canvas and dove into her work, painting darkness where red meets brown and gray meets black, moonlight stingy with every color, hoarding color to lavish on its only favorite, white. Purer, brighter than it ever was in daylight. The cops would be back. Guaranteed. She lashed herself to her work, stitching her mind into her night at the mill, recalling grain on stone, wooden chutes worn powder-smooth and glistening from a century's river of kernels. Most of all the rumble that shivers through the muscle and coats the bone.

Gradually the knowledge seeped into her as she worked. She heard Wayne die. That over-loud bang when she closed the trapdoors. The trapdoors were unnaturally heavy, weighted with an extra inch-thick layer of wood nailed to their undersides so their bulk pulled them back into place once a sack had pushed through. But she had opened them all the way, folded them back, leaving a gaping hole in the floor. She stopped and set her brushes down. She sat on her chair with her feet tucked up onto a rung and heard it again, the bang of the trapdoors and then the second sound, a little scuttle of sounds from outside, a thump, almost an echo. She hadn't made it up. That had been him.

That was the sound of him slipping or falling or landing, a tree falling in the forest. While she had raked the oats and replenished the wheat hopper he lay on the rocks dead or dying. If she had looked down from the upstairs window she would have seen him. Perhaps she could have saved him. The cops didn't say anything about that, when he died, exactly how he died. They only took information, they didn't give it.

*Don't stop,* she told herself. She signed large and clear in order to feel the message through her arms and eyes and mind. *Keep painting.* Watch the light on the rope, the shadow hiding in the folds of white. Paint. Paint while you can.

She did not look at her watch but it was deep into the night, so far into the middle that no light could be imagined on either shore, when a great roaring commotion barreled down on top of her, engine noise, headlights, cab lights, hollering. Blackwood, who had bedded down in the lee of the goose shed enjoying the coolness of the night air as he often did in the summertime, barked ferociously. Earl swung open the cab door and landed nearly in the dog's jaws. He jumped back and slammed the door, revved his engine and leaned on the horn. Fear kicked at Pipe. Disoriented in time and space she fought her way to the present trying to make sense of what was happening. Someone, a man, was yelling. At her. A gunshot cracked the sky. Blackwood! She dashed for the door, ran out into the yard and Blackwood ran to her side. Relief overwhelmed her fear.

Earl leaned out the window of his truck, his face contorted in horrific pain. Pipe had not seen such pain in twenty years. The things he was yelling at her, the wild raging horrible things flung like bricks at her head. Spit foamed at the corners of his mouth and he kept tripping over his words and having to yell them again. Pipe shrank to eight years old. She turned and ran for the house calling her dog, barred them both behind the door and huddled against it sobbing into her hands. Outside Earl fired his rifle into the air twice more before she heard the truck squeal in a tight turn and listened to its roar diminishing down the laneway.

Early the next morning Ben arrived and Pipe suspected this might be his second try—that he might have come round previously while she was sleeping. She couldn't face him. Even at the best of times she'd rather not. Blackwood was doing his job, barking like a thing possessed at the sight of the Camry. The geese swarmed. She scrambled upstairs where she could look down through the window at him, undetected. Pipe watched him sitting in the car, rolling his window down, wondering if he should risk stepping into the yard. She saw more than heard him call out to her, waffle. He eased open the car door and ventured to plant his feet on the ground, kept his back pressed against the car. Look at his shirt for Chrissake, the middle of summer and he can't even manage a T-shirt. A proper collar and buttons and little cuffs on the short sleeves. A miracle he isn't wearing a tie. Probably got a briefcase with all the specs about some new program for murderesses. That's what they thought. That's why the Mounties went to all the trouble to get the warrant. Whatever the cops say that's what Ben would believe. The proper authorities. Oh God. She had to steady herself on the window frame, ease herself to the floor while the room pitched and swirled around her. Don't go, Uncle Ben. Don't leave me. But she did not walk towards him, made no move to call in her dog and let him approach, no move to answer his calls or show her face. She covered her face with her hands listening for the car door and the engine to announce Ben's defeat. Don't go.

Pipe had only been back to work less than an hour when the dog barked again. *I can't stand it! I can't stand it!* The cops again. This time she called Blackwood in and sent him to his nest by the stairs. She wasn't going to risk his taking another shot of their pepper spray, the pigs. The same two. She ignored the fat ugly one. God, she would love to sign. She would love to insist on a translator and sign the whole goddamned story but that big bastard would take her in, no doubt about it, and make sure he took twenty-three hours getting an interpreter.

She set her paint-smeared chair out for the smaller guy, Townsend, and perched on the millstone, inviting him to sit, signing.

"Quit the ballet. And I mean it, you speak up. Unless you want to be prancing around a cell. We have a warrant, don't forget."

"I said, 'Never mind that brutal bastard.'" She didn't miss the constable's reluctance sizing up the chair, imagining the paint streaks on his uniform. "I think I know what happened." Pipe related what she remembered. The sound she heard, what may have been the fall. She wore no watch but it had been after dawn, early morning, maybe six or six-thirty.

"Oh, a mysterious noise. Imagine that. When did this occur to you?"

Over and over the ground they went. What kind of noise, a bump, didn't you look to see what made the noise, no; how come you didn't look, it was vague and muffled—the mill was running; you knew he was there, no; you saw him, no; you were meeting him there, no. What time, what time, tell us again what you did, what time did you look out the window, were you waiting for him, how come you've got your dead cousin's picture on the wall? She answered the same questions she had answered yesterday. No he wasn't in the mill, no she never saw him, no she didn't know why he would be there, no she had never seen him there before, no, no, no.

"You're a bit of an odd duck aren't you? All this historical mumbo jumbo, sneaking around, sign talk for no reason, a millstone in the middle of the house. All this muck on the walls." The big one tapped the wall behind him as though she might not have noticed the paint. "This part of being the suffering ar-*tiste*?"

She turned her attention from Townsend to the brutal bastard, looked him in the eye and knew she could not muster the indignation she sought to convey. Loneliness clung to her, dragged at her, cement-sodden. Look hard, she instructed herself, paint iron in your eyes. Don't back down.

"I can't answer those questions. They contain implied fallacies."

"I understand your mother is a severe schizophrenic. She is a permanent resident of the Nova Scotia psychiatric hospital."

Pipe slammed her ears shut. *That's it,* she signed. She jumped up and walked away from them madly slapping brain paint on the panes in her ears. There were still words being said and when she finally turned to see them again Townsend was tucking his notebook into his pocket. The brutal bastard, already nearly to the door, was shaking his head and rummaging for something in his Batman utility belt. She ran for the door and pushed by them grabbing her herding stick to keep the geese out of their way. Townsend nodded at her as he turned to climb into the Jimmy, gave her the weakest of smiles, an indication of sympathy. She would have loved to touch his shoulder, loved to ask, Was the death instantaneous? Was it worse than life? When is the funeral?

"He was my cousin," she said to him, so low it was almost a whisper.

"Yes. I'm sorry."

She shouldn't have said it. His voice was kind and this above all was what she could not stand. So much work to do, right at her fingertips, and now she hadn't the strength to hold a brush. Honestly she wouldn't have minded a visit from Cass right now. Her hand flashed the name sign she had given him. If he rode up right now, or walked, maybe they could talk again. She closed her eyes to listen to the Jimmy retreating then waited and waited for hooves or footsteps. Or something. It wouldn't kill her grandmother, would it? She signed to no one, *It wouldn't kill you, Eleanor, would it, to come by with the news of the death of my cousin?* Nobody comes. Her conscience twisted at the thought of Ben who *had* come and she quickly shifted her focus. There should be somebody.

# CHAPTER EIGHTEEN

EVERY TIME Cass thought of Wayne's body tumbling, there he was, back on the iron bridge. *Kid,* he squiggled his finger under his nose. He couldn't leave it alone. It was more real to him than the folded sheets of paper under his bed. It was more real than Eleanor's stories. And each time he visited the bridge his memory cleared and solidified and he became surer, but then he waffled again. Perhaps he was coloring it all in from nothing, making up the blank parts. And now Wayne kept getting in the way. He wanted to get this figured out before it got too snarled up to ever see the truth in it.

He should have spoken to her the day they met on the railbed but he let her get away. Once very long ago there had been a home near a railway track. Once he lay flat against the ground although the ground itself was not flat but rose steeply to the rails. The land was dark and oily and it smelled of diesel fuel. Little stones everywhere pressed into his cheek when he laid his head down, his body flat out, hugging the ground. When the train came it always had a light even in the daytime and the light was the first thing you saw, then the front of the engine barreling down. Get down tight tight to the earth, hold on to the earth, squeeze handfuls of it into your fists. The engine came and it came and it came, a force so powerful, so loud, so all-encompassing there was no world beyond. The ground beneath him quaked, all of him quaked, and he was swallowed in a physical fear that lifted him from this world. The train was upon him then, fire licking out from the rails, the heat intense upon his skin, gravel shot as if from guns, the world trembling and the roar of ten thousand lions. He could feel their teeth on him, their breath. Air shot by him poisoned, foul smelling and bitter. He squeezed his eyes shut tight and held on to the trembling, shivering earth as everything that was Casper the boy flew up into the trees above and only a sack of jelly-fear remained in the eye of terror. The train passed. Rhythmic clacking emerged from the roar then even this grew faint. Oxygen puffed by in a breeze, the earth quieted. Casper the boy lifted his head, tasted the oil smacking in his mouth, picked gravel off his skin and clothes, wiped water from his face though he had no recollection of crying, although he never cried no matter how hard he tried. When he stood, his legs wobbled like they were hollow and too light to carry him. It could be hours before his loneliness reclaimed him, hours before he was saddled with himself again.

There it was. You started out for one place and ended up somewhere else you never wanted to be. He needed to talk to her about the iron bridge. Just to have her say yes, it's true. Especially now that the cousin was dead and things would be jostled and something would fall and be spilt and then she would know about him and the land and she would not speak to him about anything. And there would be no painting. Before that he must talk to her at least about the bridge.

PIPE'S BRUSHES were too heavy to hold and she could do nothing but abandon them. She shouldn't have let Ben go, she should have called out to him. And where was Eleanor? Granny Eleanor would believe what they all believed. Eleanor would be the first to believe it. Still she couldn't stay here all alone. She had to see one other person at least, touch another human. She took her bike and pushed it along the path and out onto the railbed, rode towards the iron bridge. They thought Wayne had fallen from the window of the mill but she had been there all night so knew for certain what they didn't. When she closed her eyes she saw him falling and could find no peace from it. When she opened them still he fell, his arms open like a paratrooper, his legs kicking at the air, searching for their feet. By the time she reached the bend before the iron bridge sweat soaked her T-shirt.

She stopped and climbed off her bike, stood there staring ahead along the railbed, at the vertical line where trees cut the view, where the train would have disappeared around the bend. She pushed her palms into her eye sockets but Wayne just kept falling and falling. She could not move. A monstrous roar assailed her ears, the rushing wind of falling and then a burst before her eyes, a flash—deep river blue. She jumped. Two guys on ATVs filled the road in front of her and roared past. When she recovered she and her bike both sat in the ditch. Just ATVs. She lifted the front of her T-shirt and stretched it upwards to wipe the sweat from her face.

PIPE WAS NOT AT HER HOUSE. The bike tracks heading towards the village looked fresh although it was hard to tell with the dryness of the land. Cass followed them. Two ATVs sped down the trail towards him and the guys riding nodded from beneath helmets as they passed him and continued. Just before the turn in the track he found her resting in the ditch with her bike beside her.

"I know you," he said to Pipe, which was a ridiculous thing to say because of course he knew her. They had sat together, talked; he had seen the house. She had painted him.

She replied with tired hands. Likely some comment to that effect. He crouched beside her on the edge of the trail, pulling a blade of grass from the stalwart patch of vegetation beside him and rolling it between his palms.

"I guess I mean I knew you before. There's a few things, you know, I got to get straight. You remember I told you I was here before, uh, staying with Jack? Twenty years ago? I seen the crazy lady, your crazy mother. You were a little girl then. I seen you by the track, by the bridge. You seen me."

His sister raised her hands to speak but lowered them again. She said nothing.

"You seen me."

"My cousin died," she said.

"Wayne Holmes. Everybody's talking about that at work. Earl's boy. Cousin. But I have to ask you this. I seen you when you were a little kid." *Kid,* he squiggled his finger. "When I come back here I moved into Jack's same as twenty years ago. I was sitting in the kitchen and I knew where this train track went. I knew what it looked like. But then later on I came out here and sure it was here, and sure I knew this was the bridge and that was the river and I could find the path that went to the garage in the village—but still I got surprised. Not just the tracks are gone now and the bridge got a new deck and there's railings and some of the trees been cut and some grew bigger. You know, sure, you have to expect that. But the whole thing, even the stuff that *didn't* change, looked different from what I remembered it—sky, river, bridge."

*The iron bridge.*

Again she signed and he did not understand.

"I know I seen the crazy lady. I don't know how many times. What I know is that her eyes had that light you find in coal bits by a railroad track. You get a chunk of coal that's been sliced open and you can see the fire in it, lying flat, and it lights up like a mirror if you hold it to the sun. Her eyes had that same light. She just comes that close up to my face I see that coal glint and she got breath that smells like peanut butter so I'm not afraid but she grabs my shirt and I always pay real close attention when someone's got a hold of me. This is the word of God, she says. And she holds up a Coke can. And this is how things go funny 'cause if she had my shirt in one hand and a Coke can in the other then what about the cloth? She didn't have three hands. But this is the most important part. She had this piece of cloth, this scarf, but soft soft and thin like you could see through it and it was every color. She held it up to my face till it touched. Soft rubbing." Like she was wiping off a kiss, Cass thought, and swallowed at the memory of it. He had never felt anything like that cloth until he touched the lining of Lionel's coffin. Then he remembered the crazy lady. "It was as soft as the stuffing in a coffin but all colors, bright like fall leaves in the sun."

*The butterfly scarf,* Pipe signed.

"What's that you signed there? I don't understand."

She flailed her arms a bit then finally repeated the sign and whispered, "The butterfly scarf."

"On this one day though the little girl wore that scarf, had it all twirled around her. It was you. You were just a little girl then. You seen me."

"I never saw you."

"Yes, the girl had the scarf on the day of the iron bridge."

"It wasn't me. I was playing in the woods." Cass couldn't follow her angry signing. *I stayed in the woods. I only came out when Daddy ran by. Sometimes he needed me to help him. My mother wasn't well. My mother is ill. It isn't her fault that she's sick. It's not her fault. I can't hate her no matter what she does. I'm not allowed. It's not her fault.*

"That summer I was here I used to come up through Jack's field to the track same as I do now. I used to lay my head down by the rails so I could feel the ground shake when the train went by. I used to do that when I got lonesome. I remembered that about the trains. So that day, the iron bridge day, I'd been laying there or … no, there was no train. I don't know, maybe cooling off in the river? I never swum, never learned how, but I could duck underwater if it was real hot. It was fall that day though so it couldn't've been that hot I don't think, but I was here. I'll show you where."

She shook her head wildly no, but Cass turned away so there was nothing to receive her words except his broad back. He could hear her footsteps behind him, nothing then a short run then nothing again as though her feet were saying yes then no then yes again. Cass drew her to the spot where the railbed narrowed and joined the iron bridge. Here Pipe stopped dead.

"I'll show you where I was," he said and started across the planking. She did not follow but stood on the soft ground watching after him, alarmed. When he reached the other side he looked down the slope where the path, now the ATV trail, led to the village, then he descended a few steps down the other side where the land simply dropped off to the riverbank. "Here," he called to her and pointed with exaggerated movements so she could see across the breach. He had to yell loudly to be heard from such a distance. "I came up from here, from somewhere around here. It must have been the noise that called me up here, I don't know. There was a racket for sure, her screaming about the devil, screaming at him."

Cass scrambled up the slope and headed back towards her. Pipe did not move but stood rigid, her face wooden, and Cass wondered was she listening at all. "He stayed back like he didn't want to step out on the bridge. Well, at that time there was no railing, no deck, just the ties with spaces between, and he was trying to get her to come to him but she just kept screaming. Then she started climbing … no, see, there must have been some kind of a railing, something, because she climbed up something or over something like she was going to jump, maybe the trestle, I don't know, and he ran out to get her, I don't know exactly what happened. You saw it too. They were wrestling there on the edge of the bridge. I know when he went over it was like a spider, straight down and all arms and legs. Not that much of a splash. I remember watching for him to come up 'cause I couldn't swim, like I said. And I was watching the river for him because I didn't know which side to get on. See what I mean? If he come up over there maybe I could get him from that shore but if he come up here

I would have to run across the bridge. So I stood there and watched but he never come up. Never. It was like he dropped into that river and he kept going down forever."

She stared directly into his face but she wasn't seeing anything. Cass looked away and looked back, trying to break the spell. "That one, that Murray Holmes, he never come up again at all. Did he? Not living anyway … Was there a railing there or what? What was she climbing on? You saw her."

She signed but he could not understand.

"Come on, talk words. You were there. I gotta know."

"I wasn't there."

"You were. It was you. I don't remember what happened to the crazy one. Maybe I never saw. I guess she ran back." Cass walked past Pipe on the railbed, paced back and forth, stopped and pointed. "Yeah. You were right there. The little girl in the scarf. You ran up over the bank right here and called out, 'Daddy.' You thought I was him, Murray Holmes, but when you saw me good, up close, you stopped and backed away and ran into the woods."

Her mouth opened and closed, fishlike. He waited and finally she spoke.

"Your footsteps were just like his. I could see his rubber boots coming towards me so I climbed up. They were his rubber boots."

"I never had rubber boots."

"They were his steps. His boots." She moved a couple of steps away from him and signed. *Stay in the woods, play in the woods, make a picture for me.* Cass recognized the sign for "photograph."

"That's why people say like they know it was your mother done it, but not like they can prove it. It's true that she's crazy and she killed him and you saw her. I did too. And now Wayne—that's why the guy at work says it was you tossed him off the dam. 'Cause it was near the exact same thing happened."

"I never even *saw* Wayne," she cried out like a child wrongly accused.

"But that's why people say stuff like that. 'Cause they think you're crazy too, like your mother. But that's not true. You're not crazy, you just want them to think you are. With hand signs and that. You're really smart is all, and a bit magic. Not crazy. I seen lots of crazy people and you're not like them.

"That woman on the bridge though, she was crazy. Did they get her for what she done?"

"It's a disease. It's not her fault."

"Sure it ain't her fault. Who wants to be crazy? Nobody. She locked up somewheres?"

Pipe nodded, tears streamed down her face.

"Our father—" Cass tripped on the words and stopped. These two words so fresh they could have been born, scrubbed and shiny, from his mouth this very second, yet instantly ancient. There had been some chant, him standing in his black and white sneakers on a glistening tile floor. Our Father, Do art in heaven. The one thing he did not want to say, did not want to tell. My father, our father. Suddenly there, suddenly gone. But it would all seem more likely if there was a story, a reason, another person who knew all about it and why it had to happen the way it did.

"It wasn't her fault. He never should have gone out after her," she said, adamant yet faltering.

"What did you do? You run off?"

"I was supposed to stay in the woods but I was scared and I ran after him. Afterwards, I hid in the woods where I was supposed to be." *Mussel shells for wavy water, poplar leaves and sand dollar sun.* "That's all I ever said and everybody believed me. Sometimes I thought it was true."

Cass continued. "I figured if I seen something like that I better get to hell out, you know, because you just see trouble one minute and the next minute you're right in the middle of it. I was supposed to be in this foster home and I didn't want nobody to know I was around. I sure as hell didn't want nobody to know I seen that. So when I seen you I thought, shit, that little kid's gonna tell and they'll be looking for me. So I took off. Nobody ever come after me though and I figured I got away but now I'd say you never said nothing, did you?"

She shook her head slowly from side to side over and over again. Silently she turned and headed for home, her head still swaying on her shoulders.

"Hey, we both saw that, didn't we? You and me together." She didn't turn back.

Cass sat at the juncture where the bridge met the railbed, his butt on the wooden planking, his legs drawn in close to his body with his feet on the ground. His feet hurt with a slow aching tiredness he hadn't noticed before, as though he had just yesterday finished walking across the country. What he had was that one glimpse of his father, a second or two, as the man fell through the air before his eyes, from the bridge to the water. Passing. No sound except the splash and then the stilted running of feet on railway ties above. The crazy woman running away, the butterfly scarf trailing behind in the wind. No. The little girl wore the scarf that day. But his father fell into the Scotch River, fell down before him. He had these two seconds of unassailable truth, surely.

Surely.

# CHAPTER NINETEEN

THE MAJOR CRIME UNIT swept through with great efficiency. Wayne's footprints could be followed easily through the woods, across the railing above the dam and down onto the millrace. A couple of particularly clear prints on the edges of the flume had been made by his shoes muddied in the water. A fresh-looking skid mark on one of the waterwheel buckets marked the spot where Wayne's foot had been trapped. An officer with major crimes found the Baggie that had carried the Ritalin tablets and the rocks Wayne had used to crush them. Lab tests confirmed the presence of the drug in the boy's blood. Given Wayne's history, his fall was completely understandable. Almost inevitable. A misadventure.

While the mill itself was rife with evidence of Pipe's presence there was not one fresh print of her shoe on the walkway, the dam, the sluice, anywhere outside of where she claimed to have been. Townsend and the corporal made one more visit to Pipe's and found her subdued but unchanged in her statements. Under repeated questioning her story remained consistent and plausible within its bizarre framework. More importantly, it matched all physical evidence. There was no sign of a scuffle anywhere, no disturbance by the upstairs window. No evidence could be found to put Wayne inside the mill or Pipe on the dam. There was no evidence to put her near Wayne at all and no motive they could find beyond the month-old annoyance over his trespass on her property and the death of a goose. Most likely she had not seen him. Even if she *had* seen him, if she had called to him and thrown him off balance, seen him fall, it could never be proven in court and it would have made no difference anyway. Wayne had died almost instantly. Massive trauma to the head.

Townsend visited Earl with the results of the investigation and the final reports. Earl watched the Mountie more than looked at him. Clearly Pipe had said nothing about his late-night visit. "So that's it then?" Earl said at last.

"Yes. Everything is fairly straightforward, I'm afraid. Very sorry for your loss. I'm really sorry, Earl. Judy."

Judy showed the policeman out and thanked him.

Townsend also stopped in at Ben's house because they had so often worked together. Townsend was the favored officer for school visits with safety lectures, on career days or at special ceremonies. It was Townsend who let children try on his hat and answered their questions. (Is that vest really bulletproof? Did you ever shoot anyone?) It was his holstered pistol the boys stared at with awe and longing. Ben made them a pot of tea and the two men spoke quietly at Ben's kitchen table of Wayne and his life, of Earl, of Pipe, then of changes expected at the detachment and plans for an exploratory course in law at school that fall.

When Townsend left, Ben sat a few moments longer in the stillness of his house watching his fingers clasp and unclasp in his lap. He would have preferred to sit awhile with a deep uncomplicated grief for his fallen nephew. Instead he was ambushed by an overwhelming loneliness. When Ben closed his eyes a huddle of wine bottles enticed him. There was a half-full bottle in the fridge and several unopened bottles under the counter. He would love to go and hide for days, maybe weeks, maybe forever, in some bar in the city where no one knew him. He envied Earl his family, his irresponsibility. There must be a more generous word for it, he thought. His spontaneity. His ability to love without personal sacrifice, his ability to inspire love in return. Think of Wayne, he chastised himself. Guilt corkscrewed around the slender shoot of grief he managed to generate. He shook a couple of Advil out of the bottle above the sink and set out to check on arrangements at the funeral home.

BECAUSE HE WAS NOBODY's he was everybody's. Three-quarters of the village filed through the funeral home for Wayne Holmes's visitation. Everyone remembered the little boy who had been buffeted by loss and gossip. When he was seven and eight and nine Marnie at the Co-op had slipped him suckers at the checkout, the teachers at school had touched his shoulder when they saw him in the hall. How's Wayne today? The volunteer fire department Santa always had a special present for him. Vikki at the Scotiabank had photocopied pictures of whales and polar bears for his school projects on the bank copier for free. A village of people watched Wayne slide from a sad seven-year-old to a difficult fourteen-year-old living in a trailer. With his father. Everyone knew the score but what difference did it make? People furrowed their brows at the mention of his name. They all knew what Wayne could not, that time was short and there is an ocean of difference between a neglected child and a teenaged delinquent.

Wayne Holmes, clean and dressed in good clothes he had never owned, with his hair washed and combed and parted, and his hands folded so they didn't show the sores on his fingertips that he would gnaw when his fingernails were chewed too far below the quick to offer any purchase for his teeth, with his lips covering his stained and missing teeth and his eyes closed to hide the anger and confusion that defined him, shook everyone who looked down at his body nestled in the puff of white satin. He looked, in fact, like a handsome young man, a fallen soldier in a war only he turned out to fight.

Ben watched his brother slip out of the funeral home chapel halfway through the visitation and wander across the road for a smoke by the river. After a couple of minutes Ben followed, stood before him.

"I know what you're thinking," Earl said, bitter.

"You don't know, Earl." There was more contradiction and less kindness in Ben's tone than he had meant. What he had been thinking was how much he would love to take his brother in his arms and hold him. He was imagining their heads touching, his hand in Earl's hair and how he would love to pour what little strength he had into his brother's veins and peel his brother's pain away. He was thinking how he would love to say that there wasn't one of them that couldn't have done better by Wayne and that to the extent that anyone was at fault, they were all at fault. But sometimes fault doesn't really matter. To see his brother, his baby brother, standing there in a suit coat and pressed trousers made him sadder than he could bear. "Do you remember that time in the garden when the rope broke on the swing?"

"What?"

"You were maybe five or six, and we had that tire swing in—"

"Jeez, Ben, don't start for Chrissake."

"I'm just saying, well, there were many unfortunate circumstances in this case, circumstances beyond anyone's control." He had seen Earl tumble through the air and seen him land on the ground below. He had run over and picked him up, astonishment and fear frozen on Earl's little face. The wind had been knocked out of him and he couldn't cry. Ben remembered the physicality of lifting him off the ground, of carrying him. He had been a load because Ben himself had been only ten or eleven, but he remembered the way Earl had clung to him, gulped air and started to cry. And Ben had carried him all the way into the house, stronger than he had ever been. It had been the moment that strength and compassion met in him and he understood their power in a visceral way, a way that directed much of his life from then on.

"Earl. I'm so sorry."

"Yeah, well."

"Do you want to come over to the house for a little while when this is over? Have a glass of wine? Or I could stay with the boys if you and Judy …" He could lay a hand on Earl's shoulder but he didn't trust himself.

"I haven't been to the trailer. Someone should go by."

"I was over, looking for clothes and such." Ben didn't have to say he found nothing passable and had gone out to buy the burial suit. The facts were clear enough. "The police wanted a look around. I let them in. I stayed with them."

Earl frowned and scratched his chest.

"They took a few things away. A few VCRs and such. It doesn't matter."

"You went to the trailer?"

"It doesn't matter, Earl."

"I was going to go earlier and. And things came up. Look, could you tell Judy I'll be home later? I'm going to go out there now."

"Let me come with you."

"No. *I'm* his father, damnit."

"I know, Earl. I know."

Earl felt Ben watching him as he drove his truck across the bridge, felt the eyes of judgment on him when he pulled into the liquor store parking lot. Frig him. What would Ben know about what it was like?

The orange trailer sat a mile outside the village. The first absence to meet Earl was the little Nissan's. Wayne's truck was not in the yard. God, he was desperate for a drink, tore at the paper bag and took a long pull on his bottle, followed the burn down his throat. He climbed out of his truck, lit a cigarette and tossed the match into the grass at his feet, sucked at the bottle and the cigarette. He loosened his tie, stared up then down the highway. If Wayne had had an accident with his truck he would have heard. Earl circled the trailer and there it was, with a headlight smashed and the hood crumpled, driven into the back wall of the trailer by the corner—must have cut too soon. Earl scrunched into the driver's seat and tried the key in the ignition, to no response. The battery was dead. He tossed the keys on the truck floor where he had found them and kicked a tire on his way to the trailer door. The interior was cleaner than usual—he recognized the hand of Ben. Clothes picked up and set in a pile on the bed, garbage collected and tied in a bag behind the door, dishes washed. He checked the cupboard under the counter and sure enough the electronics equipment was gone. He chugged at the rum, impatient.

"Bastards!" Clean him up, put him in a suit, take back his goddamned stolen shit, sweep him away! Good riddance. That's what everybody thinks. Just as well, before he kills someone besides himself. Well, it wasn't Wayne that did the killing in the end, was it? Now everybody was looking at Earl like he was the one to blame. You can't leave the boy to raise himself. Those were Ben's exact words when he and Wayne moved out here. For all the false front, what his brother really thought was, I told you so. I knew you'd fuck up, you always have and you always will. Easy enough for Ben doling out advice on other people's kids when he's got none of his own. Earl had told him that too, right to his face once. That had shut him up, you bet. He had hoped the memory of the scene would cheer him up but it only made him feel worse. The pain of it cut him physically. Although he could not place his hand on the pain it burned through him like the rum. He sucked on the bottle. Fuck them all! He grabbed the garbage bag and turned it upside down on the empty tabletop spilling pizza boxes and chip bags and Coke cans everywhere. There was a bit of smelly crap in there too, and grease rags. Wayne must have been working on the Nissan. Earl wormed out of his suit jacket and tossed it on the chair.

To think just the other week he had tried to help Pipe, trying to make things decent for her, help her along. He brought her groceries for godsake. Everything! Then what does she do? Tosses his son off the dam. And what do the cops do? Nothing. Too much effort to deal with that so we just say it never happened. Misadventure, my ass! They should be able to lock loonies like her up *before* they go after innocent people. It's clear enough what runs in that family. His brother then his son. And she is still out there getting away with it. And here he is with his son, his poor son, dead in a box.

He had held baby Wayne in his arms, a soft bundle of weight like a coiled rope or a net, no bigger than a cat. Wayne's eyes would follow Earl's finger back and forth. Wayne's little fist tightened around the finger and drew it to his mouth, gummed slobber on it. Earl knew then why men laid down their lives for their families. No one is ever going to hurt you he had promised with a will so determined, so sharp and unsullied, it was as though no human being had ever made this vow before.

People had all kinds of opinions but they didn't know jack. Nobody knew what kind of hell his first marriage had been. One foot in the door and she'd be yapping at him. Ten minutes later they'd both be in a lather and half the time end up fucking like minks. His prick twitched now and he rubbed it in annoyance. No way it was worth it. He'd have been gone a thousand times but for her pleading. Don't leave me, don't leave me. She wouldn't let him go. And then what? She fucks off with that Frenchman. The lying scheming bitch. She could have taken Wayne with her, any decent mother would have for Chrissake. But no, she leaves her goddamned kid behind. What kind of a woman is that? I suppose we'll see her at the funeral all teary and sorry. She knows it's her fault, she knows I'd love to spit in her face. I will too. At the funeral. Every person there will know why I did it. I wasn't the one. I wasn't the one who left him! It was me who rescued him.

Judy had wanted him so bad then. They couldn't keep their hands off each other. They didn't. They must have done it everywhere but the post office steps in those days. Leave her, she kept saying. Come live with me.

You're looking for trouble, boy. Supporting two kids is one thing, supporting two wives is another. That's what his Dad had said, that and no more, when he got wind of Judy's pregnancy. They fished as always that day. Not another word said about it. Then or ever. His father probably understood. Sometimes it seemed the women got together and plotted to get you in a bad spot.

Wayne. Wayne, if it wasn't one thing it was another. And after that incident at school with the little boy, that was it for Judy. You could practically see her washing her hands of him like the guy in the Bible. It was Judy who kicked him out. Fine for her now, all sad-eyed at the coffin, but it was Judy said Wayne couldn't live with them anymore.

Earl patted his pockets. He had left his cigarettes on the seat of his truck. The trailer swayed when he stood. More than half the rum was gone already. He found his smokes, managed to suck the flame off a shaky match and headed back inside. He leaned back in one of the two chairs that remained intact. From that angle he could see where the truck had stove in the trailer wall. Just a bit, cracked a stud he suspected but did not care to investigate. Everybody else wanted Wayne out of the way and that was the problem right there. He couldn't get a goddamned break anywhere. Ben calling Earl in to school for "parent conferences," his mother picking all the other kids as favorites over Wayne. Even Pipe she favored over Wayne. Even *Pipe*! Make him do this, make him do that, make him stop something else. Did she think he was some kind of magician?

"Fuck!"

Grief engulfed him, spun him like a Tilt-a-Whirl, and he tipped off his chair, grabbing for the rum, cradling it close to his chest. There was not one goddamned person besides himself that gave a rat's ass for that boy. But in spite of them all he and Wayne had been going to make it. Fuck 'em all, they were going to get that license and start up the lobstering again, him and Wayne. He had it all worked out, and now look. Earl staggered to his feet, struggled to set the nearly empty bottle on the table overflowing with garbage, splashed a little. He lit another smoke, tossed the match, tried to wrangle his chair upright. He sobbed, kicked at the confusion of chrome, staggered and fell.

Earl wanted to get to his feet, that's what he wanted now. Something was going wrong. He groped at the chair, concentrated, and with a confluence of effort and luck pulled it upright, flopped his chest over the seat, his knees still propping him on the floor, his arms hanging down. I'll rest here a second, he thought. Something wasn't right. He coughed and sucked in smoke, coughed again.

Earl didn't see it start, the match landing by the crumpled flyer leaning on the cardboard pizza box, draped with a grease rag. The suit jacket caught and the remaining garbage ignited in a whoosh illuminating the trickle of spilled rum in a race of blue spikes across the table. The dish towel Ben had left drying invited the flames into one of the punch holes in the cheap paneling. Wayne's nylon jacket caught and the lighter in its pocket detonated. The flash of flame blasted Earl to his feet. Smoke blackened and twirled the air into thick woolen ropes. Thinking took forever. Water. Earl lunged towards the sink, tried to fill a pot but the pressure here was low and the flow ridiculously slow. He could see nothing now through the smoke but the piercing brilliance of the flames, could not breathe, the smoke grasping the oxygen from the air before he could haul it into his lungs. His few sober cells shook at his brain: go. Go! Now completely obscured with smoke, the door stood only a few feet away. He stepped and staggered, stepped and pitched against the counter, stepped again, his head leaden with rum, eyes running, lungs burning from smoke. The heat was almost overpowering now. Blinded and choking, he forced himself into the heat, into the smothering black abyss, towards the door.

He fell, felt the rip of the world giving way and tumbled forward and down. Tiny rocks pushed into his face, a fist grabbed grass. Go!

His legs swam, pushing and slipping in the dirt until finally, somehow, they propelled him forward, tossed him against the bed of his pickup where he clung, hacking smoke and sucking air. He made his way to the truck cab, reversed and sped over the culvert and onto the road. When the engine cut out the truck had settled somewhere low and Earl abandoned it. He struggled back towards the trailer, was swaying on the highway with the yellow line under the soles of his funeral shoes when the sparks reached the Nissan's gas tank. A flame rocket shot straight up as high as a silo and the back corner of the trailer flew apart like a jack-in-the-box gone mad. The thunderclap knocked him back onto the pavement, jarred the asphalt under him and sent barrels of debris raining onto what remained of the structure. Flames engulfed the tree where Wayne had climbed, the roof under which Wayne had sheltered. A car approached on the highway, slowed, pulled over and stopped. The next thing Earl knew a woman was helping him onto the seat of a car and he was listening to her strong clear voice as she spoke into a cell phone.

"You wouldn't want to get too much closer than this," the doctor said at Emergency where they took him to check for shock and smoke inhalation. "You're lucky it's mostly first-degree. Basically you've got a pretty heavy sunburn here." There was a burned patch on the back of his neck and when he ran his fingers through the hair above it he could feel tiny knobs where the strands had been burned off. The alcohol numbness began to ebb and a hot tenderness tingled on his back. Ben had to come and pick him up from the hospital.

"Are you okay? I'm just going to talk to the doctor a minute."

"No, Ben, they're busy, it's okay. I'm okay. A bit sore is all."

"You sure? You need to get anything at the drugstore? Did he give you anything? Are you all right? Really?"

"Yeah. Let's go."

"You gave us all a scare. Mom was worried."

"I got to go get my truck. God, I hope that truck's okay."

"I called the tow truck. They're going to take it to your place. No harm done by the looks of it. What happened at the trailer?"

"I don't know. I was just sitting there, having a drink."

"A beer drink or a forty-ouncer drink? And a smoke? Did you fall asleep smoking?"

"No. I don't know what happened. It just caught fire."

"While you happened to be sitting there drunk and smoking?"

"Shut up, Ben."

"Sorry."

"Could you pull in at a store somewhere? I got to get a smoke. I guess I lost my cigarettes. Jeez, I uh, I got no money on me."

"That's okay, I've got money. Do you want me to go in for you?"

"No."

"You know, I've been thinking, Earl. I know you want to get a lobster license. I've been hesitant in the past but maybe I could help you with a down payment. Maybe we could come to some arrangement. If it's really what you want to do." The familiar words stopped Ben's speech. For the last six years his argument had always ended with, If that's what you really wanted you would have been making the payments you were supposed to at the time.

"Be careful now, Ben. Mom won't like that—you giving in."

"It's not about giving in. She didn't want to lose you to the water. You know she never liked Dad on the water."

"She didn't like him that well on land either."

"Now, Earl. We don't know what's in people's hearts."

"Oh for the love of Christ!"

"Okay, I know. Okay. I was thinking there must be some reasonable way to approach this license business. If you feel you really need the lobster."

"Why? What's the point now? I only ever wanted it for Wayne. Him and me. I might as well just scuttle the boat now."

"Don't say that."

"I guess the trailer's completely shot, is it?"

"Oh yes. Ashes. And did you know there was a pickup parked behind the trailer that was destroyed too?"

"Yeah."

"Whose was that?"

"Never mind."

Ben opened his mouth and shut it again. "That shirt is done. I bet you lost your jacket in the fire. We better get you something for tomorrow. Something for the funeral."

"I can't face it."

"Here, I'll get you cigarettes and a couple of Tylenol, you just stay in the car. I'll go pull something off the rack at Sears. We're here anyway. I won't take more than a few minutes."

Earl said nothing and Ben pulled into the mall parking lot.

When Ben dropped him off at home Earl thrust his new clothes at Judy to keep her at bay and escaped to the shower locking the bathroom door behind him. He shivered under cold water drawing the heat from his skin. The scorched smell wouldn't wash out of the burned streak of hair.


A GREAT RESTLESSNESS propelled Cass back to the horse barn where the colt spotted him and took off in a flurry of excitement around the rails of the corral. Momentum without purpose. Cass had been over-cautious with the colt, he thought now, overly sensitive to Weidermann's view of the animals as pets. He could wait for Weidermann, have him hold the head, ease his weight onto the saddle, but really what was the difference? The colt was more than ready.

Cass caught him and led him to his stall where he saddled him, pulling the cinch snug with great care. Back in the corral he stroked the colt's neck. The difference between dead parents without names and dead parents with names he could not account for. The difference between a living cousin he hardly knew and a dead one he hardly knew was ... what? And Eleanor. She knew more than she was telling. Earl. Pipe. He eased himself into the saddle and the colt balked in surprise. Cass stuck with him, let him prance a bit then started to rein him in. Once he settled a little the colt began to recognize the commands at the corners of his mouth and, in his confusion, followed them.

Cass offered up his voice. "Whoa boy, steady there. That's not so bad now is it?" He drew him up in the center of the paddock and eased him to a stop. Every time the beast skittered Cass urged him to be still, sat unmoving with his weight bearing down on the colt's fresh back, Cass feeling his own weight as though he were the horse, as though he were his own burden. When Weidermann roared into the yard on the tractor towing a load of green feed and saw Cass sitting on the colt in the middle of the corral he jumped down and pelted over to them, ducked through the fence rails. The colt shied at the man's boisterous approach and Cass quieted him.

"Ah! You have had success!"

"Some."

"Was it difficult? Did he try to buck you off?"

Cass shrugged. He thought of his half sister's silence, her exclusive language, of her three geese and her anger and her calm and her magical painting. Weidermann was rubbing the colt's blaze, his eyes shiny with exuberance.

"It went well?"

Cass spoke. "I had a brother, sort of, who died. He told me this— that a long time ago there was whole herds of wild cattle roaming around the States, generations of 'em built up over the years from cows got loose from settlers. After the railroad came through you could take the cattle east on the train and sell beef. There was money to be made so cowboys started roping the cattle and they dragged 'em to a pen they made from sticks. Then they had to move 'em out to the train in Kansas so they took sinew and sewed their eyes shut, the eyes of the cattle, you know, and so all the cattle were blind. That quieted 'em right down. The cattle stayed close together where they could feel the others around them, got used to the smell of the cowboys and the horses. Then when the thread dissolved and the cattle could see again they still didn't run off 'cause now they had a new family and they stuck together. Herd instinct, eh? They drove them to the train like that. Together."

"Is that a fact?"

Cass understood that he was talking nonsense, that the story meant nothing, had nothing to do with here and now and that he was showing off his stupidity again. He was talking about things for no reason like crazy people did. "It takes a while to get used to things, is all. That's all I mean, I guess. The colt's good though. You gonna try him?"

Weidermann rode a horse like he drove a tractor: from the outside in, from the top down. Cass watched him from the fence rail. There was an innocence about the way he directed the colt, like he did not know that the colt carried a burden and he did not know the burden was him. When he dismounted, the colt, startled by the sudden lopsided weight on a stirrup, bolted, tipping Weidermann off balance and setting him almost gently on his backside in the dust. Cass rescued the colt, Weidermann rescued himself, climbing to his feet and laughing.

Cass led the colt into the stable. Weidermann stowed the tack then leaned on a rail while Cass gave the colt a long and thorough brushing.

"There is a lot of land in this country, very cheap," Weidermann said. "We have already a lot of land—me and my brother. More than required for the farms. The trail where the train used to go is public. My wife, last night she says to me, Hans, you have got your 'big idea' look again. First time I see that big idea look we end up in Canada. Every time I see it after, I know there is going to be a lot of money going out and a lot of work coming in." He laughed as easily now as when he had picked himself out of the dirt. "I am wondering actually about making perhaps some trails for riding."

Cass felt the colt relax into the familiar attention of the grooming. The colt had no way of knowing if or when the riding would occur again, no way to consider the future, no way to weigh possibilities. With what I know I'm like God to the colt even though it's him carries the load, him that takes the bit or don't, him that knows all about being a horse. Cass had long assumed there was no God but now he wondered. Maybe there is a God it's just that there isn't much He can do.

Once Cass had owned a pair of black jeans and a blazer that he had bought for Lionel's wedding, wore at Lionel's funeral. He didn't own them now. "I was wondering if maybe you might have a jacket I could borrow. I gotta go to this funeral and I got nothing. Jack Heighton, eh? He's way too short, too small."

"Sure, of course I can do this. Shirt and tie as well. Whatever you need, of course." He ran his eye critically up and down Cass's body. "But maybe I am a bit too fat, heh? My son is short yet, but my brother—maybe fit better. You depend on me, heh?"

# CHAPTER TWENTY

CASS CLEANED AND POLISHED his boots. He took a bath and washed his hair and parted it down the side, straight with a comb. The shirt that Hans Weidermann had passed him was fine and white and it made him wince. It felt oddly light as though its color absorbed its weight. The trousers puffed out, insubstantial against his skin, soft and loose, baggy and a little short on the leg, not like his jeans at all. He gathered in the shirttail and stuffed it into the waistband of the pants, cinched it all with his belt. Perhaps Jack would know how to tie a tie. He had only ever worn a string tie, the one Lionel had given him for special occasions. Lionel was wearing one now in that hole in the ground. The boy in the coffin today was his cousin. He closed his eyes to imagine it: his father's brother's son. All the family lined up there in a bubble, him there under the dome with his cousin. The suit coat flapped in front over his flat stomach.

Cass brought the tie downstairs and held it out to Jack. "Any chance you'd know the knot for this, Jack?"

Jack stared and blinked, then worked his way out of his chair and shuffled himself into the center of the kitchen. A gray silence had fallen over him, and Cass, thinking back, could not remember if this silence was new or if it had taken him days ago. Cass stood still, his arms hanging by his sides, as Jack turned up his shirt collar and settled the tie in place, the back of Jack's fingers brushing his neck. Cass heard himself grunt as though from pain, as if a horse had kicked him, hoof cracking a rib. Mom-Ryan had turned up his collar like this and adjusted a tie, brushed fingers and thumbs against his neck, spoke to him close to his face, patted the strip of material against his chest. Cass forced himself to remain rigid while Jack labored, his movements excruciatingly slow. The moment Jack began to tug the tie through its final loop Cass jumped back, grabbed the knot in his fist and shoved it into place. The Ryans' was the best place he had ever lived—before Dartmouth, before the boys' home. They taught the dog a trick, he and Dad-Ryan. It was called "pick up your toys" and it had something to do with a Frisbee and things on the lawn. When they cheered for the dog their voices bubbled together, different but bumped up tight side by side like marbles in a glass. Dad-Ryan always set his hand on Cass's shoulder. That's m'lad. Mom-Ryan knotted Cass's tie, light fingers on his neck. He did not know how or why his stay with the Ryans ended but he endured the sudden memory of sitting on a concrete step with too many things and other people crying.

"I got a cousin who died," he told Jack gruffly, as though Jack had been trying to convince him otherwise. He clamped his hat on top of his combed hair and headed off across the back field towards the village leaving the old man dazed in the middle of the kitchen.

ELEANOR COULD NOT BEAR the knowledge of Cass: Murray's eyes and Murray's step, so close, and her with such a need of him. Of course Cass was shocked by her story the last time they spoke and as a result he was unable to offer comfort. But now he would be longing for his new family, desperate to see her, his grandmother—his father's mother. There were things he didn't know. When Murray died she thought she would go mad from grief. And again when her husband died, the old fool, again she was tormented by grief—for Murray. Now Wayne—the fall and the water and the rocks. Again. Perhaps Wayne fell in Murray's stead, a chance for Cass to know his father, glimpse his father's life and death, share the grief. He came home to shoulder some of the grief, bring some respite. Oh, what foolishness, what nonsense, but every time she tried to think rationally a great urge to see him and touch him enveloped her. She could not bear to look down into that casket without Cass by her side. Never mind that she could not explain his presence, that Ben would be all over him, more questions than a bishop in a brothel. Never mind the funeral would start in half an hour and she ran the risk of late arrival. She climbed into her car and headed directly for Jack Heighton's.

Jack seemed inordinately stupid about her request. Eleanor could not believe how the man had deteriorated since Effie's death. She was in no mood for patience or courtesy, no mood to stand here and look upon this shell of grief. "I'll look for myself," she told him and darted past.

There were only three bedrooms upstairs. She found it on the second try. On the dresser was a portrait of Murray as a child. Pipe's work, without a doubt. And the sketches tacked all over the wall were hers too. So they knew each other. Pipe and Cass, Murray's children. Murray's two children, all he had left to the world. She sat on his bed with the painting in her hands. A deep envy brittled her edges, that Pipe could follow her father's features like this, brush him into existence, each rise and hollow of his face, the piercing gentleness of his eyes. Looking at the image, holding it, she could feel the intimacy in the act of creating a portrait. The daughter creating the father as a child, creating him as she had never known him.

If only Murray had lived, there would not be this rift between her and Pipe, the problems with Wayne, Earl's drink-soaked childishness, Ben's determined bumbling towards goodness. If Murray had lived he would have kept them all together and happy: Pipe with her easel and paints in the garden, painting the flowers that Eleanor grew. Murray, bronzed in the summer sun, placating Pipe whenever some jagged tooth of her thorny nature broke the calm. And Murray's son, a taller broader Murray, not called Casper but the sort of thing Murray would have chosen. Named for his mother, likely. Taylor. She shivered at the thought but knew she was right. Taylor folded into an Adirondack chair, one long leg bouncing slightly, leisurely, over the other. Yes, Taylor entertaining them all, reading aloud from a book of poetry or perhaps short stories in a Murray-like buckwheat-honey voice. Further back, so far beneath the shade of the maple tree that Eleanor could not see her clearly, another figure lounged, more like hovered. A grown woman a scant year older than Murray, inscrutable, yes, but Eleanor could feel her calm beauty. And in the center of it all, her Murray of course, strong and handsome and alive. Effortlessly kind. It all seemed so possible. What was unbelievable was how far everything had gone wrong, slipped off course. How she could be left here with these two strangers for grandchildren and another grandson lying dead in the funeral home where she ought to be this very moment.

Casper Hutt. She remembered now. The cleaner at the hospital, what was her name? Dead for years now but when she lived out Crooked Harbour Road, well, you couldn't stop her prattle with a cork. She said, in the greatest confidence of course, it was the pediatric nurses who provided the name. So small and pale he was—ill and not properly cared for at all, no surprise. It being Halloween that they found him, they named him for the little cartoon ghost, Casper. And Hutt, for the little shed where he was found.

You must get on with things she prodded herself, but the dictate came out more as a plea than an ultimatum. If decorum would only permit she could easily lie back on this bed of her dead son's son and sleep. Get on with things. Cass was not here. Perhaps she should check the Weidermanns', then Pipe's wretched little house. She could drive up and down the road all day long, searching. In fact she could spend the rest of her life, that rudely dangling rag of sensibility left to her, searching, looking for him.

BEN ARRIVED EARLY to speak to Lonnie MacKinnon, the mortician who owned and operated the funeral home. In addition Lonnie managed the Anglican cemetery and had one daughter who ran the flower shop and another daughter who worked in the liquor store. This daughter's husband ran a tow truck and salvage business. "They've got all the bases covered," people would say. A "MacKinnon Party" was one that ended in a drunken car wreck. It was a stage of drunkenness beyond caution: drunk enough to make a MacKinnon smile.

Because Ben asked, because he approached the subject with concern, he discovered that Earl's credit card had been refused. Earl had insisted on writing a check but Lonnie had thought it prudent to avoid the ATM and wait in the bank lineup to speak quietly to a teller who advised him not to cash it.

"It's a major expense for a family. And so sudden," Lonnie said, commiserating and shaking his head. "Normally in a situation like this we work something out later. Time payments. This has been such a shock for the family. A real tragedy."

"Don't worry about it, Lonnie. If you have any trouble collecting I'll make good on it. Here, I'll give you something to start with. I'll talk to Earl later, in a few days maybe."

Ben and his mother would have preferred a proper Anglican service in the church but Earl said no. The funeral parlor had once been a grand old home owned by a nineteenth-century shipbuilding family. It was situated a few hundred feet off the highway on a little riverside street that offered a view of the entire village. White wicker furniture sat primly on the wide front porch and it was here Ben retired to get some air before people began arriving for the funeral, where he sat looking out over the rich blue of the Scotch River and the village lining its banks. He tried to contemplate his young dead nephew. He was sitting there when he saw his mother's Honda Civic beetling over the bridge and along the highway out of the village. He glanced at his watch. Where could she possibly be going? He fussed again about Pipe. Three attempts it took before he finally managed to speak with her. This business with Earl and the shotgun was profoundly disturbing, most unfair. Even though he had assured her safety at the funeral it wasn't surprising she refused to come with that kind of intimidation. It simply was not fair of Earl. Unacceptable really, but things were complicated enough for today.

Shortly after he returned inside to the chapel Judy and her boys arrived. Judy settled the twins into seats in the front row and told them not to talk or if they had to say something to keep it to a whisper. Her older son she elbowed to the front of the chapel where Ben spoke in a hushed voice with neighbors. She prodded her son forward towards the corpse without speaking, forced him to look upon his half brother. If she had been required to speak who knows what words might have flapped from her mouth like startled partridges. This is what becomes of boys who do not do as they are told, or, Here is the boy sacrificed that your life might be more comfortable, or, Here is the beast I saved you from. The son, for his part, eyed escape routes, subconsciously fingered the scar on the back of his hand where Wayne had burned him with the blade of a hot knife. He longed to join his little brothers in their childhood cocoon. He could see them whispering, relived their covert conversation from the evening before: "I remember when he held my head underwater at the beach and wouldn't let me up. I nearly drowned.—So? Once he unscrewed my Game Boy and totally wrecked it then told Dad he was fixing it. The liar. He broke everything.—And he barfed in our room. Totally gross.—Yeah. On *my* bed!—'Cause you told on him.—That's nothing. He nearly busted my arm. I hated him.—Me too."

"Where's Earl?" Ben asked Judy.

"He dropped us off. He said he was going for a quick drive, just around the village, to get a bit of air before the funeral."

They stood together in the presence of this sentence, not believing or disbelieving, not wanting to move beyond the shape of the words to the place where their own understanding would betray the man they loved. Again Ben felt the tug of his little brother's innocent cowardice and longed to wrap his arms around him and weep.

EARL DROPPED HIS FAMILY OFF at the funeral parlor and continued on across the bridge. There was astonishingly little left of Wayne's trailer. Ben had already arranged for the site to be cleaned up. He stood in the ruins where the bed used to be, the bathroom, the kitchen, the piled-high table. He kicked the ground and a soft smoky cloud rose knee-high, settling on his navy blue trousers and dusting his polished oxfords. If there was little to see now, in a week there would be less. By winter it would be as though Wayne had never lived. "I was the only one who loved him," Earl said aloud. And with the sound of the words the truth of them resonated, convinced, confirmed, and he loved Wayne more in that moment than he ever had. That there were people in the village who thought, and no doubt behind his back would say, that he had not been the father he should have been incensed him now. The hypocrisy of it! There were people now sitting at his son's funeral assuaging their guilt, people who only a week ago were saying he should be locked away, or worse. In truth they were glad to see the end of him. Earl loosened his tie, sat sideways in the cab, truck door wide open, staring at the charred corpse of Wayne's climbing tree, into the rectangle of ash, and he thought of all the things he had done for Wayne.

Wayne would have been something. There were lots in this village, lots and lots, who were as bad as Wayne when they were young. Worse! Way worse. And here was Wayne, nearly a lobsterman. He would have been. It would show them all if he *did* get the license back, if he went ahead. He had plans, after all. Cass hadn't disintegrated. He could do it himself without Ben's candy-assed teaching money. Maybe he should go ahead—for Wayne's sake. Yeah. Wayne would have wanted it.

CASS THOUGHT IT MIGHT be considered disrespectful to ride a horse to a town funeral so he left enough time to walk the two miles along the railbed. Hank the morning milker had explained it all out to him at excruciating length, where the funeral home was, how it worked, the people who ran it, and he had appeared ready to detail the life of everyone who had ever had a funeral there. Cass had seen the building before of course but he had never gone to the work of decoding the elegant sign on the lawn out front.

Inside, the main room was quiet with carpet, white walls and polished wood. The casket was laid out up front with flowers all along it. Cass could see it was made enough like a church to show people they should take their hats off and don't talk except real quiet. At Lionel's funeral all the family sat together at the front then other people gathered in clumps with rodeo people here and cattlemen there. Here it seemed like everybody just sat as far away as possible. He kept to the wall, followed it along and slipped into a chair on the far side of the room. At the front of the room, off to the side, a little beside the casket, a small knot of people came and went, speaking to, and shaking hands with, a pudgy man who looked often towards the door. Cass knew he had seen this man before but could not remember where. A woman seated two young boys in the front row and guided an older one up to the casket.

A haggard blonde woman not much older than him with a huge handbag slipped into the seat next to his and scrunched her chair back as though she wished to hide behind Cass's broad shoulders. With all the stillness and hushed voices in the room her twitching, her rummaging in her bag, her shifting, jangled everything. She blew her nose on a tissue and tucked it back into her purse then leaned over to Cass.

"When I left here I said I would never see this place again. I promised myself. Scotch River. God. But here I am again, look. I thought I wouldn't even get here. I thought I wouldn't get a ride but then my brother-in-law, he says he'll drive me down. My Ricky, eh? He wouldn't come, hates stuff like this. Can't handle it. Anything like this, funerals and that. Even weddings or anything in a church or like church, you know. I'm serious. Then Lucien says he'll drive me. I smoked half a pack of cigarettes before I come in here and I wants another one already. I knew I would too. I'm not going back out past that one there though."

"Who?"

"I got gum. You want some?"

"No."

She rummaged some more and bent a stick of gum into her mouth.

"Ohmygod." Back she went into the bag for more Kleenex. "He's so handsome. Did you see him all laid out up there, so handsome. My boy."

"Your son?"

"Yes." She cried into her tissue, lonely soft snuffling. "I didn't know he ever got so handsome."

"Don't the mother sit at the front?"

"Oh sure, if they wants to get pucked in the nose right in front of everybody. Seven years I spends here and it was the worst seven years of my life. And that's saying something. Where's Earl anyway? Not that I cares but I figured, you know, he's the father and all. And with that one up there like a peacock. She never did have no shame. I'm surprised Earl's still with that one, I must say. Ben's put some belly on him in the last few years, eh?"

Ben, of course. The man at the front was his Uncle Ben. Earl had pointed him out. He seemed to be in charge, or at least he seemed to have some notion of a plan that needed carrying through. Sad and serious and glistening clean, Ben reminded him of his city men.

"Ben was always nice to me, I will say that," she added.

"He ever go looking for you?"

"Ben?"

"No, Wayne. He ever go looking for his mother?"

"Wayne never had to go looking—he knew where I was to. I suppose that's some lie they put around, that he never knew where I was to? Sure Wayne would come up whenever he wanted. Hitchhike up, see? Then sit around on the couch until he and Ricky starts getting into it, then up and off he'd go back home. I never ever seen him done up so handsome as that up there though."

And off she went crying again. Cass frowned. Wayne could visit his mother whenever he wanted. She wasn't gone like Earl had said, or no more gone than Earl anyway.

In mid-sniffle she started up again. "Once he done a job even. He was up and they was working on the roof of the church, big high church. Sure you know what the Catholics is like with their churches, eh? Up he goes, no bother on him. Right up that pointy part even. All week he works there with them but then it's Saturday night and off he goes getting into some racket with somebody over nothing and that's the end of that."

"There's nice people up there. Not like here." She leaned into him, whispering. "They was always stuck-up around here, that's what I find. But I guess you're prob'ly from here so I shouldn't say that."

"No, I been away."

"You a friend of Wayne's?"

Cass waffled. He touched his tie hanging there against his borrowed shirt and he leaned into her ear as she had leaned to his. "He's my cousin," he whispered and glanced around.

"Oh."

Cass wondered if she was figuring that out, if she was going to ask more, but she just rustled in her bag, her hand finally emerging gripping a pack of Marlboros. Ben kept looking at his watch and the door. He conferred with Judy and then another man.

"It's not very nice," the woman said. "No matter what anyone says, it's not very nice to have somebody coming to your door and telling you your son is dead. It's a terrible thing is what it is." Wayne's mother was crying now for real but quiet about it. "If I don't gets a cigarette I swears I'll be good for nothing more than that one laid out." The organ gave out a long sad chord that slid into a plodding tune. "There now, no one can bother me once the music's started." She squeezed past him and fumbled her way along the wall and out to the porch, cigarette waiting between her lips.

Cass crossed one leg over the other trying to get comfortable in his baggy, too-short pants with people all around. Cass tried to imagine a snow globe with the new handsome Wayne. He tried to collect the family and stand them all together: Wayne's mother off on the porch smoking cigarettes, his father not here although he had sent his wife and children in his place, his grandmother Eleanor absent, his cousin Pipe home, he supposed, with her painting, his Uncle Ben struggling to keep things looking normal. And in the middle, one dead boy. Cass did not bother putting himself into the picture. The Holmes family was just a string of holes. Missing, wandered off, other things on their minds. Useless.

The Holmes family. None of them were any good. The world picked them off one at a time, and what did they care about it? People left like those whales on the beach in Jack's newspaper picture, like that baby abandoned in the village. From far away on the horizon his anger began as a speck, somewhere off in an appendage, a toenail. It galloped towards him on thudding hooves but from so awfully far away Cass had a great deal of time to watch it approach. From several provinces away across the prairie. He felt it reach his fingers and elbows, his knees and scalp, plunge into the pit of his stomach, clatter over his ribs overtaking confusion and frustration. Anger settled in a dark nest on his forehead where his eyebrows tilted towards each other, burned through him as the funeral progressed. Where was his family? Nowhere.

When the final hymn sounded everyone stood as the casket was wheeled out and the crowd shuffled forward. Carefully, carefully, because there is nothing as dangerous as anger, Cass descended the steps from the funeral home with the others. He would not stay to see the boy lowered into the ground. Let the Holmeses look after themselves. The boy was nothing to him. Carefully, carefully, he monitored his steps down the street past Eleanor's, on through the gas station lot and at last to the cover of the bush where he broke into a run. Anger spit flankers from his belly, chased him along the ATV trail, across the iron bridge, family falling everywhere, and up the railbed. Like a dog flushing rabbits, like a coon in the henhouse, his anger snarled and snapped and sent everything flapping and squawking into the air. The letter under his bed. Only paper. Flimsy as a feather, sure, but more than that useless lot. Corpses and paper. Like those scrapbooks of Jack's, paper stories cut and glued to paper. Whales, strong men, babies on doorsteps. He would hear from his mother now. He didn't care, had nothing to lose. He could be no worse off than the rest of them.

## CHAPTER TWENTY-ONE

CASS'S ANGER JOSTLED EVERYTHING, painted colors brighter, drew lines sharper. The back door hitched when he tugged on it though he had never before noticed that it stuck. His hand seemed foreign on the knob, his boots too large on the mat. Dirt mottled the floor tiles. They must have been dirty for some time. In the kitchen the old man leaned into the stove, hefting a kettle of water onto an element with more effort than it once had taken him to swing a loaded milking machine. The room was dingier than he remembered.

"Jack! I need your help, Jack." Cass watched Jack turn slowly, peeping around his own shoulder, clutching the oven door handle for support and squinting. Reedy and hollow, his sparse body had shriveled into a skeleton so loose that Cass feared it might rattle. There were hollows in his skull, pools of gray where his eyes had been. The man was helpless and Cass did not know how long this had been so, when this had happened. "Jack!" It came out in a bark, spiked and accusatory.

The old man looked up startled, scared even, certainly confused. Hobbling, Jack made for his rocker, grabbing it and almost crouching behind it for protection. "Oh my. I guess I didn't … I don't …"

"You're fucking starving to death, old man!"

"Here, here, there's no need for language like that. Don't you let Effie hear that kind of language."

"Effie's dead."

Jack crumpled into his chair.

Cass hated this helpless out-of-control feeling. Free fall. He rubbed his face, desperately trying to rein himself in. "Jesus-Jesus-Jesus, Jack. The thing is I've got all mad and I'm not really the type, you know. I'm not the type for getting mad." The old man hunched over, sad and quiet. "How long since you ate a meal, Jack?"

"Oh, I'm uh, I was, uh, just making a cup of tea there now."

Cass looked around the kitchen as he hadn't in weeks. He approached the wooden breadbox painted with birds and flowers that sat on the counter. The half-full bread bag inside was puffed with green powdery mold. You growing a new carpet, he was going to say, but stopped at the sight of the back of Jack's head. Simmering, he dropped the bag into the garbage. There in the garbage can lay a stack of disposable pie pans, each covered with tinfoil, each, when he eased back the cover, containing an untouched dinner. Another stack of untouched dinners sat on the top shelf of the fridge.

"I can't have you starving to death here before I get everything figured out. You were supposed to eat those dinners, I suppose?"

"I guess I forgot."

The problem was, once angry, everything fired anger. Cass concentrated on keeping his movements slow and even. He opened a can of stew, placed a bowl of it in the microwave and toasted bread. He set the meal on the table fighting the pressure within him.

"Here's your supper now, Jack."

"No, no. I'll just have a cup of tea there in a minute."

Cass hauled a kitchen chair out from the table and into the middle of the floor where it wobbled and tottered from the force of relocation, then settled. He slid Jack, rocker and all, from his post by the window to the empty spot at the table in front of the stew bowl. Jack hardly had time to blink, he groped at the chair arms and managed a soft grunt of surprise, but he was already ensconced with Cass sitting across from him before he could manage a protest. Cass picked up Jack's spoon, pressing it into the spidery shaky hand.

"You eat that there, Jack." Easy boy, easy. Cass watched him lifting a shaky claw, raising one spoonful of stew to his mouth then another.

"Did Effie say—I can't remember, did she say when she's coming back?"

"No. She said for me to give you your dinner. She said for you to eat it all." He watched the old man sip and chew and swallow obediently.

"I'm not the type for getting mad, like I said. It don't sit well with me. Don't sit well at all." He rubbed his bad shoulder. "Sometimes you hear stories. And you can't figure out what really happened unless you know the guy that's talking. You ever notice that, Jack? You got twenty guys, you got twenty stories. All different. So then if you see the thing happen you think you got the truth, eh? But all you really got is twenty-one stories. Funniest goddamned thing. Doesn't help that everybody's a horse's ass. The world is just a big pit full of horses' asses."

Jack peered over his bowl, lifted an eyebrow at the language, but before he could interrupt Cass continued, "Effie said for you to eat that." His anger tipped and there beneath it trickled a deep and narrow sadness, a well down through the middle of him. That was where Jack was caught, Cass thought, turned inside out and trapped, squeezed tight inside there. Probably felt like he was being crushed alive. Maybe like he could crawl out of the tunnel if he got skinnier. Maybe his brain thought that up all by itself and told his stomach without mentioning it to the rest of Jack on account of the foolishness of the idea. Your brain could come up with any goddamned thing and make you crazy before you knew it. End up worshipping Coke cans on a railroad track.

"Hey, Jack …?" The old man looked like a child with his low rocking chair pushed up to the table. He could have spun the man up across his shoulders and carried him with no more effort than carrying a newborn calf. He could have broken each brittle bone in Jack's body with his bare hands. He could have worked and eaten and gone about his business while the old man shriveled and died and he saw nothing at all.

"Can you eat another piece of toast there?" Jack shook his head. "I'll make us tea in a minute. Maybe slip a bit of whiskey into it, eh? For strength. You know, we gotta get you fixed up here 'cause if people see you like this they're gonna sweep you outta here so fast your head's gonna spin. Know that? What if your daughter sees you like this? What then? And what about me? I'll be out on my ass. You ever think of that?"

Jack shook his head sadly.

"Listen now, Jack. I know you feel bad. I know, but listen to me. I want you to do something for me. The truth is I was never so good in school and I know you're real good with reading and writing and that stuff. You and Effie both. I got these pages, this letter I guess, a message, but it's all written in joined-together writing, by hand, you know." He lowered his voice although there were only the two of them. "I'm no good at that. I can't make head nor tail of it to tell the truth. But I guess I gotta read that letter. Fact is, I guess I figure it's kind of prob'ly from my mother. I got to know what's in it, Jack."

Cass wasn't sure how much of the old man was present and accounted for but maybe it didn't matter all that much. "Do you think you can give it a try? I got it just upstairs. I'll go get it, okay?"

"What's that?"

"Hold on there, Jack. Don't go away."

Cass whirled away, took the stairs two at a time, careened into his room and smacked his head on the angled ceiling of the dormer. Cass's head snapped back and tiny silver slivers of ice floated before his eyes. The wall grunted from the blow, the room resounded with the crack. He sank to his bed, doubled over with his head shouting pain into his hands. A low moan curled in his throat, his stomach lurched then righted itself.

"Fuck."

He sat until his mind cleared and the wound settled into a quiet throbbing. He fingered the tender area where a lump had already begun to grow. Too big to move so fast in such a small space. And what's the rush? Thirty-five years without a mother, what's a few minutes? Still sitting he slowly and carefully loosened his borrowed tie and set it over the bedstead. He wiggled his jacket off and worked his way down his shirt buttons releasing himself. He felt his shoulders relax into their intended dimensions. He unbuckled his belt and pulled it through the loops of his borrowed trousers with one graceful tug. Then he stood and stepped out of the pants and into his jeans. All of the Weidermanns' clothes he folded meticulously and returned to the plastic bag they had come in. He pulled on a T-shirt and gingerly lowered himself to the floor where he pulled his pack out from under the bed and fished out the letter. Holding it there in his hand he was glad of the pain in his head and the heavy deliberation in his movements. Like Wayne's pallbearers he carried his burden, heavy with solemnity, down to Jack, unfolded the letter with quiet reverence.

"What do you think, Jack? Can you read this out to me?"

"Oh well yes, I suppose I can."

*To Casper Hutt*

*I have started this letter a thousand times on paper. A million times in my mind. This attempt, for better or worse, I am determined will be submitted to my lawyer. My medical prognosis is bleak and if I do not act now I may lose my chance. For myself, I am content to let questions lie unanswered. What is done is done. However I cannot pass you this deed of land without some explanation.*

*I am your mother. I did not know for certain until I saw you, touched your arm and looked into your eyes. But it is true. You are my son. Perhaps you hate me. Perhaps you spent your life imagining I was better* than I am. I did what I thought was best at the time. I can see there were mistakes made. I don't ask you to forgive me, only to believe this one thing — that I did what I thought was best for all of us at the time. This property in Scotch River that I am passing to you ought to have been yours. You should have been raised on it. That was my intent. I never questioned that you had been.

Long ago I had problems. There were pressures. I don't expect you to understand the kind of life a girl like me had to manage but I can tell you there can be many good reasons to take a leave of absence from circumstances. I was twenty years old the year of my Nova Scotia summer, driving from beach to beach, swimming and letting time and the ocean wash over me. I met your father, Murray Holmes, on a beach outside Scotch River. He was trying to rescue a wounded seagull that had slid down between two rocks and was stuck. He was so earnest that I found him funny at first, even ridiculous, but increasingly I was drawn to him. I had never seen such innocent kind-heartedness in a man, such utter guilelessness. He would not be budged from his gentle view of the world or from his tender approach. This was my impression at the time. It never crossed my mind that he could betray you.

I struggle to recall the magic of that summer as I experienced it at the time. Murray with his gentle unshakable faith; he made me laugh. He gave me shelter. His devotion to me grew deep, wondrous, almost fanatic. All this was a mystery to me. And him with a brute of a father and a harridan for a mother. For a while I thought I could be like him, surrounded by tranquility and floating through life on a cloud of goodness. I thought I had found peace and love and a simple perfection that would last forever. So I bought a piece of land, a little paradise with trees and an old house to fix up. Murray chopped firewood. I painted the kitchen walls and planted some flowers. It was too late for them to bloom Murray said but promised there would be flowers the next spring.

*As the months slipped by and summer faded the truth began to dawn on me. Winter blocked us in, held us hostage, froze the water and the air. All around people led their dull simple lives with their dull happy children. They played cards and went to church and talked about the weather and bantered stupidly until I thought I would scream. They did not see what I had seen or know what I knew.*

*I realized this country life had been a childish dream. I could never be happy there. Murray's goodness would never rub off on me. Moreover I would only pull Murray down, away, eventually destroying all he was. At this point I began to suspect I was pregnant. Try as I might I could not bear to see myself stuck in the bush with a baby while the rest of the wide world tumbled on without me. I needed to find some place on my own where I could think my situation through. I slipped away swiftly and quietly.*

*You were born in the city of Boston amid the anonymity of a metropolitan hospital. I was not, have never been, the mothering type. Although I was fairly sure of this, in the days following your birth I came to understand it thoroughly. I could not make you happy. But your father had patience and love and a caring hand just waiting for such a project as you. Or so I believed.*

*I bought a bright-colored plastic laundry basket that could not fail to be noticed. I drove north through New England and back into Canada, over rough roads crowded by trees clutching their last brilliant leaves of fall. Outside Scotch River I bundled you against the October chill. I wanted a clean break, nothing jagged to mar my memories. Perhaps I was afraid to face your father. Perhaps I was a coward but as I said, at the time I thought it was for the best. I drove in the laneway and carried you, basket and all, up to the house where I knew your father would be sleeping. What explanation I could muster I left folded in a little pink envelope that I tucked in with your blankets. When I left you on my land, in your father's care, you were sleeping peacefully. As far as*

*I knew Murray respected the wishes I had spelled out in the note and never tried to contact me. As far as I knew the two of you were growing happily together. I arranged for a legal firm to look after the land so you would always have a place to live. I picked up the pieces of my life and carried on.*

*Secrets abound everywhere. On the whole I believe it is best to let sleeping dogs lie but several years ago in a wide-ranging cocktail party conversation I dropped a passing tidbit that as a girl I had vacationed a summer in Nova Scotia. Immediately I was set upon by one of those annoying small-town people who delight in finding others who may once have trod on the same path as some far-off relative of theirs. She pressed me for specifics and was overjoyed to find me vaguely acquainted with Scotch River. Being from that very village herself she had to discover exactly who I had met during my stay and tell me every detail of their lives in the intervening decades. I was about to shut her down when I realized my opportunity and enquired about Murray Holmes and his son. This is how I learned of the unfortunate circumstances of Murray's death. This is when I discovered, no matter how I pressed and insisted, that Murray Holmes had never had a son. The woman insisted that Murray married a very troubled lady from the area and together they had a daughter. He had no son. No other child. No rumors of you, no adoptions, nothing. Perhaps if Murray Holmes had not died I would have confronted him with my questions.*

*As it was I hired a detective, a man famous in small circles for his discretion and his resourcefulness. He confirmed that Murray Holmes was never known to have had a son. But he brought me the story of a baby found abandoned in the village the same day I left you with your father. I had no inkling Murray was capable of such a thing. To transport the child to the village and leave him — you — there for discovery, to live the rest of his life with this knowledge. I had no idea he could hate me so much for leaving him. This was my mistake. It*

*was always my mistake to have too much faith in people and I am
sorry for it.*

*The foundling was registered with the name Casper Hutt. I do not
know why they chose such a name. I do not know why you still carry this
name. My detective presented me with a photograph of a full-grown
man, a man of precisely the right age, a rodeo rider from Cotton Creek
Alberta who called himself Cass Hutt. "You might want to take a look
and see what you think," he said.*

*So I did. I found your rodeos loud, noisy affairs, dirty and hard and
cruel as life itself. I watched as they called your name and you were
released into the dirt ring on the back of a wild beast. I watched you
hit the ground and spring to your feet. My eyes followed you as you
climbed over the boards and out of the ring in your deep red shirt with
the white piping at the yoke. I made my way down out of the stands
towards you always keeping the red of your shirt in my mind so I
would not lose you, Cass Hutt. Other men leaned on fence rails but as
I approached I saw only you, tall and strong and solid. You had that
wide flat chest of Murray's and the Taylor forehead and cheekbones but
you were a distinct man entirely. I could see that, hear it in your voice.
I stood beside you, watched you unbutton your shirtsleeves and roll
them up two turns of the cuff. I moved towards you staring at the fine
black hairs on your forearm. When I set a hand on your arm you
turned and I looked directly into your eyes. I knew without a doubt.
You were there and whole and real. You were your own man and had
nothing to do with me, there in spite of me, no thanks to me, in a world
utterly foreign to me. Strong. Singular. For a moment we stared at each
other then you cricked your eyebrow perhaps in a question, perhaps in
annoyance. You drew your arm away. I heard myself apologize, "I'm
sorry, I was looking for someone else. I'm sorry." You turned away. And
in the end, so did I. There was nothing more I could do. It is unlikely
that you remember the incident.*

*The scrap of land represented by this enclosed deed was always meant to be yours. Use it now as you see fit. Sell it if you like. I left you with your father. I never meant for you to be abandoned. I hope your life has gone well enough, despite the misadventures. You look like a fine man in your own way. I hope you will not judge me too harshly. In the end, I am sorry.*

*—C.T.*

# CHAPTER TWENTY-TWO

CASS SAID NOTHING. If he had been back in Cotton Creek he would have ridden off somewhere to be alone under the sky but here one farm led to another, houses lined up along the roads every quarter of a mile, sometimes every couple of hundred yards. Trails through the woods kept leading to clumps of settlement and nowhere was there unbroken space. He thought briefly of the expanse of sea he had experienced on the boat. That was not a place he ever wanted to revisit. I could go back west, he thought, but the notion petered out before it was even fully imagined.

He climbed the stairs to his room and lay on his bed with his mother's letter spread open on his chest, unconsciously stroking the pages. His mother had touched his arm, she had looked him in the eye then turned and left him. Twice. You won't remember me, she said. He remembered her. It was in Medicine Hat. That was the year the Canadian bull riding circuit started up, separate from the full rodeo. To start the show they lit a trail of gasoline into a wall of fire across the front of the arena. All the cowboys lined up behind it, "appearing" as the flames died down. Then they were introduced one by one over the loudspeaker. There were fireworks after. All that became old hat to him soon but at that time it had been new and startling to find himself, his name, his riding, such a public part of a show. Lionel had been racking up the points and looking at the finals for that year but it was Cass who won the competition that day. He won. His mother didn't mention that in the letter, maybe she didn't notice. It wasn't the first time he won of course but that was the year he decided to concentrate only on bull riding. No more roping or wrestling. The win was an omen, Lionel said. Proof that he had done the right thing, put all his eggs in the right basket.

That day in Medicine Hat she came down from the stands. It was impossible not to notice her. She looked like someone in a movie, completely lost but moving through the crowd as though it was not her but everyone else who was out of place. She kept coming, swimming through the crowd. Her clothes flowed like a river, silky, a dress, yes. Fire colors, orange and red, and a sun hat with a brim the size of a trash can lid, and shoes with heels that made her rickety, but somehow more graceful in spite of it. She moved as though she expected seas to part in front of her. People stepped out of her way out of surprise at first then probably because everyone else did, figuring she was someone famous. He remembered the confused embarrassment when her trail stopped in front of him, his sense of exposure, and he remembered scanning the crowd for Lionel, thinking she must be looking for Lionel. She was tall for a woman but with that same brittle twiggy body that women have. Breakable.

Yes, she touched him like she said in the letter, but she also said his name. She didn't mention that. She reached out and took his arm and looked in his eyes and said, Cass Hutt. He waited. She said it again but more a question this time, *Casper* Hutt? He didn't like that name and turned away and when he turned back the crowd was parting and closing behind her and all that was left was the flutter of her dress. Later there were rumors that she was an actress or singer or something.

He thought of the flutter of clothes again, afraid now he might have mixed it up with the butterfly scarf. But the odd feeling she had given him—that was true. His stomach turned liquid again as it had that day, and again he was on the seat of a car heading towards the end of the road with a cardboard box on his lap. Pain corkscrewed through his intestines and he slapped the bump on his head in a vain attempt at distraction. She should have said something, why didn't she say something? From then on she could have found him any day; she knew where he was, who he was. She could have spoken to him. Told him. They could have fixed things. But he was not what she wanted.

She had looked at him, touched him, knew him and walked away. Twice. The letter lay in one great undigested ball in his stomach. She had been young, drove with the baby across the border, left it, drove away. Each time his hand stroked the letter smooth the paper sighed with a soft crinkle where it had been folded.

Time passed, daylight faded, night approached. He had to milk the cows. And so he sat up, pulled on his boots and placed his feet flat on the floor. He stowed the letter back in the pack under his bed, rose, walked across floorboards, stairs, lawn, road, farmyard, concrete. One foot in front of the other, one cow after another, Cass moved forward, the heartbeat of milking machines carrying him through the shift. That night a cow calved, the calf removed and stowed in its own pen, another cow returned to the herd. Cass tried to bend his mind to the facts. There was comfort here, thinking of the movement of solid things, the progression of the visible. He rubbed his hand against the newborn calf's head and let it push against him, butting and wobbling. The baby left at Murray's but found in the village. Murray, his father, supposedly so kind and gentle, but he had risen in the morning and found the baby there, read the note, tore it up, drove the child to the village, abandoned it. Mad, Cass imagined, cursing Catherine Taylor, fuming that the baby was not his. He had handled it roughly, careful to touch only the blanket and not the skin. He looked around, three times over each shoulder, before he shoved it into the corner of the doorway, cursing it to shut up when he jarred it into crying. On the way home he pulled off the road and tossed the laundry basket into the sea. Yes, where the inlet came in by Wayne's trailer where everything is tossed. Like Wayne.

Cass grabbed at Wayne and hung on to the lone boy in the coffin. They should not have left the boy alone. They should not have left Wayne alone at his funeral. They should not have—all those Holmeses. There was that rip of green in Pipe's painting, that yellow yearning.

At dawn Cass left the calves and leaned against the barn to watch the sun come up. Sun, he said to himself. East. West. Ground. Sky. Barn. Easy boy. He strolled over to the paddock where he ran his hands over the mare's withers, stroked her nose, searched her eyes. Millad. He leaned on her back, crouched on his haunches and ran his hands down her withers and leg. Hock, pastern, fetlock, hoof.

At eight o'clock, one foot in front of the other, he carried himself back across the road to Jack's, focused his eyes on Jack's skinny body huddled over a scrapbook open on his lap, nodded at him when he looked up, so sad and small. Keep this man alive, he told himself. Feed this man, make sure he eats. Feed the horses. Feed the cows. Feed the calves.

"Breakfast time, Jack."

"I've been reading the foundling story again. See here in Effie's book? I never knew it was you. What a terrible thing. If Effie were here she would know what to do."

"What was that word, Jack? Found—something?"

"Foundling? The Scotch River Foundling. Everyone knows about the Scotch River Foundling."

"Yeah. What's that mean? Foundling?"

"That's what you call a baby that's been abandoned, left on a doorstep or suchlike for someone to find."

"How can there be a special word just for that? There can't be too many kids like that, can there? Enough to get their own word?"

"Enough, I guess."

"That's something though, eh Jack? To get your own word." It *was* something, too. To imagine a group, a line of people, or a herd, all foundlings. Not lost-lings or left-lings but *found:* bonuses, windfalls, clear profit. His brain jerked sideways and he thought of steers who were all ancestors and no descendants, the end of a line, the final product. The foundlings were the opposite, no past; they were their own beginnings.

"Eleanor Holmes was here again, looking for you. I didn't say anything but I think she knows about the foundling. I think she knew before this."

"Yeah, I reckon you're right."

Eleanor knew. You bet. That was the other thing that kept popping up every time he managed to surface and grab a breath. Eleanor knew everything. She picked what she wanted and made up the rest and handed to him whatever she felt like. Murray had probably told her all about it, or maybe she found out some other way after Murray died. Either way, Murray was dead now and Eleanor wanted to go on thinking he was perfect. She didn't want to think about him leaving a baby, a foundling, just because he was mad at some girl. She didn't want people to know what he did. That's why Eleanor wanted everything kept secret. But now … when it leaked out that Cass was the Scotch River Foundling she was going to blame everything on Catherine Taylor.

Sure Eleanor knew. Eleanor wanted to see him? Well, he would see her all right. And there it was again, another flare of anger, another fire to slap out with his coat, exhausting himself, only to have another tuft of flames break out a few yards away. Rage spread in no time. Prairie fire.

"Breakfast now, Jack." He bent down in front of him, bounced on his heels in front of the rocker but did not look at him. He stared at the baseboard where dust was beginning to build up into gray fluff. "I keep getting this anger, Jack. It don't sit well with me at all."

"Ah, you're easygoing like me. Effie too. No point getting all worked up."

"Like swallowing a whole nest of hornets, eh Jack?"

Jack chuckled, shook his head a little and looked off into another time beyond the windowpane.

CASS SADDLED THE MARE. He saddled her slowly and with great care, settling the saddle blanket just so, polishing the rings on the bridle with his sleeve. He constructed an entire windowsill full of snow globes in his head: A young woman driving a car through forested hills. A woman alone, carrying a laundry basket up out of a long lane flanked by uncut weedy brown hayfields, the night sky crisp and moonless with a million stars. She struggled, carrying the basket awkwardly far out in front of her, making it heavier than need be. Murray he could not see at all except as a speck falling, falling from the iron bridge. Wayne falling, his half sister painting, Wayne laid out. When he veered too close to Eleanor an electric charge sizzled through him and he doubled back, riding out around her, circling, watching from a distance. The wrapped baby by the shed, a man and a small sniffing dog at dawn.

The gray sky hung close to the earth, noncommittal about rain, as Cass led the mare out of the barn, mounted and set her trotting across the road and through the field behind Jack's to the railbed. Eleanor would have to tell him what she knew. He had decided.

The moment she saw him, even before he got the mare tied, she strode from a flower bed across the pond. "Cass. You're here. I need to speak to you. I've been looking for you since before the funeral. I couldn't get any sense out of Jack Heighton at all. He's gone dotty."

Cass stepped back from her and his arms folded across his chest. "There's things you know, I guess, that you never told me. All about the foundling. That's a big thing to forget to mention to a person."

Fear froze the skim of her eyes like ice on a puddle.

"I was going to tell you. That's why I was looking for you. Who told you about the foundling?"

"Everyone knows about the Scotch River Foundling." Repeating Jack's words sounded truer, less disputable, than anything he might say. "You knew that foundling was Catherine and Murray's baby."

"No, I didn't know the foundling was Murray's. I never suspected until that day you came and you looked at that turtle."

"You knew it was Catherine's though."

"How would I? She must have—well, obviously she did—leave here pregnant. How would I know that? How would I connect her to the foundling?"

The questions were half dismissal, half challenge. But no denial.

"'Cause Murray told you? And you didn't want to say nothing in case Murray got in trouble."

"Murray! Murray never knew."

"That ain't so. That's the lie right there. He knew it was his baby 'cause Catherine wrapped up a note with the kid and left it by his door. Murray didn't want a baby. Murray didn't care about no baby. He dumped it in the park, didn't care if it got ate by dogs or coyotes or nothing. All you say about Murray, all kind and sweet and that, that's crap. He could of give it to someone who wanted a baby. He just didn't care."

Eleanor reached out for him, grabbing. "Don't you ever say that about your father! Don't you blame Murray for that! I won't have his name sullied, I warn you! Murray never knew about that child. I knew there would be nothing but lies and gossip spread. That's not the way it was at all. Who is talking about this? Pipe, I suppose, making that up just to get a rise from me. That is why I told you to speak only to *me*! Catherine Taylor abandoned you, not my Murray. There was no note found with that child. There was an investigation."

"What you don't know is I got proof—in black and white. My mother, she left me a letter with that deed I showed you. My mother told me she left the baby with Murray. Up the lane by the house. Not in the park."

Cass watched the color drain from Eleanor's face. "There is no letter." But this was more a plea than a declaration. "And—and at any rate Catherine Taylor was a liar."

"Well, I guess it turns out I know more about it than you. I know it was Murray. You got nothing to say to me but lies."

The rumble of a passing transport truck left a quaking trail in the air, a bird chattered somewhere off to the west, across the river a car door slammed, its impact muffled by distance. When Eleanor spoke her words came out both soft and clipped. "Please come and sit." She turned towards the bench by the pond and settled onto one half of it, patted the seat beside her, pulling him with her proud, muted voice.

He felt the will on both ends of an invisible lunge line, the play of a dozen different shades of power. Wary, he approached and propped one foot on the bench seat, leaned forward on his knee looking out to the pond.

"I know your mother abandoned you. I know for a fact. This is terribly difficult. I thought I would take this secret to the grave. I saw your mother one last time—that autumn, specifically October thirty-first. I often have trouble sleeping at that time of year. We all have our burdens. I went out for a bit of air that morning—earlier than morning, it was dead black out. We were still living out by the Crooked Harbour Road then, where the road meets the highway. My husband always kept a streetlight at the end of the lane. There was a great old maple tree back from the road, it's still there, actually, and I used to sit on the garden swing on its shadow side away from the light. Anyhow, that's how I saw the car pass on the highway. Well, you couldn't mistake it, bright yellow. It just lit up, driving through the pool of light. I saw her all right. It was her. That morning they discovered the foundling. I never for a moment believed that baby was Murray's. Of course it is clear enough now that I was mistaken. She was carrying you in the car that night, brought you and left you."

"She left me at Murray's."

"I said nothing at the time. Perhaps some would consider that wrong. I meant it for the best. I couldn't bear to see him tied to her with some child, likely not even his, forever chasing after her, tied to something that was never more than a mirage. I would never let him suffer so. If there was any justice he should never have had to think of her again. But there is no justice. I can assure you Murray never knew."

"She left him at Murray's. Murray knew. Murray took him to the park."

"He never knew! Murray spent all his life taking in strays and derelicts and orphans—the walking wounded. Look at your mother, look at that one he married! He would never have given up a baby in a basket—his or not."

"See there's the lie right there—there was no *basket* in the park. You only know about the basket 'cause Murray told you." She did not deny it. Towering over her at his end of the bench Cass watched her gaze melt into the middle distance, somewhere in the air over the pond. She touched her white hair with her hands, patted her knees, light as the flutter of birds' wings, folded her hands in her lap.

There, he thought, she can't deny the truth. He straightened himself, backed away from the wrought iron bench, watching the space grow between them. The silence of the morning filled his ears—the sound of his story—and with the thought flashed a tug of yearning for his silent sister. The mare dipped and tossed her head as Cass fixed the reins and stepped into the stirrup.

Perhaps the creak of saddle leather broke the spell or perhaps it forced her hand. Perhaps causality was an illusion. When Eleanor spoke she did not turn her head or lift her voice, seemed not to be speaking to him at all but simply speaking. "Murray couldn't have brought you to the village. He had no car." She paused perhaps as long as it took for a silent sigh. "That was the most hideous plastic turquoise hamper ever manufactured. That color has stuck with me like gum to the sole of my shoe."

Cass heard her words and for a moment the information hesitated like a ball bearing balanced on a peak, trembling. Consider or disregard? It tipped, rolled through him, bouncing off fact, possibility, likelihood, rumbling inexorably home: Eleanor absorbing the color, Murray the rescuer asleep in bed. Cass urged the mare forward and around the bench where he stared down at her from the saddle.

"You," he said.

She sat motionless, did not look at him, while the truth bled all over them. Again Cass saw the bull's horn scraping an arc under Lionel's rib cage, life tumbling out all over and nothing could be done.

"You saw her car. But then you followed it. *You* found the basket at Murray's. You moved the baby to the park."

"She was the one who left you. She *decided*. Never forget that." Now she stood and looked him in the eye, steady and resolved. "You were found and adopted. Lots of families wanted babies by then. All that is in the past. What's past is past and can't be helped. You are here now and you are all that is left of Murray, Casper Holmes. Never mind the past."

Never mind thirty-five years filled with all the houses and all the cardboard boxes and all the emptiness, and never mind the Ryans or Randy or Lionel and his family or the One Bar None or all the cattle or horses or bulls or trophies or city men. Never mind Cass Hutt. Leave him out by some shed. She confesses and she forgives herself all in one easy breath! Never mind Wayne or Pipe or Earl or Jack or anyone. "Past is past, my ass! I'm the past! You're the cause of every goddamned thing gone wrong."

She stood, reached up to the saddle for him. "You are my Murray's." He met her with his foot. The sole of his boot square on her shoulder spun her around, tipping her backwards where she glanced off the bench and sprawled out on the grass.

"You get out of my way!" He took off leaving her trail of words disappearing behind him. His one glance back caught the old woman on her hands and knees, struggling for her feet. Gravel flew out behind the mare's shoes on the verge of the road. When Cass pulled her tight into the turn onto the path to the railbed she nearly stumbled on a root, just regained her balance.

Shit. Shit. Shit. His heart pounded in his head, blurring his eyesight, setting every muscle atremble. Rein in, he commanded himself. He brought the mare to a walk but even then did not trust himself and so dismounted and led her off the path and out to the riverbank to drink under the bridge. Think of the chute, the anger below, outside; think of riding the storm. Circle around, look back from the outside. A woman in a yellow car carrying a basket up a laneway, a baby wrapped in a blanket and a note tucked in a pink envelope by its feet, leaving it near the door where the man will hear its cries as he comes out at dawn to piss against the clapboards. She runs, arms flapping, back to her car and drives off forever. A second, older woman, who has seen the yellow car and followed it, arrives soon after and turns up the lane. She does not see the yellow car as she expected but finds instead a bright basket, a babe, a note. She cuts her headlights. She picks up the basket and all and backs her car ever so silently down the lane. Returning the way she came the woman finds the village utterly still, black and deserted. She lifts the wrapped baby from the basket and sets the parcel snugly on a shed step in the middle of the village. She arrives home as dawn is breaking. The basket she hides, maybe cuts up to dispose of later. She lights a fire in the stove to boil the morning tea. Flames lick a pink envelope, taste it, devour it. The ashes mix with all the other ashes to be sprinkled later on the garden.

Murray didn't even know he had a son; never even saw him, although he might have seen if he had turned his head to the right in the last moment of his life. Looked right here, right where he stood now. Murray would have seen but not known.

Eleanor. His head throbbed again and he jerked his thoughts sideways. There was his mother in her flowing costume with her hand on his arm and saying nothing. That part was no good either, made him mad. His mother had arranged for him to live on her land, inherit her land. She didn't know Murray wouldn't get the baby, wouldn't get the note even, would marry a crazy woman and have a daughter who thought the land was hers. The further the story moved away from him the more his anger dissipated, the more calmly he could approach it. All Catherine Taylor's life she thought of the child. She had meant the land for him. She knew he might not understand the story in the letter but the land was proof of something. I have thought of you always; I have given you something; I am your mother. She left him. No, she gave him. It was Eleanor who left him.

Cass pulled off his boots, sat on the rock by the bank with his feet in the water, hurting. The dull pain that often crawled into his left shoulder escaped and invaded his entire body. He did not move to shrug it off. He sat and hurt while the story swirled around and around him.

More than ever he needed his half sister to paint for him. But more than ever he wanted his own land, his mother's land, beneath his feet. One canceled out the other though. Pipe would not paint for him if she knew he would evict her. Still, he sat and hurt.

ELEANOR FELT PHYSICALLY ILL. How could everything of Murray's become so tainted? Even Wayne's death with the deafening echo of the tumble and the water and Pipe in the background. She had mangled that, missing the funeral and feeding who knows what rumors. Fumble after fumble she had lurched through life. Everything turning out wrong, every decision turning back on her, teeth bared. Wayne's funeral, and before that the ridiculous fishing license. Her whole married life tied up in that wretched fishing license, she herself snared and tangled like a whale in great knots of netting never meant for her. Yet they would drag her down until she couldn't move, couldn't breathe. Peter and his holy fishing, his lobster and herring, didn't want to do anything, go anywhere, hear anything, be anything that didn't involve a smelly bait tub and waterproof clothing. Her whole life strangled and drowned. Wasted. And when she was finally cut free and she sold the cursed thing there was nothing but trouble from Earl. As though Peter, not content with damage done, kept spitting at her from beyond the grave. There could have been another life, an English life, a passionate English botanist not sacrificed to a uniform, a beautiful English daughter. War takes everything. Was that her fault too? All that? She did not have the luxury of decision. Barely more than a girl then, but she forged her own salvation, such as it was, her own comfort, her boy Murray.

She only did what she had to do to save him. Did Casper honestly think she enjoyed that? Her one monumental act of heroism. He had no idea what it cost her to set a baby free. The child would be adopted. The harm is to the one who loses, not the one who finds. How could she know how twisted everything would become? Perhaps if Murray had had a son to tend to he would not have married that crazy Lucy and they would have all been spared the horrors that followed. The thought drained the blood from her brain, churned nausea through her stomach. She was sick, sick, sick. Ill down so deep she knew this would kill her. To lose Murray from her home and then finally and forever to the river, this was the last ring of hell she had thought. But to almost have him back, some part of him anyway, to be tantalized and taunted, to have him so close, this could not be borne. And then to carry the blame.

She had spent days preparing Cass's room, rearranging all of Murray's things to make way for him, imagining their future. But now this. Him standing there with his father's eyes in his head and speaking to her as bold and impudent and cold as the others. And then that push, that kick! A kick was what it was. Murray never got angry. Well, seldom. Perhaps Cass would come around, perhaps … Already she felt herself leaning towards him again. Cass would be back. She had no choice but to believe it.

Belle barked and Eleanor twisted her poor wretched body around far enough to see Ben heading towards her across the lawn. "There's no mercy," she whispered. Ben had not given her a moment's peace since she missed the funeral.

Today he almost cried out, "Mom! Mom, you look awful."

"Thank you very much. I've been meaning to mention just how gray you're getting around the temples. Not to mention that stomach. You look like you're carrying a pet raccoon around under your shirt." Eleanor found some mild relief in seeing him stricken, as though *he* was the one who had just been kicked to the ground.

"Really, what's wrong, Mom? You're not looking well. Have you been to see the doctor? I have to insist you see the doctor."

"Stop your fussing, Ben. If I were half the old woman you are I would do away with myself."

For a moment he stood there examining his hands in that exasperating way of his, as though he were not the principal but the little boy caught with the stolen crayons. Finally he sat in the wrought iron chair next to her bench.

"Maybe I should have taken Wayne in, Mom. Back when Judy couldn't keep him anymore. Remember? I know Earl didn't want that. He said he was looking after him but he wasn't and I knew that. I knew it, Mom. I mean, I don't mean Earl wasn't trying his best. He was torn, I know. But maybe I could have kept Wayne in school a little longer. I don't know what I should have done. Earl doesn't want to talk about it. I can understand that." Ben searched his mother's face. Of course she did not answer him. Anyone could see his mere breathing annoyed her. For the ten thousandth time in the last twenty years he sat with the knowledge that she would trade his life for Murray's in a heartbeat. And if he had died in Murray's stead she seldom would have thought of him again—a maudlin moment on his birthday perhaps.

Eleanor concentrated on keeping her jaw unclenched enough to speak. "Why don't you make some ice tea? And bring me a couple of aspirins." She braced herself for the sigh.

Sure as the sunrise, Ben sighed.

# CHAPTER TWENTY-THREE

PIPE SIMPLY WORKED. Way too much had happened too fast: Wayne's death, the cops, Earl in the night. But her work had carried her through, righting her every time, keeping her above water and facing into the storm. She painted the surmounting of deceit and tragedy. She painted dogged determination, persistence, resilience, drawing it out of the woodwork, making it live, absorbing it into herself and propelling herself onward. She could see every detail; she was so close to finishing that the work itself pulled her forward. And then Cass with his story at the iron bridge. That had stopped her cold and she could only sit and stare into her dark blue past, swirling, denying, wondering, then finally knowing.

Through the years she had kept one of her very first paintings despite its roughness and its poor technique and its jumbled and confused composition: a child's collage rendered in acrylic—an ocean of mussel-shell waves, dried spruce-needle sand, a sand dollar sun, and amongst the shells a small sprig of lichen, white as a splash. Often she had hovered over this piece, hesitated, ultimately unable to consign it to the trash where it belonged. It was stored up under the rafters of the goose shed, she knew, and this was where she found it before she carried it into the woods behind her house and affixed it to the trunk of the particular maple tree where her forest studio had been. This tiny sheltered nook in the woods had seemed immense to the child she had been. Merely a spot, an identifiable patch of earth selected and named. This was where she had run to on that day and this was where they had found her that evening building her picture, dismantling and reassembling it over and over.

There was a more recent, more sophisticated work. Upstairs, stacked face in against her bedroom wall, sat a series of canvases, her thesis project from school, entitled *Falling*. She set them out, one through five, falling from frame to frame to frame, over and over until time bloomed up and out and then retracted back into the dimensions of the canvases, contained in squares, finite and complete. She did not know where Cass was or why he had not come back. Cass Hutt, who had witnessed what she had witnessed at the iron bridge and who, after all this time, could help shoulder a corner of the burden. Perhaps he had discovered the fraud in the portraits she had done for him, discovered it was Murray and not Cass himself that had carried them. Still, after all this, Cass would be back surely, and when he came he must see her gristmill work completed.

Finally she gathered up her canvases, carted them downstairs and tucked them into a corner. She was not finished with them but she must set them aside and return to her waiting work. If she did not move forward she would simply flounder and drown. Concentrate, she told herself, come closer, remember your night in the mill. Once she re-entered her creation completely, it would shield her.

The final panel of her work encompassed the door, approaching the corner where the journey began, completing the circle. Here a baby girl turned and stood, growing and maturing as she turned: the girl, the young woman, the wife and finally her Nan, the grandmother Pipe had known. Then as she walked towards the viewer Nan was replaced by Lucy, Pipe's mother, painted from photographs not from a memory stained and torn and dirty—a beautiful woman with a war behind her eyes, pausing, looking back before she stepped out of the picture. And then, at the door, at the end of the road, the self-portrait. She had left this for last and was modeling with a mirror, not the frozen slice of a photograph. It was going well. She repositioned the mirror on her easel, found her angle, and resumed.

WHEN CASS ARRIVED he did so on foot. His mother's land rose up to meet his every footfall as he made his way up the laneway with his shirt pocket full of Milk-Bone and his head cluttered with shards of stories but no plan at all as to what he should do. So much had happened in the last few days with the funeral and the letter and Jack and the foundling and Eleanor and the clouds of anger it seemed a great deal of time had elapsed. It was possible that Pipe already knew about them being related, about Catherine Taylor and the ownership of the land. Eleanor could have told Pipe by now, or Earl could have figured it out or Jack could have told someone from the village. Cass did not meet the dog on the way to the house but was greeted by the geese, which he distracted with bits of Milk-Bone.

The dog barked from inside the house. Cass heard it through the window glass before Pipe appeared looking out, slightly confused, maybe worried. Neither of them moved then the dog barked again and she brought her eyes into focus on Cass and smiled. They stood not four feet from each other. There was no doubt about it, she smiled at him. When she signed through the glass between them it was an ordinary sign, the kind anyone could understand—just a second, hold on, I'm going to open the door in a minute.

A goose snapped at his pant leg and he tossed it another half dog biscuit. There were scraping, moving sounds from inside the house then the door opened.

"Don't touch the door. There's wet paint," she said.

Cass turned to look. The last empty spaces had been filled, the end blended into the beginning, the last face straining towards the first. It was Pipe, looking in as though the top panel in the door was really a window and she was looking in on the very world she had created herself. Before that a woman taking a last look around before stepping behind the door, before that another woman growing from a child to an old woman before his eyes.

"That's you," Cass said, pointing to the door panel. "That's your mother before she went really crazy, that's your grandmother, not Eleanor but the other one. The one I never seen."

The miracle of it was not just her ability, the breathtaking magic of it, but that he could understand the pictures of people he never met. Anyone could understand if they kept going around and around and around. No matter how stupid you were, eventually you would know all about the story. How was it possible? The intensity of his desire for such a work pressed on his lungs. She had said nothing about their being related or about the land. No one had told her.

"Are you going to do my paintings soon?"

"Soon." She signed simultaneously, *soon*. "I brought some old paintings of mine downstairs in case you came by. You can look through them. I didn't completely understand them myself until, well, you know, the last time we talked. At the bridge. I knew, I guess. I guess I always knew but not really—until you told me all that. I know that doesn't make much sense but like you said, I was a kid. I have to keep working here or my paint will dry out." She set her mirror back in place by the door and did not look his way again.

He knelt by the collection she had indicated and flipped through the images. She had painted the space with nothing in it. Five canvases showing the space from every angle, just the space from the deck to the river, each one closer, falling from blue to muddy brown, a picture of the fall from behind Murray's eyes. It was all true, already recorded, captured, made real.

"You didn't come to Wayne's funeral."

"I didn't want to meet Earl. He's gone off his nut—came by here a couple of nights ago shooting off his rifle. He would have killed me for all I know."

"Oh. Well, Earl weren't there neither."

"Why not?"

"Don't know."

The millstone was scattered with photographs. Everyone had so many, Lionel's family, Jack, Pipe, probably anyone you asked, they could toss them around like nothing. He searched the faces, placing them in little piles in his mind. From the portraits on the wall he could sort out Pipe's mother and Pipe's Nan. In the pictures Pipe's mother was young. Cass remembered the crazy lady as ancient like a witch but that was not so. There were photos of Pipe as a little girl. Half the photos included Murray. Just like that, pictures all over the place, no mystery at all, common as dirt. Murray about the age Cass was now, about the age of his death. Murray a bit younger but not much, always old enough to be Pipe's father—she was sometimes in the pictures with him.

Cass sat on the millstone for a long time, the little house in silence. She hardly remembered that day on the bridge and still she painted it. She could do anything. Here in his mother's house. Cass didn't know which way to go, what to tell, what to do. He stood and looked across the room at her back, busy painting herself from mirror to window, painting then stopping and studying her reflection. Engrossed. Cass signed *my father, your father,* then forefingers together in the sign for *the same* or *together,* the same sign used to express *brother* and *sister. Pipe, my sister, my half sister. Cass, half brother.* He signed over and over, practicing perhaps, watching his hands form meanings. When he raised his head again she was staring at him, her mouth open slightly, her eyes tight and scared. Not painting at all and who knows how long she had been sitting so still, staring. She signed quick and waited as though he would understand but he did not.

She spoke slowly and quietly. "Why did you sign that? My father, your father. Pipe, my sister, my half sister. Half brother."

Cass could not move.

"Why did you say that?" she persisted.

"You—you couldn't see …"

She tapped the mirror with a forefinger.

"Oh."

"Why did you come here? Why were you on the bridge that day? Why does Earl think you own my land? Why are you crinkling my photographs?"

"I want you to paint me."

"Who are you?"

At that moment he was the closest he had ever been to answering that question and also the farthest away, everything there and too much blocking the view. "Cass Hutt," he whispered. He flashed his name sign, the silent rapping on air. Suddenly between his ribs there was way too much air and not enough space. He choked out a rasping cough, tried to suck in enough oxygen to breathe but the space was clogged. A couple more gasps but he could pull nothing through. I'm drowning. The notion whizzed by. Then something broke, stabbed through him like puncturing a tire, and he could breathe again. In panting, ragged huffs, but he tasted oxygen, sobbed air. He didn't know at first that this was what it was to cry.

He jostled past her easel, through her door-canvas, her protestations, and fled to the pump where he splashed water over his face until his hair and shirt were soaked. She followed him, her face dark with alarm.

"You'll still paint for me, right? Murray had a woman before your mother, see? Murray was my father. Eleanor knows. That woman, Catherine Taylor, that's my mother. She left pregnant, before Murray knew. She's dead now. Ask Eleanor. It's true. I want you to paint for me. You still gonna paint for me?" He avoided mentioning the land but knew she would figure it out. As soon as the rest of the information settled she'd get to the land part, no doubt about it.

"Wait. Who? Your mother was the girl he left home for?"

"You know about her?"

"It's part of the legend, The Ballad of Murray Holmes. A terrible girl. Stole him from his home and never cared a fig for him. Ruined him for life. Made him a soft touch for sick crazies ever after. Specifically my mother. Never mind that my mother only had sporadic episodes at first, that she could have been treated, that he probably made things way worse for her, 'protecting' her. Then they blame everything on my mother. Blame her for getting sick. Well, I got way more from my mother's people than I did from any of the Holmes crowd. All that in there, that's my *mother's* people."

Cass struggled to follow but she was talking about a different story from the one he was trying so hard to piece together. The main characters and the minor characters were switched around. "You knew about her? My mother. Catherine Taylor." She had lied about that earlier.

"I never knew her name. Far as I knew she never had a name, she was just the one that caused the big fight. That was your mother?"

"Yeah. I got a letter from her and everything. It's for real. There's proof. It's all figured out. Murray was my father. Eleanor knows. Eleanor—"

"Jesus H. Christ."

He couldn't lift his eyes off his boots. He patted the side of his leg, whoa boy, hey boy, tried to force his chin off his chest but it would not budge. He had stepped back without realizing it, stared at his footprint in the soft earth by the pump. Here, class, is a little boy who can't write his own name. A yellow puddle growing around a sneaker toe, spreading over white-flecked tile.

"Eleanor knows?"

"Yeah."

"Murray's son? Murray's son. Did she try to smother you or strangle you?"

"I'm not sure. Both, I guess. She pissed me off. So I kind of upset her."

"Really? That's a crying shame."

There was music in her voice, almost laughter, not like she thought it was a shame at all. Look up, he commanded himself again. He squatted on his haunches, could not lift his eyes.

"That's why you look like him. You've known this all along. When you came to visit me the first time—"

He shook his head. "I didn't know then."

"That day on the bridge—"

"No. Eleanor told me just—not long ago. I only knew—" He was going to say "about the land" but stopped himself in time. "All I knew was that I was born here." But he wasn't after all, not as it turned out. "I thought I was." He hunched there in the grass while she figured everything out, while she stripped his life off his body one thin layer at a time, until his muscle lay raw and exposed on his bone, drying in the sun. Slowly and tentatively he lifted his eyes, broadening the sphere of grass in his vision. She had stepped back and huddled against the house in much the same way she had on the day he first saw her when she drew the mare. She picked a long blade of grass and was examining it between her fingers. The dog nestled in beside her and Cass saw them encased in a dome, alone. She pulled the blade apart opening it like a zipper and tossing the halves onto the grass on either side of her then picked another. Cass remained where he was, crouched, silent, waiting.

A good deal of time passed. He took a Milk-Bone from his pocket and broke crumbs off it, tossed them to the chickens that lunged for them in twos and threes, gobbled the crumbs, tugging them from each other's beaks. This brought the dog trotting over. He nosed his pocket and gobbled the biscuit Cass held out to him. While he waited for another Cass scratched his ears. "What's the dog's name anyway?"

Pipe drew three fingers across her eyebrows. "Blackwood." At this the dog disappeared and returned to Cass a moment later with a stick in his mouth. Cass tossed it for him.

The next time Cass looked over at his sister she was staring at him, more like waiting for him. He didn't look away. *My brother, my half brother,* she signed to him. He answered her, *My sister, my half sister.*

She circled her forefingers around each other and Cass wasn't sure what she meant. He hesitated and she beckoned him with a more traditional wave. Come here, she was saying, come over by the house, crouch down there. She'd be good with horses, he thought, she knows about sending messages, understanding you have to imagine the eyes and ears on the receiving end. She would know you had to listen for what they were saying back.

"So Earl thinks you own this place."

"I got this deed. Catherine Taylor left me this deed …"

Cass positioned himself just as he had the first time they met when she had drawn the mare. When Pipe spoke again it was with vehemence. "You think Catherine Taylor owned this place, don't you? And she passed it to you? Well, don't try to tell me this house was never Dad's, that it was not left to my mother and that it's not mine, 'cause this house is *mine.* It has always been mine and it's all I have. I will burn this house down before I let you take my work from me."

"The house is yours, I know. I don't want the house. All that painting is yours. I know it is." He pounded his fist to his heart so she would know he understood about the house. "I want you to paint for me. There's lots of bits I remember, some stuff from Dartmouth and the Ryans' and their dog and other stuff before that too. Bits. And now all this new stuff. I got this plan, sorta." A plan was exactly what he did not have. But there weren't that many choices when it came down to what to do. He couldn't leave. She couldn't leave. "The land, this land …" The dog stood panting in front of him, grinning, his feet planted, poised in anticipation of the next throw. Cass bounced a couple of times on his heels then let the stick fly in a great arc over the pump and nearly to the ruins of the old barn.

"This is my house. And my trees. You're not taking down my trees," she said.

"No." *Half brother.* "I could take that part on that side of the laneway. Down by the road. You wouldn't see me. You won't see me."

"Right, sure. Till Earl gets in on it or you get some other bright idea. Cut everything. Sell everything."

"No, I don't want money, I don't like … No saws, no bulldozer. But I have to have land. It's from my mother. All I got, same as you. But I want you to paint me."

Again silence. After a while she squinted at him. "If Catherine Taylor had a kid he wasn't born here."

"No." Cass told her what he knew while she listened with a ferocious intensity.

"The Scotch River Foundling." She painted silence around them like it had its own color. "What proof have I got that you won't wreck everything?"

"I'll deed you half the land, your half, all legal. You'll have a deed, same as me. The house, land from the east line to the lane, all the way back." *Half,* he signed. *Half. Half.* "Will you paint for me?"

"And I get half of what I've had all along? Oh, that's just great." She sounded incredulous, sarcastic, but not exactly angry. They took turns looking at each other, stealing glances and looking away. The more he looked at her the more he saw. Her shoulders were broad and flat like his. The Holmes eyes.

"So it turns out our father never left either one of us a pot to piss in," she said.

Our father. Cass nodded, trying to still the storm in his chest.

Only Blackwood remained unruffled by the changes snapping through the air all around. A crow called out from the woods warning of an overactive dog and the dog barked his excitement at this new stick-launcher who could send a projectile farther than he had ever experienced before.

"Dad used to do that too. I forgot until this minute."

"Play with the dog?"

"Well, yeah, but I mean he used to sit like this, on his heels, like we're doing. I think I learned that from him. Where'd you learn it?"

"I don't know. I always done that."

"A half brother. Jesus! The foundling. A brother just dropping out of the blue." She shook her head in disbelief then smiled a little. They sat and waited some more, all the pieces of the story falling around their shoulders. "You gonna build on your half?"

Cass dipped his head and brought it up slowly in what felt like something very close to a nod.

"There's still great old timbers in that mess of a barn. The barn's on your side."

"The well's on your side. I'll need water."

"We can deal."

*Stay there.* Pipe fetched her sketchbook and pencils from the house. When she returned she dipped down beside him close enough for him to catch her painty-smoky smell and she lifted his hat off his head. Cass jerked to grab it back but stopped in mid–muscle twitch. For a moment her hand rested on his cheek, soft as grass in a breeze, her fingers brushed his jaw following the bone from his ear to his chin. Then she nestled back into her spot with his hat on her head and her pencil busy on the page in front of her.

She studied him and drew, looked at his eye, the bunching at his eyebrow, the way he held his left shoulder as though carrying a pain in a pouch. She sketched. All her life, her striving and bucking, her silent language, her reconstructed history, her running away and running back, had been an exhausting attempt to fill in holes, paint over blank spaces, contain a loss that had the potential to swallow her. Now here was a real live half brother. And she was a half sister. That was exactly how it felt. A half of something. He felt it too, she could tell. He thought she could paint the rest of him in, thought she could perch here on the ground and draw his life around him. Good as new. Never mind what she knew. The walking, talking half a brother with skin and muscle and bone, he was real and he was here. The warm horsy scent of him seeped from his Stetson and shimmered around her. A person could never tell what two halves might make. Her pencil danced over the page.

"Tell me what you know," she said.

CASS LEFT SLOWLY, stretching out his journey down the laneway. He peered into the bush on the right—his sister's land—and into the bush on the left—his land. As he knew, there was no brook or stream on the property so one spot was as good as another. All he had to do was pick a spot to his left. Here, somewhere here. This is the land my mother bought for me, kept for me, gave to me, the land I am sharing with my sister. I will build …

He breathed deeply enough to quiet the fear that spread through his rib cage like a fever. He thought of the cardboard box under his bed at the ranch, under countless beds, on his lap on the way to the end of the road, beside him on a concrete step, waiting. Of having, and losing. "There's lots of time," he said aloud and wished he had the mare here for company, for strength. Just a shack, a cabin, just a small one. No big deal. A chimney, a roof, four walls. No big deal. Still, he knew, if he could manage it, it would be the bravest thing he would ever do.

# CHAPTER TWENTY-FOUR

PIPE CURLED into her grandmother's garden furniture as best she could but it was hard and unforgiving, designed for those who sat up straight with their hands in their laps. Of course she could go to the door but she would rather wait in peace, rather sit here on her own as though her life was just like everyone else's and here she was a young woman enjoying the sun in her grandmother's garden. What remained of her gristmill work required little of her. In fact she found herself stretching out the finishing touches, details almost clerical in nature, reluctant to finish absolutely. Today she had a preliminary sketch of her new commission to show her grandmother, a scroll of pure vengeance. Today she had her grandmother helpless at the point of the knife, the thrust and twist glinting off the blade. And Pipe could not approach the spirit of revenge. She called up every nasty interchange, every blaming, every slander Eleanor had heaped on her mother, and she could not stir the ashes. Eleanor's secret was as sad as the day on the iron bridge.

Pipe had half a dozen drawings of a maintenance shed with an untidy bundle lying by the door. But Pipe had never seen the shed, had no idea of its size or shape, because it had been torn down before Pipe was born. Eleanor could tell her which hut was closest to the truth.

"I didn't realize you were here," Eleanor said when she finally wandered out of the house and down towards the pond where Pipe waited. Her tone lacked its usual crisp judgment; she sounded tired, spent.

Pipe bobbed her head and looked away. She wished her grand-mother would just sit sometimes and not have to talk, never mind the lecture voice, but she knew that would never happen. Indeed, Eleanor immediately started to speak.

"I understand you have met Cass Hutt. I saw a portrait you did for him. You must be pleased to get a commission. Was he happy with it?"

"It's supposed to be Cass as a boy but it's mostly Dad."

"I could see that, yes. Have you spoken much with Mr. Hutt?"

"Yes. Quite a lot." Pipe nodded slowly letting scarce silence pool around them.

"I see," said Eleanor.

Eleanor would never be able to sit quiet, not like Cass, her brother, Cass.

"I need your help," Pipe said. Slowly she unfolded the sketches of the sheds and handed them to her grandmother. "I'm doing a mural for Cass."

"Oh my. My, oh my," Eleanor sighed.

"Just the baby and the shed. Nothing else, nobody else. Perhaps the blur of a retreating hand. I want to preserve the air of mystery, I guess."

ONE, TWO, THEN THREE DAYS passed after Eleanor's revelation, after his deal was struck with his new half sister. Nothing further happened, nothing fell apart; nothing died or ceased to be. Every day he dropped by his place and stood on his land, stared at a spot just up from the road, the plans for his cabin solidifying in his head. Three times a day Cass put a plate of food before Jack and sat across from him at the kitchen table pointing to one of Jack's photographs, or a page in Effie's old scrapbook, or pulling out a memory, prodding the old man to speak. "What's this here, Jack?" he would ask. Or, "Who's this, Jack?"

"Remember that summer I was here, Jack? And Effie had those fancy chickens? Didn't she have some funny-looking chickens with big feet or something?"

"Oh yes," Jack chuckled and started a tale about Effie at the agricultural fair with her hens.

After lunch while Jack dozed in his rocker Cass cracked open a cold beer and tipped it down his throat. Balancing on the back legs of his chair he practiced saying sentences with words like "my sister" and "my place" in them.

"I'm giving half my place to my sister," he said aloud. Talking to a sleeping man is almost as good as sign language, he thought. "I'm gonna live next door to my sister, but down nearer the road. My sister's old barn got some beams good enough to salvage for my—my new, um, cabin. Just down the road at my place. My place, that's down towards the Crossing. I got a deed."

Jack snuffled a little in his sleep. Cass padded upstairs in his sock feet and retrieved his letter from under his bed, returned to the kitchen and spread it out on the table in front of him. There sat the three of them—the somnolent Jack, Cass, and the letter—alone with the ticking clock. "To Casper Hutt": he could make that out at the beginning of the letter—that was easy. And at the end, the two initials, "C.T." Again he tried setting everything in place, the foundling, the day his mother had come to him, the land.

"Eleanor made me mad, Jack," Cass told the sleeping old man. "Knowing all about me and saying nothing, then trying on lies to cover up the truth. She was the cause of everything gone wrong. Turns out it was her that put the baby in the park, moved it from Murray's next door here—my place—to the park so Murray wouldn't know. How 'bout that? There's a bit of news that never made the scrapbook, eh Jack? What would Effie think of that? The whole goddamned mess is Eleanor's doing.

"She made me real mad. And you know why? I been doing some thinking about it and I'll tell you why. 'Cause it's the same for her today as it was then—take the foundling and do what you want. Same as now—here's the foundling back again and she makes me up in her head, tells me anything, like I belong to her. Jesus, that don't make no sense, do it, Jack? But anyway she made me so mad I give her a shove with my boot. Knocked her right over on the ground. Fling. Splat. Tough luck. Left her there crawling around on the grass. Fucking cow."

"Hey!" Jack sat up, suddenly alert, his eyes fierce as a hawk's trained on Cass's face. His hands trembled on the rocker arms.

Cass reddened. "Um, ah, I mean *darned* cow."

"Is that true? Did you knock down Eleanor Holmes?"

"I didn't know you were listening, Jack. I thought you were asleep."

"Did you hit Eleanor Holmes? Did you knock her over?"

"I guess, yeah."

"You don't ever hit a lady, Cass. Not while you're living here. Not while you're living anywhere. It's not right."

"But you know what she did?"

"I'm not saying nobody ever *wanted* to hit her. But it's not right. Effie wouldn't have it. Not at all! You go and see if she's all right. You apologize to her and that's it."

Cass might have been back on the deck of Earl's boat the way the world kept slipping out from under him, the way the tiniest ripple sent his insides splashing up against his rib cage, sloshing around uncontained, the way his head swam with dizziness. He grabbed his beer and stomped off, pink with embarrassment, leaving Jack alone with his opinions. He propped himself up behind Jack's empty barn and tried to settle his brain in neutral. Maybe if he drank enough now he would fall asleep later, get five or six hours of oblivion before work. Five or six hours free of the past, the present and the future.

That night Jack would not eat his supper. When Cass put a fork in

Jack's hand it simply clattered to the floor. Then suddenly Jack was back again with snapping eyes and the it's-not-right business about Eleanor. And Effie won't have it—you here in her house! Sleep, Cass thought. Please, just let me sleep.

He picked up the fork and tried again, touching the old man's arm. "Remember the old Case tractor, Jack?"

What Cass remembered was how that summer he had arrived never having driven anything more complicated than a shopping cart and Jack had put him on that tractor. It never crossed Jack's mind that Cass wouldn't be able to learn, that Cass was stupid, that he would make a mess of things. "The thing about a clutch …" Jack had explained the whole thing as though it were the most natural thing in the world for a person not to have heard of one, as though this were specialized, almost confidential information. Later when Jack had showed him the mechanism Cass remembered how the understanding of the clutch had filled him like Effie's roast beef. Filled him not only with the specific understanding but also with the possibility of further understanding. The clutch. Looking at him now it was easy to forget how much Jack knew about just about everything.

CASS RODE THE MARE into the village and up Eleanor's drive past a creaky Chevette and the little red Civic. It wasn't so bad when he thought in generalities—someone's grandmother's house with bright blue paint and flowers everywhere. A perfect grandmother's house with big trees and a golden dog and a pond with special pond flowers and a fountain and a live turtle. Cass rounded the house and there, across the yard, was Earl whom he hadn't seen since the day of the bulldozer and Ben from the funeral. The two men stood conferring by the pond and did not see him at first. Eleanor, not fifteen feet to his left, quit fussing with a plastic tablecloth on the patio and bolted over, almost running. As he swung down off the saddle she reached out then suddenly pulled her arms in by her sides in a jerky wooden way that looked painful, as though she were cracking her bones to force them into position.

"Casper."

"It's Cass."

"Yes, of course, Cass. You've been upset. So have I." She was rushing her speech trying to get as much as possible in before interruption.

"Jack says I gotta tell you I was wrong about that shove, you know, with my boot that day. And I hope you wasn't hurt or nothing. I never meant nothing by it. It weren't right, striking out like that, even if you did, you know—"

"You're here now. That's the main thing. Pipe knows our secret. Have you told anyone else? I haven't told anyone. Not even Ben or Earl. I have to tell you all about your father. You'll come by later, won't you? When there's just the two of us. Tell me that you will—"

"Hey, Cass!" Earl caught sight of him and strode over, fast enough to leave Ben behind, fast enough to throw Eleanor off guard. The dog trotted alongside. Half a smile crooked Earl's face and Cass couldn't read him. He could see him on a talk show, soaking up the camera's attention, yeah, this is my nephew, the famous Scotch River Foundling.

"Hey, Earl."

"We got unfinished business, you and me."

Earl's face had lost some of its animation, his voice some of its life. There was a fatigue about him and a forced joviality.

"I guess you didn't understand the plan completely, eh? Had some trouble with that? I've been tied up with a bit of a tragedy here." His face winked in a tick. "We better talk, buddy."

Ben caught up to the action and was waiting to be introduced but when that did not happen he stepped forward. "Ben Holmes. I saw you at the funeral. Thank you for coming. I didn't realize you were an associate of Earl's, Mr. …?"

"Cass," said Earl, his resentment clear. "Cass Hutt."

"Pleased to meet you, Cass," said Ben.

Cass nodded. Eleanor fanned her face with her hands, flapping. She looked around, lost. "Are you all right, Mom?" Ben stepped towards her.

Earl maneuvered Cass to the far side of the horse as though this provided them with some magic privacy. He bent his head into Cass's. "The phone company took my cell and the goddamned power company's after me now, thanks to your stalling."

Cass looked away. Don't fuck me over, Dogshit. "I guess I decided not to sell. Not going into the land business—gonna keep her like she is."

"No. You've been talking to—"

Eleanor, pursued by Ben and the golden retriever, darted round the back end of the horse startling the mare, who pranced sideways a few steps and whinnied in surprise.

"Cass, listen—"

Cass steadied the mare's head.

"Now listen, buddy, there's a few things you need to—"

The kitchen door burst open and Earl's twins raced into the yard. "Hey, a horse, can I ride, me too, I said it first, so what ..." And an older boy. "Cool, whose ..." Followed by Judy with a tray of drinks. "Earl, I—oh look ..." The mare reared a foot off the ground as the mob rushed her. Cass reached to steady her as one of the twins, the chunky one, hauled on a stirrup and the other one, the freckled one, dipped under her front legs.

"Hey girl, easy, girl."

The chunky one kept hauling on the stirrup as the freckled one scrabbled up onto the saddle on his belly, mounting from the wrong side, flailing. The mare snorted and lunged forward. The freckled one was propelled headfirst off the saddle onto the ground where he lay wailing. The chunky one, now with his arm caught in the tack, shrieked as he was pulled off his feet. Judy screamed, Earl bellowed. Ben ran for the captive twin, Judy for the tossed one.

The teenaged son charged forward, berating his younger brothers, Eleanor jumped back, Ben flapped around searching for order.

"Whoa girl, good girl, hey pet, whoa girl." The bit pulled at the horse's tender mouth and Cass felt it on his flesh as he tried to haul her in. The teenager bounced directly behind the mare with his arms wide as though he were a goalie waiting to stop a shot. "Don't stand behind the horse." Cass tried to be heard without adding to the din. "Get him away from the back of the horse."

"Brad, get to hell away from there!" Earl hollered in the mare's ear and she twisted away from him.

"What?" the boy barked and leaned to the left just as a shod hoof whizzed by his ear missing him by inches. Judy screamed again, Eleanor wailed, "Murray, do something!"

"Murray? Why'd you say Murray?"

"Stand away from the horse. Steady, girl, good pet. Stand back from the horse. Here, girl."

Ben caught on and began collecting the family one at a time and corralling them against the house. "Here, Judy, take him to the kitchen, Brad, take your brother to the door there, Mom, go with Earl, tie up the dog, Mom, before she gets hurt, call the dog, here, Belle, come on, Earl ..."

Bit by bit the area cleared and those still bawling at least were not doing it in the horse's ear. Gradually the mare steadied under Cass's hand. That Ben's as good as a goddamned cattle dog, Cass thought as soon as he was free to think anything beyond restraining the mare. He led her away from them, her still nervous and prancy, towards the pond where she could drink and settle herself.

"Those are my tiger lilies he's trodding down! And my irises!"

"Can we go see him now, Mom? He's quiet now, see?"

"No thanks to you, bonehead."

"You're the one who nearly got your head kicked in."

"No loss." Children's laughter.

"I'm not going, the stupid thing broke my ribs."

"Don't be mental."

"You guys stay here, I gotta talk to Cass for a—"

"Earl, I really think—"

"I'm going with Dad."

Cass stepped closer to his mount, slender leaves of some flower giving way under his boots. The whole family began to trickle forward as though the bucket they had been scooped into sprang a leak. Earl headed the parade, the chunky twin running after him with the dog by his side then Eleanor, Ben's containment efforts disintegrating entirely. "Here they come again, girl. Let's trot."

He tucked his toe into the stirrup, hopped into the saddle and lifted his hat to them. "We'll take the back way out," he called and clicked the horse into a trot, guided her around the far side of the pond, through a border of flowers scattering a splash of red and orange petals, and out onto the road. In no time they were safely out of sight on the trail leading to the bridge.

At the railbed he slowed to a walk and patted the horse's neck as she stepped onto the iron bridge where her horseshoes clattered on the wooden deck. In the middle of the bridge he reined her to a stop and sat in the saddle looking out over the Scotch River watching the sky's blue deepen on the western horizon. He thought about the coming of fall at the One Bar None and the bull riding championships and he touched the ribs he had broken several times and felt the memory of Lionel lying between them. His land. Half a property, land to share with a half sister. Two dead parents, two living uncles and a grandmother. An aunt by marriage. A dead cousin and three live ones. It was an awful lot for one man. "It's likely as much as I can stand," he told the blue sky above the bluer river. He thought again about the little cabin he would build, a miniature of the first bunkhouse he had lived in. Not the new one built at the One Bar None but the older one it had replaced. All along one wall would be his painting, and although from here he could not see the details it contained, he felt its acorn of truth in the pit of his belly. If he looked long and hard he could see the outline of what might be a tiny stable joining the north wall of his little cabin to a stall that opened into a corral where bush had been cleared and there was Millad tossing her head above the flakes of hay on the ground in front of her.

His sister, Pipe Holmes—she had been misplaced too, not like him but set aside all the same. But she was as smart as Lionel, kind in her own way, and with hands of magic. She had power enough in those hands to save them both. Saddle leather creaked when he stood in his stirrups, extending his legs, feeling the weight of himself on the balls of his feet. He plucked his wallet from his back pocket and flicked through its empty cellophane windows to his chipped and worn birth certificate, passed a broad forefinger under the print and read it aloud: "Casper Hutt, Scotch River, Nova Scotia."

He folded his wallet, tucked it back into his pocket, clicked the horse into a trot and headed for home.

## Acknowledgments

FOR THEIR WISE GUIDANCE, many thanks to my agent, Dean Cooke, and my editor, Barbara Berson. For financial contributions, thanks to the Canada Council for the Arts and the Nova Scotia Department of Tourism, Culture and Heritage. And thanks, as always, to Joel.